DARCY BURKE

USA TODAY BESTSELLING AUTHOR

LADY of DESIRE

LEGENDARY ROGUES

Lady of Desire

ISBN: 1939713552
ISBN-13: 9781939713551

Book design © Darcy Burke.
Cover design © Sweet 'N Spicy Designs/Jaycee DeLorenzo.
Copyediting: Martha Trachtenberg.

For my Grandma Finney.

I miss you so much and wish you'd had
a chance to read my books.

I know you're smiling down on me,
and my heart is full of love.

Chapter One

Gloucester, July 1794

"THIS IS HOPELESS." Margery Derrington closed the lid on the third trunk she'd searched in her great-aunts' attic. Though they'd accumulated a great many things in nearly seven decades on this earth, not one of them was valuable enough to save their little family from financial ruin. Even piling all of it together wouldn't be enough.

Aunt Eugenie, her aunt with the most common sense, looked around the cramped space with a grim expression. "How many trunks are left?"

"Just two," Margery said, pushing herself up from the floor and moving to one of them. It was small, and unless it held some priceless jewel her aunts had somehow misplaced or forgotten about, Margery couldn't imagine anything of value fitting inside of it.

"I'll try the other trunk. We're bound to find something. Don't lose faith, Margery." Aunt Agnes turned and scooted to the last one, which was considerably larger than the one sitting before Margery. With sparkling blue eyes and a charm to match, Aunt Agnes possessed enough optimism and cheer for all three of them.

Margery opened her trunk and stifled a groan at its contents. Papers. Stacks and stacks of what looked to be ledgers. She rifled through them, finding nothing but the mundane accounting of her great-grandfather.

"I suppose I must consider marriage." She'd reached the age of four and twenty without having to submit to matrimony, but it looked to be her only alternative unless they wanted to surrender the modest town house in their quiet little Gloucester neighborhood.

"Now, Margery, don't be a defeatist," Aunt Agnes said sternly. "We'll come up with something, won't we, Genie?"

Aunt Eugenie made a noncommittal sound as she continued going through the large trunk she'd been searching with Agnes.

Margery cringed. The last time her aunts had "come up with something" was the reason they were in their current mess. Financial investments were not their area of expertise. "Please don't."

Aunt Eugenie's excited inhalation drew Margery and Aunt Agnes to stop what they were doing.

"What is it, Genie?" Aunt Agnes turned and leaned toward her younger sister, trying to peer into the trunk.

"My goodness, Aggie, do you remember this?" Aunt Eugenie pulled a book from the trunk. Bound in dark brown leather, the tome appeared quite old. The spine was scuffed and the edges frayed.

Aunt Agnes scooted back to her former spot and gasped. "Is that what I think it is?"

Aunt Eugenie grinned as she set the book on the floor and opened the cover. *"The Ballads of Sir Gareth."*

Sidling up close to Aunt Eugenie, Aunt Agnes touched the first page. "I haven't seen this in decades."

"Since we were children," Aunt Eugenie said.

Margery set her trunk aside and went to kneel beside Aunt Eugenie. "What is it?"

"A medieval manuscript," Aunt Agnes said. "It's

about the tales of Sir Gareth, one of King Arthur's Knights of the Round Table."

"He has to complete a series of quests so that he may marry Blodwyn. The other knights—and King Arthur of course—provide assistance." Aunt Eugenie pointed to an illustration. Full of brilliant color and accompanied with precise, beautifully written text, it depicted a knight kneeling before a king, beside whom stood a young woman.

"Is that Blodwyn?" Margery asked, instantly enthralled with both the detail of the work and the stories.

Aunt Agnes nodded. "And her father. My favorite tale is the one where Gareth defeats a boar. The beast is so fierce in the picture."

Aunt Eugenie flipped ahead to the image Agnes had described, but Margery wanted to see the entire book.

"Wait, I want to look at it," Margery said.

Aunt Eugenie smiled. "Of course. We got a bit excited. Our father used to read this book to us when we were children."

Margery reached out. "May I?"

"Certainly, dear." Aunt Eugenie slid it over in front of her.

Margery closed it so she could savor it from the beginning. Faded remnants of the title were all that remained on the cover, but it was printed in vibrant letters on the first page. "You said this is medieval?" Margery had never heard of *The Ballads of Sir Gareth*.

"Yes," Aunt Agnes said. "Or so Father said."

It certainly looked and smelled old. The pages were made of vellum, and the style of calligraphy appeared medieval, but what did Margery know? Only one thing really mattered. "Is it valuable?"

Her aunts exchanged looks. "I don't know," Aunt Agnes said. "But I remember Father telling us about a collector in Monmouth." She tapped her finger against her chin. "What was his name?"

"Alexander Bowen," Aunt Eugenie said. Her mind retained all sorts of details, which made the sudden appearance of a potentially valuable manuscript perplexing.

"You didn't remember this was here?" Margery asked. If it *was* valuable, it could've saved them months ago.

Aunt Eugenie pursed her lips, her silvery eyes dimming. "No."

Aunt Agnes patted Aunt Eugenie's shoulder. "Don't fret about it. I didn't remember it either. The important thing is that we have it now. We shall have to contact this fellow in Monmouth."

"I'll do it," Aunt Eugenie said, "after we finish going through these last trunks. There's no telling what else we might find."

The firm set of her mouth told Margery how disappointed she was in herself for not recalling the existence of this book. But then Aunt Eugenie had been acting rather depressed of late. She took the downturn of their finances as a personal failure, and hated the thought of Margery having to marry to save them from ruin. Oh, she *wanted* Margery to marry, but for the right reasons—for love.

Margery stroked Aunt Eugenie's arm. She didn't want her to feel bad, not when they finally had something to perhaps be optimistic about. "Where did your father get this?"

"I don't know. It's been in the family for as long as he could remember."

Margery turned the page, taking in the meticulous drawings and rich color. It was breathtakingly beautiful, and its age only increased its attraction. To think of the effort it had taken to create, and the fact that it had survived for centuries, was awe-inspiring. It had to be worth *something*.

Aunt Agnes seemed to read her mind. "This is going to solve our woes. Margery dear; you won't have to marry." Aunt Agnes had never married. She'd fallen in love with a gentleman who'd been promised to another. When he' offered to make Agnes his mistress, she'd accepted—to Aunt Eugenie's horror. During the twenty years that Agnes was his paramour, the two sisters didn't speak, only reconciling after he died.

"Unless you want to," Aunt Eugenie said, with a disapproving glance at Aunt Agnes. Aunt Eugenie had also fallen in love, but she'd married her gentleman. However, her husband hadn't shared her emotions and had soon taken a mistress. He'd died five years into the union, leaving Eugenie alone, childless, and at the mercy of his creditors. Despite this, she still believed in marriage, provided one found the right man. Margery doubted such a person existed.

Aunt Agnes smiled and winked at Margery. "*If* she falls in love. And even then," she shrugged, "she needn't give up her independence if she doesn't want to."

Aunt Eugenie lifted a brow and peered at her sister. "So that she, too, can worry over finances in her golden years?"

Margery returned her attention to the book. Marrying for love didn't interest her. *Love* didn't interest her. Life was far easier to navigate if she kept that sort of emotion at bay. She'd buried her sentimentality deep after her parents had died, but had allowed a gentleman to court her five years ago. When he'd learned of her less than favorable financial circumstances—even when they hadn't been bankrupt, they'd never been more than mildly comfortable—he'd disappeared like a plate of Shrewsbury cakes at teatime. That had ensured that she kept herself from getting too close to anyone besides her aunts. They'd taken her in after her parents had died in a carriage accident when she was ten, and they were the only people she trusted. Everyone else she'd met had wanted something from her or expected her to be someone she wasn't. She was quite content to remain unmarried and take care of her aunts.

Aunt Agnes sent her a giddy smile. "Only think of what might happen if this book could finance a Season."

Margery's head snapped up. "Let's not get ahead of ourselves. This book may be worthless." She fervently hoped that wasn't the case. Just as she fervently prayed she'd never have to endure a Season. She couldn't think of anything she'd rather do less than parading around in search of a husband.

Aunt Eugenie tucked a wayward gray strand of hair into her cap. "Help me up, dear. I'll start drafting that letter while you two finish up."

Margery stood and helped her aunt, who was taller than her by at least two inches. Aunt Eugenie smiled down at her with love in her gaze. "It's going to be just fine, Margery. In this instance, I wholly support Aggie's dogged optimism."

Aunt Agnes made a noise that sounded suspiciously like a snort.

After Aunt Eugenie had departed to write to the

collector, Aunt Agnes went back to the other trunk to complete her search. "Did you find anything?" she asked Margery.

"Just accounting papers." Margery went to help Aunt Agnes. "What's in there?"

"Hats and . . . this." She held up a headpiece with a half-dozen feathers in a rainbow of garish colors.

"Did that belong to you or Aunt Eugenie?"

Aunt Agnes stared at it bemusedly. "I'm not certain." She set it aside and rifled through the remaining items. "Nothing valuable in here, I'm afraid. Ah, well, the book will come to our rescue."

Margery wished she could feel as confident that things would be so easily solved. "We'll see."

Aunt Agnes gave her a scolding look. "Now, Margery, you mustn't be pessimistic. Things will work out. We'll take a nice little jaunt to Monmouth to see this fellow, he'll give us an enormous sum for this book, and all will be well."

"And if it's not?"

"Things always work out, dear." Aunt Agnes's eyes widened briefly. "Oh! I nearly forgot. Mr. Digby will be arriving in town in the next few days."

The gentleman had come to town last month, and Margery had met him at the local assembly. After dancing with her once, he'd affixed himself to her side and asked to call on her. She'd politely declined. He'd seemed a decent enough fellow, if a bit awkward, but she wasn't interested in another courtship. "I didn't know he was coming."

"We didn't tell you, dear. You seemed so uninterested in him."

Margery's gentle rebuke hadn't stopped him from writing to her. After receiving three letters over three consecutive days, Margery had asked her aunts to keep from giving her any others should more arrive. "I gather he's continued writing?"

Aunt Agnes replaced the various items in the trunk. "Oh, yes. Say what you will, but he's quite charming on the page."

"I'll take your word for it." Margery didn't remember him that way. He'd talked to her about animals and the weather, and all manner of mundane topics without once endeavoring to determine her interests.

"It's a shame you don't like him. His family is well-respected. I believe his grandfather was a knight or some such."

"Yes, but how is his fortune?" Margery asked drily. She found it a bit odd that he wasn't in London for the Season if he was searching for a wife. If he was without funds, he would soon vanish like her previous suitor had.

Aunt Agnes tapped Margery's arm. "Oh, stop. Not every gentleman is concerned with a young lady's fortune. I'm not familiar with his financial state, but it's quite possible he simply liked *you,* dear. Now, help me up."

Margery stood and helped the still beautiful woman to her feet. Though approaching seventy, Aunt Agnes looked far younger, with her porcelain skin and her ready smile. While her sister was quite tall, Aunt Agnes was more petite.

"Not every gentleman is as heartless as Jennings was five years ago. Genie is hoping you'll give Digby the courtesy of an audience."

Margery stifled a groan. "I don't want to encourage him. I don't want to encourage *anyone.*"

Aunt Agnes nodded, her eyes sympathetic. "I understand, dear. Perhaps we should just travel to Monmouth to see Mr. Bowen about the book."

"Forgo a letter, you mean?"

"No, we'll still post the letter, but it will inform him of our arrival for an appointment—in say, three days. That will expedite the process of selling the book with the added bonus of saving you from Mr. Digby's attentions."

Margery felt a pang of guilt. Mr. Digby wasn't a bad sort; he just wasn't the sort for her. Who was? Did she even have a "sort"? "We'll leave tomorrow?" Margery asked.

"The day after, I think. I daresay Harker won't be able to prepare us for the journey that quickly."

Harker, their housekeeper, cook, and ladies' maid, was a gem, but to say she was overworked was an understatement. Margery looked forward to when they could hire someone to lighten her workload.

"The sooner we can sell this book, the better." Margery bent down and picked it up. She caressed the worn leather and felt a jolt of sadness over having to part with something of such beauty and value, especially if it had been in the family for a long time.

Aunt Agnes's blue eyes brightened with purpose. "I'll speak with Genie."

Margery was grateful for her understanding. "Thank you." She looked down at the book and flipped to somewhere in the middle. "I can't believe you both forgot about this." Reverently, she stroked the page and drank in the gorgeously meticulous illustration.

"It's extraordinary, isn't it?" Aunt Agnes asked softly. "Though we haven't looked at it in years, it's a piece of our shared past. Genie and I had so many years apart and this reminds me of the time before, when we were young and innocent. I admit it will be a touch difficult to let the book go."

Margery raised her gaze to her beloved aunt's. "You don't have to. I don't want to ask it of you."

"You aren't." She reached over and patted Margery's hand, her fingers lingering over Margery's knuckles. "You know that Genie and I would do anything for you, including selling a silly, old book."

Margery tamped down a burst of emotion. "I feel precisely the same."

"Yes, but you agree that marrying someone like Digby isn't nearly as easy as selling a book. Our sacrifice is far less intrusive. It's scarcely a sacrifice at all."

"I *would* marry him, or someone else, if it was our only option."

Aunt Agnes shook her head firmly. "It isn't." *Yet.* The word was unspoken, but it hung between them like a living, breathing animal. Margery was going to do everything in her power to ensure that never came to pass—she didn't want to sell herself, even for financial security.

Margery's gaze dropped to the book once more. The illustration of a knight slaying a boar was so vivid. She traced her finger along the edge. Centuries had passed since the person who'd drawn this had toiled over its creation. How long had it taken? Where had this story originated? Who had written it? She hoped Mr. Bowen could answer these questions in addition to providing the text's value. He was a collector himself. Would he offer to buy it? Were her days with this book, already too short in number, limited to single digits?

"Margery, why don't you take the book to your room?" Aunt Agnes suggested. "I can see you long to peruse it at length."

How well her aunt knew her. Margery closed the book and hugged it to her chest. "Thank you."

As they left the attic, another, more disturbing thought encroached. How many days did she have left with her aunts? When they were gone she would be truly alone in this townhouse—if she were lucky. If she were unlucky, she could be alone and destitute.

No, she wouldn't think like that. This book was going to change their fortune and she'd do whatever necessary to ensure they lived in at least a modicum of comfort. Maybe they'd move out to a cottage in the country. Yes, she could see herself living a simple life, even after her aunts were gone.

Determined, she made her way to her room and vowed to keep them all safe and happy.

RHYS BOWEN CRACKED an eyelid at the sudden invasion of light into his bedchamber. His valet, the beast, had opened the drapes on one of the windows just enough to illuminate a section of the room. Thankfully, the beam didn't shine directly over Rhys's bed.

He turned away from the window and pulled the cover over his aching head. "Was that really necessary?"

"I do this every day," Thomas said stiffly.

Yes, but Rhys didn't wake up with a thundering headache every day. Only when he infrequently attended one of Trevor's bacchanalias, which Trevor threw for soon-to-be-married gentlemen who came up from London or somewhere. He hosted a few days of feasting, drinking, and whoring, then everyone embarked on a tour of the River Wye, except for Rhys. One night of debauchery was more than enough to tide him over until the next event a few months later.

Rhys peered up over the edge of the coverlet, sensing his valet's presence near the side of his bed. "Would it pain you to skip it this morning?"

"You have guests arriving soon, if you recall."

No, he hadn't recalled. Blast, how had he forgotten that a widow and her spinster sister were coming to visit him about a medieval text they'd found in their attic? Because he wasn't terribly enthused about seeing them. It was probably a forgery, like so many of the works brought to him, and his father before him, for estimation.

He sat up begrudgingly, wiping his hand over his chin. The scratch of his whiskers reminded him of last night—and of the woman who'd appreciated the feel of them against her flesh . . .

The sound of Thomas clearing his throat interrupted Rhys's salacious thoughts. "Mrs. Thomas recently learned a recipe for a headache tonic and prepared a batch for you earlier." Thomas left the side of the bed and came back a moment later with a mug he offered to Rhys.

Rhys took it, but looked up at his valet in doubt. "This smells like horse piss."

Thomas didn't dispute him. "Nevertheless, she assures me it will eliminate your headache in a trice. There are certain things one does not question Mrs. Thomas about." He gave Rhys a haggard look.

Though he was purposefully unmarried, Rhys understood the state of matrimony enough to know that sometimes one absolutely did *not* question one's wife. With a silent toast, he quaffed as much of the drink as he could. With a cough and a sputter he handed the mostly empty mug back to Thomas. He started to settle deeper beneath the coverlet, but Thomas's sharp look froze his movements. "Now what?"

"Your visitors are arriving in a little over an hour."

How long had he slept? "What time is it?"

"Half-noon."

"Hell." Rhys threw off the coverlet and set about his toilet. His day-old beard might have pleased his companion last night, but he doubted the widow and her spinster sister would approve. He might be a bit of a hermit, but he wasn't a boor.

After a quick—because he unfortunately couldn't summon an appetite after downing the vile tonic—meal, he awaited his guests in his office. The room was quite large, more a library really. Father had filled floor-to-ceiling bookshelves with ancient texts and academic papers, a collection Rhys had only enlarged in the three years since his death. A long table filled one side of the room, while a collection of chairs and a settee were situated in front of the windows that looked over a wide lawn.

The door opened and a young woman stepped inside. She was followed by a slightly older woman—but only slightly. These were the women who'd written him? He'd been expecting women past middle age at least. He supposed either one of these ladies could be a widow, but a spinster? The one who'd come in second lingered in the background and kept her head bent, so he couldn't really discern her features, but the woman standing before him now was, in a word, breathtaking.

"Miss Roper?" he asked.

"No." She shook her head, sending the honey blond curls that were just visible beneath her hat swinging. "My great-aunts weren't able to make the journey with me. I'm afraid my Aunt Eugenie fell ill."

Mrs. Eugenie Davenport. *Her great-aunt.* So this beautiful creature was neither a spinster nor a widow. As far as he knew. And, surprisingly, he wanted to know.

"Miss Margery Derrington," Thomas intoned from the doorway rather tardily.

Rhys peered around his guest at his valet, who also served as his butler. "Thank you, Thomas, would you bring tea, please?"

He nodded in response and left the room. The other woman remained by the door.

Miss Derrington must've noted the direction of his gaze. "This is my companion, Mrs. Edwards."

"Please join us, Mrs. Edwards." He indicated the seating arrangement near the windows.

"I'll just stand over here." Her voice sounded pinched, nervous. "Thank you," she added hurriedly.

Miss Derrington threw her a reassuring glance before moving to the settee, where she perched at the edge of the ruby-colored cushion. She set a book—obviously the item they wished for him to inspect—beside her.

Rhys sat in a chair across from her and stared at the tome, wondering why he hadn't noticed it in her grasp straightaway. He'd been too entranced by his guest's bright hazel-colored eyes, smooth cheekbones, and the clever little dimple in her chin. "You've brought the manuscript for me to review?"

"Yes. I realize it's a bit presumptuous, not giving you an opportunity to decline our request, but I was most anxious to obtain your opinion."

Presumptuous. Anxious. *Beautiful.* He directed his attention to the book instead of the provokingly lovely Miss Derrington. "Your aunts said it was a medieval Arthurian text?"

She picked up the book and held it in her lap. The way she touched it, the glide of her fingertips across the flat plane of the cover, revealed her affection. He recognized her attachment since he felt it for nearly every medieval manuscript he happened upon. In a moment, he'd ascertain whether this one was worthy of his interest.

"I understand you'll be able to ascertain its actual age and perhaps its origin?" Her gaze was deeply inquisitive. She wanted to learn everything she could about this book. He could see the curiosity burning through her placid expression.

"Yes, and I understand you'd like to know its value, that you're interested in selling it?"

Her fingers tightened ever so slightly around the tome. She looked at him skeptically. "Forgive me, I thought you'd be . . . older. My aunts said you'd been a scholar of medieval texts for decades."

"That was my father, Alexander Bowen. He died three years ago." And he was still the one they'd written to. "I'm Rhys Bowen, and I assure you I'm every bit as knowledgeable as my father was."

She gave a subtle nod. "Where shall I put the book for your investigation?'

He'd thought he'd have to sit and endure tea for a few minutes, and was intrigued by her eagerness. More intriguing was the fact that he'd been looking forward to conversing with her.

"Let's move to the table." He already had several manuscripts out, including a text written in medieval Welsh that he'd been translating. He hesitated, wondering if she would hand him the book, but she didn't.

She went to his work area and set the manuscript down. Rhys moved to stand beside her. He caught the scent of apples and honey and forced his attention to what she was doing, instead of at her directly.

Once it was out of her grasp, he could finally see the book in its entirety. Glorious illustrations emblazoned the edges of the pages, visible only while the book was closed. The title had been stamped on the front, but what would have been gilt at one time had worn away from centuries of dirty fingers and haphazard care. He just made out the letters:

The Ballads of Sir Gareth

Excitement pulsed through him. They hadn't revealed the title in their letter. If they had, he would've jumped on his horse and ridden straight for Gloucester—and likely passed them on the way. If this book was what he thought it could be . . . His name would become as synonymous with the study of medieval texts as his father's.

Rhys reached for the tome, but she flattened her palm atop the cover and turned to face him.

Her gaze was guarded, her hold on the book protective. "You must be gentle."

Irritation dampened his enthusiasm. "Look around you. I deal with manuscripts like this every day. My hands have been thoroughly cleansed in preparation for touching this, though if its condition had been poor, I would've donned gloves. Do you take the same precautions?"

Her eyes widened slightly, and he felt a moment's validation.

"Now, may I please look at it?" Rhys kept his tone even, though his pulse was racing. If this book was authentic . . .

She pushed it toward him slowly.

He settled himself in a chair at the table and brought the book in front of him. "Please sit." He didn't look at her, but knew there was a chair to her right. She dragged it closer and sat beside him.

With a silent prayer, he opened the cover. He lightly ran his fingers along the edge of the page. The workmanship was exquisite. This had to be the book he thought it was, written by the scribe he suspected. The formation of some letters was similar to his, if not identical. More importantly, the illustrations were reminiscent of a second book, but he'd only viewed it once and that had been three years ago, just before his father's death.

Rhys turned his head and met her searching gaze. "How much do you want for it?"

She cocked her head to the side, her hands folded primly in her lap. "How much is it worth?"

This book alone was an excellent specimen of medieval illumination and worth a decent sum. But if he could get his hands on the other book and put them together, the value was incalculable. He didn't want to get ahead of himself. He offered what the book was worth on its own. "Twenty-five pounds."

Her mouth turned down—not a frown exactly, but

an expression of disappointment. He couldn't help but stare at her pink lips for what was probably a moment too long.

"That's not a paltry amount," he said.

"No," she said slowly, wariness creeping from every corner of the word. "However, I was hoping. . ." She reached out and tried to take the book. "Perhaps coming here so hastily was a mistake."

He couldn't let her leave with the manuscript. "No, it wasn't." He gently rested his palm across the page, as she'd done with the cover. "I have the impression the book belongs to your aunts—they didn't even mention you."

"Yes, it belongs to them." She pressed her lips together, which accentuated the dimple in her chin. "I should've waited for my aunt to feel better before coming. This isn't my decision to make."

He didn't believe her. She'd come with the intent of striking a deal. If she didn't have the authority to make the decision, why would she have come at all? "Well, since you *are* here, why not let me make my full assessment? You do want to know more about it, don't you?" He watched the battle behind her eyes. This book wasn't hers, but she wanted it to be. Why were her aunts selling it if she wanted to keep it so badly? *Because they likely didn't have any other choice.* They were in a perhaps desperate situation—one that he could turn to his advantage if necessary. Not that he wanted to cheat them. He was prepared to compensate her fairly for the book.

"Yes." She cleared her throat. "I should like to hear what you know of it."

Thomas came in with the tea tray. He stopped short at seeing them at the table instead of at the window.

"I'll just set the tray over here." He indicated where Mrs. Edwards perched on the settee near the window. Thomas knew better than to serve refreshment on Rhys's sacred workplace, where spilled tea or an errant cake crumb could cause irreparable damage.

Rhys nodded. "Thank you, Thomas. I'll ring if we require anything further." He doubted they'd get to the tea tray at all, not when Miss Derrington looked as if she was going to snatch the book up and dash back to Gloucester.

The sound of Thomas departing was accompanied by the clink of dishware as Mrs. Edwards saw to her tea. "Will you be having tea?" she asked them.

"I won't, thank you," Rhys answered. He turned back to Miss Derrington and noted that her gaze was pinned to his hold on her book. Rather, her aunts' book. He exhaled, his fingers tingling as he realized anew what he was touching. The lost text by Edmund de Valery, which some scholars doubted existed. Clearly it did—but did it contain the secret code that supposedly led to an Arthurian treasure?

A sense of alarm slammed into him. "Does anyone else know you have this?"

Her brows drew together. "No. At least not that I'm aware of."

He relaxed against the back of his chair. *Good.* If certain others knew that this book had surfaced, they'd go to great lengths to possess it. Just as he was prepared to do.

He turned the page to an illustration of several knights battling a giant. "These tales are a series of tasks that a knight—Gareth—had to complete in order to win the hand of his true love. He obtained several items, which her father demanded as her bride price."

He pointed at one knight in particular. “This is Arthur.”

“Yes, I’ve read it.” She leaned closer, and once again her scent assailed him. “Is that Excalibur? It doesn’t say.”

He shook his head, turning another page. “This story is before Arthur purportedly found that sword. Every tale is a bit different.” And based on pure fantasy. There was no actual Excalibur and no King Arthur.

“Why is this book so special?”

He felt her eyes on him, wondered how she’d detected that this book was indeed special. He had no plans to tell her about the code, particularly when it might not even exist. “It’s an excellent piece. I assume you’ve studied it intently.”

Her brilliant eyes met his. “Every word, every stroke, every color.” Her passion for the book was palpable. Perhaps equal to his own. But no, that couldn’t be possible. His entire life had been dedicated to books like these, and this was the discovery of a lifetime. A discovery that would do much to establish Rhys as a leading scholar outside of his father’s shadow, even without the code or treasure.

Rhys flipped ahead, though it pained him not to linger over each page. There’d be time for that. He’d pay any price to make sure of it.

There were more stories. An illustration of men around a table.

Her hand fluttered over his. “The round table.”

“Mmmm.” He turned the pages faster, using great caution so as not to damage the aged vellum, eager to reach the final page to confirm that this was, in fact, the treasure he believed it to be.

Finally, the last page. And there it was, in the corner, so small as to be mistaken for a smudge or a bit of graffiti. He lightly touched the mark, as if he could feel the imprint of the man who'd made it centuries before.

"What?" She'd caught his reaction and leaned closer. "What is it?"

He turned his head. If the excitement coursing through him hadn't pushed him to the edge of joy, her proximity might've done so. She was lovely. And desperate—but for what? He realized he didn't care. He only knew he had to have this book, even if it didn't conceal a secret code that led to a mysterious treasure.

"Name your price, Miss Derrington."

Chapter Two

IF AUNT AGNES and Aunt Eugenie were here, they'd ask for maybe fifty pounds, he'd likely accept, the book would trade hands, and they'd be on their merry way. But the words stuck in Margery's throat. Why couldn't she just name a price?

Because in the days since she'd laid her hands on the manuscript, she'd devoured every page dozens of times. That first night, she'd stayed up into the wee hours poring over every drawing and every line of text. After so much time with it, the thing felt like it was hers.

Too, there was his reaction. His interest had been evident, but the way he'd held the book from her had taken his interest to an entirely different plane. He desired this book quite fervently. Why?

She glanced at the open book where his long fingers splayed across the bottom corner. "You didn't answer my question." She was guarding her answers because she didn't want him to know how desperate she was. Why was he guarding his? "Why is this book so special? Knowing that might help me come up with a price."

He cleared his throat as if he were about to deliver an oration. "It's a singular artifact. On their own, these stories aren't necessarily original or extraordinary, but in this state, they are elevated to art. It's the scribe who composed this book that makes it so important." He pointed to a small, black drawing in the bottom left corner of the last page.

She tried to make sense of the swirled ink, but it just looked like the scribe had blotted his pen there. "What is that?"

"The scribe's mark—Edmund de Valery. It's hard to discern, but this is an E, D, and V written over each other." He stood and reached for a magnifying glass sitting at the other end of the table and handed it to her. "Look."

She held the glass between her eye and the page. "Yes, now I see the V and the branches of the E." She turned to look at Mr. Bowen and realized just how close they were. She could feel his heat. His mouth was only inches from hers.

With a jolt, she set the glass on the table and averted her gaze from the absurdly handsome Mr. Bowen. He was an antiquarian, his nose buried in books all day. Why then did his appearance make her think of the knights in the book before them? Likely because he was uncharacteristically tall with broad shoulders. He had the look of a Welshman with his jet-black hair, earth-brown eyes, and dark complexion. If she hadn't known his occupation, she might have assumed him some warrior of old.

She forced herself back to the matter at hand instead of romanticizing Mr. Bowen. "How did you recognize this?"

He kept his focus on the book, something she should endeavor to do. "I've seen his mark before. I have another document written by de Valery."

She expected him to get it or at least offer to show it to her. That he didn't filled her with suspicion, as did his reluctance to tell her why this book was so important to him. "May I see it?" she asked, infusing her question with sugary politeness and offering her most charming smile.

He blinked at her, his terribly long, ink-black lashes briefly shuttering his dark eyes. He studied her at length, then stood, though she sensed he was hesitant. His fingers pressed against the book before releasing it as he stepped away from the table. As he went to his desk, she resisted the urge to pull the book back toward where she was sitting.

A moment later, he returned with a slim, leather-bound manuscript and set it on the table in front of her. "This is a poem from the late fourteenth century. My father had it bound to protect the vellum. If you turn to the last page, you will see a better representation of de Valery's mark."

She hesitated and shot him a saucy look. "May I touch it, since I'm wearing gloves?"

The corner of his mouth lifted in the barest hint of a smile, and he tipped his head. "Please."

Something about the way he delivered the word made her shiver. She opened the cover and flipped past a few blank pages before reaching the text. The document wasn't illustrated, beyond colors used in some of the lettering, but the handwriting was an art form in and of itself. "I can only imagine how much time it took to compile these."

"Years in some cases, though this poem probably only took several weeks. It's not terribly long."

No, just a handful of pages. As he'd said, the last page contained a larger, more legible version of the mark. She looked over at him. He was watching her. "Are you certain this is the same?"

"If you'd studied the written word for as long and as extensively as I have, you could identify the similarities in the letter shape and the stroke of the pen." His tone was smooth, certain.

"Has anyone ever told you that you're arrogant?"

He lifted a shoulder. "On several occasions." His nonchalant response only underscored her assessment. "Has anyone ever told you that you're immoderately direct?" The question sounded more curious than judgmental, maybe even a little bit flirtatious.

She decided his answer suited her just fine. "On several occasions."

He inclined his head. "I didn't mean to be arrogant; I take the study of manuscripts quite seriously."

"It's your life's work," she said, wondering what that felt like.

"It is." His contentment and confidence conveyed an emotion that told her what it felt like, at least, to him. It also filled her with a sense of longing. She wished she felt like that about something.

She looked back at the scribe's mark. "This is Edmund de Valery's work, you say. But you still haven't told me why my—our—book is important or valuable."

He glanced at Mrs. Edwards, her neighbor from Gloucester who'd consented to accompany her on this errand when Aunt Eugenie had taken ill. Unease flashed in his eyes, as if he was reluctant to share his thoughts in front of the woman. He lowered his voice. "To any scholar this is a highly important text, but I am not any scholar. I believe this book might be one of a pair of the finest representations of medieval documentation ever created. As a singular specimen, the book is worth what I offered you. The books together are worth significantly more." He leaned forward. "I want the book, Miss Derrington. Enough that I am willing to risk my coin to pay the elevated amount now, before I ascertain if it is indeed the text I believe it to be."

She ought to just sell it to him, would be deranged not to, but she'd seen the gleam in his eyes before. It was the one a gentleman who was light in the pockets wore when he acquired the attention of a debutante with a fat dowry. Could there be more wealth involved than the amount she required to solve her immediate problem? Could there be enough to live independently without worrying about every shilling she spent? "Where is this other book?" Perhaps she'd appeal directly to that person.

"It belongs to my second cousin, the Earl of Stratton."

Drat. She'd heard of Stratton, a dissolute beast with a penchant for drink and a constant stream of women who weren't his wife. Every young lady, even those who couldn't afford a Season, had been warned of Lord Stratton as an example of why to approach the Marriage Mart with great caution. He'd duped not one, but two young women into wedlock after wooing them quite earnestly. Not for their money or their position, but for their beauty. He saw women as objects for his lust and little more.

No, he was not the sort to deal fairly with a lady. She couldn't risk going to him directly with her text. She was stuck then with Mr. Bowen—unless she could find another buyer. But first, they needed to appraise the book, apparently.

"It sounds as though the books ought to be compared side by side so that a true value can be ascertained," she said.

"Yes, that is what I would propose. If you would consent to lend me your book, I'd be pleased to take it to Stratton Hall and conduct the comparison."

Margery stared at him. Was he daft? "I'm not going to let you borrow it. I'll go with you. I should like to see Stratton's de Valery manuscript."

Now he stared at her as if she were daft. "Out of the question. Have you any idea how loathsome my cousin is?"

"All of England does. That is neither here nor there. I'm not letting you take my book."

"Your *aunts'* book."

She gritted her teeth. His condescension was quite frustrating. She kept her chin up and tried to exude a measure of hauteur. "You've no choice in the matter. If you wish to analyze the books together, you must take me with you."

His jaw worked, and she could tell he didn't like being forced, but that he also realized he was cornered. "Very well."

She relaxed slightly, but kept her guard up. "When shall we leave?"

"The sooner the better," he said, glancing at the book. "I can arrange for us to depart in the morning."

This was happening so quickly. Margery thought she had enough money to pay for the journey, but wanted to be certain. "How long will we be gone?"

"Stratton Hall is outside the village of Leominster—two days' travel to the north. We'll have to lodge in Hereford tomorrow evening."

Margery mentally calculated her funds. Yes, she had enough to suffice. She'd post a letter to her aunts explaining the extension of her trip. But would Mrs. Edwards consent to accompany her? If she did not, the entire enterprise would fail before it even began. And she believed it was necessary—both to determine the book's true value and to ascertain what Stratton might pay her.

The voice of Aunt Eugenie, of common sense, railed inside Margery's brain. She ought to sell the book to Mr. Bowen right now and return home. However, the voice of Aunt Agnes, of a romantic nature Margery hadn't even realized she possessed, rose and demanded she embark on this quest. It was a risk, but if it paid off, she would solve all of their financial problems.

"I'll send a note to let Stratton know we're coming."

"How will you explain my presence?" she asked.

"I'll tell him you're interested in seeing his de Valery manuscript. Sometimes the simplest explanation is the best."

The truth, then, or at least a portion of it. "I need to speak with Mrs. Edwards. Please excuse me." Margery stood and went to where her companion sat near the windows.

The woman, just three years Margery's senior, lowered her empty teacup to the saucer perched on her lap. She showed no indication of having paid any attention to the discussion at the table. "Ready then? Too bad we can't just return home now, but I suppose an afternoon of shopping won't come amiss." Shopping was all Mrs. Edwards had talked about during their journey from Gloucester yesterday.

"I need to extend my trip. Mr. Bowen and I must travel to Leominster."

Mrs. Edwards blanched. "I agreed to this short jaunt, not a lengthy expedition. I must get back to my house, to Mr. Edwards."

Margery supposed she could hire a new companion, but preferred not to. "I understand. You'll be compensated for this additional time. It won't be more than a few days and we're going to see an earl."

As Margery had hoped, Mrs. Edwards' eyes lit up at the mention of an earl. "I suppose I can be away a little longer. But what will your aunts say?"

"They will support the journey. I'll post a letter when we return to the inn."

Mrs. Edwards glanced at the door, clearly eager to depart. "Are we going back to town now?" Their lodgings were in Monmouth, a short carriage ride away.

"Not yet. I'll be just a moment." She returned to the table where Mr. Bowen was studying the book and reclaimed her seat. "That's my favorite page."

Toward the end, this particular page bore the most elaborate illustration—a large group of people surrounding the knight kneeling before a beautiful lady dressed in blue robes. He offered her a heart-shaped stone as she beamed down at him.

Mr. Bowen's fingers, so long and lean, traced the decoration at the edge of the page. "This stone is called the Heart of Llanllwch. It isn't typically one of the thirteen treasures in these sorts of tales. It's particular only to de Valery's version. And unlike the thirteen treasures, this stone actually exists."

"It does?"

"It's in the Ashmolean Museum at Oxford. I've seen it, though it's been dipped in gold and has five different gemstones affixed to its exterior."

"Sounds lavish. And quite different from that one." She pointed at the simple stone, a pale yellow, on the page just as he moved his hand. Their appendages collided and she felt the contact as though her hands were bare. Perhaps traveling with Mr. Bowen, even with a chaperone, wasn't such a sound idea after all.

He quickly moved his hand back to the margin.

"The stone was likely augmented later. Underneath the decoration, it's a simple yellow tourmaline stone."

"So de Valery somehow knew its original state?"

His brow furrowed as he stared at the page. "So it seems, which is intriguing, given the stone was just discovered less than fifty years ago."

She began to see why Mr. Bowen was so fascinated with this text. "Do you think he saw the stone before—when he wrote this?"

He shot her a provocative glance that further kindled her enthusiasm. "I don't know. I would guess he based this drawing on whatever source material he used to record these stories."

She found herself drawn into his knowledge on the subject. Yes, he was arrogant, but about this, it appeared he had a right to be. "What sort of source material?"

He shrugged. "It could be another document or oral stories. Or de Valery could have simply made them up." He closed the book and looked at her, apparently finished with their interesting discussion. "Where are you staying in town?"

"The White Lady." She picked up the book and was mildly surprised when he let her take it without comment.

He stood from the table and went to his desk, where he opened a drawer and withdrew a sturdy linen bag. He came back and handed it to her. "Carry the book in this to protect it. Be ready to depart at nine." No please or other politeness, just directives he expected her to follow.

Margery slid the book into the back and got to her feet. She hoped she wouldn't regret not selling it to him immediately. "We'll be waiting for you, Mr. Bowen."

And because she couldn't bear to let his superiority win the day, added, "Don't be late."

AFTER HE'D WRITTEN a letter to Stratton, Rhys set about organizing the details of their journey. He preferred to avoid visiting his odious cousin, but it was, unfortunately, necessary.

Was it, however, necessary to embark on this adventure with Miss Derrington? Apparently it was, since it didn't seem she was going to sell him the book straightaway.

When she'd tried to leave, he'd reconsidered his position. She'd sensed how important the book was to him because he'd been foolishly excited about its existence. *The lost de Valery manuscript.* Paired with Stratton's text, there would be a secret code that would lead to a treasure—if the legend were true.

And he wanted that treasure. If the de Valery manuscript on its own would elevate his reputation, solving de Valery's secret code and discovering the treasure would guarantee his renown as a leading antiquarian. He felt sad that his father wouldn't be able to share in his success, but the accomplishment still meant everything to Rhys.

Rhys looked at his workspace where her book had sat and frowned. Traveling with a young, unmarried miss—chaperone or not—bordered on scandalous. Yet, propriety wasn't something he typically worried about. He was, as so many purported, practically a hermit.

Thomas entered the office, his black costume

impeccable. "I have informed Craddock of your travel plans."

"Thank you. Here is the letter to dispatch to Stratton." He handed over the missive, which Thomas would have Craddock take into town for a courier to deliver.

Pinching the letter between his thumb and forefinger, Thomas made no move to leave.

"Is there something else?" Rhys asked.

Thomas's brow creased. "Your charge is in the rear yard with a . . . whip."

His charge. *Penn.*

Damn, he'd been so overwhelmed by first his aching head and then the arrival of Miss Derrington and her astonishing book that he'd failed to recollect the newest member of their household. "A whip you say?"

"A whip. And he's . . . how to put this . . . using it for target practice of some sort."

Rhys pushed back from the table and stood. "I'll investigate."

"Mrs. Thomas is worried he'll hurt himself."

Of course she was. She'd been mothering the eight-year-old since Rhys had agreed to foster him scarcely a fortnight ago.

"Sir," Thomas said somewhat hesitantly. "Are you sure taking Master Penn in was the right decision?"

Rhys paused on his way to the door. "What choice did I have?"

Without Rhys's intervention, Penn would have nowhere to go, except to his father—who thankfully didn't even know Penn existed—and Rhys had promised he wouldn't allow that. He would *never* allow that. He might not appreciate the sudden invasion of a child into his well-ordered life, but he wouldn't consign the lad to the alternative.

"You could send him off to school," Thomas suggested.

Rhys had pondered that. In addition to agreeing to keep the boy safe from his father, Rhys had promised to see Penn educated—those were the two things Penn's dying mother had sworn him to do. "I may, in time."

Thomas nodded. "I suppose if you tried to ship him off now, Mrs. Thomas would likely revolt."

"Yes, she would, and I don't want to inflict that upon you, Thomas," Rhys said.

Turning, Rhys made his way to the back of the house and onto the small terrace that overlooked a tidy garden. Beyond that, a green space stretched before a thick wooded area. Penn was whipping rock targets he'd set along the top of the stone wall that separated the garden from the greenway. He scarcely missed, each stroke of the whip knocking the objects down one by one. With long strides, Rhys approached him from the side.

Penn darted his bright blue eyes toward Rhys, showing that he was aware of Rhys's approach.

Rhys eyed the whip. He had no such implement in his possession. Though Penn's mother had assured Rhys that he was a well-mannered boy, Rhys didn't know if he'd be inclined to steal. But from where? He hadn't left Hollyhaven since arriving. "Where did you get that?"

Penn didn't stop his movements, arcing the whip out until it snapped another rock from the top of the wall. "Found it."

"Where?"

Another crack.

"Digging over by the trees."

Penn had a habit of digging holes. If Rhys hadn't known better, he might've thought he'd brought a dog with him.

Rhys looked toward the treeline where Penn had pointed, but didn't see anything. "Show me."

Penn took out the last rock and shrugged. He coiled the whip and loped toward the trees.

Rhys walked swiftly beside him. "You're very good with that whip. And you just found it?"

"This morning." The boy was frustratingly light of speech, but what could Rhys expect? Penn's mother had begged Rhys to foster him, stayed for two nights, and then left him there. Rhys doubted he'd be able to find much to say in those circumstances either.

They reached the wooded area. Along the edge was a series of holes. Penn went to the one at the far end and stood.

"This one, eh?" Rhys asked, studying the boy. His hair was a bit too long, falling over his forehead, but Mrs. Thomas had insisted they not try trimming it until he'd settled in.

But how would they know he was settled? Rhys had no siblings and, of course, no children of his own. He hadn't the slightest notion how to read a young person, particularly one who only spoke the bare minimum.

Penn didn't say anything, nor did he nod. He just looked down at the empty hole.

Rhys couldn't contain himself any longer. "Why do you dig?"

Penn looked up at him, the strands of his hair partially obscuring eyes that seemed alert, intelligent, though Rhys had seen nothing in his behavior to confirm that. The boy could read and do sums, but he showed no interest in continuing his education. This was a fight that was coming, however. Like his father before him, he'd ensure Penn learned what he must.

Penn shrugged. "I find things."

"What else have you found?"

Digging into his pocket, Penn withdrew a fistful of items. He opened his palm and exposed them: a piece of metal, a bone fragment, a shard of pottery, and two coins.

Rhys had expected a verbal list, not the actual things. He leaned forward and examined the treasures. And they were treasures—at least the coins were. Rhys recognized them as Roman. He reached out to touch one, but Penn pulled his hand away. "Where did you find these?"

"I dug them up last year." He gave his head a defensive shake and looked at the ground. "I don't remember where."

Rhys was frustrated by this answer, but not surprised. "You don't have to hide things from me. When I agreed to foster you, I promised your mother you would be safe and that I would treat you fairly."

When Penn raised his eyes, his gaze was wary. "I'm not hiding anything."

Rhys endeavored to keep his expression open and friendly to keep the boy talking. "Did you dig up *all* of those things?"

"All but the piece of dish." He turned the pottery, which had dulled to a murky gray, though some sort of etched design was visible on one side. "A man gave it to me. He said Wales was full of hidden treasures."

Rhys nodded, thinking of whatever might be at the center of de Valery's code. "He's right. And you like doing that, digging for treasure?"

Penn shrugged again.

"You're welcome to dig wherever you like around here, so long as you replace the dirt when you're finished." Rhys glanced at the holes as he made the gentle admonishment.

"Yes, sir."

Rhys nearly smiled at the resignation in the youthful tone. How he remembered being a lad and not wanting to do the things his father required—calculations, memorizing scientific theories, learning Latin. Yet now he was incredibly grateful for his father's care and tutelage, even if it had been demanding. Could he do the same for Penn? Did he even want to?

He was surprised to find he did. Maybe it was time for him to become less of a hermit. And he could think of no better reason. Penn had no one else—his mother was dying and his father was the worst sort of human being. Just as Rhys had grown up with only his father, Penn would grow up with Rhys. There was a certain poetic symmetry to it that appealed to Rhys's ordered mind.

"I didn't just come out here to talk about your holes," Rhys said slowly. Though he hadn't yet formed a bond with the boy, he felt a bit of regret over having to leave him so soon. "I need to take a trip for a few days—four or five at most."

Penn's gaze shot up, his pupils dark and heavy with vulnerability. Caution dropped its veil once more, hiding whatever his true reaction might be.

Rhys wasn't sure why he continued, but maybe it was the regret. "I'm actually going after a bit of treasure myself."

Penn brushed his hair from his eyes as he looked up

again, this time his gaze full of unguarded interest. "Like my coins?"

"No." At least not yet. "I'm going to decipher a code."

"A secret code?" Excitement tinged Penn's question as he leaned slightly forward.

Rhys smothered a smile at the boy's response. Perhaps they'd find some common ground after all. "When I get back, I'll show it to you. Would you like that?"

He nodded briskly. "Very much, sir. Thank you." The lad's manners and method of speech revealed he'd been well-born.

Penn squatted down and set his whip on the ground before he began to fill in the hole. Rhys blinked as a thought struck him: how odd it was to have a child before he had a wife. He'd never given marriage much thought, always thinking he had plenty of time, likely because his father hadn't wed until he was forty. Also, Rhys had yet to meet a woman who piqued his interest enough to even consider it. Until today. Miss Derrington was quick-witted, capable, and, it seemed, adventurous. She was also beautiful into the bargain.

He shook the ridiculous notions from his head. He was no more ready for marriage today than he was yesterday, even with the presence of a young, now-motherless charge. Miss Derrington was a necessary component to fulfilling his aspirations and nothing more.

What he really ought to be considering was how he was going to face his cousin while fostering the son Stratton didn't even know he had.

Chapter Three

THE MORNING WAS cool and damp as Rhys's coach turned onto the High Street in Monmouth. He heard the commotion before he saw it. He barely waited for Craddock to bring them to a halt before throwing open the door.

A line of coaches were stacked along the street, and a group of men clustered in front of the White Lady, where Miss Derrington was lodging. What the devil was going on?

Craddock met him as he stepped from the coach. "Sir?"

"Find out what's happening." Rhys moved toward the men, his body tensing. But then just as quickly, he relaxed as he recognized one of the gentlemen, then a second, then a third.

"Bowen!" Lord Alfred Trevor, one of Rhys's oldest friends, stalked toward him, a wide smile curling his slender lips. "You've decided to join us."

Blast, a lapse in memory from the other night's festivities it seemed. "Ah . . ."

Trevor laughed heartily. "You don't remember. I could see it in your eyes before your coachman dragged you off. Yesterday must've been a pisser, eh?"

"Somewhat, yes."

"Come on then." Trevor clapped him on the back and guided him forward to the group. "We're just waiting for a slug-a-bed before we continue to the river. We're off on the second half of the Wye Tour for

Gillivray's prenuptial celebration. Septon was most insistent that you join us."

Now he remembered the event, if not the invitation to join them. His eye found Septon chatting with another gentleman. Five years Rhys's senior, Septon was a close friend and a fellow antiquarian. Following the tour, he planned to visit the Roman ruins at Caerwent for several days of study.

The academic in Rhys wanted to tell Septon about Miss Derrington's de Valery manuscript, but the adventurer that was emerging from within him insisted he keep quiet. It was a shame, for Septon was particularly adept at ciphers and would undoubtedly thrill to the prospect of studying de Valery's code.

Rhys turned toward Trevor, halting their progress and dislodging Trevor's arm. "Actually, I'm afraid I must decline your kind offer. I am embarking on an important errand this morning."

Trevor frowned, his disapproval apparent. "Something academically-related, I'm certain. You need to put aside your musty texts once in a while before life passes you by."

"I just did that the other night. Pardon my preference for moderation," Rhys said wryly.

Trevor laughed again, his rich, booming voice drawing the attention of some of the other gentlemen. "So you did." He glanced at the doorway. "Good Christ, what is taking Howe so long?"

Rhys also scanned the inn's entrance in search of Miss Derrington. Though she was suitably chaperoned, he didn't want to advertise their joint venture to this group of rakehells.

As Trevor was joined by a pair of gentlemen who were positing reasons for Lord Howe's delay, Rhys edged back toward Craddock. "Would you go into the White Lady and see if you can escort Miss Derrington out via a less conspicuous door?"

With a brisk nod, Craddock hurried inside.

Several minutes later, a tall, slender gentleman garbed in a dark suit of clothes that was quite at odds with the bright colors worn by the rest of the lot exited the inn.

"At last, His Highness deigns to join us!" Trevor offered an exaggerated bow. "We aim to serve at your pleasure, my lord."

The others guffawed while Howe's lips curved into a regretful smile. "My apologies. I'm afraid I was busy . . . lording over the inn's staff." His eyes crinkled with his sarcasm. Howe had a reputation for trying to tumble anything in a skirt—good-naturedly, of course. He wasn't a brute, just a charming viscount with a penchant for women.

The group erupted into even louder laughter, which was accompanied by slaps on Howe's back as they ushered him toward the line of coaches.

Trevor paused before following them and turned to look at Rhys. "This is your last chance to abandon your boring academic quest and come with us."

Rhys smiled and waved him off.

A few minutes later, Craddock called to him from down the street. He carried two valises—one in each hand. Miss Derrington, holding the protective bag he'd given her for the manuscript, and Mrs. Edwards walked beside him.

Rhys hurried to meet them.

Mrs. Edwards frowned at him. "Why did your coachman have to drag us through a back alley?"

Rhys frowned at Craddock. "Didn't you explain?"

"Left that to you, sir." He shrugged as he belatedly pulled down the steps of the coach before climbing up to his seat and securing the luggage.

Opening the vehicle's door, Rhys held it ajar and offered his hand. "My apologies for the inconvenience ladies, there was some congestion at the front of the inn. Please allow me to assist you."

Miss Derrington placed her hand in his and ascended into the coach. He provided the same service for Mrs. Edwards, who looked skeptically at the now-empty street but said nothing further about their detour.

Rhys climbed into the coach just as the ladies had situated themselves on the forward-facing seat. He deposited himself in the seat opposite.

"What precisely is our itinerary?" Mrs. Edwards asked.

As the coach moved forward, Rhys braced himself against the squab. "We'll spend tonight in Hereford, and we should arrive at Stratton Hall by early tomorrow afternoon."

"Is there shopping in Hereford?"

"I'm afraid we won't be there long enough to do that," Miss Derrington said. "Perhaps Leominster boasts some shops."

Rhys vaguely remembered the small village and thought there might be a milliner's, but couldn't say for certain. "We shall find out when we pass through, and I'm certain we can make an accommodation for you to tour the village, Mrs. Edwards."

"That would be most diverting, thank you." She settled into her corner and looked out the window as the coach traveled down the High Street.

Rhys turned his attention to Miss Derrington. She

appeared fresh and lovely today, garbed in a blue traveling costume edged with black velvet. A wide-brimmed bonnet shielded her blond hair, but a few curls brushed her temples.

He oughtn't look at her so closely. They were business associates at best. At worst, adversaries vying for the same treasure, which she didn't even know existed. *Yet.* He'd thought about whether he should have told her, but until he was certain there was even a code to decipher, why bother?

"We should discuss our visit," he said. "You must never go anywhere alone, and you mustn't do anything to encourage Stratton's interest." Though she'd likely do that by simply breathing.

Miss Derrington eyed him inquisitively. "I'm well aware of your cousin's reputation. I shall be on my guard."

"You must be. Stratton is a dissolute fiend. Make sure Mrs. Edwards is with you at all times. In fact, I will insist that you sleep in the same chamber."

"There you go with 'must' and 'insist.' Have you always been so dictatorial?" she asked.

Mrs. Edwards shrugged. "It's no trouble; we shared a room at the White Lady."

Rhys gave Miss Derrington a look that communicated something to the effect of, *not everyone thinks I'm dictatorial.*

Miss Derrington exhaled softly. "I suppose adjoining chambers will suffice. Thank you so much for consulting with us," she said with false sweetness.

He ignored her sarcasm. Protecting her was his responsibility while they were traveling together, and Stratton was a legitimate threat to a young lady like herself. "I worry that I should have come alone," he muttered.

"With my book?" She shook her head. "There was never any chance of that."

Right. "Then you must adhere to my guidelines. You'll leave the door between your adjoining chambers open so that Mrs. Edwards can hear you if you need assistance." Rhys would request a nearby chamber as well, though that would undoubtedly pique Stratton's curiosity.

In fact, perhaps Rhys ought to infer that Miss Derrington was already taken. It wouldn't be foolproof—things such as marriage and engagements hadn't always prevented Stratton from attempting scandalous behavior—but it might work. There had to be some honor among families, even for Stratton, didn't there?

Was there honor in keeping a man's son from him? For the boy's well-being, yes.

Miss Derrington set her hand atop the bag that held the book nestled beside her. "I shall be cautious."

They fell into silence for a good quarter hour or longer. Soft snores emanated from Mrs. Edwards's corner.

Miss Derrington turned her head from the window to look at Rhys. "Are you and Stratton close? While you possess a somewhat irritating predilection for condescension, your behavior is at complete odds with his scandalous reputation."

Rhys fought the urge to smile at her description of him. He ought to find her irritation annoying, but was instead charmed. He decided he might enjoy tormenting her—at least a bit. "Our familial connection is distant. I've only visited him a handful times: a few occasions as a child, his weddings, and once with my father to see his de Valery manuscript. I did attend one of his house parties, left early, and swore never to repeat the mistake."

"I see. I understand Lady Stratton simply disregards his mischief?" Her tone held a strong note of disbelief.

Rhys had met her twice—the wedding and the house party—and found her to be lovely, if withdrawn. He felt sad for her lot and wondered what she would say if she knew the first Lady Stratton was still alive—at least for now. "She has little choice in the matter, unfortunately."

"Indeed," Miss Derrington murmured. "It doesn't recommend the institution of marriage, does it? Is that why you are unmarried, Mr. Bowen?"

Her gaze found his, and he was struck by the frank curiosity in its depths. There was something more. Her eyes reminded him of a hothouse—a mix of earthy brown and vivid green. Exotic. Sultry. Perhaps he'd been reading too much romantic poetry of late.

"I haven't felt the need to take a wife."

She cocked her head to the side. "Too wrapped up in your books?"

"Perhaps." *Definitely*. "And why do you remain unwed? I can't believe you haven't had offers." She was far too lovely, too intelligent, too bewitching.

Bewitching?

"Believe it or not, I haven't," her answer came quick and carried a touch of irritation. "Furthermore, I haven't felt the need to marry either."

He'd been jesting with his answer. It wasn't so much that he hadn't felt the need, just that he hadn't considered it at all. But with her, he imagined she had to have considered it—women in her position really had no other choice. Sooner or later, she'd likely marry.

And he suddenly envied that faceless man.

MARGERY OPENED HER eyes in the fire-lit room and took a moment to register her surroundings. The chamber at the inn was small, which was why she was huddled on a pallet between the narrow bed she'd given to Mrs. Edwards and the small fireplace in which the remnants of an earlier fire glowed orange. Based on the color of the embers, Margery hadn't been asleep terribly long, but it wasn't unusual that she would wake up when lodging in a strange place. Especially when the thin padding separating her from the floor did nothing to provide comfort.

Creak.

Now *that* was unusual.

Margery turned onto her back, expecting to see Mrs. Edwards getting out of bed perhaps. Yes, there was a dark figure. But it was much too tall . . .

A muffled screech, like someone was holding his hand over Mrs. Edwards's mouth, drew Margery to sit up. She looked frantically for some sort of weapon. Her gaze landed on the fireplace poker.

"I'll slit yer throat if ye scream," hissed a masculine voice. "Where's the book?"

The book?

It was stuffed beneath Margery's pillow. She bolted to her feet and lunged for the poker, grasping the handle with a tight grip. Spinning on her heel, she nearly lost her balance as fear and anger coursed through her. Lifting the poker, she brought it down on the intruder's head, but he moved to the right and she just grazed him.

It was enough to dislodge his hand, for Mrs. Edwards let loose a high scream that was bound to bring the inn down around them. The intruder raised his arm and the blade in his hand flashed, reflecting the scant light from the embers.

Margery swung the poker again, this time hitting him square in the side of the head.

He roared, nearly as loudly as Mrs. Edwards had screamed, and swung around. There was enough light for Margery to make out the nasty scar that disfigured his mouth and his long, misshapen nose.

"Ye shouldn't have done that," he growled. He reached for her arm, but she flailed backward, trying to escape his reach.

The door slammed against the wall as a second large figure dashed inside. And then the would-be-thief was gone, or at least no longer pursuing her. The two men tussled for a moment, but it was so dark, Margery couldn't tell who was who or what was really happening. There were grunts, a curse, and a sharp intake of breath.

Then one of the men—the intruder, she was almost certain—fled the room.

"Mr. Bowen?" Margery moved cautiously toward their rescuer.

He lifted his head, and the firelight revealed it was he. "Are you all right?" His gaze raked her thoroughly before he turned to look at Mrs. Edwards. She sat up in the bed, her eyes wide, and clutched the coverlet to her chin.

Margery dropped the poker and rushed to her side. "We're saved. Are you hurt?"

Mrs. Edwards shook her head, her long, dark braid

curling along her collarbone.

"Are you both well?" Mr. Bowen asked from just behind Margery.

She turned to look at him. "I think so. He asked for the book." She returned her focus to Mrs. Edwards. "Did he say anything else?"

"That he was going to . . . to . . . slit my throat." Her face was the color of ash.

Margery leaned closer and slid her arm around Mrs. Edwards's shoulders in a half hug. "You're going to be fine. We're safe now."

"I think I'd prefer to return home in the morning. After Mr. Bowen's talk of Lord Stratton and that . . . that . . . brigand, I'm afraid I . . ." She dropped her face into her hands and began to cry.

Margery's heart ached for the poor woman. It must've been terrible to wake up to a strange man standing over you with a knife. Margery's own heart was still beating a horrendous rhythm in her chest, and she couldn't shake the icy sensation lodged in her spine. She rubbed her hand over Mrs. Edwards's back as she cried.

"What happened?" A new masculine voice came from the doorway as light flooded the chamber.

Margery looked over to see the innkeeper, a lantern in his hand.

"There was an intruder," Mr. Bowen said. Now that she could properly see, Margery was shocked to realize Mr. Bowen's chest was bare. And quite muscular. "A would-be thief." He shot Margery a glance that was meant to convey something—probably not to mention the book, though she'd already made that determination for herself.

The innkeeper moved farther into the room. "He

make off with anything?"

"No," Margery answered. "He was tall, slender, with a scar cutting across his mouth and a long, crooked nose, as if it had been broken several times."

Mrs. Edwards had stopped crying, though her frame still felt quivery beneath Margery's touch. Additional figures stood in the corridor outside the room. Other guests, certainly—the inn was full to capacity—which was why Margery and Mrs. Edwards were sharing such a tiny room.

"Everyone all right?" The innkeeper's gaze settled on Mrs. Edwards, whose head was still bent.

"She'll be fine," Mr. Bowen said. "You ought to do a thorough check of the inn and the stables. Probably the grounds. He had a knife and threatened the ladies. I know we'd all feel better if we could be certain he was gone."

Mrs. Edwards nodded, but didn't say anything.

"I'll come with you," Mr. Bowen continued. "Allow me to attire myself appropriately."

The innkeeper nodded, then turned. "If any of the lot of you care to help, follow me."

Mr. Bowen made to leave, but Margery gave Mrs. Edwards a gentle pat and hurried to stop him. She touched his elbow just as he was crossing the threshold to the corridor. The connection of her fingers with his bare flesh banished any residual chill that was resting in her bones.

She jerked her hand back as he turned. "Thank you."

His eyes reminded her of the blackened pieces in the fireplace, dark as pitch but smoldering with undeniable heat. "You're certain you're all right?"

"I am. Though I am concerned for Mrs. Edwards.

She's had a terrible fright."

"Unsurprising. That was quite an event." He blinked at her. "Did you hit him with the fireplace poker?"

She nodded, feeling exceptionally good, maybe even a bit pleased with herself. "Twice."

"What a dangerous vixen you are," he murmured. His gaze caressed her, lingering on her hair, which she'd unpinned before bed and left to hang loose past her shoulders.

"Perhaps, but your arrival was most opportune." She suddenly noticed a small trickle of blood on the side of his neck. Her fingers were against his flesh again before she could censor herself. "You're hurt."

His hand came up and their fingers collided. "Just a scratch from his knife."

She ignored the sensations rioting in her belly and poked at his skin. Yes, just a small scratch, but it would require cleaning. "You're lucky it wasn't worse."

He arched a brow at her. "Luck had nothing to do with it. I can move rather quickly, Miss Derrington, despite my size."

Yes, his size. She'd likened him to a warrior and now, with his bare torso exposed to her perusal, she was certain he was some reincarnated hero. Perhaps one of the knights in the book. The book!

She dropped her hand from his neck and rushed back to the pallet. Throwing the pillow aside, she scooped up the tome and clutched it to her chest. The attempt to steal the manuscript had changed everything. Mrs. Edwards wanted to return home, Mr. Bowen had been injured, and someone was most definitely after her book. *Who?*

Mr. Bowen had followed her. "It's safe?"

"Yes, I had it under my pillow."

"A good thing." His tone was grim. "However, it might be best if you gave it to me for safekeeping."

"Why? Whoever's looking for it knows I have it. They'll still try to come after me."

"But they won't find the book. Not that I'm going to let anyone come anywhere near you." His pledge was dark and glorious, almost romantic. She shivered.

Perhaps she *should* deliver the book into his custody. No, she had too many unanswered questions.

"Please give it to him," Mrs. Edwards said.

Her tone was so forlorn, so frightened that Margery nearly relented. "I'll consider it."

He frowned at her. "We'll discuss it after I've helped with the search."

"Must you?" Mrs. Edward's voice croaked. "I'd feel safer if you or someone else stayed with us."

Margery went back to the bed and patted the woman's shoulder. "Whatever you'd like."

"Give me a few minutes to get dressed and check on the search," he said. "I'll feel better when I know the bugger—pardon me—is gone." With a final probing stare, he turned and left.

Mrs. Edwards's gaze fixed on the book Margery cradled against her right side. "What's in that anyway?"

"Just old stories recorded by a fourteenth-century scribe." Now Margery was certain there was more to this book than Mr. Bowen had revealed. And she was going to demand he tell her the truth. "The book is highly valued."

"But why are you taking it to Stratton Hall to compare it with this other book?" Her eyes narrowed. "This whole endeavor is suspicious."

Margery couldn't disagree. "Do you truly want to return to Gloucester in the morning?" This was by far a better topic than the book. Besides, if Mrs. Edwards meant to leave, Margery would have to make other arrangements for a chaperone.

"I do, and you should come with me. This is a dangerous escapade." She said this in her best I-know-better-than-you-and-as-your-chaperone-it's-my-duty-to-remind-you-of-that tone.

"I trust Mr. Bowen to keep me safe." She was surprised when the words escaped her mouth. She might not trust his motives regarding the book, but he'd jumped to their defense with alacrity and vigor—and she didn't think it was just because of the manuscript. The way he'd looked at her . . . She suppressed another shiver. "He can keep us both safe. Plus, I'll sleep with a poker."

This earned a smile from Mrs. Edwards. "That was rather brilliant of you. Your aunts will find this tale most diverting."

Her aunts. Oh dear, this would worry them needlessly. She didn't want to keep it from them, but there would be time to tell them later. "If you do return to Gloucester, please don't tell them what happened. Just say you needed to come home." Margery touched her hand, which sat atop the coverlet in her lap. "Please, this errand is absolutely necessary and I won't have them upset."

After a long moment, Mrs. Edwards nodded. "Let me consider whether I will continue with you to Stratton Hall. After I sleep. *If* I sleep." She lay back against the pillow and brought the bedclothes up to her neck.

"That sounds like an excellent notion." She brushed her hand against the worn cotton of the quilt. "I'll just wait for Mr. Bowen to return."

She partially closed the door and moved into the corridor, leaning against the wall. A few minutes later, the light of a lantern flashed down the hallway and Mr. Bowen came into view. He'd donned a shirt and waistcoat, though his neck remained bare.

"There's no sign of the brigand yet. I'm sure he's gone and won't bother us again tonight."

Holding the book to her chest, she pinned him with an intense stare. "I think it's past time you told me the truth about this book. What are you hiding about its value?"

He hesitated a moment too long, his mouth pulling down.

"Tell me now or I'm returning to Gloucester in the morning—with my book." Her voice climbed. "That you would put me and Mrs. Edwards in danger—"

He pressed his fingers against her lips. "Enough. The book holds a secret code." He gritted his teeth as if he'd hated letting the words out. Which he probably did.

She moved his hand away from her mouth, though his touch hadn't bothered her nearly as much as it should have. "A secret code for what?'

"A treasure."

Margery resisted the urge to kick him. "You bounder!"

He took a small step back. "I don't even know if the code is real. I wanted to make sure before I told you."

"So you planned to tell me after you did whatever you were going to do at Stratton Hall? Forgive me if I don't trust you at all just now."

His dark eyes glittered in the lantern light. "This book . . . this treasure . . . They're important to me in ways you can't understand. To you, they represent a monetary find, but to me, they are the discovery of a lifetime."

"And your discovery is more important than my need for money?" She pressed her lips together, wishing she could take the words back. "What is this treasure?"

"No one knows for certain. The pair of books is alleged to be coded with information that will lead to something important. Perhaps another of the thirteen treasures, like the Heart of Llanllwch."

"You were never going to tell me about the treasure, were you?" Suddenly the book felt like a possible weapon in her arms. One she could bludgeon him with. "You planned to solve the code at Stratton Hall and probably send me on my way back to Gloucester without ever even purchasing the book."

He had the grace to look aghast. "That isn't true. I wanted to buy the book. I still do. You're the one who changed their mind about selling it. I'll buy it from you right now—name your price." He leaned toward her, his features harsh. "*Any* price."

"Oh, I'll sell you the book. *After* we find the treasure and split it."

His nostrils flared, and his eyes narrowed almost imperceptibly. "*We* find the treasure?"

"You need this book to find it. And I'm not letting it out of my sight, especially not after you tried to swindle it from me without disclosing its true value."

"Swindle?" His voice rose, but he reined it back by clenching his jaw. "I did no such thing. I offered you a fair price."

"Fair for what? A rare medieval text? Perhaps. For a treasure that you called the 'discovery of a lifetime'? Your offer didn't even come close to paying for something of that value." She notched her chin up and straightened her spine. "Take my offer or leave it. It's the only way you'll have access to my book."

He crossed his arms over his broad chest. "That isn't going to make for a very solid alliance."

"You're right. Perhaps we should part ways right now. I can visit Stratton on my own and solve the code."

"The devil you will. I'm not letting you anywhere near him without my protection." He dropped a glance at the book. "And just how do you purport to solve this code when you don't even know what it looks like?"

She eyed him with a generous dose of skepticism. "I suppose you do?"

His muttered epithet gave her a notable amount of satisfaction.

"Do we have an accord?" she asked.

His eyes were still dark as pitch, but there was a glint of something in their depths—begrudging admiration perhaps. "Yes."

Margery exhaled, not realizing she'd held her breath. "Have you any idea who tried to steal this?" She tightened her grip on the book.

He crossed his arms and leaned his shoulder against the wall. "Did you speak to anyone about it?"

"No." She'd kept it close and hadn't discussed it with anyone. "My aunts had forgotten all about it until we found it in the attic just the other day."

His expression mirrored how she felt—utterly confounded. "Well, someone knows you have it. We'll need to be very careful."

"This someone is after the treasure, not just the book."

He inclined his head. "I think it's safe to assume that, yes. But Stratton has the other book and without both, the code can't even be detected."

She knew that to be true, since she'd spent countless hours studying the text and hadn't noticed anything that could be interpreted as a secret code. She supposed that was what made it *secret*. "Even *with* both, the code might be meaningless, unless we can decipher it."

"We will." He spoke confidently, but she had to admit she found his streak of hubris somewhat attractive. Probably because he had the intelligence and wit to support it. "Does Mrs. Edwards really want to return home? I suppose I can have Craddock drive her, and I can hire a coach to take us to Stratton Hall. Then there is the matter of a chaperone—"

"She's pondering it while she sleeps. I'm hopeful she'll just continue with us, though she is quite upset."

He cocked his head to the side. It was a slight, innocuous movement, but it put his head at an angle that made him seem even more attractive, if that was possible. "I'm a little surprised you're not."

Margery appreciated the admiration in his tone. "It takes a great deal to rattle me. However, I didn't wake up with a large, ugly man waving a knife in my face, so I reserve the right to behave precisely as Mrs. Edwards did."

"You're an extraordinary young woman, Miss Derrington." He moved subtly closer, and it was as if the air in the corridor thinned. "But if that ever happens to you, I pity the man, for I'll ensure he won't live to see the morrow."

Chapter Four

THE EARLY AFTERNOON sun shone bright as Rhys helped the ladies—Mrs. Edwards had decided to join them after waking up feeling better that morning—from the coach in the drive at Stratton Hall. The butler, whom Rhys vaguely recalled was Post, met and led them into the wide marble entry hall.

Unable to keep his eyes open after a mostly sleepless night, due to the intrusion on Miss Derrington and Mrs. Edwards, Rhys had dozed off for a bit in the coach. He'd dreamed of treasure and verbally battling with his lovely partner. Until their sparring had turned into seduction. When he'd awakened, Miss Derrington had thankfully been too engrossed in her book to notice his half-aroused state.

Shooting a glance at his companions, he wondered how they were faring. Mrs. Edwards had also slept, but Rhys didn't know if Miss Derrington had rested. The flesh beneath her eyes was stained a faint lavender, but didn't detract from her striking beauty. Hopefully his cousin wouldn't find her as attractive as Rhys did.

"Bowen, my good man!" Stratton's voice echoed through the hall as he strode from the base of the staircase at the far end. "It's been far too long. I'm delighted you've come to visit, even if it is to look at some musty old book."

Right away, Rhys noted the resemblance between Stratton and Penn. It wasn't strong, the boy favored his mother, but there was something about the cut of their jaws and the shape of their noses that revealed their familial connection. Rhys would endeavor to ensure the two were never together.

The earl was darkly attractive, which only aided his lecherous behavior. He was also erudite, deceptively charming, and a callous prick. He stopped short upon seeing Miss Derrington, and though Rhys hadn't seen his cousin in a few years, he recognized the look sparking in his eyes—and it wasn't good.

Rhys edged closer to Miss Derrington, who stood to his right. "Hello, cousin. Thank you for accommodating us on such short notice."

Stratton's gaze didn't stray from Miss Derrington. So much for Rhys's hopeful thinking. "I've said you're welcome any time." He moved forward and took her hand, bowing gallantly before pressing a kiss to the back. "A pleasure, Miss Derrington. Welcome to Stratton Hall."

"Thank you, my lord. This is my companion and chaperone, Mrs. Edwards."

"Chaperone, eh?" He darted a glance at Rhys, who had moved even closer to Miss Derrington—close enough that they nearly touched.

"I believe I included that fact in my missive," Rhys said, perhaps a touch too coolly. He looked at Post. "Please see that they lodge together and that the accommodation is sufficient."

Post nodded. "Of course."

"In the east wing," Stratton said.

Rhys wasn't completely certain, but suspected that was where Stratton's quarters were located, and that was unacceptable. Rhys did the only thing he could think of: he sidled closer to Miss Derrington and slid his hand along her waist. She tensed, but didn't flinch away from him. Her lush eyes turned toward him, their depths burning in quiet question.

Rhys gave an almost imperceptible nod trying to communicate that she should just follow his lead. If Stratton believed Miss Derrington and Rhys had an *arrangement,* he would probably leave her alone.

Stratton took the bait, his gaze noting Rhys's possessive touch. Thankfully, Mrs. Edwards was busy studying the artwork in the hall instead of paying close attention to her charge.

The earl turned to his butler. "I know precisely where to house our guests, Post. Put the ladies in the Orange Chamber and Mr. Bowen in the Knight's Lounge." Stratton said this with a smile and a conspiratorial wink directed at Rhys. If he had to guess, he would say his and Miss Derrington's rooms were in close proximity, which meant Rhys could keep an eye on her. After last night's invasion, he was loath to let her—and her book—out of his sight. Not just because he would be upset if the manuscript went missing, but because he suspected Miss Derrington would be devastated.

The question was, how serious would the devastation be? Simply emotional or were the financial implications of losing the book and the treasure disastrous to her and her aunts? He suspected the latter was a very real concern.

Stratton pivoted and motioned for them to follow him through the hall. "Come, let us take refreshment after your journey. Post will oversee the transport of your luggage upstairs."

Rhys kept his hand at the small of Miss Derrington's back as they trailed their host. He led them through a large drawing room and into a smaller sitting area bedecked with flowers and decorated in a cheerful yellow and blue theme.

Stratton stood to the side as his guests entered and waited for the ladies to seat themselves on a settee that faced the windows. He leaned close to Rhys. "The countess says this is the best room to greet guests, and she insisted on stuffing it full of flowers from the gardens." His distaste showed in the pinch of his nose and the slight roll of his eyes. "Later, we'll repair to my study and have a proper glass of whisky."

Rhys figured he'd have to endure at least one evening of ribaldry with his cousin, but that didn't mean he wasn't hoping to avoid it. With a nod, he took a chair across from Miss Derrington and Mrs. Edwards.

"Your flowers are lovely," Mrs. Edwards remarked.

"Thank you." The response came from a beautiful woman who strolled into the sitting room holding the hand of a young boy—maybe four years old.

Rhys jumped to his feet, recognizing Lady Stratton from his previous visits. He hadn't, however, met his cousin's presumed heir.

"Ah, my wife, and she's brought down my son. This is Viscount Kersey."

The boy clutched his mother's hand and stuck close to her side. His eyes were round and gray as he contemplated his father, who paid him absolutely no attention.

A pang of sympathy struck Rhys square in the chest as he looked at the small boy. He would be raised as the heir until such time as Rhys decided Penn should know his true heritage. Was it possible that day would never come? Would it be it fair to deny Penn his birthright forever? No, just as it wasn't fair to allow this boy to grow up in deception. But then life was rarely fair. If it had been, maybe Rhys would've had a mother and his life wouldn't have revolved around books—something that had never bothered him until Miss Derrington had shown up. He banished the troubling thoughts from his head.

Lady Stratton moved forward so that Rhys could offer a bow and take her hand. "It's lovely to see you again, Mr. Bowen." She spoke softly to her son. "This is Papa's cousin. Say hello."

Kersey looked up at Rhys, the square set of his jaw mirroring that of his father and his unknown half-brother. "Hello."

Rhys glanced at his cousin and saw the resemblance, but like Penn, Kersey was fortunate to take more after his mother. Rhys squatted down so that he was almost at eye level with the boy. "I'm pleased to meet you, my lord."

"All right then, that's enough of that," Stratton's voice jolted Rhys. "Time for Kersey to return to his nurse."

Lady Stratton gave a slight nod, then turned and led her son from the room. Stratton murmured, "Pardon me," and followed them, leaving Rhys alone with Miss Derrington and Mrs. Edwards.

Miss Derrington got to her feet and strolled toward the fireplace, a fair distance from where Mrs. Edwards sat. She inclined her head for Rhys to follow, which he did with alacrity.

Her hazel eyes were dark, the brown seeming to devour the green, as she peered up at him from where she pretended to study a figurine on the mantle. "What was that about, in the foyer?"

He kept his voice low. "I didn't like the way Stratton was looking at you. I told you what to expect."

"You did *not* tell me to expect groping from you."

"Groping? I was hardly—"

"Never mind. If you have to put your arm around my waist from time to time to keep his attentions at bay, so be it." Her gaze became more intense. "*Will* that be necessary?"

God, he hoped so. Touching her had given him a welcome shock of yearning. "I think it's best that he believes we have a *tendre* for each other."

She pressed her lips together. Lips that suddenly tempted him. "I see. How . . . lurid."

"It doesn't have to be. I can tell him we're engaged, if you prefer."

Her eyes widened. "I don't think *that's* necessary, is it?"

A perverse part of him was enjoying her maidenly shock. "I believe I'll see how things go."

Stratton reentered and they broke apart. Rhys watched her return to her place on the settee as Post brought in a tray of tea and refreshments. After a few moments, during which Miss Derrington and Mrs. Edwards helped themselves, Rhys and Stratton took the chairs opposite them.

Stratton leaned over toward Rhys and spoke quietly. "Had to have a word with Lady Stratton. Can't imagine what the hell she was thinking, bringing the boy downstairs."

If Rhys had any lingering doubt about harboring Penn from his father—and he didn't—it would've evaporated. In fact, he wished there was a way to take the other boy from him as well.

Miss Derrington set down her teacup after taking a sip. She offered a dazzling smile that Rhys made a note to tell her never to display for Stratton again. It was the antithesis of what she needed to do to dissuade his attention. In fact, it might be best if she wore a sack over her head, particularly given *that look* had entered Stratton's eyes once more. "Thank you for your hospitality," she said. "After tea, might we inspect the book?"

"In a hurry, I see." Stratton's tone held a note of admonishment. If he became annoyed, he might turn obstinate and refuse their request to view it.

Rhys shot Miss Derrington a cautionary glance before turning to placate his cousin's changeable mood. "No, we are not. We shall be delighted to peruse the manuscript when it's convenient. We realize we came on very short notice. For all we know, you're engaged this evening."

"As it happens, I am. I have, ah, some entertainment coming later. Nothing suitable for the ladies, I'm afraid, but I do hope you'll join me, Bowen." Another artful wink at Rhys.

Blast. Given Stratton's peccadilloes, tonight's "entertainment" could be just about anything, but Rhys would wager it involved women and spirits, based on his cousin's preferred vices.

"Tomorrow then," Miss Derrington said, persisting in securing a time for seeing the manuscript.

Stratton waved his hand. "Certainly. I want to show it to you personally, so it must be after I'm up and about. I shan't be rising terribly early." This time he sent a smirk in Rhys's direction.

Rhys was fast approaching his endurance and they hadn't even been there an hour. He'd have to come up with a good reason to beg off tonight's "entertainment" and only hoped his cousin didn't become difficult.

They endured another quarter hour of stilted conversation, mostly led by Mrs. Edwards, before Miss Derrington declared her intent to rest before dinner. "We will be having a dinner, won't we?"

Rhys worried that her tone might offend Stratton, but he laughed. "Of course. We serve at half-six. I've assigned a housemaid to see to your needs, she will help you prepare."

Miss Derrington stood. "Thank you, my lord." She flicked a glance at Rhys. "Mr. Bowen."

Rhys got to his feet as she and Mrs. Edwards left the room.

They'd barely crossed the threshold when Stratton turned toward Rhys, his blue eyes animated. "Eye of Christ, she's a beauty! I could barely wait to sink my claws into her porcelain flesh, but then you had to go and ruin it for me. Though I find it difficult to believe you're dipping your cock in that well without the aid of the parson's trap. You're far too prude for such proclivities, particularly with a miss like her."

Rhys didn't bother trying to persuade him that it wasn't "prude" for a gentleman to refrain from seducing a young, unmarried woman. "It's nothing so . . ." He borrowed Miss Derrington's word. "Lurid. We're to be married." He latched on to the excuse both to give credence to their ruse and to hopefully avoid having to participate in Stratton's festivities later. She'd understand, he hoped.

"You held out on me!" Stratton stood from his chair, having failed to get up when the ladies had left, and slapped Rhys on the back. "Now, you must join in the fun later. Very soon you'll be leg-shackled, not that I let that stop me." No, he didn't, and he was fixated on coercing Rhys into joining him.

"I'd rather not," Rhys said. "I hope you understand that though we aren't yet married, I am committed to Miss Derrington in my heart."

"Not surprising that you're a romantic. All those damned books and poems you're obsessed with. I'm just glad you're finally living in the real world. She's a fine piece. In fact . . ." He leaned closer. "There's a secret door between your chambers. It's visible on your side, but not hers."

The vile bounder. How many unsuspecting female houseguests had been set upon via that scheme? "I'm afraid I can't contain my disgust. That you would allow men to raid a woman's bedchamber—"

"Don't get yourself in a dither." Stratton frowned at him, his thin lips pulling taut. "We only give the chamber to women who are expecting visitors and who might have a companion with them. Exactly like your Miss Derrington. You don't need to use it, but it's there if you change your mind."

As horrified as Rhys was by the secret door, he had to admit it was comforting after what had transpired at the inn in Hereford. "Thank you, cousin. I didn't mean to offend." *Not that everything you do isn't offensive in some way.*

"I accept your apology. Care to join me for that whisky?"

Rhys rarely drank before dinner and even if he did, he would've begged off. He'd had enough of Stratton for a while. "Thank you, but I think I'd like to clean up before dinner."

"As you prefer." Stratton shrugged and led him from the room. They encountered Post as they exited, and the butler guided Rhys to his chamber.

Situated in the west wing, the Knight's Lounge was

a large chamber with a massive bed dominating the space. It included an expansive fireplace, a small antechamber for a valet, and that secret door. Set in the corner of the room, it screamed its presence and also that of the woman residing on the other side.

Rather, *women.*

Rhys would do well to remember that Miss Derrington wasn't alone. He would also do well to remember that she was a young, unmarried miss with whom he could never dally—secret door or no. The fact that he'd contemplated it, even for a second, scared him witless.

THOUGH MARGERY WAS tired from the long day, she couldn't sleep. She turned over in the large bed, having lost count of how many times she'd sought a new position. But it was no use. She simply couldn't turn off her mind.

Dinner had been an odd affair. Lord Stratton had spoken freely of his plans for later that evening *in front of his wife.* And Lady Stratton had seemed not to care. Margery had practically choked on her stuffed pheasant.

She'd snuck a look at Mr. Bowen to gauge his reaction and had been pleased to see the flesh around his mouth whiten and his jaw clench. She'd also been pleased to hear him decline Stratton's offer of entertainment, pleading exhaustion after their journey. Did that mean he might've been interested in participating on another night? Tomorrow evening, perhaps?

She didn't think so. She'd come to know him, at least a little, in the few days of their acquaintance and he struck her as an honorable sort, even if he had lied to her at the outset. Part of her worried that he was angling for priority access to the book—that this was why Stratton wasn't showing *her* the manuscript until tomorrow. What if he'd already shared it with Mr. Bowen? She shook her head, annoyed by her own suspicion. Even if Mr. Bowen *had* already seen the text, he would've had to have detected the code, something he couldn't do without her book in hand.

She sat up and tied the curtain back to allow the light from the lamp on the side table in. After everything Mr. Bowen had told her about Stratton, she'd left it lit. And now she could look through the book for the hundredth time.

Opening it, she ran her fingers over the title page. Where was the code embedded? Was it in one of the pictures? Was it somehow buried in the text? Since learning of the code's existence, she'd spent countless hours at the White Lady in Monmouth and at the inn in Hereford trying to discern where it might be and what it might say. Having to wait to see Stratton's book until tomorrow frustrated her greatly.

Partway through the book, a loud mumbling came from the small chamber where Mrs. Edwards was asleep on a comfortable, but narrow bed. After running afoul of sleeping in the larger bed at the inn in Hereford, she'd insisted on taking the maid's room.

Margery got up from the bed and went to peek on her. She was asleep, just muttering indecipherable words. Perhaps a code. Margery grinned to herself and went back to the bed. Caught up in her amusement, she tripped over the leg of a chair situated opposite the bed. She landed on the floor with a loud "oof" and worried she'd awakened Mrs. Edwards.

Getting to her feet, she froze as the corner of her chamber simply opened up and a large figure strode into her chamber. A scream formed in her throat, then died as Mr. Bowen came fully into the lamplight.

He charged in, his dark brows drawn dangerously low over his eyes. Unlike last night, he wore a shirt.

Pity, that.

She, however, was garbed in nothing but a nightrail. She ought to be dashing to the bed to shield herself beneath the covers, but her feet were rooted to the Aubusson carpet.

He took a step toward her. "Are you all right? I heard a noise."

"I think the more pressing question is how you came into my room through the wall." She wanted to go over and investigate how he'd done it, but that meant walking past him and just now, she didn't think increasing their proximity was a good idea.

"It's a door in my room."

"It's *not* a door in mine."

He glanced away, but only for a second. "I didn't mean any harm. After last night . . . I preferred to err on the side of caution as opposed to propriety."

She was certainly glad he'd done that last night, and she could understand why he'd done the same tonight. Now that he was here, the question that had been burning her mind rose to the fore and begged to be asked. "What did you and Lord Stratton do this afternoon?"

"Scarcely anything, why?" He studied her with a bit of skepticism, or maybe that was just her own silly suspicion reflecting back on herself.

"I was only curious."

He made a sound that might've been a stifled laugh. "You're a terrible liar. You thought I'd received a private viewing of the book, didn't you?"

She raised her chin and crossed her arms over her chest, again aware of her lack of covering. "Perhaps."

His gaze was warm, engaging. "I wouldn't do that."

"You've proven yourself to be untrustworthy."

"Only by omission and that was before we forged a . . . relationship . . . an alliance. I promise you can trust me completely."

She suspected she could, but the notion frightened her. Trust opened one up to a level of emotion that she shared with very few people—two, to be exact. Better to keep her guard up. "You didn't tell me about the secret door."

He leaned against the bedpost. "And how would I have done that? Blurted it out over the soup course at dinner?"

"Why not? Your cousin doesn't censor his tongue."

His mouth curved up. "Forgive me if my manners are just a smidgeon better than his."

She couldn't keep from smiling at that.

"Be careful, Miss Derrington. I've successfully warned Stratton away from you, but if you dazzle him overmuch with your beauty, he'll throw what little discretion he possesses to the winds."

His words heated her darkest places, made her think of what it might be like to encourage Mr. Bowen. Here he was, standing in her bedchamber, leaning on her bed . . .

"You should go," she said, finally pushing herself to turn from him and go to the side of the bed. But she couldn't actually get *in* it. Not while he was still standing there. Heavens, now she was imagining him watching her climb into the bed and joining her there . . .

He stood straight and shook his head as if cobwebs had formed between his ears. "Yes, I should. Again, pardon my intrusion. I just wanted to ensure you were all right."

"Fine, thank you." Did he suddenly feel as awkward as she?

"If you need anything . . ."

"I know where to find you." She planned to scrutinize that corner as soon as he left.

He turned and went to the doorway, pausing to say "Good night" and to deliver the most provocative stare she'd ever received.

As soon as the door closed behind him, she rushed over with the lamp and studied the seam in the wall. She'd never have noticed it in the pattern of the wallpaper if he hadn't come through. She also looked for a way to lock it from her side, but there was nothing. The chair that had tripped her in the first place was an option, but she suspected the noise of moving it would only encourage him to come back. Plus, it might wake Mrs. Edwards, who'd apparently slept through the entire encounter with Mr. Bowen. Chaperonage was not her calling.

Margery went back to the bed, replacing her lamp on the side table. This time, as she tried to find sleep, only one thing kept her from slumber: the tempting vision of a shirtless Mr. Bowen and those dark, dark eyes of his promising something she didn't even know she'd wanted.

Chapter Five

RHYS PACED THE gallery for the fifth time as Miss Derrington and Mrs. Edwards sat on a bench near the center beneath a large painting of some former earl. Stratton kept his de Valery manuscript locked in a closet with other valuables, and they were waiting for his arrival. Post, stationed in front of the door, had directed them to come, but there was no sign of Stratton yet.

In an effort to keep from looking at Miss Derrington, Rhys tried to study the paintings on display. Despite this, his gaze kept straying toward her. Her hair was swept up, with curls grazing her neck, a smooth, pale expanse of flesh that longed for someone's—*his*—lips to caress it. She wore a muslin gown with a yellow floral pattern that outlined her form and reminded him of the curves he'd glimpsed in her chamber last night.

That had been a near thing. She'd almost looked at him in invitation, certainly with curiosity. If she'd beckoned him closer, he didn't think he could've resisted.

What folly. Or was it? Would she be open to courtship?

His thoughts were interrupted by the typically boisterous arrival of his cousin.

"Ready to see the book?" he asked loudly, offering smiles all around. He appeared freshly groomed, though his cheeks were ruddy and his eyes bloodshot, likely an aftereffect of his excessive evening.

Miss Derrington stood. "Yes, please."

"I'll just wait here," Mrs. Edwards said primly.

Rhys came to a stop near Miss Derrington and escorted her to the closet, lightly touching the small of her back. Post turned and unlocked the door. Stratton went first. The room was equipped with shelves and cupboards. A small table sat in the center.

Stratton fixed Miss Derrington with a probing stare. "First, I should like to see your book."

She held it beneath her arm, but hesitated, shooting a questioning glance at Rhys. He nodded. She went to the table and set the manuscript upon it.

Stratton moved forward and touched the cover. "It's very similar to mine. But you'll see that in a minute." He flashed her a grin. Opening the book, he studied each page, making occasional remarks. "The stories are different, though it seems there are a handful in each book. Yours includes the Heart of Llanllwch."

Rhys cringed at his butchering of Welsh. "It's pronounced thlan-thlooch."

Stratton waved his hand, unconcerned with such trivial things. "Have you seen it in the museum at Oxford?"

"I have not," Miss Derrington said. "But Mr. Bowen has."

The look Stratton cast Rhys was a mix of humor and disgust. "Of course he has. Bowen has bored himself with all manner of academic nonsense. The heart, however, isn't nonsense. I saw it last year—it's quite a treasure. Makes one wonder if the other items in these books might be real, doesn't it?"

Rhys's heart seemed to stop for a moment. Did he know about the treasure, the code? He exchanged alarmed glances with Miss Derrington, but quickly looked away before Stratton could detect anything. If he *wasn't* aware of de Valery's code, Rhys didn't want to alert him.

"One might also wonder if King Arthur is real," Rhys said evenly.

"I think he must have been. What a boon it would be to find his sword, wouldn't it?" Stratton looked between them. "He's supposedly buried in Glastonbury. I presume you've been there, Bowen?"

"I have not." It was not an academically important site, just a place where some medieval monks had claimed to dig up the bodies of Arthur and his queen, Guinevere. Some believed it to be real, but Rhys thought it nothing more than fancy to encourage pilgrims to visit the abbey, which was now only ruins, having been destroyed by King Henry VIII. From *that* perspective, it was an interesting destination.

"I think I might like to visit," Stratton said. He turned the final page and closed the book. "This text is very similar to mine, perhaps a bit longer. It would be something to own them both together, wouldn't it?" His fingers rested possessively on the cover, and Rhys could practically feel the tension emanating from Miss Derrington.

"It would." Rhys lightly touched her elbow, hoping to assuage her concerns. "Although Miss Derrington is not interested in selling. I am, however, still interested in buying yours." He hadn't been certain if he would offer after Stratton had flatly turned him down three years ago, but presented with the perfect opportunity to ask, Rhys couldn't pass it up.

Stratton smiled, baring his teeth in an inhospitable manner. "It's not for sale." He turned his head to focus on Miss Derrington. "Name your price. I'm sure we can come to an accord. I'm trying to build a little medieval library for myself. Once I learned how much Bowen's library is worth, it inspired me to increase my collection."

Rhys stifled a frown. Yes, his father's library was extensive and quite valuable, but its true value lay in the academic riches it offered. The books were meant to be studied and broaden one's knowledge, not line the shelves of some nobleman's locked closet.

Miss Derrington flashed an inquisitive glance at Rhys before offering a placid smile to Stratton. She was either annoyed or had taken Rhys's advice about not smiling too prettily. Both, probably.

"My lord, I'm afraid I couldn't part with my aunts' book. It really isn't mine to sell. Our visit is purely academic. Might we see your book now?" she asked sweetly, deepening her smile, which only proved to accentuate her dimples, particularly the one in her chin.

It worked however, as Stratton seemed to relax. He held his hand out. "The key, Post."

The butler, who'd been standing silently in the corner, handed him a key and Stratton went to a cupboard and unlocked it. He stared at it a long moment. "Post, have you been in here?"

Post rushed to Stratton's side. "My lord?"

"I don't see it. Where's my book?" Stratton leaned in and studied the cupboard more closely. "Where is my *goddamned* book?"

Post began pulling books from the shelves inside. "You're certain it's not one of these?"

"I think I know what the bloody thing looks like." His words dripped with such venom and he sent his butler a look of such contempt that Rhys grew uncomfortable. Plus, there was the language that was wholly unsuitable for a lady's ears. However, he didn't think it wise to mention that.

"Is it on one of these other shelves?" Rhys asked, turning to look for a book that resembled Miss Derrington's.

Stratton began rifling through the books, but it didn't take long as there were only a dozen or so. "It's not fucking here."

Rhys couldn't keep his mouth shut any longer. "Stratton, there's a lady present."

"A lady who has the partner to my most valuable book." Stratton regarded her with a malice that was akin to the way he'd just looked at his butler. "Perhaps she found a way in here last night and stole it. Post, search her bedchamber."

Rhys's muscles tensed and anger spiraled in his gut. "Wait, you can't do that." But the butler was already gone. Rhys turned on his cousin, no longer caring if he offended him. "Stratton, you're crossing the line. Miss Derrington did not steal your book."

"How do you know that? Because you spent the night between her legs?"

Rhys heard Miss Derrington's intake of breath, but didn't turn to look at her. "Your vulgarity only discredits you. We're leaving."

Stratton grasped Rhys's forearm and squeezed. "Not until I've searched your chamber as well."

Rhys threw him off. He had two inches on the man and an athleticism his cousin couldn't hope to match. "For heaven's sake, if we'd stolen your book, we would've left already. Why would we wait around for you to be sober enough to show us the manuscript if we'd taken it?"

Stratton's jaw worked, but he didn't say anything.

"Furthermore, how would we have gotten through the locked door?"

Stratton's eyes glittered with malice. "Someone did."

"Yes, *someone* did, but it wasn't us."

Now that the situation was at least partially defused, Rhys wanted to focus on the disappearance of the book. Finding it missing when someone had just tried to steal Miss Derrington's book was disturbing. It seemed certain someone was after the code and the treasure. If the same person who'd tried to steal her book already possessed Stratton's, they had the upper hand. Rhys didn't like that scenario one bit. He was also disgruntled not to be able to see the book. The dream of deciphering the code and finding the treasure seemed just that—a dream.

He took a deep breath and addressed Stratton. "Perhaps we can try to figure out who stole your manuscript. When was the last time you viewed it?"

Stratton was quiet a moment, his mind working. "A month ago, perhaps?" He shook his head. "I hosted a party and some of the guests came in here to look at the books."

Rhys glanced at Miss Derrington, who'd gone a bit pale. He knew she was worried. She wanted to find the code and the treasure as much as he did. "Do you remember who?"

Stratton massaged his temple. "There were several people. I don't know . . . it was a hedonistic party."

Did he host any other kind? "Perhaps Post will recall the guests and we can go from there."

"You think one of them stole it?"

"I think it's possible. Recovering it, however, will be difficult."

Stratton bared his teeth again. "Horseshit. You find out who took it, and I'll make sure the son of a bitch returns it. I'll go talk to Post." He turned to go, but stopped short. "You need to leave. I don't trust anyone in here now."

Miss Derrington plucked up her manuscript and exited first. Stratton locked the door behind them and took himself off without another word.

Miss Derrington wasted no time. She turned on Rhys, her gaze dark and troubled. "What are we going to do now?"

"Try to determine who might've stolen the book. It's the only thing I can think of."

"And then what? Encourage Stratton to storm into the person's house and take it back? This is hopeless."

He touched her arm again, then chastised himself. He couldn't take liberties. Though she didn't object. "Don't think like that. We'll find it." He wished he believed that, but he was fairly certain she was right. And damn if that didn't frustrate the hell out of him.

"In the meantime," he said, lowering his voice, "you should give the book to me for safekeeping."

She clutched it more tightly to her chest. "I don't think that's a good idea."

"Didn't we agree to trust each other?"

"You *ordered* me to trust you," she said defensively.

"Am I that much of an autocrat? Have I not demonstrated that I have your best interests at heart? That I will protect you?"

"Me or the book?"

Frustration erupted inside of him, and he simply couldn't stand still. "Walk with me." He retreated and paced to the opposite end of the gallery, away from Mrs. Edwards, who was knitting, oblivious as usual.

Miss Derrington followed in his wake. Her suspicion was completely unfounded.

When he turned to face her, he barely kept a handle on his ire. "Yes, I omitted the purpose of the book when we first met, but I quickly told you the truth and have vowed to continue to do so. I'm afraid we cannot continue this alliance if you are going to doubt me at every turn. Furthermore," he moved close to her, far too close for propriety, but he didn't care, "if I wanted your book for myself, I could've had it a hundred times over and there is nothing you could've done to stop me."

Her eyes widened and her breath caught. An overwhelming urge to kiss her leapt forward and he barely tamped it back.

She gave the smallest of nods. "What do you want to do now?"

He exhaled, reining in the emotions that had overtaken him. He was a universally pragmatic and reticent gentleman, unmoved to passion. Yet, just a few days with Miss Derrington had provoked him to romantic sentimentality, lust, and now an emotional outburst. Perhaps *he* should sever their alliance.

"I'll obtain the list of guests from Post and we'll review the names. Perhaps one of them will lead us to think of something pertinent."

"Do you think whoever stole Stratton's book was behind the attempt to steal mine? That man at the inn never would've come to one of Stratton's parties."

He was impressed she'd come to the same deduction he had—that whoever had tried to steal her book in Hereford was a hireling. "I think it's likely."

She looked pensive. "I can't imagine who that would be."

"Hopefully the list will spark something. In the meantime, we have to assume this person will try again to steal your book, and if they've already successfully stolen from Stratton, they might be able to do so again."

"Meaning we aren't safe here."

He pressed his lips together. "Not as safe as I'd like to be."

Her gaze was cloaked with uncertainty. "And where would that be?"

He hadn't thought it through yet. "I don't know, but we should plan on leaving tomorrow in any case."

"I suppose I should just go home. I know Mrs. Edwards is eager to get back." She shot her chaperone a worried glance. "We can't tell her about this. I don't want to frighten her."

"No, and for her safety, we should consider sending her back to Gloucester tomorrow. I can hire a coach in Leominster." His gaze fell to the book Miss Derrington held so close to her chest. Would she consent to give it to him in the name of her own protection? "I don't suppose you'd consider going with her and leaving the book with me? For safety's sake?"

She shook her head. "You know I won't."

He sighed. "Yes."

"I'll be in my room with Mrs. Edwards. Let me know when you have the list." With a prim nod, she turned and went back to Mrs. Edwards and they departed the gallery.

Rhys watched the sway of her hips as she went and desire fired through his groin. If they sent Mrs. Edwards away on the morrow, that would leave him alone with Miss Derrington. Just the notion was scandalous, but add in the way in which he wanted her and it was positively . . . lurid. How he was beginning to curse that word.

"I'M SORRY THIS errand was for naught," Mrs. Edwards said after they returned to their room. "Does this mean we're returning to Gloucester in the morning?"

"Yes." Margery had thought about Mr. Bowen's suggestion and agreed it was for the best. She didn't want to frighten Mrs. Edwards and certainly didn't want to endanger her.

Yet, would she allow herself to be endangered? Margery's emotions had bounced back and forth since finding Stratton's book missing. She'd been shocked, bitterly disappointed, and frightened by the larger situation they'd inadvertently stumbled into.

And she couldn't dismiss the timing. Her aunts' book had been forgotten until very recently. Then they'd shared its existence with Mr. Bowen and since then, things had become quite complicated. And perilous.

Did she really think Mr. Bowen was behind the disappearance of Stratton's book or the attempt to steal hers? As he'd so aptly pointed out, if he'd wanted to take her book, he could've done so many times. She shivered as she recalled his proximity—he'd smelled of sandalwood and man, a scent she'd never dreamed could be so tempting. And the way he'd looked at her . . . It was more than just wanting her; she'd seen that look on men before, including their host. No, he looked at her as if he *needed* her.

"I'm going to rest for a bit." Mrs. Edwards disappeared behind the partition into the maid's room.

Margery set her book on the bed and hoped Mr. Bowen would arrive with the list soon. Was that because she was eager to peruse the names or because she couldn't wait to be in his presence again? She chose not to answer that question.

A few minutes later a rap sounded on her door. She jolted, her pulse picking up speed as she moved through the chamber to answer the summons.

She opened the door and realized she should've asked who it was before doing so because it wasn't Mr. Bowen.

It was Lady Stratton.

The countess tossed a furtive glance over her shoulder. "Might I come in?"

"Certainly." Margery held the door open and then closed it securely after Lady Stratton came inside.

"Where is your chaperone?" she asked.

"Resting."

Lady Stratton nodded. "Can she hear us?"

"Not if we speak quietly over here." Margery led her to a small sitting area situated before the fireplace. She found Lady Stratton's demeanor puzzling. "Is there something the matter?"

Lady Stratton sat at the edge of one of the chairs, arranging her skirts around her ankles. "I heard my husband's de Valery manuscript has gone missing and that you and Mr. Bowen plan to help him determine who may have stolen it."

Margery took the opposite chair. "Yes," she said slowly, unwilling to reveal too much.

Lady Stratton nervously patted the back of her upswept dark hair. "Forgive my boldness, Miss

Derrington, but may I ask why you really wanted to view the text?"

Trying to disguise her dismay, Margery worked to keep her features serene. "Purely academic interest. I only wanted to compare it to my book."

Lady Stratton's gaze moved about the room before settling on the manuscript sitting atop the bed. Margery stifled the urge to go and snatch it up.

The countess turned her pale gray eyes on Margery. "Miss Derrington, you strike me as an independent young woman. Is it true you're engaged to Mr. Bowen? My husband says it is so, but I watched the two of you at dinner last night and did not have the impression you are in love."

In love. Margery wasn't sure she knew what that would look or feel like, and suspected she never would. Nevertheless, she sought to maintain their ruse. "What does love have to do with marriage?"

"Absolutely nothing, of course. I'm pleased to hear you realize that too." Lady Stratton smiled, and Margery saw a glimpse of the vivacious young woman she must've been. Before marrying Stratton, perhaps. "Is it possible you aren't actually interested in marrying Mr. Bowen, that you've only agreed to it because you felt you had no other choice?" She leaned forward, her eyes narrowing and gaining intensity. "What if you had another choice? What if you didn't have to rely on a man ever again?"

Margery's breath caught. She'd embarked on this adventure to improve their situation—that of her and her aunts—but she never truly believed it could change their financial standing forever. That would be . . . liberating.

"What are you saying, Lady Stratton?"

"You must promise never to reveal what I'm about to tell you. My husband would be quite unforgiving." She rolled back the edge of her sleeve, which hid her elbow, and revealed a dark bruise.

Margery gasped. Stratton was a profligate and a drunk, but an abuser into the bargain? "I'm so sorry."

Lady Stratton readjusted her sleeve and sat back in her chair. "I've accepted my lot, however you are in an altogether different situation. You can change your future and own it. Are you aware that your book carries a secret code?"

Margery had a split second to determine her reaction and in the end, she couldn't muster the necessary shock to sell the fallacy that she hadn't known. So she nodded.

"I thought as much. Can I also correctly assume that Mr. Bowen is aware of this code?"

"He's the one who told me. I brought him the book to sell it, but he . . . eventually revealed that it held a code."

"Because you forced him to." Lady Stratton grinned. "How brilliant of you. Are you partners in this endeavor, then?"

"Yes. He says he can decipher the code."

Her eyes crinkled with mild amusement. "Perhaps, but I don't know that anyone is aware of how to do that. My father knew of your book, but couldn't find its actual location. He'd tracked it through a handful of generations before it became lost."

Margery's brain tripped up. "Wait, how is your father involved?"

"Didn't my husband tell you? The book belonged to my father. He gifted it to us, as a wedding present, for our future child—for Kersey."

"No, Lord Stratton didn't tell us how he came to have the book. I'm sorry your father's book was stolen. You must be devastated." Which perhaps explained this visit, though there was still something off about Lady Stratton. She didn't seem upset.

"I would have been. If it had been the actual book." Her lips spread into a satisfied smile, the likes of which Margery imagined she didn't often enjoy. "After we realized Stratton was a brute and an ass, pardon me, and couldn't be trusted with such a valuable item, my father exchanged it with a copy. He simply couldn't let Stratton possess such a treasure, even in custody for Kersey. And it is a treasure, Miss Derrington, I assure you."

Margery's heart hammered at her chest. "Your father has the original text?"

"Yes, and you're going to take your book to see him. I'm certain he can help you decipher the code and then you will have at least a portion of the treasure for yourself."

Instead of sharing it with Mr. Bowen as they'd agreed, she'd share it with Lady Stratton's father. "But how am I to do that? I made an agreement with Mr. Bowen, and I should return to Gloucester. My chaperone is weary." Something kept Margery from sharing that someone had tried to steal her book. Trust, it seemed, was a difficult thing to give, even to someone who was trying to help her.

"Do you believe that Mr. Bowen will honor the agreement? Has he discussed with you how you will split the treasure?"

Margery shifted uncomfortably. "No."

Lady Stratton's tone turned hard. "If you put your faith in him, you're a fool. Men aren't to be trusted. I'm giving you the opportunity to take your life into your own hands. Go to my father, he will help you, especially if it means saving a young woman from a marriage she doesn't want."

But that was all a lie. She wasn't betrothed to Mr. Bowen and even if she were, would it be awful? He was kind, if somewhat pompous, and despite his initial deception, he seemed to genuinely want to work together to find the treasure. Oh, but the chance to be in control and not have to choose either of the paths her aunts had been forced down was incredibly attractive.

"Your father doesn't want the entire treasure for himself?"

Lady Stratton cocked her head as she considered the question. "He might. Even if he does, he'll ensure you're compensated for your half. He's quite fair, the most honorable man I know." Her voice had turned wistful and Margery suffered a pang of loss she hadn't felt in many years. The image of her own father, cloudy and distant, filtered through her mind and tears stung the backs of her eyes.

Swallowing back her long-buried sorrow, Margery asked, "How will I get to your father?" She glanced toward the maid's quarters. "I must go alone. Mrs. Edwards needs to return home."

"My father lives two days from here in Westbury. You'll stay at a small inn in Church Stretton the first night. I will write you a letter of introduction and they will take care of you, even keeping your identity and presence secret."

Margery stared at her hostess. She'd thought of everything. Almost everything. "What about transportation?"

"I'll arrange for you to take a private coach out of Leominster. From the King's Arms. We just need to find a way to get you there in the morning." She tapped her finger against her lip as she thought.

"If we're taking Mrs. Edwards into town to take a coach to Gloucester, I can pretend to go with her. Then I can have the coach take me to the King's Arms." It suddenly seemed not only possible, but *easy*. Margery's pulse quickened. Could she do it? What of the men pursuing the book? "If I'm to travel alone, I should have something to protect myself."

Lady Stratton smiled again and Margery had the sense that she hadn't had this much fun in a long time. "I have just the thing. I'll deliver it—and my letter for the innkeeper at the Crooked Cat—later tonight. Leave the rest to me." She stood to go.

Margery's mind was swirling with possibility. And questions. "Wait. You're an adept planner. Why don't you escape from Lord Stratton? I can see you're unhappy."

Her soft smile was sad. "Only with him. I could never leave my son and taking him from his father isn't an option. Stratton would hunt me down and make my life even more difficult than it is now. He's grown kinder since Kersey came along. He focuses most of his time on his women, which suits me just fine."

That explained the tolerance she displayed for his blatant philandering.

"I see. Well, if there is anything I can ever do for you, I hope you'll let me know."

Lady Stratton took her hand and squeezed it. "Just live your life the way you choose. Don't let a man dictate what you must and mustn't do or how the world perceives you. Knowing I've helped one woman will give me great satisfaction."

Margery nodded, her mind returning to its whirlwind. After Lady Stratton departed, Margery thought through the plan. It meant lying to Mr. Bowen—not omitting, not misleading, outright *lying*. She'd accused him of being untrustworthy, and now she was going to completely disregard their understanding.

Doubt lingered in her brain, but her heart soared at the chance to undertake an adventure that would give her complete freedom. Lady Stratton's father knew of the code and treasure, and Lady Stratton believed it would be enough to give Margery absolute independence. How could she ignore such an opportunity? Particularly when Mr. Bowen clearly didn't need the money. His library was apparently worth a fortune and since he'd offered "any price" for her book, she had to assume he'd meant it. He didn't need the treasure like she did. But he was still going to be angry when he discovered her deception. Hopefully, however, that wouldn't be for quite some time—if ever. As far as he knew, she'd be back in Gloucester.

There was still the matter of this list. If they reviewed it and recognized a name or several names, what would he do? She realized it didn't matter. He could run off on his fool's errand while she went directly to the real book. She cringed inwardly, hating how mercenary that sounded in her head. Mercenary, but necessary. She didn't owe Mr. Bowen anything, and she needed to remember that.

Chapter Six

WITH STRATTON'S PERMISSION, Rhys spent an hour investigating the book closet while a footman watched over him. There'd been no sign of anyone forcing their way inside or having to break into the cupboard. Whoever had stolen the book had used the requisite keys to accomplish their objective.

At long last, Post arrived with a handwritten list of gentlemen. Several of the names leapt off the page and were men Rhys had seen recently: Trevor, Septon, and Holborn, to name a few. He immediately thought of Septon, an antiquarian who knew of the de Valery code and would recognize de Valery's work if he encountered it. But Septon wasn't the sort of man to steal something, even to rescue an important text from a gluttonous ass. Also, Septon wouldn't accost a pair of women to steal the second manuscript, nor would he hire others to do it. However, he might be able to help Rhys analyze the rest of the men on the list for a motive. Septon had finished the Wye Tour two days before and would now be in Caerwent to conduct his studies.

Rhys scrubbed his hand over his eyes and left the closet, leaving Post to lock it back up. He made his way to Miss Derrington's room to share his plan of action. When he arrived, the door was open so he walked inside. "Miss Derrington?"

A housemaid stopped short upon seeing him. "Begging your pardon, my lord. The miss and her chaperone are out in the garden for a walk."

"I see, thank you." Rhys doubled back and went downstairs. He circumvented the direction of Stratton's study as he took a path to the back terrace. A footman opened the door for him and he stepped outside to scan the gardens, which were laid out below. He sighted the pair of women a hundred yards or so distant and quickly sought to catch them.

A few minutes later, he'd finally run his quarry to ground. His breath hitched at Miss Derrington's beauty, her face perfectly framed by her delicate curls and the brim of her bonnet. "I didn't realize you were going for a walk."

She arched a slender blond brow. "I didn't realize I needed to ask your permission."

Is that what she thought, or was she trying to be quarrelsome? "You don't, of course. I merely thought we'd arranged to review this list together." He withdrew the parchment from his pocket.

"I had no inkling of when you might arrive, and Mrs. Edwards and I cared to walk in the garden." Her response was cool.

Rhys resisted the urge to frown. What was wrong with her? "Would you care to review the list now or after you finish your stroll?"

"Now would be fine." She turned to Mrs. Edwards. "Feel free to continue on to the rose garden. You can see us from there."

Mrs. Edwards nodded and went along the path to the rose garden, maybe thirty feet away.

Miss Derrington led him to a bench beneath a tree and sat. A bird chirped nearby, and the subtle scent of roses wafted over him. A perfect summer day, yet things were far from perfect.

He sat beside her, still unsure of her mood. Peering at her askance, he unfolded the paper and handed it to her.

She perused it for a long moment. "Do you recognize any of these names?"

"Several. You?"

"Mr. Digby and Lord Trevor. And Lord Holborn, but then everyone has heard of him, haven't they?"

Yes, he was one of the eminent dukes of the realm. "How do you know the others?"

She looked up from the list. "Lord Trevor is a bit notorious for his Wye Tour parties and Mr. Digby visited Gloucester recently. I danced with him at an assembly."

A bolt of jealousy—strong and shocking—smacked Rhys in the gut. "I know Trevor, and I don't believe he has any awareness of the de Valery code," Rhys said.

Trevor was smart and gregarious, but he found Rhys's academic pursuits to be positively mundane. He would likely find a treasure hunt exciting, but wouldn't undertake the exercise on his own. Still, Rhys would question him, especially about some of the other names on the list who were also in attendance at Septon's Wye Tour party, such as the Duke of Holborn. Rhys could scarcely imagine that fearsome gentleman occupying himself with something so banal as a treasure hunt.

"What do you know of Digby?" Rhys asked.

She kept her face angled away, as if she were looking at the rose garden where Mrs. Edwards strolled, but Rhys had the impression she was avoiding looking at him. Why?

"He's a bit self-involved, arrogant even, but not like you." She cast him a quick glance. "And also persistent."

Arrogant—but not like you. The glimmer in her eye as she'd said it seemed to infer that Rhys's brand of arrogance was somehow better. He liked that. "You know him well then?"

"Not really. He's expressed an interest in courting me. In fact, he was due to visit, which is why I came to see you so quickly."

"How cunning of you." That she'd worked to avoid this Digby's advances gave Rhys an inordinate amount of pleasure. But did that mean she would also reject him? Given her demeanor today, Rhys wondered how welcome his suit might be. He thought he'd felt a connection in her bedchamber last night, but perhaps he'd only imagined it.

Her lips curved up, as if she appreciated his compliment. He hoped so. "Can you think of anything that might indicate he's aware of your book or the de Valery code?"

She shook her head, her blond curls lightly swinging against the back of her neck. "I can't imagine. He didn't strike me as someone who was interested in anything beyond his horses and hounds."

Nothing to go on really, but at least he had Septon to start with. "Lord Septon is actually a friend of mine as well as a fellow antiquarian."

She looked at him now, her eyes taking on more green with the row of trees that lined the garden behind her. "Does he know of the code?"

"He knows what I knew—that Stratton had this book and that the second book, your book, was lost. Until now."

She inhaled sharply. "Is he aware I have the second book?"

"I don't know." He turned on the bench to face her.

"But please don't be concerned. I've known Septon for years, and he's a good sort. He wouldn't be behind the theft or the attempt to steal yours."

"How can you be so certain? People change, circumstances change."

He shook his head. "Not with Septon. Like me, he's interested in the academia of it, not the monetary value of the treasure."

Her eyes narrowed suspiciously. "You were willing to pay any price for an 'excellent medieval specimen' or whatever you called it and mislead me from its true value. Academia seems as strong a motive as greed."

"I thought we'd moved past that." Earlier, after discovering the book was missing. When he'd nearly kissed her in frustration.

She turned her head to survey the rose garden again. "I never said."

For the love of God, the woman was going to try his patience. He opened his mouth to tell her again how wrongheaded she was, but she spoke first. "Mrs. Edwards would like to return to Gloucester in the morning, and I've decided to accompany her."

"What?" He couldn't keep his surprise—and disappointment—in check.

"I'd like to return home to check on my aunts. And perhaps . . . catch my breath. This is all so much. The attempted theft, Stratton's book going missing." Her aloof demeanor suddenly made sense.

"I'll accompany you."

She tensed for a moment. "That isn't necessary."

Or maybe it was more than discomfort or fear surrounding the book. Perhaps she still distrusted him. He didn't necessarily blame her for being careful about his motives when he hadn't told her about the treasure at the start. "I see. I can arrange for a coach to see you and Mrs. Edwards back to Gloucester. I will also be traveling south—to Caerwent, to hopefully catch up with Septon and ask him about this list."

"Will you?" She blinked at him. "Do let me know how that turns out. If you are able to locate the other book, I'm still interested in deciphering the code."

He didn't like this turn of events, and not just because he would miss her company. And he would. "I must say, I worry for your welfare. What will you do if you're set upon once more?" The more he thought about it, the more he realized he couldn't let her endanger herself—or Mrs. Edwards. "I insist you let me accompany you."

She faced him, eyes ablaze with exasperation. "You are not responsible for our welfare, Mr. Bowen. Now *you're* being an obnoxious kind of arrogant *and* persistent. Kindly stop."

Her words struck him like a blow to the groin. He was used to managing situations without argument. Working with a partner would take adjustment—if it were to continue, which it didn't appear to be. "Will you at least allow me to hire a guard?"

She frowned, but considered his offer. "No. Thank you."

"You're a stubborn female," he growled. He'd hire a guard to follow them at a discreet distance, and *he'd* follow behind that. She couldn't control what road he traveled nor what lodging he obtained.

"And you're a managing gentleman. Perhaps it's best our alliance is at an end."

He stood, angry at her obstinacy and at the fact that he was still drawn to her while she was ready to push him aside. "Be ready to depart at eight."

She nodded and he strode away. Maybe he *should* steal the book from her. Then she'd be safe, and he could find the treasure without worrying about having her in tow. Her presence wasn't the problem, however; it was the way her presence made him feel and behave. He prided himself on being calm, polished, unaffected. But now he was riled, hotheaded, passionate. The sooner he could leave her behind, the better—with or without her book.

THE FOLLOWING MORNING, Margery and Mrs. Edwards met Mr. Bowen in the drive. His coach was ready and only Lady Stratton came to see them off. Presumably, Stratton was sleeping off another night of debauchery. Margery noticed Mr. Bowen looked a little pale this morning. Had he participated in Stratton's lecherous activities? She tried not to think of it.

After saying good-bye to the countess, they all climbed into the coach. The tension between her and Mr. Bowen seemed to tighten the air, but Mrs. Edwards appeared unaware.

"I can't say I'm sorry to be leaving," she said disdainfully. "Lady Stratton seems a kind sort, but that husband of hers . . ." She shuddered.

The ride into Leominster passed quickly and quietly. The bag holding the book perched on the seat beside Margery, next to a second bag Lady Stratton had given her. It contained a luncheon and a pair of pistols. In addition to the pistols themselves, Lady Stratton had given Margery some quick lessons on how to fire one. However, Margery doubted she'd remember how.

Thankfully, the man who was to drive her to Westerly Cross, Lady Stratton's father's estate, would know how to use them.

As soon as they neared the coaching inn, her pulse began to thrum.

Mr. Bowen fixed her with a dark stare. "Stay here until I organize your transportation. Are you sure you won't let me send a guard?"

Mrs. Edwards leaned forward, her face lighting. Margery put her hand on her arm. "No, thank you."

After Mr. Bowen departed the coach, Mrs. Edwards turned sharply toward her. "Why did you do that? A guard would not come amiss."

Margery's mind scrambled to come up with something to say. "I don't trust Mr. Bowen." She might not trust him not to take the book, but she didn't think he would do anything to frighten them. That made the lie taste especially sour. "I've begun to doubt his motives. He's obsessed with finding the missing book and taking my book with him. I just want to return home, without his presence." Margery nearly cringed as she was going to completely confuse Mrs. Edwards as soon as they departed and she instructed the driver to drop her at the King's Arms.

Mrs. Edwards mashed her lips together. "I disagree, but I shan't convince you otherwise. Remind me never to play the part of your chaperone again. I can't imagine a more intractable charge."

Margery sought to placate the woman. She hadn't agreed to such a long journey, or the trouble they'd encountered. Margery touched her arm and offered a conciliatory smile. "Did I not save you the other night?"

Mrs. Edwards didn't look convinced. "At first, but it

was Mr. Bowen who fought him off, if you recall."

She did recall, and Margery had her own fears about traveling to Westerly Cross by herself, but she trusted in Lady Stratton's plan.

A short while later, Mr. Bowen returned and they transferred to their new coach, which would take them all the way to Gloucester. As he helped them inside, he said, "The coachman is armed and I've told him you carry something of value. If you change your mind and would like a guard, he will hire one for you." He gave Margery a handful of coins. "This will accommodate a guard, your lodgings, and your food."

"This isn't necessary." Margery still had funds, but was glad to receive his offering. Now she could transfer it to Mrs. Edwards, instead of having to halve her money.

He looked at her intently. "I've let you decline my other offers, but I'm afraid in this I absolutely must insist."

Margery tipped her head down demurely. "Then I shall be gracious."

"What a novelty." His tone dripped sarcasm, but when she shot a look at him, a smile played at his lips. "I will send word as soon as I can. Our alliance may be over, Miss Derrington, but our association is not."

The promise in his words sank into her and made her deception cut like the edge of a piece of parchment. "Good-bye, Mr. Bowen."

"Until we meet again, Miss Derrington." He closed the door and the coach moved forward.

She waited until they had turned a corner and were making their way out of town, in the opposite direction of where she wanted to go, before rapping on the roof.

Mrs. Edwards's forehead furrowed. "What are you

doing?"

"I'm so sorry," Margery said and meaning it quite sincerely. "I'm afraid I need to continue on my journey—alone. I have a letter for you to give to my aunts." She withdrew the missive from the front flap of the book and handed it to Mrs. Edwards. "Please tell them I love them and that I'll see them soon."

Mrs. Edwards' eyes were wide, her jaw sagging. "Wherever are you going?"

Margery spoke quickly as the coach slowed. "I'd rather not say, but I've disclosed everything important in the letter to my aunts. You'll be safe now that I and the book are not with you. I'm certain anyone following our path will have their eyes on me since the book is consistently in my possession."

"But what about you?"

The coach came to a stop. Margery patted Mrs. Edwards's knee. "Don't worry, I have things all planned out. I will be quite secure."

The coachman opened the door. "Yes, miss?"

"There's a change of plan. I need you to take me to the King's Arms."

Beneath the brim of his hat, his brow furrowed. "But the gentleman said to take you to Gloucester via Ledbury."

"The gentleman is no relation of ours and we are glad to be rid of him. You will still take my companion to Gloucester, but I need to continue on to visit my family." She donned her brightest smile and silently thanked Mr. Bowen for pointing out how she could use it to her advantage.

The coachman looked unsure, but ultimately nodded. They were quickly on their way back into town and to the King's Arms, which was thankfully at the other end of Leominster from where they'd parted with Mr. Bowen.

Mrs. Edwards gave her a swift hug. "I didn't mean it when I said you were difficult."

Margery smiled at her. "I know."

"If anything happens to you, I'll never forgive myself."

"Nothing's going to happen to me, but in any event, I absolve you from all guilt and blame. Here is the money Mr. Bowen gave me—I don't need it." Margery transferred the funds to a grateful but worried Mrs. Edwards. Taking her book, Margery stepped out of the coach with the aid of the coachman and gave Mrs. Edwards a final wave. "Have a safe journey."

She picked up her valise and went into the inn, where she found the innkeeper. After she provided him with the name Lady Stratton had given her—Mrs. Dunlop—he immediately led her to a small curricle.

"Wait, there's no driver?" Margery asked, thinking she'd somehow misunderstood Lady Stratton and suffering a bout of panic. She could no more drive a vehicle than fire a pistol—and Lady Stratton had only versed her on one of those topics.

The innkeeper chuckled. "'Course there's a driver. Me nephew, John. He's a good lad."

Relief seeped through her frame. "Thank you."

Shortly, John, a boy of about six and ten, came outside. Tall and lanky, he seemed unlikely to be able to protect her, but then not everyone could be built like Mr. Bowen. She shook her head, dismayed that he'd come so quickly and effortlessly to mind.

The innkeeper introduced Margery to his nephew, and after he tied her valise to the back of the curricle, they set out. As they left town, John leaned toward her.

"I understand ye have a pair o' pistols should we need 'em?" he asked.

"Indeed I do." She patted the bag nestled between them. "Right here."

John grinned, then urged the horses into a faster trot. The summer day was beautiful, the scenery incomparable, but Margery still felt a nagging bit of remorse at lying to Mr. Bowen and leaving Mrs. Edwards on her own. She also felt a surge of excitement as she considered meeting with Lord Nash tomorrow. Lady Stratton's note of introduction was also tucked into her book, between the pages depicting the knight's offering of the Heart of Llanllwch.

"Now might be a good time to hand me one of those pistols," John said quietly.

Margery's insides froze as she caught sight of the man stepping out of the shrubbery that lined the road. With shaking fingers, she opened the bag and removed one of the pistols. John snatched it from her just as the brigand held up his own pistol and called, "Stand and deliver!"

"Put your head down, miss." John drove straight and discharged his pistol.

Margery squeezed her eyes shut at the sound, but quickly opened them. John's shot must've gone wide, for the thief was still in the road. "That was foolish, mate. There's another bloke behind ye. There'll be no escape for ye now." He pointed his pistol and Margery didn't think, just shoved the boy out of the moving curricle as the shot fired.

Then she threw herself to the floor of the vehicle and prayed the horse would run the man down.

Chapter Seven

IN PURSUIT OF Miss Derrington since she'd bloody changed transportation and direction after leaving him, Rhys swore as Craddock brought the coach to a halt. Rhys assumed they'd caught up to her, but a premonition of dread washed over him. The unmistakable sound of a gunshot confirmed his fear and prompted him to race from the coach.

The curricle she'd taken out of Leominster sat in the middle of the road. A darkly-dressed man ran toward it.

"Craddock!" Rhys called.

The coachman was off his seat, tossing a pistol at Rhys as he descended. They ran forward, and Craddock fired at the man, hitting him in the leg. Rhys hoped to God that had been a villain. He circled the curricle and caught sight of a lad lying in the ditch, then heard the struggle in the curricle.

He leaped toward the fray. A sinister-looking man with a pock-marked face and several missing teeth was wrestling Margery for her book. She clutched it tightly, holding on as if her life depended on, while he did the same.

Rhys held up his pistol and spoke loudly. "Let go of the book and step away from the lady."

The man snarled, revealing more gaps in his mouth. "I didn't really want to hurt no one, but you aren't givin' me no choice." He plucked up a pistol from somewhere beside Margery and fired it at Rhys. However, he wasn't as good or as fast as Rhys, whose father had also required he fire a pistol with speed and accuracy. Rhys's bullet winged the brigand in the shoulder, just as Rhys intended. The bloke fell back over the front of the curricle and slid to the ground.

Rhys hurried to the curricle. "Margery, Miss Derrington, are you all right?" He longed to caress her face, smooth his hands all over her to ensure she was whole.

"I'm fine, thank you."

Fine? She was *"fine, thank you"*? Rhys's temper exploded. Why wasn't she grateful for his arrival? Or at the very least, relieved she was safe? "In case you hadn't noticed, I just saved you from certain death."

Instead of appearing grateful, she looked annoyed. "Aren't you being a bit dramatic? I had a pistol at my side."

"That you weren't using!" Rhys's temple began to throb. "Taking off by yourself—"

"John!" She surged past Rhys, jumped down to the road, and rushed to the lad lying in the ditch. Kneeling beside him, she cradled his head. "He's bleeding. Oh, John." *Now* she sounded concerned. Not for her safety, but for this boy who hadn't been able to protect her.

John groaned as his eyes fluttered open. "Miss?"

"Yes, I'm here. The danger has passed. You were quite brave."

The lad smiled faintly. "Did I hit me head?"

"I think so," she said. "But I think you'll be fine."

"Craddock," Rhys snapped. "Please help John into the coach and drive him back to the Knight's Arms. We'll follow in the curricle."

Craddock helped the boy to his feet while Margery stood. She brushed off her skirt as John wobbled alongside Craddock. They passed the second would-be-thief, whom Craddock had shot in the leg. He moaned piteously and clutched his thigh.

Rhys ignored the injured man and turned his attention to Miss Derrington. "That was the most foolish thing I've ever seen. It's a good thing I was following you."

Her eyes flashed. "I didn't ask for your help. I had things quite well in hand."

"You had nothing in hand." Rhys could barely find words amidst his overwhelming anger. "That brigand was going to take the book at any cost. Not to mention the second brigand Craddock dispatched in the road."

She looked over the curricle and wrinkled his nose. "You shot him. I don't think he'll bother me anymore. And that one," she tossed a glance to the wounded man in the lane, "can't follow me either."

"You're just going to jump back in the curricle and drive yourself to who-knows-where?" He crossed his arms lest he decide to shake her. "I never took you for an imbecile, but I clearly need to revise my opinion."

She pursed her lips. "There's no need to be rude. Fine, you can drive me."

He could drive her. She was going to allow him to help her after she'd lied to him and put herself in unnecessary danger. He moved closer, backing her up to the side of the curricle. "You think you're safe right now, but I would caution you not to be too comfortable. You see, I'm furious and I was scared. " All the emotion of the last quarter hour erupted inside of him. "Oh, to *hell* with it."

Rhys snaked his arms around her waist and pulled her against him. Her mouth formed an O just before his lips descended on hers. He wanted to unleash his anger, his desire, his utter need. When their mouths connected, he held her close, pressing his hands into her back.

He expected her to pull away, but her lips softened against his and he nearly dropped to his knees. Her hands came up to his shoulders and settled there, neither encouraging nor denying. But her mouth told a different story as he angled his head and slid his tongue along the crease, begging for access. She opened slightly and allowed him into her wet heat.

His tongue searched for hers, met its sweet softness and coaxed her to play. She was timid at first, then became bolder. She was the most courageous woman he'd ever met, and he wanted her like no other.

I'm kissing a young woman in the middle of a road in broad daylight. What in the devil has she done to me?

Reason drew him to pull away. He loosened his hold and she sagged back against the curricle. Never before had his passion overtaken his logic and caused him to completely lose control. There was a sense of liberty, but also fear. He couldn't let it happen again.

However, for the first time in their acquaintance he felt as though he had the upper hand, and he liked it. Swallowing back his apprehension he held out his arm. "Come along, Miss Derrington. While we journey back to Leominster, you can tell me all about your failed attempt to cheat me out of the treasure."

AFTER RETURNING JOHN and the curricle to his uncle, they traveled to Church Stretton as Lady Stratton had directed. The journey took longer than expected due to having to double back, which meant suffering Mr.

Bowen's brooding anger for an extended period of time.

Margery had tried to explain her position—that the book was hers and that she didn't owe him anything. He hadn't argued with her, just grunted occasionally and shot her resentful looks.

As they drove into town, he sat straight on the opposing seat. "When we arrive at the Crooked Cat, you'll let me do the talking with the innkeeper."

She'd told him the name of the inn where she'd planned to stay in an effort to demonstrate that her scheme hadn't been ill-conceived. His directive made her suspicious, and stoked her ire, given the tone he employed. "What do you plan to say?"

"I'm not letting you or that book out of my sight. As of right now, we are officially married."

Married? "No."

He crossed his arms over his chest and arched a brow. "I wasn't asking. For your protection and for the safety of the book, you will masquerade as my wife." He looked away. "I don't expect you to behave like it—at least not in private. There will be no more kissing."

"I'm relieved to hear it." *Liar.* She'd rather liked his kiss. That thing he'd done with his tongue had heated her in places she never imagined could burn. Her only regret was that it had been over too quickly. But he was right—they couldn't do it again.

Yet that didn't keep her from being disappointed. She began to imagine, for the first time, how Aunt Agnes could've chosen ruination. If her gentleman had kissed her like that as well as treated her kindly and with charm, he would've been hard to resist.

Wait. Was Margery actually thinking she could do the same if properly motivated? *No.* She wouldn't become a pariah, even for a life-altering kiss. *Definitely not for a life-altering kiss.*

Her anger rekindled and she tossed a glare at her captor. "You realize you're kidnapping me."

"I am not. You are free to return to Gloucester at any time." He smiled coldly. "I'll even fund the trip."

She was tempted to take him up on it, but she was desperate to see Lord Nash and his book. And at present, Mr. Bowen was ensuring that would happen. Still, she couldn't resist provoking him and disturbing his aura of superiority. "What if I did just that and took my book with me?"

His dark eyes smoldered. "You won't."

"You're awfully certain of my behavior. I don't think you know me that well."

"I know you aren't to be trusted, which is why I'm not letting you out of my company until we arrive at Westerly Cross."

So the marriage ruse was only for their stop at the Crooked Cat? They'd go back to being whatever they were when they arrived at Lord Nash's estate? She supposed she could put up with him for one night. "You're sleeping on the floor."

He arched a brow at her and sat forward as the coach came to a halt. "If the bed is large enough, you just might have to share."

She opened her mouth to argue, but he exited the coach and she refused to shout after him like some harridan. No, she needed to compose herself. Long ago, she'd learned to keep her emotions in check and Mr. Bowen wasn't going to be the one to unharness them. In fact, no one but Margery would ever have that power.

Craddock helped her from the coach, and as she

stretched her muscles, she watched her "husband" speak to the innkeeper, a stout man with a shock of white hair. The letter of introduction from Lady Stratton was pressed between the pages of Margery's book, where it would remain, unused. Pity, for she'd been rather excited about undertaking this adventure on her own. Instead, she was saddled with Mr. Bowen, his superiority, and his outrage.

They took dinner in the small dining room on the ground floor. Mr. Bowen invited Craddock to join them and the two men shared stories and conversation while Margery ate in silence. If Mr. Bowen sought to make her feel isolated and excluded, he'd be sorry to know that she was content to be left out of their discussion. She busied her mind with how she might evade him once they arrived at Westerly Cross.

After the sun set, he led her to their room, a large, comfortable accommodation with a table and two chairs, a cheery fireplace, and an unfortunately wide bed. It looked as if she was going to have to sleep with him.

"Mr. Bowen." It seemed a touch odd to be addressing him so formally after the way he'd kissed her earlier, but she didn't want to encourage further familiarity. "I'd rather not share the bed with you."

He removed his hat and shrugged out of his coat, hanging both on hooks set into the wall by the door. "And where shall I sleep? On the floor?"

"If you don't, I will." She went to the bed and removed the coverlet. There was only a sheet, so that if she took the quilt, he'd have no covering. Not that she cared. "You can ask for a blanket if you desire."

She pulled the coverlet from the bed and laid it near the fireplace, where the poker would be within reach in case there was another invasion. Or in case Mr. Bowen decided to renege on his no-kissing edict.

He gave her a bemused stare. "I *desire* you to be logical. It's silly of you to sleep on the floor. I *will* ask for a blanket, but I shall roll it up and place it between us. The bed is plenty wide enough for us to share without touching. I've already promised to keep my hands to myself." His gaze was icy. "Wild dogs couldn't drag me to touch you again," he muttered.

Since their room was the finest in the establishment, it contained a bellpull to summon a member of the inn's staff. Mr. Bowen rang for them, and when the innkeeper's wife arrived, he asked for a blanket, which she delivered moments later.

Mrs. Walters hesitated after setting the blanket on the bed. "Would you care for assistance with your clothing, Mrs. Bowen?"

Margery had considered whether she wanted to disrobe in front of Mr. Bowen, since he'd made it clear he refused to leave, but the notion of sleeping in her stays made her cringe. Even so, she could manage them without Mrs. Walters's assistance. "Thank you, but no."

Mrs. Walters nodded, then left.

"I can help you," Mr. Bowen offered. "If you need it."

"I do not," she said frostily. "I do, however, require you to turn away."

He did as she requested, presenting his back without a word.

Margery tugged at the laces of her gown and loosened it enough to pull over her head. She laid it over the back of the chair. "I look forward to having a room to myself at Westerly Cross."

"Too bad that won't happen," he said.

Her fingers stalled before she could move on to her stays. "What do you mean? You said you weren't taking your eyes off me until we reached Westerly Cross. I presumed you meant to abandon this ridiculous charade after tonight."

"I meant no such thing. If you misunderstood me, that's your problem."

She hadn't misunderstood him! Glaring at his back, she worked the laces of her stays until she was able to wriggle free of the garment. "You can't order me to play your wife at Westerly Cross. Furthermore, Lady Stratton sent a note to her father and he's expecting *Miss* Derrington, not *Mrs.* Bowen."

"That's *his* problem."

Her frustration bloomed into full anger. "You're being beastly. I *promise* I will not try to leave with the book. I want to review it with Lord Nash's book as much as you do."

"Your promise holds little credibility." His tone was vexingly even, as if he were orating a lecture. "Actually, it holds *no* credibility."

Margery fought the urge to throw something at his back. She kicked off her shoes and retrieved a robe from her valise. After shaking the garment out to the best of her ability, she wrapped it around herself. "You may turn."

He did so, his gaze landing on her for a bare moment before diverting toward the fire.

She went to the table and began removing pins from her hair. She eyed him warily, coming up with a new tactic. "You do realize this book belongs to me? That without this book you won't be able to solve the code, which means you won't be able to find the treasure."

He glanced at her, again keeping it brief. "And you realize that without me, you won't be able to solve the code?"

He was probably right, but she would never agree. "So you say."

"So it *is*." Oh, his smugness was maddening.

Searching through her hair, she located another pin and dropped it onto the table. "I had thought you to be merely smug, but it happens that you are domineering as well. You would force me into a contentious alliance."

"No, you forced it by lying to me."

She supposed she had, but Lady Stratton's situation had quite persuaded her to the advantages of establishing her independence, and now that she'd had just a small taste of what that could be, she was afraid she couldn't relinquish the idea. Still, she'd made an agreement with Mr. Bowen, and she supposed she owed him an apology.

"I regret deceiving you," she said quietly, hating that he would probably respond with his typical haughtiness.

"Thank you."

The simplicity and solemnity of his response rattled her. And provoked her to keep the discontent between them alive. "It seems to me you aren't in need of the treasure. You appear to be a wealthy gentleman."

He looked at her fully, then. "I told you I didn't want it for its monetary value. Its historical and academic importance is what matters to me."

Yes, his books were paramount. His library might be worth a fortune, but she couldn't envision him ever liquidating it.

"Well, the monetary value is very important to *me*.

How will I be rewarded for my portion of the treasure when we find it?" She didn't even mention the half that would belong to Lord Nash as owner of the other manuscript.

He moved toward her and braced his hands on the back of one of the chairs. "I will still pay you whatever you ask for the book—and I can make it enough to compensate for the treasure."

She could take his money and return to Gloucester as the independent woman she wanted to be. However, that meant abandoning her quest *and* yielding the book, two things she'd developed a surprising passion for. "I'll consider it."

His eyes widened, drawing her attention to his darkly lush lashes. She could get lost in his eyes—or worse, she could find something.

"You will?" he asked, disbelieving.

"I'll decide when we get to Westerly Cross. *After* we see the other book." She at least wanted to go that far. And she suspected that once she saw the code and key in their entirety, she'd be too excited about deciphering what it meant to walk away.

He looked back to the fire. "We needn't pretend to be married at Westerly Cross."

She suspected he didn't like making the concession, but appreciated him for it. "Thank you."

He went to the bed and rolled the blanket, placing it in the middle as a divider. It was a well-intentioned thought, but the barrier was meager at best. Either one of them could easily breach it and touch. Or kiss.

She fought to keep the heat from rising in her body and flushing her face. He couldn't know how his kiss had affected her. And *she* couldn't allow herself to succumb to another.

Picking up the coverlet, she laid it back atop the bed. Then she climbed into the far side and turned her back toward him. Though they'd reached some sort of mild accord, she purposely refrained from saying good night. She was still annoyed with his cavalier behavior.

She closed her eyes and tried to sleep, but the sounds of him moving around—probably undressing—were too distracting. Instead, her mind turned over the events of the day and every time they landed on the kiss, she forced herself to think of the book, what the code might be, and how close they were to finding it.

The situation only worsened when the bed dipped as he climbed in beside her. She scooted as far away him as possible without tumbling over the edge. It seemed to take an eternity, but his deep, even breathing filled her ears and reminded her, as if she needed reminding, of his proximity. She contemplated what it would be like to be married. Sharing this bed with him, being so . . . *intimate,* made it seem . . . possible.

And that made her want to run screaming from the room.

Chapter Eight

"I'M SO SORRY, but Lord Nash is not currently at home."

The declaration, uttered by Lord Nash's butler, Godfrey, nearly caused Rhys to swear. What on earth had happened to his even temper? He slid a look at Miss Derrington standing beside him and had his answer.

"When will he return?" she asked, her shoulders dipping with disappointment.

"Tomorrow. I received Lady Stratton's note yesterday, and I've prepared a room." Godfrey looked at Rhys. "I apologize that I didn't know you were coming."

In spite of his annoyance at finding Lord Nash absent, Rhys offered a congenial smile. "Nonsense, you can't be expected to read minds."

Godfrey nodded deferentially. "Of course. Let me alert our housekeeper, Mrs. Oliver, and she'll prepare your room. In the meantime, allow me to provide refreshment."

He led them into a sitting room with dark oaken beams stretching at intervals across the ceiling. A large painting of what had to be Lady Stratton with her parents hung above the fireplace. A housemaid entered with a tray and arranged tea and cakes on a table near the center of the room.

Rhys watched as Miss Derrington set her book on the table and helped herself to a plate of cakes and a cup of tea.

She looked up from stirring sugar into her tea. "Do you suppose the book is here somewhere?"

"In his office, perhaps?"

"Not that it matters. We have to wait for him to return." She shot Rhys an inquiring glance as if she *wasn't* certain they had to wait.

But no, they couldn't go looking for it. Could they? He'd sensed her dismay at finding Lord Nash absent, and now he could feel her desperation to see the book. It matched his own.

After sharing tea, they were shown to their rooms, which were, coincidentally, right across the corridor from each other. They exchanged glances, and Rhys was curious to know what she thought of that. He found it bloody tempting.

Though he'd told her there would be no more kissing, last night's sleeping arrangements had sorely enticed him. He'd managed to keep his hands to himself, but only because she'd made it clear she was more than happy to forget the kiss had ever happened. A shame, since he was fairly certain she'd enjoyed it. He knew he had.

He went into his chamber and closed the door. His luggage had been brought up and his clothes put away. The room wasn't as large as the Knight's Lounge at Stratton Hall, but it was well-appointed and lacked the disturbing presence of a secret door. Or so he presumed. After his experience at Stratton Hall, he might take it upon himself to thoroughly investigate any room he stayed in from now on.

He glanced at the clock on the mantel. Half-five. Dinner was to be at seven. Should he change for dinner? It wasn't likely necessary, but he wanted to tidy up after the trip anyway.

After removing his boots and stockings and stripping to his waist, he filled the bowl on the washstand and washed. As he was drying his face, a rap on the door startled him.

Tossing the towel aside, he drew a fresh shirt over his head and padded to the door in his bare feet.

Miss Derrington's fair countenance blinked at him. "Pardon me for disturbing you, but I wanted to let you know that I've decided to take dinner in my room."

He wasn't surprised. No, what surprised him was that she'd come to tell him personally. "I see. An excellent idea. I shall do the same."

She nodded, then turned to go back to her room, the door of which was ajar.

He noticed her feet were also bare, as he saw her toes peeking out from the edge of her gown. Turning, he closed the door before he could follow the mental vision of where those bare feet led . . . bare ankles . . . bare knees . . . bare thighs.

He went back to the washbasin and splashed more cold water onto his face. He rang for the footman and informed him that he would also take dinner in his room. In the meantime, he went to the bed and lay down, crossing his ankles and folding his hands behind his head.

The canopy that stretched over his bed was a dark blue. He stared at it for a long time and tried very hard not to think about Miss Derrington's bare anything.

Think about the book.

Both of de Valery's manuscripts were about to be in his presence, if not his possession. How he wished even one of them belonged to him, but he didn't see how that would be possible. At this juncture, he couldn't see how even the treasure would belong to him.

What would it be? One of the thirteen treasures like the Heart of Llanllwch, which sat in the Ashmolean Museum? Some other Arthurian item that would prove the hero king's existence? Or something else entirely?

Or maybe nothing at all.

No, there had to be something. De Valery wouldn't be that cruel, would he? But Rhys was getting ahead of himself. Putting the books side by side was only the beginning. Then came the hard part: discerning the key so they could use it to decipher the code.

The urge to find Nash's library or office to search for the book nearly overwhelmed him, but he would wait. Besides, the baron would likely keep the book locked up, wouldn't he?

Rhys thought of the men who'd accosted Miss Derrington the day before. Upon returning to Leominster, he'd alerted the constable, who'd taken care of dealing with the wounded brigands. Rhys had never shot a man before and was surprised at the ease with which he'd done it. But upon seeing Miss Derrington in danger, he hadn't hesitated. Did that mean she meant something to him? Given how badly she upset his equilibrium, he had to consider that she did.

He sat up, frustrated with the direction of his thoughts. *Book. Think about the book.*

He got up and dressed and let himself out of his room. He stopped short, as Miss Derrington was doing the same.

They stared at each other a moment before closing the doors and meeting in the center of the corridor.

"Where are you off to?" he asked, taking in the fact

that she'd donned a fresh gown, the only one she had that was appropriate for dinner. Had she changed her mind about where she planned to dine? The book was tucked beneath her arm. With a jolt, he realized he could try to take it from her while she slept, but what would be the point? He took their partnership, however untenable it might be, seriously.

She glanced to the side. "I'm just taking a short walk."

He didn't believe that for a moment. "To find a book perhaps?"

The corner of her mouth inched up briefly, but she worked to keep her face straight. "Perhaps."

"I was going to try the library."

Her gaze sparked with mutual understanding. "Yes, let's."

Side by side, they made their way downstairs with haste and quickly found the library. It was quite large, and Rhys decided he could giddily spend the next month here perusing Nash's collection. Rhys went to the nearest bank of shelves and ran his forefinger along the spines. He loved the feel of the leather and the smells of old vellum and new paper.

He recognized a title and pulled it down to look at its interior.

"Did you find something?" Miss Derrington came toward him, her voice laced with excitement.

He sent her an amused look. "Not *the* book. This is an Old Welsh manuscript. I have a copy myself."

She nodded, her mouth turning down with mild disappointment, and went to investigate another bookshelf.

They spent the next hour searching the library and though he'd been entertained, he could feel her rising frustration like a living thing. He strolled toward where she stood frowning at the last shelf. "You didn't really expect to find it, did you?"

She exhaled and turned to face him. "No. I suppose we should go back up for dinner."

"We should."

They climbed the stairs with none of the enthusiasm with which they'd descended them earlier. Outside their rooms, he paused, wondering if he should suggest they eat together.

She made the decision for him by saying, "Well, good night then." Then she turned and went into her room.

Rhys stared at her closed door for a long moment. He ought to retreat to his room and forget about her and the damned book, at least for tonight. After dinner, he could go back down to the library and lose himself. Yes, that's precisely what he would do.

Determined, he went into his chamber and closed the door. And promptly went back to thinking of Miss Derrington and the bloody de Valery manuscript.

MARGERY PUSHED HER plate away, unfinished. She'd thought Mr. Bowen had perfected the art of brooding, but she was currently in direct competition and might actually demonstrate a superior ability.

She'd been crushed to find Lord Nash wasn't in residence. Working up the courage to search for his de Valery text had taken some time, and when she'd found Mr. Bowen doing the same, she'd nearly laughed.

Perhaps they had more in common than she wanted

to admit.

What *did* they have in common besides wanting to decipher the code and find the treasure? She leaned back in her chair and studied the ceiling with its ornate ivory painted scrollwork in the corners.

They were both intelligent, capable, and unmarried by choice, which for him was fine while it cast her as peculiar. What else? They were driven, as evidenced by their jaunt to the library. They were also cunning, as evidenced by his attempt to keep the true value of the book from her and her deception to keep him from searching for the treasure.

A soft rap on her door drew her attention. The housemaid came in and removed the dinner tray. "I'll be back later to help you dress for bed, miss."

Margery nodded. As the door closed, she stood, suddenly in need of movement. Perhaps a book from the library would divert her thoughts from Mr. Bowen and the de Valery manuscripts. She plucked up her book because she couldn't possibly leave it unattended.

She opened the door and nearly stumbled, as Mr. Bowen was doing the same.

His lips curled into a disarming smile. "Again?"

Her pulse quickened and the heat she'd felt after his kiss raced through her. "So it seems. Where are you going this time?"

"To get a book."

"From the library?" She nodded. "That's where I was going."

They moved toward the staircase in unison. Though several inches separated them, she felt his proximity. He'd removed his coat, but still wore his waistcoat. He was still "dressed," but some women would be horrified. Margery was not. In fact, she was disappointed he was wearing so much. It was *that* which horrified her.

When they reached the base of the stairs, she hesitated. He did the same.

"Do you think his office might be this way?" She gestured to the right, opposite where they would go to return to the library.

He stroked his jaw, which had darkened at this late hour with the onset of his beard. "It might be."

"Do you think it would be open?"

"There's only one way to know for sure." He turned and led the way.

She stifled a smile as she followed him down a short corridor. They tried two rooms, but they weren't his study. The last door, however, proved successful.

"Aha!" His tone implied he might've found the treasure they sought. His half-smile was charming and did completely inappropriate things to her belly.

The office was very masculine, with a pair of bookshelves and a large mahogany desk. Mr. Bowen went immediately to the desk and sat behind it.

"What are you doing?" she asked.

"Looking for the book." He peered up at her. "Or are we still trying to disguise that's what we're doing?"

She suddenly felt ashamed. They had no right invading this man's privacy.

Mr. Bowen's brow gathered and he abruptly stood. "I'm afraid I've changed my mind. I'm as desperate as you to study his book, but I can't bring myself to be rude."

She retreated to the door. "Nor can I."

He joined her and they exchanged what had to be mutually appreciative looks before trudging back up the stairs. Outside their rooms, Margery faced him, lacing her fingers together in front of her waist. "Good night then. Again."

"Yes, good night." He inclined his head, then went to his room.

Margery frowned at his closed door, feeling strangely . . . empty. She pivoted slowly and reentered her own room. A short while later, the maid returned and helped her prepare for bed.

As Margery was about to climb beneath the coverlet, she realized she hadn't obtained a book and would likely never fall asleep without something to distract herself.

Wearing a robe over her nightrail, she went back into the hall. She half expected Mr. Bowen to be there and was disappointed when he wasn't. Making her way along the sconce-lit corridor, she tried to focus on what to read. A novel or a book of poetry? Perhaps some Shakespeare. She'd seen several of his plays on the shelves.

When she arrived at the library, she froze at the threshold. Mr. Bowen removed a book from a shelf and turned, pausing as their gazes connected.

"It's not the corridor, at least," he quipped.

Margery's insides melted at the warmth in his tone and the tilt of his head as he regarded her. His eyes swept her from head to foot, making her think he didn't want to miss a single detail. Men that had expressed any interest in her in the past had never looked at her like that—as if they were memorizing every part of her. For a man who professed there would be no kissing, he certainly seemed as if he wanted to. Maybe he was fighting to overcome his attraction, just as she was.

Turning from him, she went to where she'd seen the

Shakespeare. Perusing the spines, she selected *Twelfth Night*.

"An excellent choice," he said, close behind her.

Startled, she spun about and flattened her back against the bookshelf.

Unlike her, he was mostly dressed, though he wore a banyan over his shirt instead of a waistcoat and coat. The garment, crafted of gold silk, buttoned closed and looked absurdly handsome on his frame. The absence of his cravat revealed a small triangular space of flesh. Overall, he presented an alluring example of masculinity.

"Though," his deep voice drew her attention back to his face, "I might've chosen *Taming of the Shrew*."

She resisted the urge to smile at his wit, but she didn't want to call attention to the fact that her deceptive behavior could be considered shrewish. She'd only been protecting her own interests.

She tipped her head to read the cover of the book he held, but there was no title on it. "What are you reading?"

He glanced down at the tome. "A book of poetry from the twelfth century."

"What language?"

His dark gaze found hers and held. "Welsh."

"You speak medieval Welsh?"

"I *read* medieval Welsh. There is a massive difference."

She smiled at the humor in his tone. "I'm sure. What other languages can you read?"

He leaned against the bookshelf, which brought his chest almost in contact with her shoulder. "Latin, Greek, medieval English of course, Italian, French, some German."

She also turned so that her side was against the bookshelf, so she could face him straight-on. "My goodness, that must've taken years to master." How old was he anyway? She'd guessed him to be within five years of her.

He shrugged, and the familiar touch of hubris that she found attractive—in moderation—came out. "Once you learn one, the rest come easily."

"I can't imagine it's that way for everyone. I'm sure you worked hard."

"I did." There was no sense of pride in his answer, just a confidence that she found ridiculously alluring. "Do you read any languages?" He reached out and tucked a loose curl behind her ear.

She struggled to remember his question. Languages? "Um, yes. French and a little Latin. I actually speak the French in addition to reading it, however."

"Well done." His whispered words caressed her, and the heat swirling in her belly heated to a slow burn.

The moment stretched into something she couldn't define. She could see him kissing her again, wanted it to happen. She arched forward as he bent his head.

"Oh! I didn't realize you were in here." They broke apart as the housemaid moved into the library. "I came in to tidy, should I come back later?"

"No, it's fine," he said, while Margery answered, "Please come in, we were just leaving."

They exchanged heated looks as they walked toward the door.

"Good night," Margery said as she passed the maid and made her way toward the stairs.

Mr. Bowen followed her, and this time they ascended more quickly than on their previous trips. Outside their rooms, they faced each other.

Margery hugged her book and the play to her chest, as if she could armor herself against the sensations Mr. Bowen made her feel. "We should really stop doing this."

He nodded. "We should."

"Good night then."

"Good night."

Neither of them moved.

Suddenly he stepped forward and cupped the side of her face. He kissed her, trapping her hands with her books between them. Unlike the day before, this kiss was soft, gentle, and so sweet she thought she might sigh with the loveliness of it.

His fingers stroked along the underside of her jaw as his mouth worked over hers. She tipped her head to the side and kissed him back, though she lacked the experience he clearly demonstrated.

He glided his hand back along her neck and she did sigh then, which opened her lips to his tongue. Then he did that thing again, where he slipped it into her mouth, and now she wanted to groan instead of sigh. It was hot and wet and delicious and she couldn't get enough. And her bloody hands were engaged. Just as she was about to drop her books, probably on his feet, and grasp the front of his banyan, he lifted his head.

"My apologies. I said there'd be no more kissing." His voice was dark and heavy. "I'm afraid I simply couldn't resist, but I shan't do it again. Good night, and this time I mean it." He tucked his book beneath his arm, went into his room, and closed the door.

Margery stared at the door, her lips still wet and her insides still molten. If Aunt Agnes were here, she'd tell Margery to go after him. To ask him to finish what they'd started. If Aunt Eugenie was here, she'd instruct

Margery to hurry back to her room and endeavor never to be alone with him again without the benefit of a chaperone or a marriage proposal—and she'd advocate for the latter.

But Margery didn't want a marriage proposal. There was no such thing as a happy ending—just look at her aunts. Oh, they were happy, she supposed, but men played no part of it. That wasn't precisely true. Aunt Agnes spoke fondly of her protector. She'd loved him and he'd loved her. And after some of the moments Margery had shared with Rhys—Mr. Bowen—particularly the kissing . . . She began to wonder if she could allow the possibility . . .

No. Lady Stratton was right. Independence was far preferable, and it was in Margery's grasp. She just needed to keep her distance from Mr. Bowen. Tomorrow's appointment with Lord Nash and his book couldn't come soon enough.

Chapter Nine

RHYS WAITED IN the corridor for Miss Derrington, which felt odd after last night's repeated unintentional meetings. He was also surprised she wasn't out here pacing a hole in the carpet, since Lord Nash had returned and summoned them to his office.

Maybe she'd already gone down.

With a frown, he went to her door to knock. It opened just as he lifted his hand.

She stopped short of barreling into him. "Oh! I was just coming to knock on your door."

He glanced at the ever-present book in her embrace. "You were?" *She was.*

He closed his eyes briefly, irritated with himself for assuming the worst. He didn't want to return to their warfare of two days ago. Last night's accord had been pleasant. Dangerously so. He'd tossed and turned half the night recalling her kiss and chastising himself for initiating it.

"Shall we go down?" He presented his arm.

She set her hand in the crook of his elbow. "Thank you."

Their pace quickened as they neared Lord Nash's office. The door was open, and the baron, a man of middling height with a slight paunch and wearing a white queued wig, stood as they approached. "Come in, come in!"

He gestured for them to come and sit in the pair of leather chairs that faced his desk. "I'm so pleased to make your acquaintance. Artemisia's letter explained why you've come, of course." His gray eyes were alight with excitement as he retook his seat. He set his palms flat on the desk. "May I see it?"

Miss Derrington glanced at Rhys and he gave her a look that said, *yes, show it to him.*

She set her book atop the desk. "This is my de Valery manuscript."

The baron's fingers caressed the edges of the book before he opened it. He smiled as he read the title page. "Exquisite." He looked up at Rhys. "It bears de Valery's mark?"

"On the last page, yes."

Lord Nash sat back in his chair and looked as though he might cry. "After so many generations, for my family to see it again . . ." He dabbed at his eyes. "You must understand, the books were split up between the brothers—one who fought for Owen Glendower and one who did not. I've tried to trace this one, but it's long been feared lost. Can I ask how you came to have it?"

Miss Derrington smoothed her hands along her skirt. "It belonged to my great-grandfather. I don't know how he obtained it."

Lord Nash shook his head. "A shame, but I suppose all that matters is that it's come to light at last."

Rhys was terribly interested in the history of the manuscripts. "Your book has been in your family since de Valery drafted it?"

Lord Nash's smile turned sly. "Who do you think commissioned them?"

Rhys scooted forward. "Wait, your family commissioned de Valery's work? Do you know why?

From what source?"

This discovery was huge. If they could trace these actual stories to a specific source, they vaulted from romantic tales to potential history. What if these were based on actual events? What if King Arthur and his knights were real? Rhys's head spun with the possibilities, and yet the skepticism he held with regard to Arthurian legend as fact still lingered in the back of his mind.

"Unfortunately I don't know the source." Lord Nash's brow creased. "I can see that disappoints you greatly, however perhaps the code will tell you more of what you want to know."

Perhaps it would. Rhys really had no idea what it would say. "I've always assumed it would lead to another of the thirteen treasures."

Nash nodded. "Like the Heart of Llanllwch. Although, I must admit there are those in my family who think the heart *is* the treasure and that this code will simply lead the searcher to where it was found outside Carmarthen."

"That would be disappointing," Miss Derrington said. She sat forward and rested her hands on the edge of the desk. Her fingers were pale and slender, the nails perfectly rounded. Confound it, she distracted him far too easily.

"I agree with you, Miss Derrington, and I don't agree with that theory," Nash said. "I think there are thirteen treasures and de Valery's code could unlock the secret to all of them. What if it leads to each?" His tone increased in volume as his eyes danced.

Rhys shared the baron's enthusiasm. He could scarcely wait to see the other book. "There's only one way to find out. May we see your de Valery manuscript now?"

He opened the drawer of his desk, so near where Rhys had sat last night, and withdrew a book that was clearly the twin of Miss Derrington's. "Reuniting these texts has been a lifelong dream that I never hoped to realize."

Rhys itched to touch the book, but waited for Miss Derrington. She looked over at him, her eyes inquiring. He inclined his head toward the book, silently telling her to go ahead. Her lips curved up and she slid the book closer. Gently, she opened it to reveal the title page.

"It's so much like ours," she whispered.

Rhys leaned forward, bringing his head alongside hers. "You can see that it's de Valery by the slope of the letters."

"And the weight of the pen." She lightly touched one of the words and traced a letter. "You can tell by its width."

He tipped his gaze toward her briefly in admiration. She'd not only studied de Valery's manuscript, she'd been an excellent student. "Very observant, Miss Derrington."

They turned through the pages, scrutinizing each one as Lord Nash did the same with Miss Derrington's book. When they got to the last page, Miss Derrington's finger immediately went to de Valery's mark. "It's here."

They all sat back, satisfaction gleaming in their eyes as if they'd just partaken of a spectacular meal.

"Now, the hard part," Lord Nash said, steepling his hands beneath his chin. "How do we solve the code?"

"You don't know?" Miss Derrington asked, sounding slightly alarmed.

Nash shot her a bemused glance. "I've only just seen the second book. And as you can tell, they both appear to be illuminated texts and nothing more." He looked back down at Miss Derrington's volume. "It could be any number of things—something in the illustrations, a numbered cipher—"

"But there are no numbers," she blurted.

"The key, whatever it is, could correspond to numbers," Rhys explained. "We'd just have to figure out how."

She turned to face Rhys. "How will you do that? And what's the key?"

"I'm afraid we have no more answers than when you arrived, but at least we have both books." Nash set his hands down on the arms of his chair and seemed content.

Rhys, on the other hand, wanted to jump up and pace as he contemplated how to solve this mystery. "Because there are two books, I assumed there would be a key and a code. You'd need one to decipher the other."

Nash watched Rhys walk along the carpet. "That makes sense. But there's no way to discern what those might be, I'm afraid."

"Why go to the trouble of developing a code if it wasn't meant to be solved?" Miss Derrington asked. "My lord, you said your family commissioned these volumes. Did they also commission the code or was it de Valery's invention?"

She posed an excellent question. Rhys only hoped Nash knew the answer.

Again, Lord Nash's brow wrinkled in dismay. "We don't know. It's a question my father and his father before him asked many times. We'd hoped there would be something more to the other book—your book."

Just as Rhys had hoped there'd be more to Nash's. "You say you don't know the source of the material, but you never answered why they commissioned the work in the first place. Is that because this is another answer that's been lost to history?"

His gaze dimmed with regret. "I'm afraid so, and it pains me to say it."

Miss Derrington's shoulders drooped and her lips turned down, mirroring Rhys's own disappointment and frustration. There had to be more. It couldn't end here.

Rhys couldn't stand it any longer—he stood and walked to the window, which looked over the front drive. "Can you think of anything that might help us solve this mystery?"

"There's de Valery's house."

"His house?" Rhys spun from the window just as Miss Derrington echoed his question.

"The house where he completed the work is still in my family," Nash said.

Rhys moved back toward the desk, his blood thrumming. "Where is this?"

"About three miles from here, a little cottage near the Severn. Do you want to see it? There's a tenant, but if you think it could help, I'll arrange for you to have access."

"Yes, I want to see it." He glanced at the clock perched on one of the bookshelves. It was half-two. "Can we go now?"

Nash frowned. "I wouldn't want to put him out."

Miss Derrington smiled prettily and Rhys wanted to kiss her for thinking to employ her considerable charms. "We shan't trouble him. Perhaps we could take some baked goods from your kitchen?"

Nash's frown remained. "No, no, I must insist we wait until the morning. He'll want to ensure the place is tidy. Wouldn't do to arrive unannounced and risk embarrassing him. I'll send a message over right now."

Rhys wanted to argue, but he also appreciated the baron's thoughtfulness regarding his tenants. Miss Derrington sent Rhys a pleading glance, but he gave his head a little shake in denial. They had to follow Nash's lead.

In the meantime, Rhys wanted to make use of the afternoon. "Would you mind, if we took the books to your library and set them on the table for study?"

"Not at all! In fact, I'd be delighted to discuss them at length, if you're both inclined."

Miss Derrington's eager expression was all the response Rhys needed. "I'm sure we are," he said. "Perhaps our joint analyses will reveal some details that will help."

Nash stood. "Indeed. However, first I plan to have luncheon if you'd care to join me?"

Miss Derrington also got to her feet. "That would be lovely, thank you." She scooped up her book and turned to leave the office.

"You can leave that here," Nash said.

"I'm afraid I wouldn't feel safe."

"Because Stratton's fake went missing." Nash nodded. "I can't tell you how relieved I am that I swapped the books after learning what a bounder he is. I wish I'd never agreed to allow my daughter to marry him."

Rhys understood the man's remorse after the things Miss Derrington had told him about Lady Stratton's difficult marriage. "Someone also attempted to steal

Miss Derrington's manuscript on two separate occasions."

Nash's expression turned wary. "This is most concerning. I'd convinced myself that the disappearance of Stratton's fake was due to his idiocy. I could see him misplacing the damned thing after imbibing too much." He flashed a look at Miss Derrington. "My apologies, miss."

Ice crawled up Rhys's spine. "Why is it concerning?"

Nash picked up his book and turned to Miss Derrington. "If someone has tried to steal the book, you're right to keep it with you at all times. The code has long been sought after by those who truly believe that Arthur and his knights lived. These people seek to obtain and conceal all evidence that proves the existence of these legendary men. Some say this group, the Order of the Round Table, will stop at nothing to achieve their aims."

"Why would they do such a thing?" Miss Derrington asked.

"I'm not entirely certain, but I've heard they believe the artifacts to be too dangerous or valuable to be exposed."

The Order of the Round Table? Not a terribly unique name, but it certainly conveyed their purpose. "I've never heard of such a group," Rhys said.

Nash shrugged. "I'm not surprised, the faction is typically very small. I'm not sure when it originated or how it maintains its perpetuity. You might ask Lord Septon. He's an antiquarian who's studied Arthurian legend and may be aware of this group. I could provide you with an introduction."

"Actually, I know Septon quite well." Though he'd

never mentioned this mysterious group. "He might also be able to help us figure out the code, if necessary."

Miss Derrington gave Rhys a vexed look, which he didn't understand and would have to ask her about later.

"Very well," Nash said. "Let us bring our books to luncheon, then we'll repair to the library. It will be like being at Oxford again!" He grinned at them as he gestured for Miss Derrington to precede him.

As Rhys took up the rear, his mind churned at the developments from the meeting. He only hoped the trip to de Valery's cottage would prove fruitful and that this group of Arthurian followers wouldn't find a way to get what they wanted.

They might stop at nothing to achieve their goals, but Rhys would do the same to protect that which he held dear. As he watched Miss Derrington enter the dining room, he realized that conviction extended beyond his beloved books.

THOUGH SHE COULD scarcely wait until they visited de Valery's cottage on the morrow, Margery had thoroughly enjoyed the afternoon's study session with Lord Nash and Mr. Bowen. She and Lord Nash had listened raptly to everything Mr. Bowen knew about Arthurian legend and medieval illuminated manuscripts, which was quite a lot. She'd like to spend some time in his library discussing his favorite texts.

She set her brush down on the dressing table and looked at herself in the mirror. What was she doing? She wasn't ever going to return to Mr. Bowen's library, and she certainly wasn't going to forge an academic relationship with him, no matter how fascinating she found his knowledge.

Academic relationship? Was that really her primary concern, what with all the kissing going on?

Margery shook her head at herself. "Silly girl," she muttered. "You've no business dawdling with Mr. Bowen. You are not Aunt Agnes." Not that she judged her aunt for her choices. She just couldn't see herself following the same path. However, a fortnight ago, she never would've seen herself chasing some treasure that might or might not exist.

What *was* she doing?

Turning from the mirror, she got up and strode from the dressing closet into her chamber. She didn't want to think about Mr. Bowen or his kisses.

At dinner they'd discussed the Order of the Round Table. Mr. Bowen was surprised he hadn't heard of it, and unfortunately Lord Nash had already shared the depth of his knowledge. Still, they theorized about its purpose and the true lengths to which they might go to obtain the de Valery texts.

The one thing they hadn't discussed was what they would do if they were able to successfully decipher the code tomorrow. Margery hoped for that, but she was skeptical about finding anything at de Valery's cottage. If they did . . . Would she and Mr. Bowen continue on their quest? Would she have to masquerade as his wife for propriety's sake? She choked on a laugh, for there was absolutely nothing proper about it.

Aunt Agnes would tell her to keep going, to pursue this adventure because it might be the only one she ever had. Margery had never imagined she'd have such an opportunity, but was she willing to risk the ruin that had befallen her aunt? If she hadn't already. Were anyone to learn that she'd traveled alone with Mr. Bowen, she'd be as ruined as Aunt Agnes, especially if they learned of their kissing.

She had to stop thinking of that.

A knock on her door made her jump. The maid had already helped her prepare for bed. It could only be one person.

She opened the door. "Mr. Bowen."

"Pardon my intrusion, but may we speak for a few minutes?"

She should decline and send him right back to his chamber, but she said, "Yes," instead. So much for putting him out of her head. And keeping him out of her room.

She closed the door after he entered and tried not to look at the way his banyan fell over his posterior as he walked further into the chamber. Things would be so much easier if he were ugly or at least unattractive to her, like a Lord Stratton or a Mr. Digby. But no, she had to suffer a pompous scholar who looked like the knights of old they'd discussed earlier that afternoon.

He stood in front of the fireplace, which hadn't been lit due to the warmth of the day, and leaned against the mantel. His demeanor and stance made him look as though he belonged here.

Margery drew her dressing gown more tightly around herself. "What did you want to discuss?"

He folded his arms across his chest. "The treasure, assuming we decipher the code and that it actually exists."

She'd begun to feel unsettled about it after making Lord Nash's acquaintance. "Actually, I've been thinking about that. I wonder if this treasure wouldn't actually belong to Lord Nash, certainly half of it, but perhaps the entirety. At the very least, I should return the book to his family."

Mr. Bowen dropped his arms to his sides and blinked at her. "You'd do that?"

She lifted a shoulder. "It seems like the right thing to do. It did belong to his family originally."

"But it may have been purchased fairly by yours." He smiled. "Don't misunderstand me, I think it's an admirable thought. I'm just not sure it's necessary. He didn't ask for its return."

"No, he didn't."

He pushed away from the mantel and took a few steps toward her, his eyes narrowed with concern. "Besides, don't you need the money? Either from selling the book or the treasure itself?"

Yes, but she still wasn't comfortable disclosing just how desperately they needed it. "My aunts were interested in selling, but that was before I learned its true value. Treasure or no, I think they'd change their mind about selling such a dear artifact." Margery wasn't certain of that, but acknowledged *she'd* have trouble parting with it—even to return it to Lord Nash.

Mr. Bowen studied her for a long moment as if he didn't believe her. She turned and took several steps to increase the distance between them.

"Is that all you wanted?" she asked, facing him once more, wondering if he felt the heat swirling in the air, or if it was just her fancy.

"Not quite. I also wanted to, ah, apologize for last night. For kissing you again. Particularly after I said I wouldn't." His complexion darkened.

She fought to cloak her smile. His discomfiture was surprisingly attractive. Like his arrogance. Mr. Bowen was more complicated than she'd initially thought. "I wasn't exactly blameless. However, we can't let it happen again."

"Of course not." His tone was strong, definitive. "I give you my word."

She considered making a jest about him already breaking the pledge, but decided not to. They shouldn't flirt anymore. It encouraged things better left alone. "Thank you."

"Well then, I suppose I must say good night. Unless you want to take another trip to the library?"

Part of her, the part that was rapidly beginning to appreciate Aunt Agnes's way of living life, wanted to, but Aunt Eugenie's reason and pragmatism won out. "Thank you, but no. I'm anxious for tomorrow, so I'd just as soon go to sleep and get to it as soon as possible."

"I can't argue with that." He offered a bow. "Good night." He turned and went to the door, but paused before leaving. "I really did love that you thought of returning the book to Nash." His tone was warm, appreciative, and it made her regret her decision not to flirt and to decline his invitation to visit the library, and most of all their mutual anti-kissing pact.

With a slight nod, he turned, his hand on the door.

She rushed forward, but stopped a few feet from him. "Mr. Bowen? I told you I'd consider selling you the book and returning to Gloucester."

He stared at her and her body hummed with the energy crackling between them.

"Even if I gave the book and the treasure to Nash, I'd still want to find it with you. It's not at all proper or acceptable, but I don't care."

His gaze heated. "Neither do I, Miss Derrington.

And *that* is why we make an excellent team."

Chapter Ten

RHYS DIDN'T KNOW if Miss Derrington had been able to find slumber, but he'd lain awake most of the night, his thoughts consumed with today's excursion and Miss Derrington's mouth. And her eyes. And that delectable dimple in her chin. Hell, every single damn thing about her.

Except the lying. That was something he'd like to forget, but was that smart? She'd deceived him once and he had to assume she might do so again. Her words last night, *I'd still want to find it with you,* had lessened his doubt—and fueled his desire. Thank God he'd had the sense to get the hell out of her room before making another scandalous mistake.

He finished his toilet, drawing his coat on, and made his way across the corridor to Miss Derrington's room. She answered his summons immediately.

His breath stuck in his lungs as he stared at her. She wore her wide-brimmed hat with a green ribbon that tied beneath her chin. The ribbon brought out the green in her eyes, making them look vivid and lush against her pale flesh. She wore the ivory muslin dress with the small yellow flowers again. She looked fresh and lovely, like his favorite berries of summer or the winter's first snow.

She stepped into the corridor, her book tucked beneath her arm. "Good morning."

He shook himself from his fancy and offered his arm. "Good morning."

She wrapped her hand around his elbow and they went downstairs.

Godfrey met them in the foyer. He held a bag that was similar to the one Rhys had given Margery for her manuscript. "I regret to inform you that his lordship suffered an attack of gout in the night. He is unable to accompany you to Mr. Hardy's this morning, but he's asked that you take his book in case you require its presence. He trusts you will ensure its safety."

Rhys accepted the bag. "Please convey our concern and sincerest hope that he will feel better quickly. I will care for this book as if it were my own."

Godfrey nodded. "I'm sure he'll be able to join you downstairs later. Your coach is waiting in the drive."

Rhys had arranged for Craddock to convey them to the cottage. "Thank you."

A footman opened the door and Rhys gestured for Miss Derrington to precede him. Once they were ensconced in the coach, she said, "How disappointing for Lord Nash."

The coach started forward and Rhys braced his feet on the floor. "Perhaps. Let us not convince ourselves that we'll find anything."

"I didn't take you for a pessimist," she said wryly.

"I prefer pragmatist."

"That would describe me as well. Though, I must admit this treasure hunting business is quite invigorating." She looked out the window, but cast him a covert glance.

He could see that she was a reasonable young woman, not moved to sentimentality or excessive emotion. He should find that attractive, given that's how he would've described himself until several days ago. Until he'd met her. Now he felt passion whenever he looked at her or thought of her and a desire that was fast pushing the bounds of reason. He needed to rein himself in.

"What will we even look for?" she asked, turning her head to look at him.

He shrugged. "Some sort of documented clue would make sense, but I don't think we can count on that. It's been four centuries since he wrote this. We have to consider the possibility that whatever we need to decipher the code may no longer exist." Yesterday, they'd discussed taking the books to Septon for his educated opinion regarding the code, but Miss Derrington had seemed reluctant. "If we don't find anything, we still have Septon to consult."

Again, she seemed less than enthused with this idea. Her lips pressed into a line and she looked outside.

"You don't like this plan. Why?"

She shot him a noncommittal look. "I don't know that it's smart to share this with anyone, particularly someone who might be behind trying to steal the books." She must be thinking of Septon's presence on Stratton's list.

"I would be willing to stake my reputation on him having nothing to do with the theft of Stratton's fake or the attempts to steal your book."

She said nothing, just continued to look out the window. Her stubbornness sparked his ire. More excessive emotion provoked by her. He tamped it down.

The coach passed a few small dwellings before turning down a narrow road that terminated at a stone cottage with a thatched roof. A rush of excitement shot through Rhys. He looked at Miss Derrington and her eyes found his. He read the same thrill in their depths.

Craddock opened the door and Rhys stepped out before turning to help Miss Derrington to the dirt track.

They walked to the door, crafted of thick, weathered oak, and he knocked sharply.

A long silence answered them, followed by the sound of trudging footsteps. The door creaked open to reveal a small man with very little hair. He looked up at Rhys and squinted. "My lord?"

"No," Rhys said. "I'm Mr. Bowen, and this is Miss Derrington. Unfortunately, Lord Nash was unable to join us."

"Ah." The confusion that had clouded the man's blue eyes dissipated. "I wondered why ye looked so young. Thought I'd lost me mind for a moment there. Everyone looks young to me anyway." He opened the door wider. "Come on in then." He turned and walked stiltedly into the main room.

Rhys gestured for Miss Derrington to precede him, then had to duck to follow her over the threshold. Once inside, he was able to stand straight. He closed the door behind him and blinked to adjust his eyes to the dim interior. A window beside the door and another on the opposite wall provided the only illumination.

"Have you lived here long, Mr. Hardy?" Miss Derrington asked as she took in their surroundings: a fireplace on the opposite wall, a small arrangement of rudimentary furniture, and, in one corner, a somewhat primitive kitchen.

"Me whole life," he said. "I was born in that room, though it's me bedchamber now." He pointed to the doorway on the right side of the cottage. Another door sat in the center of the opposite wall, leading to the left side.

"And in that room?" Rhys asked, indicating the left chamber, trying to envision how this might have looked four hundred years ago.

"That was our bedroom when we were children. I had eight brothers and sisters, most of them are gone now, though."

Rhys took a step toward his bedchamber and looked inquiringly at their host. "May I?"

"Aye." Mr. Hardy rubbed his mostly-bald head. "His lordship's footman said ye wanted to search the house, but he didn't say what ye were looking for."

Rhys smiled weakly, realizing how foolish this errand must seem. "We're not exactly sure. A scribe lived here four hundred years ago and we're looking for something he might've left behind. I don't suppose there are any pieces of furniture that might be that old? A desk, perhaps?" It was far too much to hope for. He glanced at Miss Derrington, who stood near the fireplace clutching her book.

Mr. Hardy's eyes clouded again, looking as they had when he'd first come to the door. "I'm afraid there isn't anything like that. No desk, anyway. I don't rightly know how long me bed's been here. It was me parents'. There's a table in the other room, and I've only kept one of the small beds that we shared when we were young. Ye're welcome to look about."

"We'll be tidy about it," Miss Derrington said, offering a warm smile. "You keep a lovely home, Mr. Hardy."

The old man shuffled toward her. "Not as lovely as ye, miss. Or, are ye married?" He glanced over at Rhys.

Miss Derrington didn't look at Rhys. "No, we are not."

Mr. Hardy cackled. "That means I have a chance then."

She grinned. "You most certainly do."

Rhys's heart thudded in his chest as another chink in his emotional armor splintered. He turned abruptly to go into the bedchamber. "I'll look in here."

The room wasn't large and contained just a bed, a small fireplace, and a narrow armoire in the corner. He went to the piece of furniture and judged it to be far less than four hundred years old. The room had one window, which though clean, didn't allow much light. The walls were whitewashed and undecorated.

He glanced around in frustration. What had he expected? He walked back into the main room where Miss Derrington was poking about the cupboard in the kitchen area. She turned when she heard the floor creak beneath Rhys's feet. He shook his head at the question in her eyes.

As he crossed to the other room, he addressed Mr. Hardy, who'd sat in a chair and was watching them. "Is there anything extraordinary about the cottage? Any hiding places or unusual things you've noticed in your time here?"

He pursed his lips and rubbed his pate again. "Not that I can think of."

This was proving to be a complete waste of time. Rhys stalked into the other room, which was much brighter than the others. There were two large windows, which he found odd for a cottage of this age and size. And they weren't new. He'd guess them to be from de Valery's time. Had this been his writing room? The addition of so much light would've made a desirable workspace.

Rhys stood in the middle of the chamber and

surveyed the scant furnishings—just the bed and a rickety table set beneath one of the windows. He went to the table and rubbed his hand over the scratched top. It had once been an excellent piece, but the legs had been so oft-repaired that it didn't sit square any longer. Could it date from de Valery's time? Had he worked on this table?

Rhys studied the top, looking for something that might not be random. But what would that even look like? Seeing nothing, he dropped to his knees to investigate the underside.

"Did you find something?" Miss Derrington asked.

Rhys looked up at her as she came farther into the room and stood beside the table. "No, just looking. This table could be from de Valery's time, but I can't say for sure."

The underside was rough, as if it hadn't been finished in the same manner as the top. Again, he looked for any markings, but it was too dark underneath to see anything. He got to his feet and handed Nash's book to Miss Derrington. Then he flipped the table to its side.

She joined him to peruse the underside, but it revealed nothing. "There's nothing here," she said flatly.

"I've always liked that table." Mr. Hardy's voice came from the doorway. "Our father taught us sums there. And we'd play games on it sometimes. We didn't have much, not like you folk, but we had a good time." He smiled and revealed a few gaps in his teeth.

"Sounds like it," Rhys said. He turned the table back upright and brushed his hands together. This couldn't be the end. Perhaps they should investigate the exterior of the cottage. He withdrew a few coins from his pocket and held them out for Mr. Hardy. "I hope you'll accept this as our appreciation for allowing us to intrude upon you."

"I can't take yer money."

Rhys smiled at the man. "I insist. Truly."

The man frowned at the coins, then his face suddenly lit. "Can I give ye something in return?"

"That isn't necessary," Rhys said, pressing the coins into Mr. Hardy's wrinkled hand.

"It's me turn to insist." He took the coins and tottered back to his room.

"We can't take anything from him," Miss Derrington whispered, handing him back Nash's book. "He doesn't have much."

"I know, but we also can't insult him." Rhys gestured for her to go back into the main room.

He followed her as Mr. Hardy was emerging from his bedchamber. "I found just the thing."

He came to Rhys and held out an object in his palm. Round and made of glass with a thin frame of metal, it was maybe three inches in diameter. It almost looked like a magnifying glass without a handle, but it was terribly scratched and the glass appeared clouded. The item appeared worthless, but if it gave Mr. Hardy pleasure to give it to them, Rhys would be happy to accept it.

Rhys took the odd glass and inclined his head. "Thank you."

Miss Derrington peered at the glass with interest. "What is it?"

"A curiosity," Mr. Hardy said. "When ye look through it, colors change as ye rotate it. We had fun with it when we were children."

Rhys couldn't imagine they could look through it

anymore, not the way the glass appeared to have been damaged. He held it up and tried to see through it.

Mr. Hardy shook his head. "It's better if ye look at something with color, such as Miss Derrington's dress."

Rhys felt strange doing so, but directed the glass toward Miss Derrington. He was surprised he could see her through the object, quite well in fact. He rotated it in his grip and gasped. The yellow flowers disappeared.

"What is it?" Miss Derrington took a step toward him.

Rhys lowered the glass. "When I turned it, the yellow flowers on your gown vanished."

"Let me see." She held out her hand and pointed the glass down at her skirt. "I see the flowers, but nothing else."

He took the device back from her and looked again. He didn't see the flowers. Confused, he turned the glass. The flowers came back. "It changes as you rotate it. The colors come and go." He worked to contain his excitement. "Mr. Hardy, wherever did you get this?"

"Found it under the floorboards beneath our bed one night. I might've been about ten years old."

Rhys and Miss Derrington exchanged delighted glances.

"I thought you said you didn't recall anything unique about this cottage?" Rhys asked, wondering how credible the man's memory was.

Mr. Hardy's already wrinkled brow creased even more. "I did? I might've misunderstood. I do that from time to time." He tapped his head with his forefinger. "Me mind doesn't work quite the way it used to."

"Are you sure you remember this correctly?" Miss Derrington asked gently. "Is there a chance you didn't actually find this object here?"

"No, that I can tell ye for certain. It's funny, but I recall the old stuff pretty easily."

Miss Derrington shot Rhys a skeptical glance, and he couldn't deny sharing her doubt. Still, if what he said was true, could this object somehow fit into de Valery's code work?

Perhaps if they heard the tale of Mr. Hardy's discovery, it would provide some details. "Will you tell us how you came to find it?"

"Me brother Peter used to like to hide under our bed—the one I shared with me brother James. He thought he could scare us by pretending to be a monster or summat." Mr. Hardy shook his head as a smile tugged at his lip. "Peter was so little, we went along with it and acted terrified. One night, Peter wasn't in his bed so James and I assumed he was playing his game. But when we got into our bed, we waited and waited. We got worried, so we climbed down and looked under the bed and saw a hole in the floor. We had to move the bed—real quietly so our father wouldn't hear. One of the floorboards had been taken up and moved to the side. The space was just wide enough for Peter to slip beneath the floor. Poor bloke got stuck, but was too afraid to shout for help. When we pulled him out, he had that." Mr. Hardy inclined his head at the object Miss Derrington still held.

"He found it under the floorboards?" Rhys asked.

Mr. Hardy nodded. "Said it was his treasure."

Rhys couldn't resist looking at Miss Derrington, whose lips had curled into a jubilant smile. "Mr. Hardy, would you mind if we looked beneath the floorboards? Do you remember where you found it exactly?"

"Sure I do, it's still loose. Over in the corner." He led them back to the other room, to the far corner on the outer wall. "Third one over," he said. "I'd get down and pull it up for ye, but me back'll likely give out."

Rhys was already kneeling. "It's no trouble. You're doing us a favor by allowing us to look." He pulled up the wide plank and peered underneath, but it was too dark to see. "Miss Derrington, might I ask you to fetch—"

"A lantern?" she finished.

"I'll get it," Mr. Hardy said, ambling from the room. A few moments later, he returned and passed the light to Rhys.

"Thank you." It was tricky, but he was able to get his arm down the hole with the lantern. He couldn't see terribly far—and he certainly couldn't fit between the planks like Hardy's brother had done.

"Do you see anything?" Miss Derrington asked.

"No, but it's devilish hard at this angle."

"Mr. Hardy," she said, "I wonder if we might remove a few more boards so that I can look beneath the floor. It's terribly important."

"Let me see what I can find to help you pry them up." His uneven gait sounded across the room as he went in search of a tool.

Rhys sat back on the floor and set the lantern beside him. "I daresay Mr. Hardy is enjoying this."

Miss Derrington smiled, clearly enjoying this herself.

A sense of glee filled his chest. He'd never expected to be so inspired on this quest or to delight in Miss Derrington's company so thoroughly.

Several minutes later, he pulled up the floorboards until there was a large enough space for Miss Derrington to fit. "Are you certain you wish to go down there?" he asked.

Her answering look was almost coquettish. "Someone has to." Her indomitability astounded him.

Unfortunately, her daring was unnecessary, as she found nothing but dirt and some sort of—thankfully empty—nest. As she stood back in the room and brushed off her dress, she thanked Mr. Hardy again.

"I'm sorry ye didn't find anything."

"It's quite all right. I think we have what we need." She glanced at Rhys, who'd stashed the glass device in his coat pocket and was now restoring the floorboards. "Are you sure you want to part with your glass?" she asked, voicing the thought that had just risen to Rhys's brain. Though she was the better person, because he wasn't sure he could ask. He was too overcome with what this discovery could mean.

"I'm happy to give it to ye. Peter passed when he was fifteen. Caught an ague and died within a few days. I never had any children of me own, so it gives me pleasure to give this to someone who might appreciate it." There was a touch of sadness to Mr. Hardy's eyes. Rhys imagined you never fully recovered from the death of a loved one, whether it had happened the day before or a lifetime ago. "Besides," Mr. Hardy continued, "The memory's what's important, not the thing. I've still got what I treasure most."

Rhys hoped he could live to be as wise and grateful as Mr. Hardy. After replacing the final board, he stood. "Thank you. I think it's time we take our leave."

They said their good-byes and when they got outside, Rhys instructed Craddock to drive them somewhere private, but not back to Westerly Cross.

Miss Derrington sat in the forward-facing seat and arranged her skirts. "Why did you ask him to do that?"

"Aren't you impatient to look at the books with this glass?"

"Yes, of course. You can't wait until we get back to Westerly Cross?"

He cocked his head at her, surprised by her question. "Can you?"

She shook her head as a smile split her lips.

Rhys pulled the glass from his pocket. "This is astonishing."

"Have you ever seen anything like it?" Miss Derrington asked.

"Never. I thought it was opaque."

"So did I. Then to be able to see through it . . ."

He loved sharing this wonder with her. "And the effect it produced . . . Astonishing." He couldn't imagine how it had been manufactured. And he was skeptical that it was actually from de Valery's time.

The coach turned, slowed, and came to a stop. Craddock opened the door a moment later. "There's a little clearing here next to the river, with some rocks. Will that do?"

Rhys peered outside. The rocks were large enough to lay the books upon. "Perfect, thank you." He climbed out, then helped Miss Derrington.

They carried their books to the rocks and set them down. "Which one shall we start with?"

"Mine," Miss Derrington said.

He smiled faintly. "I thought you might say that." Holding the glass in front of his eye, he opened the book and looked at the first drawing. He squinted his other eye, but there was nothing to be seen except an oddly colored illustration. He rotated the glass slowly, but it failed to reveal anything.

"You look disappointed," she said.

"There's nothing there." He turned the page and tried again. Still nothing. Another page. Nothing. Halfway through the book, his frustration threatened to boil over and he considered hurling the glass into the river rushing not twenty feet from them. Of course he wouldn't, but it was tempting.

He put the glass down and took a deep breath. "Perhaps we should try the other book." He left her book open so as not to lose his stopping point.

She opened Nash's book on a second rock beside the other. It was shorter than the first rock, so he had to bend slightly over. As soon as he looked at the first drawing he blinked. Could he be seeing what he was seeing? The glass removed all of the blue from the illustration and, if he wasn't mistaken, the voids that were left formed numbers. What could they mean?

"What is it?" Miss Derrington's excited voice came from just beside him.

He turned, and her face was so close that he had to caution himself not to kiss her. "Look." He handed her the glass.

With a bemused expression, she took it from him and studied the picture. Her gasp stirred his enthusiasm even further. "It takes all of the red out. I think I see . . . numbers."

It worked on the red too? Just as it had removed the yellow from her dress. "Rotate the glass. It removes the red, the yellow, and the blue."

She gasped even louder, then lowered the glass to stare at him in awe. "Creating this had to have taken an inordinate amount of time. What could the numbers mean?"

"I don't know. Maybe when we write them down, we'll see a pattern."

The cock of a pistol chilled Rhys to his very bones. Stiffening, he turned toward the sound, where a man with a kerchief wrapped around his nose and mouth pointed a gun at him. He had a second tucked into his waistband. His hat was pulled low so that all Rhys could make of his features were two small, dark eyes.

The masked man directed his pistol at Miss Derrington. "Give me the glass."

She clutched it tightly against her chest. "No."

Rhys didn't fault her for refusing, he would've done the same, but the bastard was pointing a gun at her and they had nothing to defend themselves with.

"I'm only going to ask politely once more and then I'll do what I must to take it from you. *Give me the glass.*"

"Give it to him," Rhys said, his mind working out ways to protect Miss Derrington and to try to regain the glass.

"Mr. Bowen," she hissed, "we can't just relinquish it!"

The brigand held out his hand. "I'll count to three. One . . . two . . . "

Rhys snatched the glass from her and tossed it to the thief—hard. As hoped, it distracted him enough that Rhys launched forward. He yelled, "Craddock" to draw the coachman's attention. Hopefully he'd bring one of the pistols from the coach.

Rhys and the man landed on the ground with Rhys on top. The man hit Rhys in the temple with the butt of the pistol while Rhys tried to wrestle away the glass.

He caught a glimpse of Miss Derrington's skirt as she joined the fray. She tried to help him get at the glass.

The man hit Rhys a second time, causing his temple to throb and his sight to blur momentarily. It was enough for the thief to roll out from under Rhys.

Craddock appeared then, pistol in hand and fired at their assailant. Unfortunately, he missed and the bastard took off running.

Rhys jumped up, but Miss Derrington stopped him. "Let him go. I have the glass!"

Because his head was pounding, Rhys didn't pursue the fleeing brigand. He set his hands on his hips and inhaled, trying to catch his breath.

"You all right, sir?" Craddock asked, his fair brows gathering over his pale eyes.

"Yes, thank you. Excellent timing on your part."

"I'm sorry I didn't get here faster."

Rhys pivoted and took in the dirt smudging Miss Derrington's skirt. "Are *you* all right?"

"Perfectly fine. More importantly, so is the glass." She held it up in her fingers.

Relief coursed through him. That had been a near thing. Where had the man come from?

"Do you suppose he's a member of the Order of the Round Table?" Miss Derrington asked, echoing the question in his own mind.

"It seems logical." But that led to more questions. "How did he know we had the glass? Did he follow us?"

She frowned in the direction the man had fled. "Even if he did follow us, he didn't go into the cottage with us. How would he know what we'd found?" She looked up at him, her hazel eyes intense. "If you didn't know this glass existed, I can't imagine anyone else did."

"Anyone outside of this Order," he clarified. "I would not be surprised to learn they not only knew of this glass but where it was located." How else to explain the speed with which the man had accosted them? "We should return to Westerly Cross at once. I'd hate for him to come back with reinforcements."

Miss Derrington gathered up her book, while Rhys picked up the other. As he climbed into the coach a moment later, he scanned the road, wondering how the man had tracked them. The entire encounter was unnerving—the timing, the man's masked face, the fact that he'd known they had the glass.

Though he wanted very badly to decipher the code—now more than ever—and find the treasure, he began to consider that it may be too dangerous. At what point would he make that determination and abandon the quest? And if that moment came, could he actually do it?

That was a question he didn't want to answer.

Chapter Eleven

MARGERY WATCHED MR. Bowen surreptitiously from beneath the brim of her bonnet. The coach swayed as they traveled back to Westerly Cross, and she wondered if the movement caused him pain. She'd had to severely stifle the urge to look at his temple and gauge the damage the brigand had done. From a proper distance, she could at least tell that the skin wasn't broken. He'd likely sport a nasty bruise, however.

She jerked her gaze to the window before he caught her looking.

They'd reached a tentative alliance, she thought. She wasn't sure if he trusted her again—she doubted *she* would in his place—but they had at least agreed that they were committed to the hunt, together.

She squeezed her eyes shut briefly in an effort to banish last night. There hadn't been any kissing, but she'd wanted there to be, and she'd spent far too long thinking about that after she'd gone to bed.

Her gaze darted to him again, but this time it connected with his and she went back to looking at the window. Those dark eyes of his seemed to bore straight into her soul, as if he could see things she didn't even know were there.

But that was absurd. What would he see? That she was a heartless female, incapable of love? Was that how she saw herself?

She was saved from further annoying introspection as the coach pulled into Westerly Cross's drive. When the coach came to a stop, she scooted forward on the seat, impatient to disembark.

As they waited for Craddock to put down the stairs and open the door, Mr. Bowen said, "You've gone quiet."

"Just thinking about what happened," she lied. Why *wasn't* she thinking about that?

"I was doing the same. Shall we take the books directly to the library and begin our research?"

"Yes, let's." That would keep her mind off Mr. Bowen and her inconvenient attraction.

Godfrey met them at the door. "His lordship wanted me to ask if you have anything to report."

It seemed Lord Nash was as eager for information as they were.

"Indeed we do," Mr. Bowen answered. "If his lordship is well enough to join us, we'll be in the library."

Godfrey nodded. "Would you care for tea?"

Mr. Bowen smiled politely. "No, thank you. I don't allow liquid of any kind around the manuscripts I'm working with."

"Very good, sir. You can find your way?" At Mr. Bowen's nod, he bowed. "I will notify Lord Nash."

The butler turned and went to the stairs, while Mr. Bowen led Margery to the library.

Once inside, he closed the door behind them. "We should keep what we've found between us and Lord Nash. I'd prefer the servants didn't even know what we're doing."

She could well understand his reticence, and she shared it. They had no idea where or when the group would attempt to steal the books or the glass—or likely both—again.

They laid the books out, and Mr. Bowen went in search of writing implements. Finding none, he rang for a footman and requested them. He waited at the door for the footman's return, received the items, and asked that they not be disturbed.

Margery considered pointing out that their being closeted alone together was highly inappropriate, but just about everything they were doing was highly inappropriate. What was more, she didn't care. What sort of reputation was she protecting? She'd never go to London and attend the Marriage Mart. Rumors and gossip still circulated in Gloucester, but she wasn't an active member of its small society and doubted anyone would even be aware that she'd gone anywhere, let alone what had happened on her journey. In her letter to her aunts, she'd suggested they tell anyone who asked that Margery was visiting out-of-town relatives.

"Shall we start by going through each illustration and simply writing down all of the numbers we see through the glass?" he asked.

"That sounds reasonable." She sat at the table in front of Nash's book and waited for him to give her the glass. When he didn't, she looked up at him curiously. "Did you want to look through the glass and I'll write?"

"Let's take turns, actually. I'll look, you write, then you take the glass and review my work." He sat beside her. "This will, hopefully, minimize any mistakes."

He was quite thorough in his methods. She liked that. Which made her want to scowl. She'd prefer to stop learning things about Mr. Bowen that she liked.

Why was she so set on disliking him? Because he was a danger to her well-mannered life. He made her consider things she ought never consider, such as initiating an affair like her Aunt Agnes had done.

No. She could never.

"Five." His deep voice jolted her to pick up the pen and record the number. He continued until he'd read all of the numbers from the first illustration, six in all.

He handed her the glass and she scanned the picture, reading the numbers she found. Just before she finished, the door opened and Lord Nash came in, leaning on a cane.

The baron's blue eyes were animated, his mouth split into a broad smile. "You've found something!"

"We have." Mr. Bowen stood. "Come and we'll show you."

Lord Nash took Mr. Bowen's vacated seat, and they explained the glass and how it worked. When they were finished with the tale, Lord Nash shook his head in disbelief. "Mr. Hardy has had this glass all these years?"

"Yes, he had no idea what he possessed," Mr. Bowen said. "*Someone* did, however. As soon as we left, we were set upon by a masked thief who attempted to take the glass."

"The devil you say!" Lord Nash looked between them, his expression concerned. "You're both all right?"

"Yes, thankfully." Margery glanced at Mr. Bowen's temple, which had started to turn purple.

Lord Nash sat back in the chair and stared at the open book, his mouth turned down. "I take it this brigand followed you to Hardy's cottage?"

"It's possible, but I find it strange that his goal was the glass and not the books, as if he knew its location and its importance."

"Why didn't they steal it from him?" Margery asked.

Mr. Bowen's expression was troubled. "I don't

know, but someone knows an awful lot about de Valery's code—more than we do, I'd wager."

Lord Nash looked between them. "Do you think they know the glass is here?"

"Perhaps. Though, I don't think we were followed after the brigand ran off," Mr. Bowen said. "However, we didn't realize we were followed from Mr. Hardy's either. I'd like to know why the Order of the Round Table wants these items."

"As would I," Nash said.

Mr. Bowen's mouth set into a grim line. "I'd like to speak with Septon."

Margery sat straighter. Why did he keep mentioning this man who'd been on the list of potential suspects from Stratton?

Nash nodded. "Perhaps you should go to him as soon as possible. He's in Caerwent, you say?"

"Is that really necessary?" Margery couldn't help herself. "Mr. Bowen, you've already stressed the importance of keeping our findings secret."

He looked at her and acknowledged her point with a slight nod. "Yes, it's critical that we keep our work covert. Lord Nash, I think it's best if your staff isn't even aware of what we're doing."

"Godfrey will be the soul of discretion, but I will tell him this is particularly important."

"Thank you," Mr. Bowen said. "Miss Derrington, as for Lord Septon, he is completely trustworthy. We may need his help with this code in any case."

She wasn't ready to say that yet. "We've barely started. It may be that we can solve this on our own." She didn't flinch from his gaze. Her opinion mattered, and she would ensure he knew that.

"Shall we get back to it?" he asked.

"Let's." Lord Nash looked between them. "How can I help?"

They took turns decoding the numbers hidden in all of the illustrations. By the time they were done, they'd assembled a list of eighty-four numbers. At first glance, the list made no sense whatsoever.

"What do we do with this now?" Margery asked, feeling a mix of satisfaction at having completed the task and frustration at the next step not being immediately clear.

Mr. Bowen looked up from studying the list. "I would think these numbers would apply to something in your book."

"But there aren't any numbers in the book," she said.

"No, there aren't." Mr. Bowen rubbed his hand over his eyes and flinched as his fingers brushed his temple.

"I am quite famished for luncheon," Nash declared. "Let us take a break and perhaps we'll come up with something. Mr. Bowen, might I have a word?"

He hadn't said so, but the question implied he wanted to speak with Mr. Bowen privately. Margery glanced at Mr. Bowen, but his answering look was one of curiosity, as if he didn't know why the baron wished to speak with him.

"Certainly." Mr. Bowen stood as Margery got to her feet.

She picked up her book—if they'd hoped to look at it with the numbers without her, they were to be disappointed. Now more than ever, she wasn't letting the text out of her sight. "I'll see you shortly for lunch."

As she left the library, she wondered if the men

were colluding to exclude her from the treasure. But why would they do that? Mr. Bowen had already stated his intention to work with her to find it, even after *she'd* tried to exclude him.

Stop being so suspicious. You can work with Mr. Bowen without encouraging something more . . . intimate.

The problem was that while she could, she was afraid she wouldn't. The more time she spent with him, the more she enjoyed his intelligence, his wit, his touch. And right now, that seemed far more threatening to her than anything this mysterious Order could do.

AFTER THE DOOR closed behind Miss Derrington's delectable backside, Lord Nash drew Rhys from thinking about her finer attributes—something he really ought to stop doing without assistance.

"I didn't want to discuss this in front of Miss Derrington, but I think you should leave as soon as possible. These people know you have the cipher glass and the books. I fear they'll come here, and I'm not . . . prepared to fight them." Lord Nash's eyes drooped. "I wish I were younger."

Rhys clapped the baron on his shoulder in an effort to convey his sympathy. "It's all right. I understand your position. We'll leave for Caerwent at once." He fetched Nash's cane, which rested against one of the bookshelves and held it out for the man.

Nash put a hand on the cane and held his other out for Rhys to help him up. "Miss Derrington seemed reluctant to talk to Septon."

Yes, she'd stated such on multiple occasions now.

Was there another reason behind her hesitation, or was it simply Septon's presence at Stratton's party? He thought it was probably just the latter, but she'd already demonstrated her ability to deceive. He'd do well to remember that.

"We can leave immediately after luncheon." Rhys eyed the baron, who now leaned on his cane. Would he let them take his book? Though they'd already extracted the numbers from it, Rhys couldn't be sure they wouldn't need it again. "Would you allow us to borrow your manuscript?"

Nash surprised him by nodding vigorously. "I think you must. I'd like to have it back when you're finished, of course. I'd also like to ensure Stratton never learns he had a fake. Things could become . . . difficult for my daughter if that were known." Nash's eyes clouded, and his expression was pained.

Rhys understood and felt a surge of compassion for the man. "I'll make sure he doesn't. I do think it's best if the book came with us. That way if these men come calling, you can simply tell them you don't have any of the items they want—assuming they even want the books. The man today only wanted the glass." Rhys had put up quite a fight, so perhaps the brigand had decided having the glass was enough. Without it, the code couldn't be deciphered. "I would love to know why they're so opposed to anyone solving the code."

"Yes. Hopefully Septon will have information for you," Nash said. He stroked his chin. "One other thing . . . I'm not sure how to say this. Traveling with Miss Derrington as you are isn't terribly appropriate. Rest assured that I will keep your visit secret—for a variety of reasons, not the least of which will be to protect her reputation. However, the longer you travel alone together, the more you risk scandal. Please don't take my comments poorly. I'm a father, after all, and seeing as Miss Derrington hasn't one . . ."

Yes, she was an orphan. Not completely alone, since her aunts had raised her, but she had no male figure in her life. She'd given Rhys just the cursory overview of her parents' death and going to live with her aunts. He sensed a lingering sadness, but perhaps he was seeing his own grief in her. He'd taken the loss of his father hard and didn't think he'd ever completely recover. For as long as he could remember, it had been just the two of them, and despite his father's high expectations, he couldn't imagine a better mentor or friend.

Rhys had thought about this, but unless they hired another chaperone, there was nothing to be done. He didn't want to do that, not when the Order—if that's in fact who they were—was following them. Instead, they'd go with the other method they'd already employed. "We'll be traveling as husband and wife." *And hope they didn't run into anyone who would recognize her.* He'd deal with explaining their situation to Septon if the time came.

Nash peered up at him. "Have you considered actually taking her as a wife? She's quite lovely and in possession of a fine wit. I have always preferred a woman with mental acuity. My wife was the smartest person I knew." He smiled fondly.

Make Miss Derrington his wife? He did find her brain attractive, along with nearly everything else about her, save her untrustworthiness. He couldn't marry someone who would lie to him. "I don't know that Miss Derrington and I would suit."

Nash's smile turned discerning. "You might be surprised. Perhaps things will come to light on your travels." He shook his head and glanced at the carpet. "But listen to me, prattling like an old romantic fool. I'll instruct Godfrey that you'll be leaving after luncheon." He turned and ambled to the door.

Rhys watched him go, bemused by the man's observations. Yes, there was *something* between him and Miss Derrington, but not enough to build a marriage on. It was, however, enough to tempt him during their journey south, and he'd need to be on his guard to keep her at arm's length.

He slipped the glass into his coat pocket and scooped up the list of numbers, folded it inside another piece of parchment, and tucked it inside the cover of Nash's book. He was still eager to seek the treasure, but his enthusiasm was tempered by the Order's pursuit. He would have to be vigilant.

Why was the Order so committed to preventing the code from being deciphered—assuming that was their goal? The logical answer was that the treasure was exceptionally valuable. Did they know its location? Were they trying to protect it from being discovered or did they want it for themselves? Hopefully Septon would have answers. In the meantime, Rhys would focus on keeping the books and the glass—and most importantly, Miss Derrington—safe.

AS THE CARRIAGE drove away from Westerly Cross, Margery thought about the numbers and how they could possibly relate to her book, which she figured had to contain the coded message. It made sense, given Nash's book had yielded the numbers.

Thinking about the code solved multiple problems: it took her mind off her attraction to Mr. Bowen and it would hopefully help her solve the code before they arrived in Caerwent and shared the lot of their findings with Septon. Margery barely trusted Mr. Bowen, and with the repeated attempts to steal the book, she didn't dare trust anyone else.

She looked askance at Mr. Bowen seated opposite her in his coach. "If we solve the code before we get to Caerwent, do you agree that we needn't share any of this with Lord Septon?"

Mr. Bowen's dark eyes found hers in the dim light of the coach. "I do. In my letter to him, I only said I wanted to discuss some research."

He *had* sent a letter. She'd assumed as much and was glad to hear he'd been vague. She'd done the same with her aunts. Before leaving Westerly Cross, she'd posted a letter notifying them she was on her way to Caerwent and that she would hopefully be home soon.

The longer she was away, the more uncomfortable she felt. Not because of her reputation, but because she worried about her aunts. She was especially anxious to hear if Aunt Eugenie had recovered from her cold. She was not, however, eager to hear Aunt Eugenie's reaction to her unplanned jaunt across western England with a man who was neither her husband nor her relation. At least Aunt Agnes wouldn't disapprove.

"When we get to Shrewsbury, I'll hire a pair of men to ride with us as protection."

"Thank you," she said. "We still have Lady Stratton's pistols, as well. I don't suppose you've changed your mind about forcing me to act as your wife?"

His answering exhalation was full of resignation.

"I'm not 'forcing' you. It's the only way to protect both your reputation and your person. I can't allow you to sleep in a separate room."

"I understand." Begrudgingly, she did. "However, if you hire someone, can't they guard my room? And before you say I still have to act as your wife as a means to avoid scandal, can't we say I'm your sister?"

His brows dipped so hard, she thought they might crash into his eyes. "No one would believe that," he muttered. He looked out the window. "It's only for two nights. Shrewsbury, Ludlow, then we'll be at my home, and you can have your own room."

"We're staying at your house?" She'd been so focused on not thinking about Mr. Bowen and spending time with him that she hadn't considered their route past Shrewsbury.

"It makes sense. Ludlow's too far from Caerwent to make the journey in one day, so we'll stop over at Hollyhaven."

Yes, it made sense. And now she need only spend two nights sharing a room—and a bed—with him. What about when they traveled to Caerwent? Hopefully it wouldn't come to that. She planned to decipher the code before they reached his house. They'd still have to travel together—just to a different destination. Assuming the code pointed them to a destination. What if it went nowhere? Or it was unsolvable? She refused to think like that. She hadn't come all this way and put herself at risk for nothing.

She set her hand atop her book, nestled beside her on the seat. Mr. Bowen kept Lord Nash's book in similar close fashion and the cipher glass hidden deep in his pocket. "I'll go along with your scheme, but only because sharing a room will allow us more time to work on deciphering the code together."

He inclined his head, an impassive expression flattening his features. "My plan has many benefits. You should realize I always think everything through."

She nearly smiled. It had been awhile since he'd displayed his characteristic conceit, and, strangely, she'd missed it.

Now she was appreciating things about him that she shouldn't even *like*? The sooner they solved this code and found the treasure, the sooner she could get back to her life and he could go back to his.

Chapter Twelve

RHYS DIDN'T KNOW what was more frustrating: their inability to make progress in solving the code or spending so much time in such close proximity to a woman he desired and who clearly didn't desire him in return. Thank God they'd arrived at Hollyhaven.

Thomas greeted them at the door. "Good afternoon, sir, miss." He inclined his head toward Miss Derrington. "I've prepared the garden room for you. It's situated in the northeast corner and offers an exceptional view of the garden. Hence, its name."

"Naturally." A smile teased her lips, drawing Rhys's attention to them, as if he needed a reminder of their lush softness. He'd relived their kisses a thousand times over the past two days and nights as they'd struggled to endure each other's company. Or maybe that was just how he saw it. Spending time with her, exchanging information as they studied the texts, *sleeping* beside her . . . It was more than enough vexation to send a man to Bedlam.

As they moved into the foyer, running footsteps tapped against the wood floor. Penn, approaching from the back of the house, came to a sudden halt just inside. "You're back," he said, his voice heavy with exertion—and maybe something else. Maybe something like . . . relief.

Rhys went to him and touched him on the head. "I'm back." Penn's eyes darted toward Miss Derrington. "This is my friend and colleague, Miss

Derrington." Colleague was perhaps stretching things, but how else was he to describe her? The object of his unrequited lust? Blast, as she'd once asserted, he *was* beastly. He cleared his throat. "Miss Derrington, this is Penn. He's my . . . foster son."

Penn glanced up at him, his blue eyes wide. Rhys held his breath for a moment, wondering if he'd said the wrong thing. They barely knew each other, but he'd agreed to manage the lad's welfare and Rhys took the assignment very seriously. Penn said nothing, much to Rhys's satisfaction.

Miss Derrington offered a curtsey. "How do you do, Penn?" She shot Rhys a quizzical look, clearly asking why he'd never mentioned Penn.

"Pleased to meet you, Miss Derrington." Penn bowed before quickly turning his attention back to Rhys. "Did you find it? The treasure?"

Miss Derrington sent Rhys another look—this one sharp with surprise.

Rhys captured the boy's gaze. "Not yet, but we are well on our way. This is just between us, though; you understand?"

Penn nodded. "I won't tell a soul."

Rhys gave him an encouraging smile. "Very good. Now, Miss Derrington and I would like to rest after our journey. I'll see you in a while, all right?"

After another bow toward Miss Derrington, Penn turned and took himself off, though with considerably less enthusiasm than when he'd arrived.

"Shall I show you to your chamber, Miss Derrington?" Thomas asked.

"I'll take her," Rhys said. He extended his elbow, which she took, and they ascended the stairs.

As they neared the top, she sent him an inquisitive

glance. "Why didn't you tell me about Penn?"

Because he was just beginning to adjust to the change. Because the true reason behind Penn's being here was something he couldn't share. So many reasons. "He only came to live with me a short time ago. His mother is dying, but he doesn't know that. She wanted to ensure her son was cared for after she was gone."

"Why did she choose you? Is he yours?"

Rhys nearly stumbled on the last step as they reached the landing. "No. Heavens, no. I realize you don't know me, but my reputation is that of a hermit—and rightly so. She chose me because of my academic reputation." That seemed as good a reason as any. "She wants her son to learn and to go to school."

Her brow furrowed. "She trusted you to raise her son, and yet you have no prior relationship with her at all?"

He understood her skepticism and hated lying to her at this point in their association, but he wouldn't endanger Penn. "None." That wasn't exactly a lie. He'd only ever met the first Lady Stratton at her wedding to his cousin, but he'd apparently left a positive enough impression that she trusted him to raise her son. She'd also chosen Rhys because he could verify her identity and that of Penn—when the time came for him to claim his place as Stratton's heir.

"You have to admit it's intriguing."

"I suppose." He was desperate to change the topic. "In this case, though, the explanation is really as simple and mundane as it sounds."

She inclined her head and they started moving once more. "I'm surprised you told him about the treasure, since you've been so keen to maintain secrecy."

Again, he understood her doubt. "He's a lad who likes to dig for treasure. I thought it would interest him."

She shot him an inquisitive glance. "What do you mean, he digs for treasure?"

"He digs holes in the ground and finds things. Coins, bones, things like that."

"What a fascinating boy." She stopped as they'd arrived at her chamber. "Do you think he'll be able to keep this secret?"

Rhys chuckled as he withdrew his arm. "What do you think he'll do, share what he knows at the next meeting of antiquaries? Or perhaps at the next district social event?"

"Of course not, I was merely asking," she said evenly. "Children can be unpredictable."

"What do you know of them?"

"Nothing, but then neither do you. We need to be careful. We agreed we wouldn't discuss this with anyone."

He frowned. "That agreement came after I'd told him. Anyway, he's no danger to our endeavor."

Margery nodded, but Rhys couldn't tell what she was thinking, whether she accepted that Penn could be trusted. He gave her a penetrating stare. "I sense you're uneasy about this. Why? I'm beginning to think you're looking for reasons not to place your faith in me. What can I do to prove my loyalty, that I am guarding both of our best interests?"

Her eyes widened slightly—only slightly—but it was enough for Rhys to know he'd hit a nerve. "I'm . . . It's not easy for me to trust people. I find it's better to keep to myself."

Feeling as though he'd won a hard-fought battle, he

suppressed a smile. He was enjoying peeling away the many layers of Miss Derrington. What would he find when he'd stripped them all to her core? Would she even let him get that far? He hoped so—whether she was frustrating him with her skepticism or impressing him with her intelligence, he was utterly captivated by her.

He opened the door to her chamber and her intake of breath was both satisfying and exhilarating. "What a beautiful room."

The view was not the sole reason they called it the garden room. It was decorated in a palette of colors that reminded one of a summer garden—greens, yellows, purples, reds, and blues. They shouldn't have worked together, but they did. As did the wallpaper with the dainty garden scenes and the two paintings of gardens that adorned one wall.

"My mother decorated it. She passed within a day of my birth. I worried you might find it old-fashioned." Because his mother had died nearly twenty-nine years ago, which put the décor at something between dated and ancient.

She turned her head, taking in the entire room. "Not at all. It's classic and inviting. You never knew your mother, yet you keep this room as she wanted. That's . . . nice." Her tone had turned a bit wistful. She moved to the windows and surveyed the grounds below.

"I used to come in here when I was young. That's her portrait, there." He pointed to a small painting on a table against the wall. Elena Bowen stared back at them, her eyes dark and her hair darker.

Miss Derrington studied her a moment. "She was very lovely. I see where you get your eyes."

"I liked to sit and talk to her, pretend she was actually here." Why was he telling her this? He'd never told anyone about his mother. "It was foolish."

"I don't think so," she said softly, turning toward him with understanding warming her gaze. "I have miniatures of my parents and I still talk to them. So if you find that foolish . . ."

"No, I don't. I was trying to cover my embarrassment and *that* was foolish. I've never discussed her with anyone." Why would he? He'd been intimate, meaning close, with precisely one person his entire life and the one topic he and his father rarely discussed was his mother. He'd had grandparents—his father's parents—years ago, but they hadn't known his mother well. She and Rhys's father had only been married two years before she died. "Did you have grandparents when you were young? Maybe you still do."

"A long time ago I had a grandmother and a grandfather, but they passed before my parents. I remember my grandmother—she was my father's mother. She loved lemon cakes." Miss Derrington shook her head as her lips curved into a subtle smile. "I'd quite forgotten about that—she always smelled of lemon."

"My grandmother always pretended she didn't like sweets," Rhys said, "but I caught her sneaking a custard once. It was very late one night, I couldn't have been more than six. I'd been stealing into my father's study to read one of his books. I saw her. She saw me. A communication passed between us, and neither of us ever spoke of it." Like Miss Derrington, he hadn't thought of that in years, but it was a distinct and pleasant memory.

Miss Derrington abruptly turned away.

Rhys didn't know what he'd said wrong, but whatever it was had clearly pained her. "What did I say?"

After a moment, she glanced back at him. "Nothing. I'm tired. If you'll excuse me, I'd like to rest before supper."

He knew she was lying, but he wasn't going to pry. Miss Derrington held her emotions very close, and this conversation was one of the most personal they'd ever shared. He hoped it wasn't the last, but acknowledged that he'd have to work hard to continue to chip away at her armor. Questions burned his mind: Why did she have it and why was he so determined to learn more about her? "Of course. I'll see you then."

He inclined his head, imparted a final look that he hoped conveyed his compassion, and turned to go.

Her lush voice halted him and begged him to face her once more. "We'll revisit the manuscripts after supper?"

"I'd like to, yes." He was glad she wanted to as well. They weren't any closer to solving the code, but he—rather fancifully—hoped that being back in his study would provoke ideas that hadn't yet come to light.

She nodded. "Until later then."

"Until later." This time when he turned to go, she didn't stop him. He carried the disappointment back to his chamber.

AS MARGERY MADE her way down to supper, she took in the dark oak paneling and balustrade, all of which were polished to a glistening shine. Hollyhaven felt like a bachelor residence with its woodwork and lack of feminine décor—save her chamber—but perhaps that was because Mr. Bowen seemed to dominate every corner of the house, even when he wasn't in her presence.

She kept finding herself staring at his mother's portrait and wondering what it would be like to have never known your mother. The ache of losing her parents was always with her, but she'd at least enjoyed ten years of happy memories to soothe the pain. But then, Mr. Bowen couldn't really miss what he'd never had, could he? No, it wasn't the same at all.

His story about his grandmother had sent a wave of tears to her eyes, but she'd averted her face from Mr. Bowen and blinked them back. She and her father had liked to visit the kitchens late at night when the house was dark and silent. They'd raided the pantry for whatever they could find and talked about all manner of things: what the weather might be, what they were reading, which of Mrs. Cole's sweets were best—the currant tarts or the Shrewsbury cakes. Margery could almost hear her father's deep voice extolling the delights of the currant tarts, his favorite, and she had to swallow back the tears again.

What was wrong with her? She missed her parents, but she'd long ago moved past such maudlin reactions. Why was she succumbing to melancholia now?

She wasn't. She refused. Stiffening her spine, she continued downstairs to the dining room. Then stopped short as she stepped inside.

Mr. Bowen stood near his chair at the head of the table, while Penn was positioned beside another. Children didn't typically eat with the adults, though

Margery had when it was just her and her parents. That Mr. Bowen had included his charge was yet another mark in his favor. This was most displeasing when she was working so hard to maintain a purely academic relationship.

"Good evening, Miss Derrington, you look lovely, as usual." It could've been a perfunctory compliment, but when the words were spoken with a velvety tone and accompanied a heated gaze, she had to accept he meant it most sincerely.

"Thank you. Good evening, Penn, I'm pleased to see you're joining us." She snuck a look at Mr. Bowen who seemed pleased that she was pleased.

They took their seats and a footman, supervised by Thomas, served their first course.

The conversation was stilted at first as Margery attempted to engage Penn, who was far more interested in the food than anything else. She gave up after a while, and the meal fell into silence.

During the second course, Mr. Bowen spoke up. "We should reach Caerwent by afternoon tomorrow."

Penn's gaze shot toward Mr. Bowen. "You're leaving again?"

"For a short trip. We'll likely return the following day."

Margery stared at him. Was he expecting not to decipher the code? Or that the treasure wouldn't be in Caerwent? She wanted to ask him why he thought the excursion would be brief, but didn't want to discuss it in front of Penn. He seemed upset that Mr. Bowen was leaving again so soon, which she understood. His mother had abandoned him with a stranger, and now the stranger kept leaving him.

Penn went back to eating, though with far less

energy.

Margery purposely changed the subject to something that might interest Penn—his digging for treasure. However, he still didn't fully engage until the conversation somehow turned to pets. He'd never had a dog or even a kitten and listened raptly to Margery's tales of the menagerie she'd tended as a child.

"Do you have any pets now?" Penn asked, his blue eyes wide.

"No. My aunt is allergic so I haven't had a pet in a very long time." She turned toward Mr. Bowen. "I'm surprised you don't have a dog or two. Don't most bachelors appreciate canine companionship?"

"I don't know. My father wasn't fond of animals. He said they'd interrupt his work."

"That was your father," Margery said. "What about you?" She wanted to suggest he get a dog or at least a cat—for Penn's sake.

Mr. Bowen shrugged. "I never gave it much thought, actually." He glanced at Penn for a pensive moment, then the arrival of the dessert course interrupted further conversation as Penn dove into his bread and butter pudding.

What seemed like a scant few minutes later, he asked to be excused from the table. Mr. Bowen nodded his assent, and the boy disappeared from the dining room.

Margery scarcely waited until the door closed before saying, "You should get him a dog or a cat."

"I knew you were going to say that."

"And why not? Don't use the excuse of your work. You can train it to stay out of your study."

He arched a dubious brow. "That means I must obtain a dog, as cats are universally untrainable."

Margery recalled her favorite cat, Fancy, a fluffy orange and white tabby. "That's not true. Some of them are quite able to master learned behaviors. Actually, I believe they all are. The question is whether they choose to. It's all in their temperament."

His expression shifted into bemusement. "You're saying cats selectively decide how to behave?"

"Of course. They're rather like people in that manner."

He chuckled as he set his spoon beside his unfinished pudding. "Just as you decide whether you're going to be charming, as you are now, or prickly, as you were earlier."

"I wasn't prickly." She was, but she wouldn't admit it. Because then he might ask *why*.

"I won't debate it with you, but we both know the truth." He gave her a probing stare. "I can't quite figure you out, Miss Derrington. You work as my partner and yet you try to deceive me."

"You deceived me first."

He inclined his head. "So I did. You also return my kisses and then act as though I'm anathema."

She tried to ignore his use of the word *kisses*. "That's a bit hyperbolic, isn't it?"

He cracked a half-smile that did ridiculously lovely things to her insides. "It is. I'm poking fun. I like having fun in your company." He leaned toward her and lowered his voice. "Admit it, you like me."

Far too much. "Why wouldn't I?"

His smile broadened, making him seem insufferably confident. "I can't think of a reason."

She narrowed her eyes at him. "On second thought, there's that vexing streak of arrogance."

He lowered his voice even further, as if he were

imparting a secret. "I actually think you like that too." And then he *winked.*

Margery stood before she was irrevocably drawn into his flirtatious banter. "I'm ready to go to the library. Will you be joining me immediately or are you having a glass of port first?"

He got to his feet and attempted to hold her chair, but she moved away from it quickly. "Have you ever known me to drink after dinner?"

He was inferring that they knew each other well enough that she ought to recognize his habits. Surely she did not. She chose to ignore his question as she swept from the room.

Within a few steps, he moved to walk beside her. "I've provoked you. I can't seem to help myself."

He was close enough that she smelled him—sandalwood and something else that was both dark and fresh—and concluded he'd bathed before supper. She resisted the urge to glance at him, to survey the ebony sleekness of his hair, the smooth angle of his jawbone, the oft-audacious set of his mouth.

They arrived at the library and Rhys opened the door. What they beheld inside made them both gasp.

Chapter Thirteen

RHYS RUSHED INTO the library to the table where Penn was standing over both de Valery manuscripts, which lay open. "Penn, how on earth did you get in here?" The door had been locked, and Rhys and Thomas carried the only keys. If Thomas had given the boy the key . . .

Penn glanced up from the books, but quickly returned to looking at them. "The door was open."

Rhys touched the boy's shoulder. "It was not. I won't tolerate dishonesty."

The words came easily, which wasn't surprising. He still remembered the day his father had sternly said them to him. Rhys had taken a valuable manuscript to his room and, when caught, had said a servant left it there. His father had seen through the lie, and the weight of his disappointment had ensured Rhys never deceived him again.

Penn looked at him, his face reddening. "I picked the lock."

He'd what? Surprise robbed him of an appropriate response. At length he said, "I shall have to improve the lock, apparently. In the future, if you find a door locked, there is a good reason and you are not to employ your . . . abilities. Good Lord, Penn, where did you learn to do such a thing?"

Penn shrugged and looked away. Rhys doubted the boy would tell him. The wall he'd erected was still too tall to scale. Hopefully, in time, Rhys would be able to take it down, brick by brick.

Miss Derrington joined them. She stood beside Penn and looked down at the open books. "What were you doing?"

Multiple lanterns had been lit about the room, flooding the space with light. Enough light for Penn to work. "Trying to solve the code," he said.

"Any luck?" she asked, pulling out a chair.

"I found this list of numbers." He pulled the sheet of parchment they'd tucked into the front of Miss Derrington's de Valery manuscript. "Are they in some sort of order? I don't understand why the numbers are grouped together."

Miss Derrington sat in the chair and looked up at Rhys. "You may as well show him."

Rhys drew the cipher glass out of his coat pocket. While he'd locked the books in the library, he'd decided to keep the glass with him at all times. "Look through this and tell me what you see. Point it at the book on the right—at the illustration."

Penn looked at him quizzically as he took the glass. He brought it to his eye and bent his head. He sucked in air and bent further over, practically putting the glass to the paper. "How does it work?" he asked excitedly.

Rhys had to stifle a smile. He was so pleased with the boy's fervor. It reminded him of himself at that age. Or even his current age. "It was designed to remove all but one color and the scribe who created that manuscript used it to hide his code."

"Numbers." Penn said the word with more than a touch of awe.

"Rotate the glass," Rhys directed.

Penn turned his hand and let out a bolt of laughter—the kind of joy that only boys of a certain age could release. "Amazing!" He turned it again and again. "Just the three colors then?"

Rhys exchanged amused looks with Miss Derrington. "Yes."

"And that's how you have the numbers organized—they're grouped by illustration? I recognize the numbers in this one as," he lowered the glass briefly so he could glance at the sheet of numbers and point at one of the lines they'd listed, "these numbers here." He turned the page in the book and reviewed the next illustration. He'd looked at the numbers so quickly and found the appropriate group almost without looking.

"Penn," Rhys asked slowly, "are you able to remember things you see, in exact detail?"

Penn peered around the glass at him; the guarded look had returned. "Yes."

"There's nothing wrong with that," Rhys hastened to clarify. "I was merely curious. I went to school with a fellow like you. He was first in everything, the blighter."

After Penn reviewed another illustration, he lowered the glass. "What do you think the numbers mean?"

Rhys frowned. "We don't know. That's why we haven't solved the code yet."

"We proposed page numbers and numbers of letters in the alphabet," Miss Derrington said. "We've tried any number of alphabet-based scenarios." With absolutely no effect. "We also tried counting all of the stanzas and lines, but nothing we do makes sense."

Penn looked between them, his expression more confident and relaxed than Rhys had ever seen him. "Did you separate the numbers by color?"

Rhys sent a sharp look toward Miss Derrington who'd turned her head to look up at him. Her gaze seemed to mirror the foolishness he was feeling. Why hadn't they thought of that? "No."

With a quick nod, Penn took the chair next to Miss Derrington. He flipped the book back to the beginning and set about regrouping each illustration's numbers by color. He was much faster at it than Rhys and Miss Derrington had been, but then no one was checking his work either. Rhys stood behind the two chairs and watched Penn work.

When he was finished, Rhys said, "We should check what you did."

"You don't have to. It's correct."

"I see you've already left your influence on him," Miss Derrington murmured with a small half-smile.

Rhys sent her a mock-amused glance, but in truth, he *was* amused. He liked that Miss Derrington found him arrogant and, more importantly, that she called him out on it. Instead of forcing him to modulate his behavior, he found he wanted to provoke her whenever possible.

Penn studied his regrouped list of numbers. "There's an exact number of each color."

Rhys stood over him. "Yes, I see it. It's as if they're arranged in triplets—one blue, one red, one yellow."

Miss Derrington peered at the numbers. "That has to mean something."

"Page numbers," Penn said. "One of those colors could be page numbers."

Excitement began to unfurl in Rhys's chest. They'd tried page numbers to no avail, but now there seemed to be a pattern.

Miss Derrington looked at him. "And the others?" Her question carried an undercurrent of anticipation.

They were all quiet as they fixed on the numbers. In

threes . . .

Rhys snatched up the list and Miss Derrington's text and moved to her right. He set the items down on the table and flipped to the page that matched the first number, which happened to be in the blue column. He searched for the line on the page that corresponded to the number in the next column. Then he found the letter in that line that matched the number in the third column: R.

"Paper and pen, please."

Miss Derrington picked up another sheet of parchment from the middle of the table, where Rhys typically kept a small stack, and handed it to Rhys along with the writing instrument Penn had used.

Rhys recorded the R and moved to the next set of numbers. The result was L. Which didn't make sense unless the code wasn't in English. He continued with a few more letters, but decided it wasn't correct.

Penn had come to stand on his right. "Try the middle column as the page number."

Rhys flipped back to the page corresponding to the number listed first in the yellow column. He worked through the other columns and came up with S. Moving on to the next set of three, he found the matching page, line, and letter and wrote down his findings: T. He continued, feeling a steady, building excitement that this was finally it. When he'd written STTATHEUS, which Rhys immediately recognized at St. Tatheus, he knew they had it.

"Who is St. Tatheus?" Miss Derrington's question sliced through the air of anticipation.

"St. Tathyw, a late fifth-century abbot. Tatheus is the English form of the Welsh name."

Miss Derrington's eyes clouded with confusion.

"But what could that mean?"

He had no idea, but there were a lot more numbers to decode. He gave her a long, penetrating look, trying to rekindle her enthusiasm. *Don't give up now, we're so close.* "Let us continue and see what we find."

They worked quietly and quickly, the three of them reading out numbers and letters as Rhys recorded them. When they were finished, he had written STTATHEUSANARAWDVENTASILURUM.

Belatedly, he realized he'd been standing the entire time and now his neck protested the prolonged bowing over. He stretched it, running his fingers along the sore muscles. "A chair, Penn, if you please."

There were five chairs scattered about the table, one of which held Miss Derrington. Penn brought over the one he'd been using earlier.

Sitting, Rhys gripped the pen and wrote: St. Tatheus below the deciphered code. That left ANARAWDVENTASILURUM.

Miss Derrington pointed to the latter portion of the word "That looks like Latin."

"Indeed it does." Rhys wrote VENTASILURUM below St. Tatheus. A broad smile split his lips.

"St. Tathyw was an abbot in Caerwent, which used to be known as Venta Silurum."

Miss Derrington's eyes lit, it was as if the flame of discovery burning in his chest had ignited within her. "They're connected! But what is the middle part, Anarawd?" She said the word slowly, trying to pronounce the Welsh.

"It's a Welsh name, but I don't know its significance." He looked to the boy standing to his right. "Penn?"

Penn's blue eyes widened slightly, but then he shook

his head. His face flushed and he looked away.

Rhys gripped the lad's shoulder. "You've been an incredible help; I had to ask. There's no shame in not knowing. We couldn't have done this without you."

Penn's chest and shoulders puffed up. "Yes, sir. Will you still be going to Caerwent then?"

"I think we must. It certainly seems to be leading us there." Though he didn't know what Anarawd meant, he was overjoyed at having a destination and at having deciphered the code. He looked to Miss Derrington, who was staring at the words on the paper. "What do you think, Miss Derrington?"

Her face lifted as she smiled. "When do we leave?"

"Tomorrow morning." He glanced at the clock ticking methodically on the mantel. How did it get to be nearly eleven? "I think it's past time for you to go to bed, Penn."

Penn moved reluctantly from the table, but turned before he reached the door. "Will you please take me with you?"

Rhys's chest squeezed. If it weren't for the danger the Order of the Round Table posed, he would take the boy. But he couldn't risk it. "I'm sorry, Penn. There are difficulties that prevent you coming with us. Truly, I'm sorry."

Penn's face was a wooden mask. Rhys imagined he was gravely disappointed, but the boy had learned to keep his emotions hidden. Was that a new talent since losing his mother, or had he cultivated it throughout his short lifetime? Perhaps he'd ask Miss Derrington, since she seemed to do the same.

"Good night," Rhys said, as Penn departed without a word.

"Why can't he come with us?" Miss Derrington's

tone matched the scolding look she gave him. "Can't you see he needs to feel a connection to something?"

The heartfelt plea in her question was nearly his undoing, but he couldn't endanger the boy. "I can't expose him to the Order. We have to assume they'll be tracking us somehow. If they were lying in wait at de Valery's house, I imagine they'll be watching Caerwent too."

She blanched. "Is it safe for us to go?"

Perhaps not. Was she frightened? She had yet to display that emotion, even when faced with certain violence. He turned in his chair to fully face her. "You know this quest is no longer what we thought. There are people who would prevent us from succeeding."

She gave her head a shake and looked him square in the eye. "I know what we're dealing with and I don't want to give up now, if that's what you're asking." She glanced at the deciphered code, the hint of a smile lighting her gaze. "I can't." She looked back at him. "Can *you*?"

He stared into her hazel eyes, saw the thrill and the passion simmering in their depths, and he leaned forward. "No."

He lifted his hand to her hair. A few strands had escaped her coiffure as they'd worked at the table. The blond locks brushed her ear. He tucked them back and allowed his fingers to linger against her scalp. His thumb grazed her cheek almost of its own volition. She was a magnet for his desire, and he was incapable of resisting her allure.

"I'll keep you safe," he whispered, coming closer.

She didn't move, and her gaze was steady. "Maybe I'll keep you safe."

He chuckled softly. "I don't doubt that. No, I don't

doubt that at all."

He lowered his lips to hers in what was supposed to be a gentle kiss, but the minute their mouths touched, a fiery need consumed him. He rose in his chair and cradled her scalp. She gripped the lapels of his coat and held him close, opening her mouth to coax him inside. Not coax, *demand.* Her tongue met his with a fervor that matched his own.

Lust roared through him. She tasted so sweet, felt so lush, and responded with such passion that he was unable to think, only feel. All of his senses seemed hyperaware. He heard the muted sigh in her throat as he stroked her neck, smelled the apple in whatever she'd used in her bath earlier, relished the dig of her fingertips into his chest.

He stood, dragging her up with him and turned her so that her back was to the table. He reached behind her and pushed the books to the side, careful not to harm them. All the while, she kissed him relentlessly, dragging her tongue against his. Hunger raced through him, drove him to plunge deep into her mouth as he lifted her onto the edge of the table.

She pulled away from him, but kept her hands curled against his cravat. "The table? Don't you have rules about that?"

He stared down at her, his need pushed to the breaking point. He'd wanted women, tumbled them of course, but he'd never experienced this soul-burning *need.* He was a man of discipline, of control. Or at least he had been until he'd met her. Now he was a man of implacable ardor and she was the sole object of his desire. "I'd break every one of them for you."

Her lips parted to emit a whisper-soft gasp. He kissed her again, stroking into her mouth, and clutched at her back, his hands moving over the planes of her shoulders and the arc of her spine.

Her hands dove beneath his coat, her palms gliding across his upper chest, over his waistcoat to the tops of his shoulders so that he could feel her heat through the linen of his shirt. His coat fell back and he shrugged out of the garment, letting it fall to the floor behind him.

Her initiative only fueled his desire. He brought a hand to her bodice and cupped the swell of her breast. Her fingers dug into his shoulders, which he took as encouragement. But with the multitude of garments covering her, he couldn't feel her the way he wanted. He found the drawstring for the front of her robe and loosened it. The silk gapped at the center and he slid his hand inside, separating the fabric. *So much better.* He grazed his palm over her breast, trying to detect the nipple nestled beneath three more layers of clothing.

She arched up into him, seeking his hand. He pressed harder, seeking her heat. Her fingers tangled in his cravat and tugged at the fabric. Somewhere in the back of his mind, a tiny voice of reason tried vainly to be heard, but he refused to listen. She stirred him in ways he'd never imagined, and he couldn't stop the avalanche of sensation.

He tipped her head back, running his thumb along her jaw and kissing the underside of her delectably dimpled chin. He moved his hand back down to her breast, this time seeking the closures holding her gown together. He kissed her neck, using his mouth and tongue to suckle and lick. Her low moan crested over him, urged him to move closer between her thighs, her skirts bunching between them.

She'd successfully loosened his cravat and tugged it

free. Cool air rushed over the heated, newly exposed flesh at his collar. Her hands curled around his neck, her fingers threading through the hair at his nape.

Her flesh was so soft, her scent so inviting. He worked the front of her gown open and came upon her stays, which, as a self-sufficient lady such as she would require, laced in the front.

He pulled at the laces, eager to remove this barrier. When her fingers joined his, he abandoned the fight in favor of cupping her as she worked the garment free. At last, the stays parted to reveal the pale linen of her chemise. Better still, he glimpsed the rose-tinted tips of her breasts, which strained at the garment.

He gazed down at her for a moment—again the voice in his head tried to intercede and again he swept it away. Instead, he gently tugged her chemise down and then pushed her breast up. The pale flesh swelled above the fabric, but wouldn't come free. He kissed her, suckling until he heard her moan low in her throat. He pressed her upward until the nipple grazed his lip, then he closed his mouth over her through the linen.

Cradling her back over the table, he held her breast captive to his tongue. He kneaded and squeezed as he laved and suckled. She gasped and pulled at his hair. Then her hands were at the buttons of his waistcoat, working in a frenzy. Desperate need crashed over him. He eased her onto the table and brought his hand around to her skirts. Tunneling beneath them, he found her knee and then her thigh, her flesh soft and warm.

His waistcoat opened and she pushed it from his shoulders. He had to pull back from her breast and remove his hands from her to strip the garment away. When he put them back, she stilled, her hands falling to her sides.

He looked at her face. Her eyes were open and staring at the ceiling.

"Margery?" He'd never used her Christian name before, but "Miss Derrington" seemed inappropriate given the circumstances.

She moved her gaze to his and came up on her elbows. "I'm sorry . . . Rhys." She tried his name but sounded tentative. "I should go."

"Of course." The response was automatic and didn't reflect the storm raging in his body. He was hard and ready for her, desperate to bury himself inside of her soft heat. At last the voice in his head gained volume. *What the hell was I thinking?*

He helped her to stand. She immediately pulled her stays together, but didn't bother tightening the laces. Instead, she refastened her gown and drew the drawstring of her robe. Once she was as rearranged as she was going to be, she offered him a weak smile. "I didn't mean for things to get so out of hand. After deciphering the code, I think it's fair to say we were swept away by our excitement. But it was . . . nice."

Nice? Though they hadn't completed the act, Rhys was likely to remember it as the most erotic sexual experience of his life. He'd never been so consumed, so *desperate.*

"Forgive me if I characterize it a bit more colorfully than that. Spectacular comes to mind. Or magnificent." Reluctantly, he scooped up his waistcoat and shrugged it on.

Her cheeks pinked. "I think I'll go to bed. Good night."

Before he could answer, she'd hurried from the room, leaving him with the books, the glass, the code, and the simmering remnants of a desire he knew for certain would never be extinguished.

IN HER CHAMBER, Margery readied herself for bed without calling for the maid to help her. She wasn't sure she could stand another person to see her body right now, not when it was still so hot and flushed and *wanting*.

Yes, she still wanted Mr. Bowen—Rhys. Hearing her name on his lips had nearly changed her mind. There was an intimacy to it that reminded her of how it felt to have people close, to allow people to see inside of her.

Dressed for bed, she pulled her already loosened hair from its pins and brushed the waving mass. The mirror at the dressing table showed her kiss-swollen lips and rosy cheeks. Thinking about how they'd gotten that way caused her breasts to tighten and heat to spiral into her core.

She dropped the brush on the table and turned away. The bed took up her vision and reminded her of what she *could* be doing right now.

Aunt Agnes had shared the specifics of coupling with her. She believed it was better for a young woman to be prepared. She'd also said it was a singularly divine experience, and now Margery knew what she meant. She had no trouble at all understanding why her aunt had chosen to enter into a liaison with the man who'd captured her heart.

But Mr. Bowen—Rhys—hadn't captured her heart. She *did* like him, more than she cared to admit, however enjoying his company and his . . . *attentions* didn't constitute love.

Feeling overwhelmed, she left her room and stepped into the cool corridor. The maid was just coming toward her. Her dark eyes widened. "I apologize, miss. I didn't hear you ring."

Margery offered a smile to ease the young woman's concern. "I didn't. It's fine. I was wondering if you might direct me to young Penn's chamber?" She hadn't planned to visit the boy, but decided she needed something to distract her agitated mind.

"At the end of the hall."

Margery turned her head to glance farther down the corridor.

"No, that's Mr. Bowen's suite. Master Penn is at the other end."

Now she knew where Rhys's room was located. She turned away from it lest her body decide to overpower her mind and lead her in the opposite direction. "Thank you." Margery passed the maid and went to the room at the end. She knocked softly. "Penn? It's Marg—Miss Derrington."

She heard a muffled sound and let herself in. A single lantern next to the bed cast meager illumination over the chamber, but she could see that while it wasn't overly large, it was well appointed, with a wide bed and a desk, something she found endearing. *Of course* Rhys would ensure the boy had a desk. Actually . . . She looked around and wondered if this had been Rhys's boyhood room. She moved closer to the bed, where Penn had propped himself up against a pillow. "I hope I'm not disturbing you," she said.

He shook his head, his eyes wary.

"I wanted to thank you again for your help tonight. We couldn't have deciphered the code without you."

The exhilaration of finally solving the code swept through her anew.

He almost smiled. "It was fun. I just wish I could go with you."

She sat on the edge of the bed. "I know, I do too." He looked at her skeptically. "Truly, I do. I know how you feel. At least, I think I do."

He cocked his head to the side. "How?"

"I imagine you feel alone, sad, abandoned even." She watched his features tighten and instinctively touched his hand, which clutched the coverlet to his chest. "My parents died when I was ten."

"You're an orphan?" The question carried a tinge of hope, and she knew he was trying to find some elusive connection in a world that seemed grossly unfair to him.

"Yes. I have a pair of great-aunts who took me in and cared for me. I'm luckier than most. As are you."

He looked down at the patterned coverlet. "I'm not lucky."

"I think you are. Your mother entrusted you to a good man who will educate you into manhood. Imagine if you were in an orphanage or a workhouse instead."

His gaze turned abruptly fierce. "My mother is going to come back for me."

Oh no. Why hadn't his mother told him the truth? Why would she let him harbor false hope? But was it Margery's place to tell him that she was dying, that Rhys was going to be the only family he would know? Yes, *family* because she believed Rhys would offer that. Whatever she felt for him, she could see that he was earnest in caring for this boy. He never would've consented to take him in otherwise.

How had she come to be so certain of the man's motives about Penn when she still doubted his dealings with her and the treasure? Perhaps she wasn't being very fair. Perhaps she was allowing her own emotions to cloud her judgment—emotions she'd kept at bay for far too long.

Suddenly she felt a rush of longing. Like Penn whose world had been turned asunder, she felt as though things were upside down. She'd had her parents and then her aunts and now she was here, on her own. Her aunts were still there, but for how long? At some point, Margery would be really and truly alone.

She inhaled deeply, casting her fear to the side to focus on Penn. "And if she doesn't return?"

He looked away, his jaw clenched.

Margery clasped his hand. "It's all right to be upset. I cried endlessly when my parents died. But then one day I decided not to be sad about it anymore." At least on the outside. Inside, the pain of losing them still burned her chest, especially now, as she tried to give this boy hope.

"I don't know if I can do that." His voice cracked. "I miss her so."

"I know, and you always will. Penn, do you want . . . Do you want a hug?"

He gripped her hand and nodded, but kept his gaze averted.

Margery leaned forward and slipped her arms around him. He came away from the pillow and hugged her back. She stroked the back of his head and smiled against his dark hair. He needed a bath tomorrow, something she would discuss with Rhys.

When she pulled away, Penn dashed a hand over his eye. She looked discreetly to the side.

"Will you be coming back with Mr. Bowen?" His dark eyes were intense.

"I . . . I don't know." She didn't want to lie to him, but she also hated the flash of disappointment in his gaze. "I will promise to write to you. Will you write me back?"

"Only if you promise to visit."

How could she do that? She and Rhys—Mr. Bowen—were not going to continue their . . . relationship after they found the treasure. He would eventually marry—wouldn't he?—and so would she. Or not. If the treasure was sufficient, she wouldn't have to. But then that left her alone . . . A coldness started to slither over her, but she banished it by looking at Penn, so young, so deserving of people who cared about him. "Yes, I will visit you—right after we find the treasure. You are the first one we should share it with, given your invaluable assistance."

He brightened at her words, and the sight warmed her heart, reminding her that it was there for people other than her aunts. Could she risk baring it?

She shoved the question aside, finding the events of this night far too troubling to ponder. "I've also convinced Mr. Bowen to allow you a pet. Which would you like, a dog or a cat?"

He blinked at her. "Truly? I think . . ." He dropped his head shyly.

"What is it?"

"My mother always spoke of her cat. She said it was orange, and she called it Marzipan."

Margery smiled. "I had an orange cat too. Though mine was called Fancy, because she hated to get her paws dirty, even as a kitten. She also appreciated table scraps, much to my mother's dismay. That didn't stop me and my father from giving them to her."

"May I have a cat? It needn't be orange."

In that moment, Margery might've considering trading her precious book for the prospect of an orange cat for Penn. "We'll see if we can't find one."

She let go of his hand and stood. "Sleep well, Penn."

"Good night, Miss Derrington."

"You may call me Margery," she said. "I insist."

"Good night, Margery."

"Good night, Penn." She closed the door gently and started back toward her room. Then passed it and continued to the opposite end of the corridor. Her feet carried her all the way to the door, which she knocked upon before thinking better of it.

After a moment, Rhys—Mr. Bowen—opened the door. He was wearing another banyan, this one in black silk that matched his eyes. "Margery?"

She blinked, trying to ignore the pull she felt toward him. "I've promised him an orange cat. You must find him an orange cat. With haste."

His brow gathered in confusion. "Who, Penn?"

"Yes. I went to see him just now and promised him an orange cat." She vaguely realized she might sound a little batty. This was just so important and it was vital that he agreed. "You'll do it, won't you?"

He ran his hand through his hair, mussing the black strands. "I don't know—"

She poked her finger into his chest, hard enough that he stepped back. "You will get him an orange cat."

"Margery, I don't think—"

She stepped over the threshold and poked him again. "Promise me."

"All right, yes. But it will live in the barn."

"That won't suffice. It will live wherever Penn deems best. He needs this cat, Mr. Bowen."

A shaft of disappointment muddled his gaze. "You've gone back to Mr. Bowening me?"

"Agree to my terms."

"Margery—Miss Derrington," he said, with a dose of exasperation heightening his tone. "I will not be held hostage to your demands. I will discuss the cat with Penn when we return from Caerwent."

"No, you must set Thomas or someone on this task immediately." She couldn't explain it, but she felt beholden to this boy now. Someone had to look out for him, to fight for him. "Before we leave tomorrow."

He wrapped his hand around the finger still pointed into the front of his banyan. "Why is this so important to you?"

"It just . . . is. Penn needs some security. His world is completely different. A cat will soothe him." It would've soothed her. But her aunts had made her find a new home for Fancy because Aunt Eugenie was allergic. The pain of that loss so soon after her parents had crushed her heart in such a way that she wasn't sure it had ever healed. "Please, just get him the cat." Her words were soft, broken.

"Yes, I'll get him the cat—tomorrow—and it can live wherever Penn wants." He brushed his hand against her dry cheek. "Margery?"

"You shouldn't call me that." She stood on her toes and kissed him. It came from gratitude, but bloomed into something far more devastating. The passion he'd stirred earlier sprang to life within her, and she pulled his head down so she could deepen the embrace.

He returned the kiss, his hands digging into her back and holding her tight against him. His frame was hard and strong, and in contrast she felt light and feminine. There was also next to nothing between them. Her thin nightrail and robe and his banyan. Even her feet were bare.

She swept her tongue with his, reveling in these new sensations that were both surprising and exhilarating. This was madness. She should stop him as she'd done earlier. But something inside her was singing for the first time in so long, maybe ever. It was wrong, but she just knew that if she walked away she'd regret it for the rest of her life.

With a clarity she didn't know she could possess during such a tumultuous moment, she retraced her steps and closed his door. When she returned to him, she unclasped her dressing gown and dropped it to the floor.

He looked down at her, his eyes impossibly dark in the faint light from the pair of lanterns that flanked his bed. "What are you doing to me?" he rasped.

"Consider it an invitation."

"It's a bloody seduction."

She pulled at the buttons holding his banyan closed.

He gritted his teeth. "I'm not wearing anything under this, Margery."

"Good." She let the word embolden her, though her insides were quivering—both from excitement and dread. She was opening a door she could never close again, but she simply had to see what was on the other side.

She pushed the garment from his shoulders and looked at his bare chest. Dark hair sprinkled between his nipples and led a trail downward. She jerked her gaze up before she could reach his arousal.

"Are you certain?" he asked, his hands hovering at

her shoulders.

She nodded, not trusting herself to speak. Not trusting herself not to change her mind. *No, there would be no regrets.*

But he wasn't to be satisfied. "I need to hear you say it. I need to hear the words. I like words, Margery. I *love* words."

She almost smiled. Of course he loved words. And she would give them to him. Whisking her nightrail up over her head, she tossed it atop her dressing gown on the floor. Then she speared him with a seductive—*his word*—stare. "Make love to me, Rhys."

Chapter Fourteen

RHYS'S BRAIN HAD to be failing him. Was this some fevered dream? He'd been about to climb into bed, where he'd expected to toss restlessly. Now the reason for his turmoil was here. Not just here—but ready to fulfill his fantasy.

He stared at her nude body, disbelieving. The gentleman in him demanded he cover her back up and send her away. The man in him told the gentleman to shut the hell up. He decided to listen to the man.

Reaching for her, he couldn't help but repeat himself, "You're certain?"

She arched an elegant blond brow at him. "I understand your fondness for the written word, but must it carry to speech as well? Particularly *now*?"

He laughed, but it came out as a sort of half-growl as he pulled her against his chest. The contact of their bare flesh nearly drove him to his knees. He wrapped his arms around her and held on for everything he was worth.

With a gentle caress along her neck, he tipped her head back and kissed her mouth like he was drinking a fine, rare wine. But she tasted far better. How could he describe it? Like warmth and bliss and excitement.

He trailed the kisses along her jaw until he met her ear. She shivered when he stroked his tongue along the outer shell and nibbled the lobe.

"The bed?" she asked breathlessly.

He swept her into his arms and carried her a few

long strides. She clutched at his neck and pulled him to kiss her again. They fell together onto the bed.

He rolled her to her back and came over her, his breath catching at her beauty in the dim light. Her eyes were dark and sultry, her lips reddened and parted. There'd never been a lovelier, more alluring sight.

"Aren't you going to touch my . . ." She glanced away from him demurely. "What you did earlier?"

Where was the adventurous woman he'd come to know? "Your breast? Don't be ashamed of the word or of your body, Margery. You're beautiful." He gazed down at her reverently, touched her softly, his palm grazing over her nipple.

She sucked in a breath as he kept his touch light.

"So beautiful." He leaned down and blew across the tip, tormenting her with the barest skim of his hand over her flesh.

"Please."

"Please, what? Remember, I like words. Written, spoken, *screamed*." A rush of lust jolted through him as she arched up, pressing her breast into his hand.

She cast her back against the pillow, her blond hair trapped beneath her save a small fan that grazed her shoulder. "Please touch me. Harder. Like you did before. With your mouth."

"Like this?" He cupped her, then brought his thumb and forefinger to her pebbled tip and squeezed, which he hadn't done before.

Her eyes, closed during their erotic conversation, flew open as she gasped again. *"Rhys."*

His lips curved into a satisfied smile. "I like *that* word on your lips."

He bent his head to her breast and drew the nipple into his mouth. At first, he lightly licked, but then he tightened his grip and braced her for the onslaught of his kiss.

Her hand wound into his hair and held him against her. "Yes."

She arched up again, and Rhys wasn't sure how long he could wait. He edged closer until his cock nudged the outside of her thigh. She jumped.

"Shhhh, it's fine," he murmured against her breast before moving to the other one. He devoured the second as he had the first, and her low moans filled the chamber.

When her fingers closed around his shaft, blood rushed straight to his balls and his eyes shot open. He looked up at her.

Her eyes were open, watching him as her hand moved down to the base of his cock and then up again. Christ almighty, had she done that before? No, everything else about her screamed innocence, but for some reason she knew how to touch him. He was almost afraid to ask.

"Margery, have you . . . ?"

She blushed, her hand stalling. "No. Am I not doing it right?"

"God no. I mean you're doing it fine. Better than fine. Hell, you're better at it than I am."

Her eyes widened.

"Sorry." Sometimes he really lacked finesse, damn it. "You're perfect."

She tightened her hold again and stroked him from base to tip. "It feels . . . all right?"

"Divine." He wanted to ask how she knew what to do, but that was a conversation for another time.

She rotated to her side while she continued her ministrations. "When will you put it inside me?"

God. "My cock, Margery. It's a cock," he spoke through gritted teeth because she was fast driving him to the point of no return.

"You and your words," she murmured. Her thumb brushed the head. "Oh, you're . . . wet."

Hopelessly, yes. Was she? He couldn't wait another moment to find out.

He moved his hand from her breast and skimmed over her belly, trying not to focus too hard on the sensations she was arousing. If he wasn't careful, he was going to spill himself in her palm. Yet, he couldn't bring himself to ask her to stop.

He found her blond curls and delved to the hidden flesh. "You're wet, too." Gloriously so. His cock swelled in her grip.

He stroked along her folds, creating friction. She moaned softly and her hips undulated. He pressed her back against the bed and cupped her, testing her sheath with a slight, shallow thrust of his finger. He'd never bedded a virgin, but he recalled the advice his father had given him—bring her to release first. That was *imperative.*

He bent to her breast and drew the tip deep into his mouth, sucking her hard. To counterbalance, he dipped his finger inside of her, withdrew it, and plunged forward again. She shuddered beneath him.

"Open for me," he said against her flesh, his hand nudging at her thighs.

She parted for him, but it wasn't enough.

"Wider," he beckoned, looking down at her. He pressed on her inner thigh until she complied. Now she was nicely open for him, her sex pink and exposed and oh so enticing. He found the nub at the top of her cleft and rubbed his thumb across it.

She yelped and bucked up from the bed. "Rhys!"

Her hand had stopped its delightful caress, but he didn't care. He was too focused on her now, on bringing her to where she needed to be. He moved between her legs and positioned his hands beneath her. Lifting her, he licked her flesh.

She yelped again and jumped away. "What are you doing?"

"It's called—"

"No," she cut him off, "I don't want to hear the words. I was just . . . surprised."

There was a wariness in her eyes that cooled his ardor. "Do you want to stop?"

She eased back down the bed toward him. "No. I'm ready now."

There was the adventurous woman he knew.

He laid his palm over her lower belly and held her down. "Don't move." He gave her a wicked grin and used his hand to part her legs again. She was a bit stiff, so he went slow, using his fingers to coax her flesh. She was damp, increasingly so with each touch. He concentrated on the nub at the top and then slipped a finger into her heat. She came up off the bed again, but in an effort to take him deeper. This time when he put his mouth on her, she quivered beneath him. Her thighs shuddered and she gripped his head, tugging his hair.

He kept his hand flat against her and used his fingers to pump into her cleft while he sucked her clitoris. Desperate little moans escaped her mouth as her hips rotated. He worked her flesh, alternating licks and sucks until her cries escalated and he sensed she hovered at the edge.

"Rhys!"

He moved his hand up and squeezed her breast. "Let go, Margery, let go."

Her legs stiffened, and she cried out as she came to pieces in his embrace. He rode the tide with her, soothing and stroking until she was replete.

When she lay back on the pillows, he sat back from her. Her breath came fast, but was starting to slow; her eyes were wide and fixed on the canopy over their heads.

"Margery?"

Her gaze found his. "That was . . . astonishing. I didn't know . . . never mind. I thought you were going to . . ." She glanced down at his rigid flesh. "Put your . . . *cock* inside of me."

She'd said the word. For him. He came over her, positioning himself at her entrance. "I'm going to. Unless you tell me to stop. Do you want me to stop?"

"Will it be like that again?"

"I don't know if you'll have another orgasm. That's the word, sweeting." He didn't want to make false promises. "But I will do my damnedest."

She touched his chest, tentatively at first, then more firmly as she splayed her hands over his nipples. He stifled a groan. His flesh was so sensitive, so eager to find release.

He guided his cock forward, using her moisture to glide inside. He went slow, felt her stretching to accommodate him, and paused. "Am I hurting you?" The first time was supposedly unpleasant, or so he'd been told.

"No. It's . . . tight. It feels fine." She sucked in a breath as he inched forward. "That might be far enough."

"It isn't, but I'll go slowly." He withdrew a bit, then

edged forward once more. He got farther than the last time before he felt her tense. He repeated the movement again and again until he was fully inside. "How's that?" He had to grit his teeth to keep still. She was so hot and tight.

She'd moved her hands to his shoulders and now clutched them tightly. "It's good. I think. Is that all there is?"

"No, I'd like to move. If you're ready."

"I'm ready."

"Wrap your legs around me."

She did as he bade, which opened her more fully and allowed him to sink as deep as he could go. He closed his eyes, savoring the exquisite pleasure.

Then he moved, slowly at first, until he felt her relax. He picked up his pace, increasing the friction. He braced his elbows on either side of her head and lifted his hips before driving forward again. When he opened his eyes, she cast her head back and he hoped she was in ecstasy and not in pain. He had his answer when she moaned and moved her hands to his sides and then his back and then lower until her fingers grazed his backside.

He couldn't hold himself back any longer. "I'm sorry, Margery, I have to—"

He slammed into her, pushing in and out with rapid strokes. She surprised and delighted him by rising to meet his thrusts. His orgasm built, the blood rushing to his cock, as he drove deep one final time. Then he crashed over the edge. Somehow he managed to drag himself away and spill his seed next to her. He clasped his cock, stroking it until he was spent.

Falling to her side, he fought to catch his breath. After several moments, when he'd recaptured his equilibrium at least a little bit, he focused on her. She was staring at the ceiling, as she'd done downstairs, and again he couldn't read her.

"Margery?"

She turned her head and a smile curved her lips. "You were right. I didn't have another . . . orgasm, is the word? But I was close. If you could've just kept going . . ."

He rolled to his back and brought his forearm over his eyes. "Well, I thought it best to prevent a child, given that we are currently unwed."

"Oh, I understand." She touched his shoulder. "I didn't mean to criticize. It was wonderful. And thank you for being so considerate." She sat up and looked to the side where he'd spilled himself. "I don't suppose you can move so I may get up?"

"You don't need to leave."

"I wouldn't want your staff to know what transpired."

Thomas would figure it out, but Rhys wouldn't tell her that. "I'll ensure you're back to your chamber before the household is awake."

"No, I'd rather go now."

He frowned at her, wondering if he'd done something wrong. "Have I upset you?" Oh, God, she regretted what they'd done.

"Not at all."

He didn't believe her. She'd lied to him before, why wouldn't she again? "Margery, I care for you. We'll be married of course. You needn't worry that I'm a cad."

She stiffened. "I don't think you're a cad. And we're not getting married." She scooted toward the end of the bed.

He stood as she got to her feet. "But, given what

just happened, we must marry."

Bending, she picked up her nightrail and drew it over her head. "If that's a proposal—and it doesn't particularly sound like one—my answer is no."

He retrieved his banyan and fastened it around himself, growing perturbed at her obstinacy. "But you must. I've . . . ruined you."

"Nonsense. I don't feel ruined. If that's ruination, I will gladly engage in it daily."

Christ, despite the conversation, *that* particular declaration was making him hard again. "You're being obtuse. I'm a gentleman, and gentlemen do not take advantage of unwed women."

She hooked her dressing gown together, shielding her delectable body from him. "You didn't take advantage of me. This is ridiculous. I'm quite satisfied with how the evening turned out, but now I'm tired and I'm going to return to my chamber. Good night."

She turned to go and he tried to get his feet to move so he could follow her, so he could talk sense into her. But in the end, the door closed behind her, leaving him alone. Leaving him to wonder what in the hell had just happened.

AFTER AN EXCEPTIONALLY sound sleep, Margery awoke early to go in search of Thomas. It had occurred to her—rather belatedly, given what had transpired last night—that she ought to take some manner of chaperone or companion with her on this journey to Caerwent. After she'd consulted with the butler, he said he'd organize something before they left. Margery wasn't sure how he'd accomplish the feat, but she recognized that he was terribly efficient, so she didn't worry. He'd also assured her that Penn would have regular baths, starting today.

After managing those issues, she'd taken breakfast in her room so as to avoid Rhys. Though she had no regrets about last night, she did have a bit of trepidation about seeing him. He would likely pursue the subject of marriage, but she'd only refuse him again. She wasn't going to wed him because they'd enjoyed a sexual act that no one would ever learn of. He'd asked because he'd had to, and obligation was no reason to marry. At least not to her. Maybe if he'd *wanted* to . . . No, she'd made her choice last night with no expectations and no desire for anything permanent.

Now, with the hour of their departure at hand, she couldn't hide any longer.

The morning was bright and warm as she stepped into the drive where the carriage was waiting. Penn stood beside Thomas, who was speaking with Rhys. Dressed in an olive green coat and buff breeches, he was the epitome of a country gentleman. His dark hair was brushed back from his handsome face. It was impossible to look at him and not think of his mouth, his hands, his . . . *cock*.

Heat rushed to her face and she turned toward the carriage.

"Margery!" Penn rushed toward her. "Thomas and I are going to find a cat today."

Margery smiled down at him. "How wonderful, I'm so glad."

Thomas approached her next. "Craddock's younger sister, Jane, has been employed to accompany you on your journey." He inclined his head toward a young woman with dark red hair. She stood near the coach with her brother and their driver, Craddock.

"Excellent, thank you, Thomas." Margery waved a hand to Jane. "Good morning. Shall I call you Craddock or Jane?"

"Jane, I think." She cracked a wide, pretty smile, revealing a slight gap between her two front teeth. "My brother's already Craddock."

"Jane has been working as a scullery maid for Lord Trevor, but they were able to spare her for several days," Thomas explained.

Margery glanced at him. "I hate to take her away from her regular job."

"Please don't concern yourself," Thomas said. "She was more than pleased to obtain some experience as a lady's maid."

It seemed she was helping the young woman, which made Margery quite happy. "Then I'm delighted she could join us." She smiled at Jane.

Rhys came over and set his hat upon his head. "Ready?"

She gestured toward the vehicle. "Are the books and the glass already inside?"

"The books are. The glass is in my pocket." His eyes were dark and inscrutable. "After you."

Margery turned and gave Penn's shoulder a squeeze. "I'll see you soon. Be good."

He nodded at her, and she went to the carriage, where Craddock helped her climb in.

"Are you riding inside with us, Jane?" Margery asked.

"If it's just the same, I'll ride up top with my brother."

Margery would've liked the buffer between her and

Rhys inside the carriage, but wouldn't begrudge the young woman's enjoyment of such a fine summer day. "Very good."

The de Valery manuscripts were in their bags on the forward-facing seat, where she situated herself. A few moments later, Rhys joined her, sitting on the opposite cushion. The coach moved forward and rattled along the pebbled drive.

Rhys gave her a hard look. He seemed perturbed. "Why did you tell Penn you'd see him soon?"

She brushed her hands along her skirts, smoothing the folds of her traveling dress. "Are we not coming back here as soon as tomorrow?"

"*Are* you coming back here?" His tone held a barely concealed thread of irritation.

"I, ah, I promised Penn I would come back after we found the treasure and show it to him." She cocked her head to the side, growing uncomfortable with his suppressed anger. "Do you take issue with that plan?"

"I do not. But I daresay our plans are not in alignment. I still contend we must be married."

She'd expected this, but she was resolute. "And I still contend it isn't necessary."

"I insist."

"You do like to insist on things," she muttered. "It's not up to you to insist."

"I've written to your aunts to ask for your hand."

She lurched forward in her seat. "You *what*?"

"I dispatched a letter this morning stating my desire to wed you."

Aunt Eugenie would be ecstatic. Aunt Agnes would be too—if Margery wanted this, which she did *not*. Moreover, she didn't want them involved. They'd worry or try to manage or attempt to persuade her to open herself up. "You had no right to do that, especially after I declined your proposal. I don't wish to marry you and if you want to continue our partnership to find the treasure, I *insist* you cease. Otherwise, we shall have to part company."

He muttered something under his breath. "You would be that foolish." He crossed his arms and looked out the window.

They rode in silence for a while before Margery deemed it safe to broach conversation again. Given his black mood, she thought it best to start with something pleasant. "Thank you for allowing Penn the cat."

He peered at her askance, his eyebrow climbing. "You didn't give me much choice."

Maybe not pleasant, but he didn't seem to be as angry as he had been. *Good.* She hoped they could move past their indiscretion.

"What is your plan once we arrive in Caerwent?"

He unfolded his arms and sat back against the squab. He looked at her briefly, but for the most part kept his gaze averted. "We'll go to the church. Perhaps we'll find the name Anarawd in the cemetery or somewhere inside."

"Excellent thinking." She expected him to thank her or say something else that revealed his imperious streak, but he did nothing of the sort. He was well and truly angry with her.

"If that fails, we'll visit Septon at his cottage and discuss the matter with him."

She hated to disagree with Rhys given his current temper, but there was no hope for it. "I'm not sure that's wise. We've already discussed the need for secrecy."

"Now that we know the Order has been after your

book from the start, I think it's safe to discuss this with my colleague. I've known him for years and I trust him implicitly."

"So you've said."

He threw the full weight of an angry stare at her. "I've suffered your doubt and your deception, but on this we will do things my way. If you disagree, you are welcome to return to Gloucester. As I've offered before, I will even pay your way."

Since telling her about the treasure and agreeing to an alliance, he'd given her no reason not to trust him. If he believed Lord Septon could help them and keep their secret, she shouldn't contradict him. They were, after all, partners, and they'd come too far to split up now, regardless of any threat she made. And maybe it was simply time she let faith in someone else guide her.

"As you wish. We'll meet with Lord Septon."

His eyes flashed briefly with surprise, but then he gave a nod and went back to staring out the window.

At last she felt a pang of regret about the night before. It didn't stem from the choice she'd made, but from the results of her actions. She'd pursued what she'd wanted without considering Rhys's involvement. It was one thing to guard one's heart and another to ignore someone else's.

"I'm sorry about what happened last night. Initiating that was insensitive on my part, but I did it without any expectations. You mustn't feel obligated to marry me."

His gaze was shuttered, his emotions impossible to detect. "It mustn't happen again." He clenched his jaw and glanced away as if he remembered that they'd agreed not to let the kissing happen again . . . and look what that had accomplished.

"It won't."

She was surprised by how sad that made her.

Chapter Fifteen

THEY'D TRAVELED MOST of the ride in silence and now as they neared Caerwent, Rhys finally began to relax. He'd spent the journey feeling alternately frustrated by Margery's continued refusal of his proposal and shockingly relieved by it.

He averted his eyes from her for the hundredth time and looked at the passing scenery. Last night had been revelatory—both about her and about himself. He'd never imagined he would cross the line of taking a young lady's virginity and he was thoroughly vexed with himself. He also couldn't quite bring himself to regret it. The event had been far too spectacular, and he'd recall it with fondness for the rest of his days, no matter whom he married or *if* he married.

Rhys had figured he'd follow in his father's footsteps in this, as in everything. Father had wed late in life, not because he'd planned to, but because the desire had struck. Though Rhys wasn't yet that old, desire had *also* struck. Yet, wanting Margery wasn't the same as wanting to marry her. And her point about obligation was well taken.

It would be difficult not to at least contemplate repeating last night's delightful experience, but he'd try. He only hoped they could both do better than when they'd agreed to not kiss. It was bad enough to fall into each other's arms once, but twice would be sheer lunacy.

The coach slowed as it entered the outskirts of

Caerwent. Margery scooted closer to the window and peered outside. “Is that the original Roman wall?”

“Yes, there are quite a few ruins around the town,” Rhys said. He’d visited the small village of Caerwent many times, but his first trip, with his father when he’d been nine, stuck with him the most. They’d spent several days touring the various Roman sites. The wall around the town was still quite impressive. It had ignited Rhys’s interest in antiquarian matters—something his father had hoped for.

“Will we have time to see them?” Margery asked, her face glued to the window.

He hadn’t planned on doing anything other than searching for the treasure. They’d do their best to find it in the next day or two, but if they didn’t, they’d need to assess the situation. How long could she keep traipsing across western England and southeastern Wales with a gentleman who wasn’t her husband? She’d been gone ten days. Her aunts had to be concerned.

Her aunts.

He wished he hadn’t written to them about marrying Margery. However, since Margery had refused him, it would be a moot issue and he could simply forget he’d ever done it.

When he didn’t answer her query about the ruins, she turned from the window to look at him.

“I don’t know,” he said finally. “I suppose it depends on what we find. I thought it would be best to return you to Gloucester as soon as possible.”

She pressed her hand to the side of the coach as they hit a rut. “I’ve sent word to my aunts not to worry, though now I don’t know what they’re going to think . . .” She looked back out the window.

“They’ll think nothing. You’ll tell them you refused

my offer and that will be the end of it." He glanced at the other window. "We're nearing the church."

He felt her gaze on him, but didn't return it. The coach turned up the lane to the church and finally came to a halt. He didn't wait for Craddock to open the door or let out the stairs. He jumped down, pulled the stairs free himself, and helped her step onto the dry earth. Sparks leapt when he touched her, despite their gloves, but he ignored the sensation. He'd do best to forget what had happened last night and pretend that whatever residual attraction remained between them didn't exist.

If she felt anything, her expression didn't betray it. "What about the books?"

"I've instructed Craddock to guard them and to keep watch. He's armed." He gave her a dark look. "As am I."

"How thoughtful of you, particularly since I left Lady Stratton's pistols at Hollyhaven." she murmured. "What of Jane?"

"Craddock will keep her safe." He took her elbow. "Come, let us move inside and complete our search quickly."

They walked briskly into the porch, which housed the Silurum Stone, bearing ancient, Latin lettering.

Rhys heard Margery's intake of breath and gave her a brief, whispered history. "It is thought to have been the base of a statue in honor of Paulinus, legate of the second Augustan Legion."

She looked at the stone with reverence and keen interest. "How old is it?"

"The third century." He looked around the small porch, but didn't see anything different from his last visit here, maybe three years prior. Had he expected the name Anarawd to leap out at them?

They moved into the church. It was mostly empty save a single person sitting in a pew, his head bent. Probably nothing, but Rhys didn't want to take any chances. "Let's go out to the cemetery."

He tightened his grip on her elbow and led her out through another exit into the churchyard. No one followed them and he relaxed slightly when they were back beneath the clear blue sky where they couldn't be cornered.

"Shall we split up to look at the gravestones?"

"Yes, but not too far apart. We need to be on our guard." He let go of her and moved to the corner. "Let's start here."

They walked amongst the headstones in silence. Pastoral green farmland stretched in almost every direction. The sparse buildings of the town and many cottages were visible, but the air was quiet, save the occasional bleat of a sheep or the buzz of a bee.

Some people found graveyards eerie or distressing, but to Rhys they were monuments to those who'd come before him. They filled him with a sense of gratitude and belonging. Life and death were the things they all shared.

"Do you find this morbid?" he asked her.

"Not particularly. You probably think me odd." She shrugged, but kept her focus on the stones. "I think I could spend hours here reading the headstones. All of these people and their rich lives . . . It's fascinating. And more than a bit humbling."

Then sometimes Margery had to go and say things like *that* and he wondered if he might like to pursue something more permanent with her. She was . . . a singular female.

Refusing to be distracted by her, he refocused his attention to the task at hand. They'd strolled through half the stones when the sound of a carriage approaching drew both of their heads toward the drive.

Rhys tensed. His fingers ran over the exterior of his coat pocket, which held a small pistol. He moved closer to Margery who was standing stock-still, staring at the now-stopped carriage.

The driver jumped down and opened the door. The figure who emerged was tall and when he caught sight of Rhys and Margery, he moved toward them, his long legs striding across the churchyard.

Rhys exhaled and his muscles relaxed. "We were coming to see you," he said with a grin.

"Were you?" Septon smiled in return. He reached them and offered Margery a bow. "Good afternoon, I'm Septon."

"Miss Derrington, let me present my friend, Lord Septon. Septon, my . . . friend, Miss Derrington." Rhys didn't know how to describe her, but decided "friend" would have to suffice.

She curtseyed in response. "I'm pleased to make your acquaintance, my lord."

"As am I to make yours, Miss Derrington." Septon turned his gray eyes to Rhys. "Why are you skulking about the churchyard?"

"It's a long story, but one I'm eager to share." Rhys decided they might as well call a halt to their so-far-fruitless search in favor of seeing if Septon could help them. "It's quite fortuitous that you've happened across us. Indeed, what are you doing here at the church?"

"I like to spend time meandering amongst the dead. It gives me inspiration when I'm working on a project."

Rhys hadn't known that about him, but didn't say

so. "What are you working on?"

"Just some old texts. Why don't you come for tea, and I'll tell you about it? Then you can share your long story. My cottage isn't far." Septon leased a cottage from a farmer. It wasn't grand, but he'd filled it with comforts over the past few years so that it resembled a sort of bachelor's hermitage.

He led them toward the lane where the vehicles were parked. Rhys offered his arm to Margery and they made their way to his coach.

"Why not ride with me?" Septon asked. "Your man can follow us."

Craddock, who'd stood poised at Rhys's carriage door, eyed Rhys in question. Rhys nodded in return.

"Thank you." Rhys helped Margery into Septon's carriage, where she took the forward-facing seat. Septon climbed in next, sitting beside her, which left Rhys to sit alone on the rear-facing seat.

A moment later they were on their way. Margery looked askance at Septon. Rhys recognized the shadow in her gaze—she didn't trust Septon. Rhys wasn't surprised. He was beginning to think she didn't trust anyone.

Septon leaned back in his corner. "Tell me your story, Bowen."

"We're, ah, looking for something." He looked at Margery whose mouth was tight. "You may find this hard to believe, but we've deciphered the de Valery code."

His eyes flickered with surprise and his lips parted. He looked between them. "You have both manuscripts?"

Rhys nodded. "One of them belongs to Miss Derrington. She sought me out and we were able to track down the second book." He purposely left out any other information in deference to Nash's request.

"Extraordinary," Septon breathed. "May I ask . . . What does the code say?"

The thrill Rhys had experienced when they'd solved the code washed back over him in the presence of his friend's excitement. "Three words: St. Tathyw, Venta Silurum, and Anarawd. We know the first two, but the last one isn't a name we recognize."

"It's Welsh," Septon said. "But you know that. Is that what you were looking for in the churchyard?"

"It made sense to start there since it's the Church of St. Tathyw."

Septon gave his head a brief shake, but his lips curved up. "It's called St. Tathan of course, but you know that it likely means St. Tathyw. You're a well-educated fellow."

"Thank you, but I've learned any number of things since we started this quest. We're anxious to find the treasure, but there's a group—the Order of the Round Table—that seeks to prevent us from doing so. I'd never head of them before, have you? Your Arthurian knowledge exceeds mine."

Septon leaned forward, his eyes darkening. "Do you believe they're aware you've solved the code?"

"They can't know that—we just completed the deciphering last night. They know we have the tools, however." Rhys eyed his friend, aware of his heightened interest and perhaps anxiety. "What do you know of them?"

"I know they are absolutely committed in their mission." Septon glanced between Rhys and Margery. "Did you go into the church, see anyone inside?" His question was low and urgent.

Rhys recalled the bent head in one of the pews. "We did see someone, but we didn't engage with them."

"They saw you too, I'm sure. I'd wager that was a member of the Order."

WHEN THEY ARRIVED at Lord Septon's cottage a few minutes later, Margery stepped from his coach with Rhys's assistance. Her nerves were on edge upon hearing they'd come so close to another member of this cryptic Order, and she was anxious to learn more from Septon.

Their host led them into the cheery interior of the home, which boasted a second floor. The main room was large, with a dining table on one side and a seating area clustered around a fireplace flanked with overstuffed bookshelves. The focal point, however, was the bank of wide windows along the back wall, in front of which was situated a long table covered in paper, books, and a few random objects, such as a cracked wooden plate, an earthenware crock, and a small pile of coins. It reminded Margery of Rhys's worktable at Hollyhaven.

"What are you doing over here?" Rhys asked as he approached the work area.

Septon joined him. "These are some items that were found last week. I'm just recording them for my collection."

Rhys looked over at Margery, who'd come to stand a few feet from the table. "Septon's antiquities collection is quite large. Most are on display at his estate in Somerset, but a few of his most prized treasures are in the Ashmolean Museum at Oxford."

Margery was vaguely intrigued by the items on Septon's table, but she was far more interested in what he could tell them about the Order and the treasure. She was also concerned about the de Valery manuscripts just sitting in Rhys's coach, which had followed them to the cottage.

Rhys picked up one of the coins and held it up to the window to inspect it. "Roman."

"Fourth century," Septon said.

Rhys tossed him a glance before setting the coin back down and picking up another. "Before Arthur, if you believe he existed, of course."

"Do you?" Septon leaned a hand on the back of his chair.

Rhys placed the second coin back on the pile. "I didn't, but with everything we've now seen . . ." He looked at Margery.

"And what is that?" Septon asked them both, looking from Rhys to Margery and back to Rhys.

"The de Valery code exists. It leads to something."

Septon's brow furrowed. "We don't know that for sure, but the fact that you deciphered words that led you here certainly seems to infer that there is a tangible treasure."

"Or de Valery sent us on a wild goose chase," Margery said, feeling unaccountably nervous and a bit frustrated.

"Perhaps. Let us sit." He moved to the settee and a pair of armchairs positioned near the fireplace. He waited until Margery sank to the settee before taking one of the chairs.

Rhys looked at where Margery sat, but ended up settling in the other chair, as if he'd decided maintaining space between them was for the best. She couldn't help but agree.

"What do you think the treasure might be?" Septon asked.

"I can only theorize," Rhys said. "I suppose it could be something grand like the Heart of Llanllwch."

Septon rested his elbow on the arm of his chair. "One of the thirteen treasures, you mean?"

Rhys sat straight, rigid almost. Was he feeling anxious, like Margery? "Perhaps. It could also be nothing—a whimsy. Though, given the cipher glass we found, de Valery went to a great deal of trouble to create the code."

Septon leaned forward, his eyes bright with interest. "A cipher glass, you say?"

Rhys dug it out of an interior coat pocket and held it out to Septon. "We found it at his house on the Severn."

Septon's intake of breath was audible. "May I?" At Rhys's nod, he took it from Rhys's palm, his movements slow and almost reverent. He held it up to the light streaming in from the window. "De Valery's brother was an alchemist. I wager he created this device. How does it work?"

"Look at one of your books over there—at one of the illustrations. It strips the colors from it. As you rotate the glass, it will remove all color except blue, then red, and then yellow. Doing so revealed numbers in one of the de Valery manuscripts, which we used to decipher the code buried in the other manuscript."

"Extraordinary!" Septon leapt to his feet and tried the device on one of his books. "I should like to look at your manuscripts with this, see what you saw, if you don't mind indulging a fellow antiquarian?"

Rhys smiled, his form relaxing into the chair. "Of course not."

Margery wanted to protest. She didn't want to share her book with anyone, which is why she hadn't fetched it from the coach immediately. But that was selfish of her. This man wasn't a threat; he was simply a scholar. She hoped that was all he was. What if he tried to obtain the treasure before they could? Then the entire adventure would have been for naught. She glanced at Rhys, who watched his friend with a mixture of amusement and shared excitement. Perhaps not completely for naught . . .

"If we could determine the meaning of the name Anarawd, we believe we could find the treasure," Rhys said.

Septon returned the glass to Rhys and then retook his chair. "I wish I could help you, but I don't know the name." His tone was clouded with regret. "We should read through some books later. Will you come for dinner this evening? I'm sure my housekeeper can put something satisfactory together."

"We'd be delighted, thank you," Rhys said, without consulting her.

Margery's impatience bubbled over. "Lord Septon, I wonder if you might tell us what you know of this Order of the Round Table. They've attacked us on three separate occasions and I'd like to understand why."

Septon turned his attention to her, his expression grim. "They attacked you?"

Rhys answered. "Twice, they attempted to steal her manuscript, quite violently, I might add. The third time they tried to steal the cipher glass."

Septon shook his head sympathetically. "I don't

know too much about them, just that they're a group that believes in the existence of Arthur and his knights, hence their name, the Order of the Round Table."

"Why did they try to steal my book?" Margery asked.

"Some say they seek to obtain all items that may prove the existence of Arthur." Just as Lord Nash had told them.

Margery set her palm on the settee cushion beside her skirt. "I don't understand. If they believe in his existence, why do they need further proof? Why wouldn't they want that proof made public, so that the mystery of whether he was man or myth could be answered permanently?"

"As I said, I don't know very much about them," he said. "I would guess they would prefer to have possession of all things that might lead to Arthur."

Rhys shot her a glance. "The treasure must exist then."

"If the Order has been pursuing you as you assert, then yes, it certainly seems they have something they are trying to obtain—or hide."

Or keep hidden. Margery returned Rhys's wary look. "Do you think they're trying to prevent us from finding the treasure?"

"It's possible," Septon answered. "I'm sorry I can't help you more than that. I *can* tell you the Order has been around for centuries. Before de Valery created his code."

Rhys re-pocketed the cipher glass. "If they want the treasure to remain hidden, I imagine they weren't too fond of de Valery's manuscripts."

Margery couldn't stand another moment of not ensuring the books were safe. She stood, and the gentlemen jumped to their feet. "Please excuse me, I'm going to check on Jane and Craddock. It's an awfully warm day; might I offer them refreshment, Lord Septon?"

He nodded profusely. "Of course, of course, I've been remiss. My housekeeper and valet have the afternoon off. I have some ale in the cupboard if that will suffice."

"Thank you, I'm certain it will." She smiled at both of them, lest either one detect the anxiety roiling inside of her. Then she departed the cottage and strode purposefully to Rhys's coach.

Craddock and Jane were seated on the grass in the shade of a tree. They looked to be partaking of a small meal, which alleviated at least part of Margery's concern.

Craddock jumped to his feet and met her near the coach. "Miss?"

"I'm just going to fetch the books from the coach."

Craddock opened the door and she stepped up to grab them . . . only the seat was empty.

Alarm shot through her belly and expanded until she felt quivery and hollow. "Craddock, where are the books?" Her question came out thin and raspy. She turned from the coach and speared him with a distraught stare, knowing she must look terribly upset and not caring in the slightest.

His face blanched. "They're not inside?"

"No." She stepped down, her knees wobbly.

He scrambled up to where she'd just stood and looked for himself. "They're not under the seats?" He removed both cushions and lifted the seats to the storage compartments.

Margery tried to see inside, but she couldn't imagine

how the books would have gotten there. They'd been on the seat when they'd departed the coach back at the church.

The church! Where the man from the Order had been sitting. Had he snuck into the coach and stolen the books? Margery's insides shriveled as she contemplated the loss. The book was utterly irreplaceable—and the other book wasn't even theirs to lose.

Craddock turned from the coach, his face white and his eyes distraught. "I'm so sorry, miss, they're not here. I don't know what to say . . . I take complete responsibility."

"You were with the coach the entire time at the church, were you not?"

He nodded. "Indeed. We sat in the shade, as we are here, but I kept it in my sight at all times."

Jane had come over to join them. "Except when I coaxed you to look at the baby rabbits beyond the hedge." She looked even more distressed than her brother, likely because she was afraid of failing at this opportunity to act as lady's maid. "It's all my fault, miss."

Margery sought to console them both. "It isn't, nor is the fault Craddock's. The people who stole them were assiduous in their methods. We should have provided a better defense." She was quite furious with herself for not carrying the book with her, as she'd done for so many days. Now that they'd solved the code, she'd gotten lazy. And that laziness had cost her.

She turned and went back to the cottage.

As she stepped into the cool interior, both men looked over at her.

Septon stood. "Let me get the ale."

"That won't be necessary," Margery said, her tone deceptively even while her insides were a tumultuous mess. "Mr. Bowen, I'm afraid the manuscripts have been stolen."

Chapter Sixteen

AFTER OBTAINING A pair of adjoining rooms at the Bear and Hound, Rhys paced his chamber. He could hear Margery and Jane moving about next door, but he wasn't as concerned for their safety now that the Order had obtained what they wanted.

Yet he found himself wanting to comfort Margery about her book.

The look on her face when she'd come back into Septon's cottage had nearly sent him running to her side. She'd appeared agitated, alarmed, and . . . defeated. He knew how much the book had come to mean to her, and he was damn well going to get it back for her.

Septon had been horrified by the loss. He'd felt bad for Margery, but his distress came from a purely academic place. Losing both de Valery manuscripts was a blow to the collection and study of antiquities. Rhys didn't want to contemplate how distressed Lord Nash would be when he learned his family's treasured book was gone.

And they were no closer to finding the treasure. Without it—and the book—Margery's quest to improve her fortune would end in failure. Regardless of what she said, Rhys believed she needed that treasure for financial purposes. If she had to return to Gloucester empty-handed, he wasn't sure what he might do. He doubted her pride would allow him to simply give her and her aunts money, but he couldn't see them suffer because he'd failed to keep their manuscript safe.

He held out hope that they'd find the treasure and that it would be worth something. He only prayed it was enough to compensate for the loss of the book, though he doubted anything would ever come close.

The sound of a door closing jolted him. It had come from Margery's room. He went to the adjoining door and knocked. A moment later, Margery answered.

"Is everything all right?" he asked, trying to peer around her. "I heard a door."

Margery's gaze was guarded. "Yes, Jane has gone to fetch water."

For a bath. He tried not to think of her peeling her gown away to reveal all of the tempting delights beneath. "I wanted to apologize again for the loss of your book."

"It's not your fault. I blame myself for not keeping it with me."

Her unfaltering accountability never ceased to amaze him. "I'm going to get it back."

Her lips formed a sad smile. "I appreciate the sentiment, but I have grave doubts as to the likelihood of that happening. I only wish we didn't have to inform Lord Nash that his book has been stolen. He's going to be devastated."

"No more than you," Rhys said softly. "I know how much it meant to you."

She kept her chin up, but he sensed the depth of her disappointment was far greater than she would admit. "It was a valuable piece. Irreplaceable."

"If you would allow me, I would compensate you for its loss."

Her eyes widened briefly. "No, I couldn't let you do

that. As I said, it wasn't your fault."

He wanted to argue, but he'd had enough of arguing with her, particularly when their fortunes had taken such a downturn. "Will you be ready in an hour to depart for Septon's?"

She fidgeted with the edge of the door. "I've decided to take dinner here."

"You have?" He leaned against the doorframe. "But what of researching Anarawd?"

"I'm quite fatigued from the journey, and losing the book has just . . . well, it's taken a bit out of me, I'm afraid." She offered him a weak smile. "No, please don't worry—I can see that you're considering it—worrying, I mean."

He stepped away from the jamb and toed the threshold. "I don't think you should be alone."

"I shan't be. Jane will stay with me. Besides, it's not as if the Order cares about me any longer. They have what they wanted."

"I still have the glass." He patted the front of his coat and felt the interior pocket that held de Valery's brother's device. "They might come after it. I'm going to leave Craddock here to watch over you and Jane. I'll walk to Septon's, it's not far."

"If you insist."

"I do. Insisting is one of the things I do best."

Her head snapped up, a glint of humor lighting her eyes, but it was gone too quickly.

"It's strange to not be spending the evening together," he said.

Her eyelids fluttered. "Yes, I suppose it is. After so much time in each other's company."

For ten days, they'd spent an inordinate amount of time together, particularly since they'd started this journey as strangers. They were far from that now. "I'm sorry about what happened today, but I don't regret this expedition, and I hope you don't either."

One side of her mouth turned up. "No."

A ridiculous warmth spread in his chest. He leaned close so he could bask in her scent and her heat. "And it's not over yet. We're going to find the treasure."

She looked up at him, her eyes dark and sultry. "I almost believe it when you say it." Her voice was pitched low, and it did strange and marvelous things to his groin.

He lifted his hand to touch her cheek. "Margery."

She evaded his touch, not jerkily, but with a slow, smooth movement that ended in a head shake. "Rhys, I think we both know what will happen if you touch me. We'll kiss and things will . . . progress. Jane will be back at any moment."

Did that mean that if it weren't for Jane, Margery would invite his kiss? It didn't matter. They'd agreed to keep their hands off each other.

He took a step back and schooled his features. She was too alluring, too seductive, and he was far too susceptible to her charms. "I didn't mean to overstep. I only meant to console you. Have a pleasant evening—I'll see you for breakfast and we can discuss what Septon and I uncover."

She arched a brow at him. "*If* you uncover anything."

Cheeky thing. "I'll see you in the morning."

With a slight nod, she closed the door. Rhys stared at the wood. It seemed as though their exciting adventure—and their partnership—had come to an end. Though he knew it would happen, he hadn't expected the hollow feeling expanding inside of him.

The manuscripts weren't the day's only, or even worst, loss.

MARGERY TURNED FROM the door and urged her rising ardor to cool. The slightest provocative look, the hint of a touch . . . these were things that shouldn't elicit such a strong response. However, it seemed she was utterly vulnerable to Rhys's seductive power.

Keeping him at arm's length not only kept with their agreement, it was *necessary*. It was also an excellent reason for not accompanying him to Septon's tonight.

Though it paled next to her primary reason for staying at the inn: she didn't think Septon would help them find Anarawd in some book. Her intuition said the answer to the mysterious name was in the church, precisely where the other clues pointed them. She considered going there to investigate the interior further, but had no notion of where to start.

Besides, there was the issue of the Order perhaps watching it. How sinister was this group that they had members protecting key places—de Valery's house and the Caerwent church? Since de Valery's house had yielded the cipher glass device, she had to assume the church contained something of equal importance. Yes, the church was critical to the puzzle.

Perhaps the inn's staff might be able to provide some information about the church or about Anarawd. After tidying up with Jane's assistance, Margery went downstairs.

The inn offered a small, well-appointed dining room for its guests. Margery arrived just before dinner was due to be served.

The innkeeper's wife, Mrs. Powell, greeted her with a welcoming smile. "Good evening, Miss Derrington, I'm so pleased you'll be joining us for dinner. There will be one other attendee, I hope that's all right."

"Then I shall have company," Margery said. "I wondered if I might ask—"

"And here he is." Mrs. Powell looked past Margery. "Good evening, my lord."

Margery turned to make the other guest's acquaintance and nearly fell over in shock. "Mr. Digby."

Tall, with queued brown hair graying at the temples, he wore a muted costume of dark brown relieved only by his ivory shirt and cravat. He bowed gracefully over her hand. "Miss Derrington, this is an unqualified boon. I was so disappointed that you weren't in Gloucester. To find you here . . . Well, I am the luckiest man in Britain." He smiled, his eyes crinkling at the edges.

"I'm pleased to see you, as well, Mr. Digby." She wasn't really, since he'd foiled her investigative plans. Now, she'd have to reserve her questions for Mrs. Powell for another time.

Beneath his widow's peak, his brow gently creased. "I was sorry to hear your aunt was ill, but so relieved that she was recuperating."

Was she? Now that was welcome news. "Thank you for telling me. I haven't received a letter from them, so I've been anxious to hear how she's doing." Margery felt a pang of remorse over not returning to Gloucester to check on her aunts. When had she become so selfishly driven? No, that wasn't fair. She was undertaking this entire expedition to solve their financial woes.

"Then I'm doubly glad to have found you," he said.

"How fascinating that you already know each other," Mrs. Powell interrupted. "Would you both care to sit? Dinner is ready."

"Yes, of course," Margery said with an apologetic smile.

Mr. Digby went to the long table, where there were two places set—one at the end and one to the right—and held out a chair for Margery. After she was seated, he took the place at the head.

Mrs. Powell bustled from the dining room, presumably to fetch their first course.

"I owe you an apology, Miss Derrington."

Margery snapped her gaze to his. He had brown eyes, akin to a light sherry, not dark and earthy like Rhys's. "You do?"

"I think I perhaps came on a bit too forcefully in our earlier communications. I was, quite simply and perhaps embarrassingly, swept away by your charms."

Oh dear. Margery wasn't sure she liked how this was going. She began to wish she'd gone with Rhys. "That's . . . all right."

Digby turned himself toward her. "There was actually a reason behind my initial visit to Gloucester and to my seeking you out at the assembly."

Mrs. Powell entered with the soup course and they fell silent while she served them.

Margery picked up her spoon and tested the soup, while she watched him warily.

He ignored his soup. "As I was saying, there was a purpose for my interest in you. Your aunts possessed a manuscript I was most interested in finding—a medieval text of an Arthurian legend, *The Ballads of*

Gareth?"

He knew about the manuscript and he just *happened* to find her here in Caerwent? Her trepidation crystallized into alarm. "Have you been following me?"

His eyes widened with horror. "Goodness no! I came to Caerwent to do some research—I'm a bit of an Arthurian enthusiast. Finding you here was completely unexpected, though I must say gratifying."

Her mind grappled to understand his intent. "So you attempted to court me in order to gain access to a manuscript? That's incredibly mercenary, don't you think?" She didn't bother to mask the derision in her tone.

He surprised her by laughing. "I don't blame you for thinking the worst. Indeed, when you describe it, I sound like an unscrupulous scoundrel. But, and please forgive me, when I met you, I almost forgot about the manuscript entirely. You possess such a keen wit . . . I'd never met a lady like you." He looked down as a flush spread up his neck. "I'm afraid I don't have much experience in matters of courtship."

Margery began to adjust her opinion. He seemed genuinely embarrassed, and she didn't want to humiliate him. "Social situations can be difficult to navigate. I must be forthright and tell you I'm not interested in courtship or marriage at this time."

His head shot up. "I see. How . . . unusual."

She paused in lifting a spoonful of soup to her mouth. "I beg your pardon?"

"Most young women in your station are eager to wed." He made the statement without inflection, as if they were discussing a point of reason.

She couldn't argue with his assessment. "Yes, that's true. I am not, however, 'most young women.'"

His lips curved into a smile. "No, you are not."

They discussed mundane topics during the remainder of the soup course, the warming trend of the weather and the charm of Caerwent. Throughout, she thought about what he'd said, that he was an Arthurian enthusiast. Could he know anything that would help her find the treasure?

As the second course was laid, Margery decided to broach the topic. First, however, did he know about the code and the treasure? And how had he even known they possessed the book when her aunts had forgotten it in the attic? "Why were you looking for the book and how did you learn that my aunts had it?"

He quickly swallowed his bite of fish as he chuckled. "I think you're trying to covertly ask if I'm aware of the de Valery code and the treasure it leads to. The answer is yes."

She tried not to reveal her surprise at his candor. Would he have tried to obtain the book without telling her of the code, as Rhys had done?

"I've been trying to find this de Valery manuscript for quite some time and had finally tracked it to your aunts' great-grandfather. That's why I came to see you last week—or tried to. I'd wanted to talk with you about the book."

"Why didn't you do that when we met?"

He glanced away, the color rising in his face again. "I was too overcome with my reaction to you. I'm not proud of my insecurity."

Again, she had to rethink her first opinion of the gentleman. Given her experience with all matters relating to her book, she was right to be skeptical. However, she could give Mr. Digby the benefit of the doubt—for now. "You'd planned to talk to me about the book and the hidden code, perhaps to solve it and find the treasure?"

His eyes lit. "Of course. It would be marvelous, wouldn't it? Deciphering the code? Finding the treasure?"

Yes, it would. It *was*. At least the deciphering part. She hesitated to reveal what she knew, but he if he could help . . . She forked a bite of fish and raised it. "What do you know of the treasure?"

He set his utensils down and dabbed at his mouth. "Nothing specific, as far as what it might be. I believe it's important, however, something vital to Arthurian legend. It could even be one of the thirteen treasures."

Margery swallowed the succulent fish. "Such as the Heart of Llanllwch."

He smiled. "It's pronounced thlan-thlooch, though that was a good effort. Welsh is the devil to pronounce." He said it the same as Rhys, so he was at least educated in the Welsh tongue.

"You think the treasure is valuable?"

"For its historic importance alone, yes." Like Rhys, he seemed to want to find it for the right reasons, yet . . . He looked at her intently. "I failed in our previous encounters and I don't wish to do so again," he said. "As you were forthright, let me be the same. Why are you here in Caerwent? Are you . . . alone?"

She'd been risking her reputation by traveling with Rhys, and now it seemed the threat would finally come to fruition. Mr. Digby might not be a prominent member of society, but he was still a peer and capable of ruining Margery with just one well-placed comment.

However, she couldn't think of a plausible lie, not when he would most certainly learn that Rhys was also a guest of the inn. "I've been working with Mr. Rhys

Bowen to solve the code and find the treasure."

Digby registered surprise, his mouth parting, and not in the way it would to eat the bite of turnips on his fork.

"Are you familiar with Mr. Bowen? I went to him as a medieval manuscript expert and together, we were able to decipher the code." She didn't want to get into the particulars with Digby, not when it would reveal her association with Lord Nash, and perhaps by extension his daughter. She forged ahead in an effort to stave off any questions. "The code led us here—to the Caerwent church. However, there is one piece that we don't understand."

He'd replaced his turnip-laden fork to his plate and was staring at her, enthralled. "You solved the code? I can't, I just, it's extraordinary!" His face lit with wonderment and he shook his head in disbelief. "You haven't yet found the treasure, you say?"

She nearly smiled at his difficulty in keeping up. His excitement was palpable and reminded her of that moment when they'd solved the code. The moment that had led to her and Rhys allowing their passion for the adventure to overcome their sense of reason. "We haven't. As I said, there is one piece we can't puzzle out—the name Anarawd."

His lips spread into a beatific smile. "Now *that* you pronounced perfectly," he said softly. "I can tell you precisely who he was."

Now it was Margery's turn to be astounded. She set her utensils down and leaned toward Digby. "Who?" The single word sounded quiet in the room, or maybe she couldn't hear over the blood pounding in her ears.

"Anarawd was a sixth-century monk. He lived at St. Tathyw's monastery, which was founded very near here—at Christchurch."

Margery was breathless with anticipation. "How does he figure into this? I fail to see how a monk has anything to do with Arthurian treasure."

"I understand your confusion." He laid his palm on the tablecloth. "You see, he was more than a monk. Anarawd was a scribe, and he may have documented some of the exploits of Arthur and his knights—directly from their oral stories."

Directly? "You mean he was a contemporary of Arthur?"

"Perhaps. This is all conjecture, but there are some who believe the treasure could validate *everything*." His brown eyes took on a luster that revealed a confidence he didn't possess regarding social matters.

"What do you mean by 'everything'?"

"Anarawd's role in documenting *history*—not legend." His voice quivered with excitement. "The existence of the thirteen treasures of Britain, and of course the very existence of King Arthur and his Round Table. Imagine, at last, putting the question of whether he was a man or myth to rest."

That sort of discovery would be astounding. What would Rhys think? "You believe the treasure could prove all of this?"

He lifted a shoulder. "I hope it does, but we won't know until we find it." He glanced away. "Sorry, until *you* find it."

She wanted to share in his elation, but there was still the issue of the Order and whether they would even allow them to find the treasure. "I'm afraid it might not be that easy. Even if we knew where to look—and we still don't," the revelation of Anarawd's identity didn't illuminate anything for her regarding the location of the treasure, "there are those who would stop us."

His face darkened. "The Order of the Round Table. They've intervened?"

Margery couldn't contain her intake of breath. "You know of them?"

He nodded grimly. "I've done extensive research on all things Arthurian, Miss Derrington. The Order rears its head time and time again. They will stop at nothing to prevent you from finding the treasure, and will employ methods both daring and subtle. You must be vigilant."

So far they'd opted for daring, but she would keep her senses attuned for anything. "I can't tell you how much I appreciate you sharing your knowledge with me."

He touched his chest. "I consider it a privilege to do what I can to see you safe."

They focused on their meal for a few minutes and soon the fish was removed and replaced with a course of roast pheasant. Mrs. Powell served their plates and refilled Mr. Digby's wineglass before departing once more.

Digby sampled the pheasant and leaned back in his chair as he contemplated her with a wrinkled forehead. "You say you don't know the location of the treasure?"

Margery cut into her pheasant. "No. The code was just three words: St. Tathyw, Anarawd, and Venta Silurum." She fleetingly wondered if she shouldn't have revealed the code, but Digby seemed so earnest and unlike Rhys, he'd shared information with her readily—and immediately.

"Fascinating," he breathed. "I would agree that it points to the church. I wonder how Anarawd fits into that."

"You said he was a monk in Christchurch; could we have the wrong place?"

He frowned. "I don't know. Have you investigated the church here?"

"Just the churchyard, because there was a man from the Order inside."

"I see." He cocked his head back and looked at the ceiling as if he were seeking some sort of divine direction. When he lowered his gaze, there was a determined glint in his eye. "We shall have to lure him away from the church."

Now it was her turn to frown. "How would we do that?"

"I'm not entirely certain, but I will devise a plan." A flash of color highlighted his cheeks again. "My apologies, I'm overstepping. This is your endeavor. Yours and Mr. Bowen's."

It was, but Mr. Digby had demonstrated a knowledge that surpassed Rhys's and even Septon's—neither one of them had known who Anarawd was. Did that mean she wanted to invite Digby's assistance? How would Rhys react to including him?

Wait. What was she thinking? Splitting the treasure with Rhys—not to mention Lord Nash's half—was one thing, but dividing it with Digby would diminish her share even further. She needed this treasure to keep her family from losing everything, while Rhys and Mr. Digby were merely enthralled by the potential for discovery. For her, the situation was far more desperate. She'd already lost the book. The treasure represented her last hope.

"It is our enterprise," she said slowly, "but I deeply appreciate your assistance. Perhaps tomorrow morning we could meet. If you and Mr. Bowen compare your knowledge, something might become evident."

"I shall do whatever you require." He lifted his glass. "To finding the treasure."

She raised her glass in response. "To finding the treasure."

And then what?

Chapter Seventeen

FOLLOWING A DELICIOUS dinner of kidney pie prepared rather hastily by Septon's housekeeper, Rhys and his host prepared to select books to peruse. Sconces illuminated the space, so they had plenty of light by which to conduct their research. Rhys hoped it would prove fruitful.

"Before we begin, I'd like to discuss something with you." The tone of Septon's voice carried a hint of foreboding.

Rhys's neck tingled. "What is it?"

Septon gestured to the seating area. "Please sit with me." He took the armchair he'd used earlier in the day.

Anticipation stirred in Rhys's gut as he sat in the other chair. "Why am I suddenly anxious?"

Septon smiled, but lines of tension fanned from the corners of his eyes and mouth. "I want to show you something." He pulled his boot off and rolled down his stocking. Then he presented his leg, turning it slightly so the inside of his calf was visible. A sword, about three inches long, was tattooed into his flesh. "Every member has one in just this spot."

Rhys leaned forward and studied the mark. The letters "KRT" were stamped across the guard of the sword handle. He instantly knew what it meant. Dread unfurled in his chest. "I should call you out for the danger you submitted Margery to."

He didn't care that he'd first-named her in front of a member of Society. He only cared that fury, white-hot and blinding, was coursing through him. He just barely kept himself from launching his fist into Septon's grim visage.

Septon seemed to sense the danger. He pulled back into his chair, as if he could remove himself from Rhys's reach. However, nothing would keep him safe—not after what he'd just exposed.

Septon rolled up his stocking and replaced his boot. "Before you leap to judgment, allow me to explain."

Once again, strong emotions rose up inside of Rhys, shocking him with their virulence. He wasn't a violent man, but right now he had a savage urge to inflict damage on Septon and his entire bloody Order. "You have one opportunity to convince me not to knock your head from your shoulders."

"I understand your anger. First, let me apologize for any danger to Miss Derrington. The man at de Valery's house was a bit . . . aggressive."

Rhys vaulted out of his chair and stood over Septon. "And what of the man who attacked her in Hereford? Or the pair of men who accosted her outside of Leominster?"

Septon blanched. "I didn't know about either of those events. . . I'm not in charge."

Rhys leaned forward, his lip curling. "Who is?"

"We don't reveal that information, under any circumstance." He glanced at Rhys's fisted hands. "I am not aware of anyone who might have perpetrated either of those acts. Was that before or after you took the glass from de Valery's house?"

Septon knew that? "Before," he growled.

Septon exhaled. "I doubt it was the Order. We weren't cognizant of your activity until you showed up at de Valery's. We've tracked you since, but we've kept our distance."

He thought of Margery alone at the inn. "Is someone watching her now? By God, if anyone hurts her—"

Septon lifted his hand, palm out. "No one would hurt her. We don't do that. The man at de Valery's said you fought him—we prefer not to resort to violence."

They *preferred*. "That doesn't sound like you *don't*."

"Sometimes it's been necessary. However, once I determined it was you—after I received your letter—I gave orders not to engage with you or your companion. At the time I didn't know her identity." Septon's gaze turned pleading. "Please, you must understand. The man at de Valery's, he wouldn't have actually hurt you."

"Tell that to my head." Rhys turned to show him the still-yellow bruise on his temple.

Septon cringed. "My apologies. Will you let me explain the purpose of the Order?"

Rhys had to admit he was curious. "You assure me that Margery is safe?"

"From us, yes."

Rhys had started to relax, but then remembered the bloody books—how could he have forgotten that? "Wait. Our de Valery manuscripts were stolen from the church earlier. They were taken from my coach. And you conveniently had us ride here in your vehicle." He glared at his one-time friend.

"Rhys, I swear the Order had nothing to do with that. I don't have your books. In fact, I share your concern. This is most distressing. Those are important artifacts."

"They're more than artifacts," Rhys said heavily, thinking of how devastated Margery was and how distraught Lord Nash was going to be.

"I know." Septon's agreement was sad. "I'll help you find who stole them. I'm beginning to think there's some vile plot at work here. Perhaps a corrupt member of the Order executing his own agenda."

Rhys looked at him sharply. "Is that possible?"

"Anything's possible. And sadly, there have been instances during our long history where members have taken it upon themselves to act with haste or have simply lost sight of their oath."

"And what oath is that?"

"To protect the legacy of King Arthur and his knights. Most of us are descendants of the Round Table."

Rhys blinked at him. "You can prove this?"

Septon shrugged. "In some cases. In others, it's an oral history that's been passed down."

"Your ancestor was a knight of the Round Table?"

Septon smiled sadly. "How I wish. I was selected because of my extensive Arthurian research. They approached me after I left Oxford."

And he'd apparently risen to some level of importance from the sound of it. "You're telling me King Arthur actually lived."

Septon adjusted in his chair. "Do you think you might sit down again? My neck is beginning to ache as I look up at you from this angle."

Rhys backed away. "No, I have to return to the inn. If there's a member who has, as you put it, 'lost sight of his oath,' I need to make sure Margery is safe."

Septon got to his feet. "Goodness, you're right. We'll take my gig." He grabbed his hat from a hook near the door and went outside with Rhys fast on his heels. The nearly full moon lit their way to the small stable. "Davis, ready my gig posthaste!"

A young stable lad bustled about, quickly tethering the horse to the vehicle. Rhys mentally calculated if he could run there faster, but decided the gig would be more expedient. That didn't stop him from pacing while the stable lad worked.

"I'm sure she'll be fine," Septon said, his tone laced with anxiety.

"She'd better be." Raw fury blistered just beneath the surface of his temper—a temper he hadn't known he possessed until he'd made the acquaintance of Miss Margery Derrington.

"Let me finish telling you about the Order," Septon offered.

Yes, that would keep Rhys from obsessing over Margery for the next ten minutes, though he continued to pace, elevating his already spiking body temperature. The summer night was warm and he longed to strip off his coat. "Continue. You were telling me that King Arthur was an actual historical figure."

"We believe so, yes, although there are no direct ancestors that we are aware of."

"Ready, my lord," Davis called.

Septon raced forward and climbed into the gig. Rhys followed, vaulting into the opposite side. He stifled the urge to snatch the reins from him.

Once they were moving, Septon went on, "In addition to the knights having lived, some of their stories, while exaggerated and romanticized over time, are factual. The stories in the de Valery manuscripts are based on actual events. The items in the stories—the thirteen treasures—are real."

The speed of the gig allowed a cooling breeze to soothe Rhys's raging temper. "Many people believe that since the Heart of Llanllwch was found."

"Yes, but that's only part of it. The heart isn't actually one of the thirteen treasures. It doesn't contain a magical property."

Rhys angled in his seat and stared at Septon. "Are you saying these treasures exist as written in the legends? There are magical swords and knives and chariots?" Rhys wasn't sure he could believe that, not without seeing it. Hell, he still wasn't sure he believed anything this Order purported. He was a man of academics—he required evidence to prove his theories and assertions.

"It's not quite that simple." Septon turned a corner and they raced toward the inn. "The treasures have power—for the right people. Many of the stories speak of the treasures choosing the user by virtue of their nobility or bravery. They don't work quite like that. Armed with the right information, the treasures could be very dangerous."

"What information?" Rhys was torn between Septon's revelations and the need to ensure Margery's safety. But the inn was in sight.

"That isn't something I'm permitted to discuss." His tone was apologetic as he glanced at Rhys. "You must understand—the weapons amongst the treasure could empower someone to achieve terrible things, and the items that provide comfort or ease . . . men would kill to possess such treasures. The Order's primary objective is to keep them hidden."

"Is that why you're trying to prevent us from finding the treasure from the de Valery code? You think it's one or more of the thirteen treasures."

Septon brought the gig to halt before the inn. "We don't know for certain. We can't confirm the location of any of the treasures—save the heart, which as I said doesn't seem to possess any magical qualities."

Rhys prepared to step out of the gig. "The Order doesn't sound particularly knowledgeable."

"I assure you, we are," Septon said with a touch of heat. "However, so much of the real information has been lost to history. That is why the de Valery manuscripts are so important. They were derived from another work—a work that was drafted perhaps during Arthur's lifetime or shortly thereafter. By a scribe named Anarawd."

Rhys snapped his gaze to Septon's. "You lied to us."

"To Miss Derrington. I'd planned to tell you the truth once we were alone."

Margery. Rhys jumped from the gig.

"Bowen, wait," Septon called. He stepped out of the gig and came around to speak more quietly. "If someone *has* gotten to Miss Derrington, I'd like to help. I'll remain here. If there's trouble, send me a signal." Rhys turned to go, but Septon snagged his elbow. "I've shared all of this with you for a reason. You *must* abandon your quest. I'll do everything I can to help you recover the de Valery manuscripts—but *they* must be your treasure. I'm pleading with you to leave the other treasure where it lies. This is critical." His grip on Rhys's arm tightened.

Rhys shook him off. "Is the Order threatening me?"

"No, your friend is asking you a favor."

Rhys pulled his sleeve to straighten the bunched fabric at the elbow. "I'll consider it."

Septon's gaze sharpened. "Please, this is vitally important. You must understand the danger the thirteen treasures pose. I'm appealing to your scholarly nature—leave history alone."

"My scholarly nature is precisely what demanded I

seek the treasure in the first place." He coated his tone in ice. "It could be an important artifact that we could use to learn and teach."

Septon stepped back from him, his mouth turned down. "You must do as you believe, but I am not the sole member of the Order and there are many people above me."

There was no mistaking *that* was a threat.

With a parting scowl, Rhys turned and strode into the inn. He took the stairs two at a time, but when he reached the landing, everything was quiet. With light steps, he went into his room, planning to access Margery's via their connecting door. He didn't get that far, however, because sitting in the chair by his open window, her loosened hair blowing in the gentle, night breeze, was Margery.

He closed the door behind him and in a handful of strides he clasped her hand and pulled her from the chair. "You're safe," he breathed.

Her eyes were wide, her lips parted as she nodded.

"Good." He wrapped his arms around her and kissed her. The heat of the night, the anger he felt toward Septon, the fear he'd felt for her well-being—all of it tangled inside of him into a sweltering passion he simply couldn't contain.

He swept his tongue into her mouth, ravaging the soft recesses. He dug his fingers into her back as he brought her more tightly against his hardening body.

Her fingers curled into his lapels, holding him captive to her eagerly answering mouth. She struggled to push his coat off and he was only too obliged to help her, stripping it from his shoulders and tossing it to the floor. Her fingers wound into his cravat and pulled the knot free. Then she tugged the ends so that the silk pulled against his neck as she tilted her mouth beneath his.

God, she was excitement and adventure and bliss all rolled into a tantalizing package. He raked his fingers up her back and fisted a length of her hair. She moaned into his mouth and ground her hips against his.

She whipped the cravat from his neck and replaced it with her fingers, stroking and kneading his flesh. He feasted on her mouth, unable to quell the desire raging through him.

With a gasp, she pulled her lips from his. "We shouldn't do this," she breathed, but her fingers were busy unbuttoning his waistcoat.

"We shouldn't." He worked the fastenings of her robe and pushed it aside to reveal the linen nightrail she wore beneath. A breeze from the open window rustled over her, shifting the material against her breasts so he could see their pebbled tips.

He leaned down and drew one into his mouth, suckling her through the fabric. She arched her neck and moaned softly as she pushed the waistcoat from his shoulders. She clutched his head to her chest, her fingers digging into his scalp. His lust spiraling to new heights, he tongued and sucked her, then lightly nipped her flesh. She gasped and tugged at his hair even harder. Blood rushed to his cock.

He swept her into his arms and carried her to the bed. With fast, jerky movements, he stripped his boots away and whisked his shirt over his head. He didn't have time for more because she pulled him down on top of her and kissed him again, her tongue a wildfire of need and demand.

She dragged her mouth away to press kisses along his jawline, then lower, against his neck and his collarbone. He gritted his teeth against the overwhelming sensations. She was going to kill him. Then her hands were on his fall and her fingers brushed against his erection through the fabric. Yes, death was imminent.

But oh, what a death it would be.

He grasped the hem of her gown and pulled it up over her knees and thighs, his knuckles grazing her soft flesh. She was hot, like him, the summer night fueling the heat of their desire.

Her hand found his bare cock, and he groaned with the pleasure of it. Her grip wasn't tentative or light, but sure and strong. She found the base and slid her palm up, as confidently and wonderfully as the last time.

Desperate to touch her, he found the soft heat between her thighs and stroked the sensitive folds. Her hips came up and rotated into his hand, seeking his touch while her hand continued its ascent and descent over his rigid cock.

"Miss Derrington?"

The sound of Jane's voice broke through their sexual haze. Both of their hands stilled as their heads turned, in unison, toward the connecting door. A loud knock sounded.

"Miss Derrington?"

Their heads turned again, this time toward each other, eyes wide. Then they scrambled from the bed, practically falling over each other in the process.

MARGERY PULLED HER nightrail down to cover her legs and snatched up her robe. With shaking fingers she refastened the garment. Her body was hot, thrumming with unsatisfied desire. What had just happened? If it hadn't been for Jane . . .

"Shit," Rhys muttered as he readjusted his breeches.

Margery tried to keep from looking at his magnificent chest, but failed. The muscles beneath his dark flesh flexed as he reached for his shirt.

"Yes, I'm here Jane." Shaking her lust-addled head, she went to the door and opened it just wide enough so that Jane could see her but not into the room—and more importantly Rhys—beyond. She smiled at the young maid, whose forehead was drawn with concern. "I didn't mean to worry you. Mr. Bowen and I had some matters to discuss. I'll be back shortly."

Jane nodded, her expression relaxing into relief. "I woke up and when I didn't see you, I thought perhaps I'd failed to bring you something, but then you weren't downstairs."

"Oh, Jane, you're doing a wonderful job," Margery assured her. "Just wonderful. Please, go back to sleep. I'm quite used to caring for myself, so you mustn't take my actions as a slight against your abilities. I'm learning, just as you are."

Jane's answering smile was soft and appreciative. "Good night then."

"Good night, Jane." Margery closed the door and turned. Rhys had donned his shirt but nothing else. Not that she blamed him, the night was quite warm and if he was half as hot as she was, he likely wished he was naked.

Do not *think of him naked.*

She crossed to the window and put her face into the breeze, closing her eyes. It was a mild comfort, but still a comfort. She exhaled and when her body had cooled just a little, she opened her eyes and turned to look at him. "My apologies. I didn't mean to get carried away."

His gaze was wary. "No, it was my fault. I'm the one who kissed you."

"Clearly, I was not opposed," she said drily.

"It's just . . ." He raked his hand through his hair, mussing the thick black strands. "I was worried something had happened to you and when I found you safe, I'm afraid my relief got the better of me."

He'd kissed her out of relief? That kiss had seemed to stem from something far deeper, far more primitive. She shuddered remembering the intensity of his kiss, the insistence of his mouth on her breast, the promise of what was to come next . . .

She shook her head. "I don't understand."

He pulled the second chair from the table, set it opposite the other in front of the window, and gestured for her to sit. As he took the other chair, the breeze rippled the opening of his shirt, drawing her eye to the stark contrast of his nearly-brown flesh against the pale linen. She curled her fingers into her palms as the urge to touch him again swept through her.

She sensed a tension in him that may or may not have had to do with their interrupted sexual encounter.

At last, he turned his head to look at her. His eyes were dark and vibrant, as if his passion burned just behind them. "Septon confessed that he's a member of the Order." He made the declaration with a contempt and disdain she'd never glimpsed in him before.

"I can't say I'm terribly surprised." It made too much sense, given Septon's Arthurian knowledge and the timely disappearance of the books. "Did you get my manuscript back?"

"No, but wait." He held up his hand. "You aren't

surprised? I was."

"I think you mean shocked."

"Hell yes, I'm shocked. Septon's been my friend for years. And when I thought he'd brought danger to you . . ." His hands were splayed on his lap, but they dug into the fabric of his breeches.

"He was behind all of it? The attacks on me to obtain my book, the altercation near de Valery's house?" She glanced at the light bruise still evident on Rhys's forehead and felt an urge to kick Septon where it would hurt most.

"He says he wasn't." Rhys frowned out at the night. "He insisted the Order isn't dangerous—as a rule—though they might have a member who follows their own path from time to time. He doesn't know who tried to steal your book, and he doesn't have the books now."

She leaned forward and almost touched his knee to draw his focus, but stopped herself. Touching should be avoided at all costs unless she wanted to end up back in bed with him. For a brief moment, her mind indulged her hungry body, but he thankfully interrupted her wayward thoughts.

"Septon's pledged to help us recover the books," Rhys said.

She didn't trust Septon to do anything he said. "And how does he plan to do that?"

"We didn't discuss it. I was too concerned with getting back here to you. When he said there could be another member of the Order out on his own, I immediately wanted to ensure your safety." His gaze burned into hers. He'd been afraid. For her.

She swallowed as the attraction between them coaxed her temperature past the breaking point. Sweat gathered at the back of her neck and she pulled her hair over her shoulder to expose the flesh to the somewhat cooler air wafting from the window. "I'm not sure why you would trust Septon. He's a member of the Order, and from what Lord Nash said, they're a dubious organization."

"I'm angry with Septon, but I still trust him. I've known him a long time, and he confessed his membership of his own volition." He massaged his neck. "He also told me the Order's purpose." He shot her a skeptical look. "He claims King Arthur and the knights were real people and that the Order was founded by the knights' descendants."

Margery let go of the mass of her hair. "You don't believe that, do you?"

He shrugged. "I don't know what to believe. Actually, that's not true. I don't know whether I believe *that.* However, I can tell you that his other revelation is too fanciful to be indulged."

She could hardly wait to hear. "Do tell me."

"You know of the thirteen treasures of course. The Order says they not only exist, but that they hold the magical properties as outlined in the legend."

Margery thought of the items in her book. "There's a sword that bursts into flame?"

He blinked. "Supposedly, yes."

They stared at each other a moment and burst out laughing.

"I can see you find this as compelling as I do," he said through a wide smile that made her heart turn over.

"It's preposterous. And where are these precious items?"

"He says they don't know, but I'm not sure I believe

that either. He's quite insistent that we give up our quest—to protect the world from these potentially dangerous items."

She scoffed. "How is a hamper that provides as much food as necessary dangerous?"

"Because it will induce men to fight over its possession."

She fervently wished the breeze was stronger and cooler. Her nightrail stuck to her back beneath the heaviness of her robe, but she didn't dare remove it again.

After a long pause, she said, "Septon believes the treasure from the de Valery code is one of these magical items?"

"He isn't certain, but says it's possible. He's asked that we respect history and let it remain hidden."

Anger flared in her belly. "That's fine for him to say, but I need that treasure, especially now that my book is gone." She pressed her lips together, hating that she'd said so much.

"I know," he said softly. "And we're going to get it back, I promise."

She appreciated his sympathy, but it did little to ease the sick feeling rooting in her stomach.

"Margery." The word stroked her like a caress. "You don't need to worry about needing the treasure. I will take care of you."

She snapped her gaze to his. "You'll *what*? I'm not your paramour."

His forehead creased, making him appear chagrined. "I didn't mean it like that."

"How else would it be interpreted for a gentleman to give money to an unmarried young woman?"

He looked away from her. "My apologies."

"What are you going to do about finding the treasure?"

He kept his gaze averted. "I'm not sure. I have to consider Septon's plea."

He'd really surrender their quest? She clenched her teeth, upset that he'd abandon her. She couldn't do it alone. Digby could help her. And with Rhys gone, that was one less person to split the treasure with. But could she trust Digby? It had taken time for her to trust Rhys, and now knowing Septon was a member of the Order, and that there might be another member out there with a self-serving agenda . . . Could Digby be that member? A chill raced down her back, icing the perspiration and making her shoulders twitch.

No, she'd come too far to back down. She *needed* that treasure. "I'm not giving up."

He turned his head to look at her. "And what will you do when you find it?" Sell it? To whom? How will you be monetarily compensated?"

She blinked at him, her mind scrambling. "You were going to . . ." Take care of that with his antiquarian connections. Or something. They'd never really settled on a firm plan. Why would they do that when finding the treasure had seemed, at times, like an insurmountable challenge? But if he sided with the Order and chose to leave the treasure alone, she wouldn't have his assistance. And she couldn't take any money he offered without losing every shred of self-esteem she possessed. Besides, Aunt Eugenie would never allow it. She considered Aunt Agnes's decision to become a man's mistress to be a dire mistake, one she never truly forgave her sister for. That Margery wouldn't actually be Rhys's mistress didn't matter—she'd given him her virginity and if she took his money, it would seem like a transaction.

Standing, she fixed him with a determined glare. “Never mind. I don’t need your help to find the treasure. Good night, Mr. Bowen.”

She turned to go to her room, but he lightly clasped her wrist, spinning her until she nearly connected with his chest—if not for the hand she splayed over his shirt and quickly snatched away.

He let go of her with a slight nod of apology. “I haven’t decided if I’m going to give up the quest—I’m only thinking about it. I consider things from all angles, as any good scholar would.”

“Do inform me when you’ve completed your analysis.” She quickly retreated to her room before he could stop her again.

Once inside, she hastily stripped her robe away and flung it to the floor, uncaring that it would be a wrinkled mess by morning. Jane would be delighted to have something maid-ish to do.

The single window was open, but the heat of the room was near-stifling. Between that and the lingering desire burning between her legs, finding sleep was going to be the devil.

Yet she managed to do it, and Rhys haunted every single one of her dreams.

Chapter Eighteen

MARGERY WAS DELIGHTED to find Mr. Digby in the dining room the following morning and not Rhys. "Good morning, my lord." She offered a slight curtsey.

He stood from the table. "Good morning, Miss Derrington. Your loveliness steals my breath."

He had to be lying—she looked wilted from the heat, despite employing her fan to the best of her ability.

He inclined his head toward her accessory. "This is a day I should like to carry one of those. Though I daresay I might be a laughingstock."

Her lips pulled into a smile. "Probably." She closed her fan and selected a cake from the sideboard, then took a seat at the table with Mr. Digby's assistance. "Thank you," she said, looking up at him.

He retook his seat. "I hope you slept well. I'm afraid this heat robbed me of some much-needed slumber."

"It's oppressive, isn't it?"

"Intolerable," came a deep voice from the doorway.

Margery looked over to see Rhys moving over the threshold. His dark hair was brushed back from his striking features, and he was expertly garbed from starched cravat to polished boot. He didn't look wilted at all. He looked virile and fresh, damn him.

Mr. Digby stood. "Good morning, Mr. Bowen."

Rhys scrutinized the baron thoroughly.

"Mr. Bowen, this is Mr. Digby," Margery said.

Rhys inclined his head. "I'm pleased to make your

acquaintance."

Digby nodded in response. "Mr. Bowen."

After helping himself to breakfast at the sideboard, Rhys sat beside Margery. "How coincidental to see you here in Caerwent, Mr. Digby." He shot Margery a glance that seemed to carry some sort of meaning, but she had no idea what.

Mr. Digby opened his mouth to respond, however Margery cut him off before he could say anything about the treasure. Until Rhys made a decision about whether he was going to listen to his friend from the Order or continue on their quest, she didn't plan to tell him about moving forward with Mr. Digby's help. She gave Digby a look that she hoped conveyed the message that he shouldn't mention their dinner conversation. "Mr. Digby is here to tour the Roman ruins."

Digby smiled at her, seeming to understand. "Indeed."

Rhys looked between them, a mild frown tugging at the corners of his mouth. "They're fascinating."

Digby pivoted toward Margery. "I was hoping you would join me."

She was most anxious to learn whether he'd come up with a plan to access the church. "That would be lovely, thank you."

"It's going to be quite hot again today," Rhys observed, buttering a piece of bread. "You might be advised to postpone your excursion until the weather is more temperate."

"Actually, I'd planned to go right after breakfast, before the day becomes too warm. The morning air is rather cool and refreshing after the stifling heat of the inn, wouldn't you say?" Digby asked Margery.

"I would," she agreed, noting the slight narrowing of Rhys's eyes in Digby's direction.

Rhys moved his perturbed stare to Margery. "We were to return to Hollyhaven today."

They'd discussed it, but nothing had been resolved. In fact, any tentative plans they'd made had become moot with the disappearance of the manuscripts. She gave him a questioning look. "I believe our plans have changed. I *believe* you promised to find something that was lost."

"There is that." He took a bite of bread, his eyes glittering. He seemed quite perturbed this morning. He was the one who was considering ending their partnership—why should he be angry? Because he wanted her to stop the quest too, or maybe . . . Maybe he simply didn't like seeing her with Digby.

Rhys's potential jealousy stirred a sense of feminine pride. She batted her eyelashes at him. "Unless you've decided to return home without completing your objective?"

He scowled at her briefly before schooling his expression into an inscrutable mask. "I haven't *decided* anything."

Then why was he suggesting they return to Hollyhaven? She caught the dark look he directed toward Digby and confirmed her suspicion. He *was* jealous.

"What is your objective?" Digby asked before taking a drink of ale.

Rhys sent Margery a look that clearly said, *thank you for calling attention to our* secret *quest.* She returned his regard with a subtly raised brow. He was the one who'd made it *unsecret* by telling first Penn and then Septon about it.

Rhys straightened his shoulders. "I'm cataloguing certain antiquarian finds. In fact, if you don't mind, I'll accompany you on your tour today."

Now it was Margery's turn to scowl. "You said it was too hot for such activity."

He smiled calmly, sending a nod toward Digby. "I think Digby has the right of it. If we go early and return before the sun is high, we should be comfortable enough."

Margery looked at Digby who was now wearing a vague frown. He glanced at her and they exchanged looks that said they'd have to postpone any discussion about the treasure. That, or rudely deny Rhys the opportunity to accompany them. Although, Margery wasn't sure that would be effective. In his current mood, she couldn't guess what he might do.

Digby's smile seemed forced. "Excellent."

Margery finished her cake and stood. Both men got to their feet. "I just need to fetch my hat," she said, picking up her fan.

"As do I." Rhys pulled her chair back so she could exit. "We'll meet you out front, Digby."

Margery hurried upstairs with Rhys heavy on her heels. He followed her directly into her chamber where Jane was preparing to take the laundry downstairs. She dipped a curtsey, muttered "Pardon me," then stepped around them.

Margery snatched her broadest-brimmed hat from a hook and nearly collided with Rhys, who was standing behind her. "Don't you have to get your hat? In *your* room?"

"I will. What in the devil are you doing taking an unchaperoned tour with Digby?"

"'Unchaperoned'? You must have feathers in your

head. A public walk with Mr. Digby is far more appropriate than," her mind fumbled to find the right words, but in the end she simply gestured between them, "*this*."

His brows pitched low over his furious eyes. "There's a villain out there—someone who's sought to do you harm."

"So Septon says." She set her hat atop her head. "I'm just as safe with Digby as I am with you."

"Not if he's the villain."

She glanced in the mirror hung on the wall and tied the bonnet beneath her jaw. "You're just saying that because you're jealous."

"I'm not."

She adjusted the bow before turning to give him a saucy stare. "Not *saying* that because you're jealous, or are you *not* jealous?"

He gritted his teeth, and his flesh deepened in color. He hadn't gone red—no, she didn't think his complexion was capable of that. He only looked darker, more intense. Ridiculously handsome. "I'm saying that because he was one of the men who attended Stratton's party. What if Digby's a member of the Order who's gone off?"

She'd completely forgotten Digby's name had been on the list. "Septon's name was also on the list and you trust him."

"I've known Septon a long time."

"Yes, you keep reminding me of that." She tried not to let her frustration with Rhys cloud her judgment. She would be wary with Digby. "I highly doubt Digby is a member of the Order. He had nothing but unpleasant things to say about their methods."

"What the hell have you discussed with him? The

Order? The treasure?" He stood staring at her, his hands on his hips.

Margery licked her suddenly dry lips. She felt like the time she and her father been caught sneaking into the kitchen by their housekeeper, Mrs. Ingle. "He's an Arthurian enthusiast. We discussed the Order at dinner last night."

"And the treasure, I'd warrant." He shook his head. "If he had derogatory things to say about the Order, that could support him going against them."

"Why is that a bad thing? I realize Septon is your friend, but he's a member of an organization that physically attacked you. I can still see the outline of the bruise on your temple. I think that leaving the Order would only add to Digby's credibility." She set her hand on her hip. "I've an idea. Why don't you just ask him if he's a member?"

"And if he is corrupt, how would that turn out?" He scrubbed his hand against his chin. "Members have tattoos on their legs. If we can verify he has one, we'll know for certain."

"And how on earth are we going to do that?"

He shrugged. "It's hot. Perhaps we could find some water to dip our toes in. When he removes his stocking, we'll see the tattoo."

"Or not, if it doesn't exist." She shook her head at him, confounded by how this conversation had deteriorated. "A moment ago you were lecturing me about propriety, and now you want us to present our bare feet and ankles. Have you been locked up with your books for so long that you have absolutely no notion of what's acceptable?" She ignored the irony in her question, considering that she had been the one to go to his bedchamber two nights ago.

"At least my academic pursuits provide me with an excuse. What's the reason for your lapse in rectitude?"

She gasped, then narrowed her eyes at him. "I'm leaving." She brushed past him and strode into the corridor.

"Go on ahead. I'll catch up to you," he said darkly. "I always will."

AFTER A TORTUROUS morning of enduring Digby fawning all over Margery and her seeming to not only appreciate it, but *encourage* it, Rhys was ready for a drink. And a long soak in a cold bath. He settled for a large basin of cold water and several pieces of toweling.

As he dropped his boots to the floor and peeled his stockings from his feet, he mused over his failed attempt to find even a small pond for them to plunge their feet into during their excursion. As a result, he still had no idea if Digby was a member of the Order. Which meant he had to go and ask Septon.

And that meant he had to decide what he was going to do—continue searching for the treasure or succumb to his old friend's plea.

First, however, he was going to find some relief. He stripped off his clothes until he wore only his breeches. Then he wetted a towel and dragged it over his chest, closing his eyes at the respite the cool water provided.

He heard a door close and opened his eyes. Then he heard the creak of the adjoining door as Margery stepped into his room. And immediately halted upon seeing him.

Her hand clutched the edge of the door. "You're . .

."

He nearly smiled at her obvious discomfort. "Undressed?" he offered blithely. "It's nothing you haven't seen before."

She glared at him, then closed the door. "Jane's gone to find some relief in the shade. I would've joined her, but I want an answer from you about the treasure. We can't keep bickering."

He took a perverse pleasure from bickering with her. Her cheeks flushed and her breasts heaved. It reminded him of when they'd been in bed together. "I'm still thinking about it." He was almost settled, but he was enjoying her indignation far too much. He dragged the wet cloth over his shoulders and the back of his neck and sighed.

She stared at his movements, licking her lips as she'd done that morning. Had she no idea what she was doing to him?

Rhys's cock twitched. If they weren't careful, this could turn into something they were both trying to avoid. Perhaps he oughtn't tease her.

"When are you going to make up your mind?" she asked, crossing her arms and then dropping them almost immediately, probably because such a stance was too hot. Damn, but the room was sweltering.

"Soon."

"You're only being difficult because you're jealous of Digby. There's no reason for you to be."

He lowered the cloth into the water once more. "Isn't there? You giggled over Digby's every comment. I've never heard you giggle before."

There was a glint of something in her gaze—female satisfaction probably. "Perhaps because your company isn't as diverting."

He snorted, wringing out the towel. Then, because he simply couldn't resist, he scrubbed the cloth over his stomach and lowered his lids to give her a seductive stare. "I wager you find my company *plenty* diverting."

She wore her simplest dress—it fastened in the front—and with quick flicks of her fingertips, she had the bodice open and strode toward him. "Give me that."

She snatched the towel from his hands and dipped it into the water. She twisted the excess out, but not enough, and when she brought the cloth to her chest, rivulets ran down her breasts, soaking her stays and surely the chemise beneath. He imagined the outline of her form with her undergarments plastered to her flesh and went immediately and painfully hard. Though he'd brought himself to release after she'd left last night—there'd been no avoiding it—he felt as though he hadn't achieved orgasm in quite some time.

She cast her head back and sighed deeply as she pressed the cloth against her neck.

Or maybe ever.

He took the cloth from her and rewetted it, squeezing it before bringing it back to her breasts. He swiped the towel over her garments, thoroughly wetting them, his gaze connected with hers.

Her lips parted, and he fought to keep from kissing her. He was treading a very fine line.

She reached down to the table, on which the basin sat, and picked up a second towel. She dipped it into the water and then dabbed it over his chest. A thick stream ran down his flesh. With her spare hand, she caught the moisture on her fingertip and brought it to her lips. Her gaze never left his as she sucked her finger dry.

He stifled a groan. They were playing a dangerous game, one neither of them seemed prepared to halt.

He dragged the table a few feet to position it by the bed. Then he arched a brow at her in invitation. He held his breath, waiting to see if she would put a stop to their flirtation.

Meeting his inquiry with a beguiling stare, she shrugged out of her bodice, peeling her gown to her waist. Her fingers plucked at the fastenings of her stays until it gapped away from her breasts. She pulled the garment free of her gown and dropped it on the floor.

With slow, deliberate steps, she went to the basin and soaked her towel. After barely squeezing the water from it, she swept it over her chemise, thoroughly dampening the linen until it clung to her nipples.

Rhys's mouth was dry enough with the heat of the day, but now it felt like a desert. He licked his lips as his cock turned to granite. He dropped his cloth into the basin and prowled around the table. She turned with him until her backside met the bed.

He curled his arm around her lower back and guided her backward, but kept her from hitting the mattress. He took the wet towel from her fingers and squeezed the water from it, watching it trickle down to her breasts and slide over her chemise and her flesh beneath it.

He tossed the cloth into the basin and cupped her now-cool breast. Her nipple was already stiff, but he watched as the pink flesh pebbled around the tip. Pressing his thumb and forefinger around the peak, he squeezed just hard enough until she gasped.

Sliding his hand up over breast and collarbone, he slipped it inside the capped sleeve and pushed it down over her shoulder. She tried to pull her arm through the hole, but emitted a groan of frustration when she couldn't.

He tugged at the sleeve and rent the seam. The front of the garment fell forward, exposing her breast. She threw the remains of her sleeve to the floor as his gaze devoured her pale flesh.

Her hand came around his neck and pulled his head down. He needed no further urging and set his teeth around her nipple, to graze the soft skin. She arched into him, her fingers twining in his hair and holding him tight against her.

He drew her into his mouth, tasting her sweet, wet flesh. He cupped her as he moved to the other breast, giving it the same exacting attention he'd given the first. He licked and suckled her, his fevered body reacting to the soft moans and whimpers coming from her throat.

Her once-cool flesh had heated again. He reached back for the cloth in the basin, but she pushed him upright. Then she spun him and shoved him onto the bed. He had no idea what she was about, but didn't protest.

Taking one of the towels, she wrung it out over his chest, dribbling the last of the water down his belly and onto the front of his breeches. As the cool water soaked through the fabric, he closed his eyes and cast his head back against the mattress.

He felt her tongue on his nipple, lapping the water up. He thrust his fingers into her hair and kneaded her scalp. She moved across his chest, trailing her lips over him and repeated the process of licking his other nipple clean. Then she traveled downward, her wicked tongue teasing his flesh and driving him to the brink of his control.

Down, down, she went until he felt the front of his breeches fall away. He'd been so focused on her mouth that he'd failed to notice her undoing his fall. She peeled his garments away, dragging his breeches and small clothes down his legs.

He kept his eyes closed, afraid to break the quiet spell that had fallen over the room. The afternoon was impossibly hot and hushed, like the world had ceased to spin. His awareness was full of her and the things she was doing to his body.

Water trickled over his cock and her hand worked it into his torrid flesh. Like last night, she handled him expertly, her grip precise and intense.

When her tongue flicked the head, his eyes shot open and he tugged at her hair. "Margery," he growled.

"Shhhh." Her breath gusted over him, heating him to an even higher degree. She took him into her mouth, her tongue stroking him inside.

He clutched her head and squeezed his eyes closed again, unable to stand the erotic image of her sucking his cock. No, he wanted to watch her, otherwise he might not believe it was actually happening.

He opened his eyes as she moved up and down in earnest, her mouth and tongue working over him. Sweet heavens, how had she learned to do that? Again, he didn't want to know. He only wanted to enjoy, to surrender to her completely.

She cupped his stones, driving him to lift his hips into her mouth. Lightly squeezing, she sucked him deep until he nudged the back of her throat. He moaned, his orgasm threatening.

He pulled at her head, trying to stop her before it was too late, but she refused to be deterred. He lurched back from her, scooting across the bed as he simultaneously tugged her hair. "Margery. Stop."

She straightened, her lips full and red, her eyes glazed with passion. "Why?"

He sat up. "Because." His brain wouldn't work. "I was too close."

She looked at him as if he were a lunatic. "And that's bad?"

"I suppose not if you don't mind me coming in your mouth."

Her already pink cheeks deepened with color. "I see. I don't think I'd mind."

He moved to the edge of the bed and grabbed her waist, pulling her between his legs. "You're going to kill me." He kissed her hard. "But it will be the sweetest death a man could hope for." He took her lips and devoured her mouth.

She moaned, her hands cupping his head as she returned his kiss with fiery need. "I'm . . . so . . . hot." She let him go to fumble with her dress. There was a drawstring at the waist. He pulled it loose and she shoved the dress to the floor. The chemise soon followed, leaving her clad in nothing but her stockings and shoes, which she kicked off.

She reached down to undo her garters, but he brushed her hands aside, impatient for his turn with her body. "Leave them."

He turned her, reversing their positions. "Get on the bed." Copying what she'd done, he picked up a sodden cloth and sluiced water over her bare flesh. She gasped, her body arching as the coolness met her heat. He twisted the excess over her mound and watched the water slide between her folds. He dropped the towel and licked her, tasting both the water and her.

She twitched and cried out. "Rhys."

He smiled against her and dipped his fingers into the basin. Then he slid them over her, loving the sound of her rasping breath as he massaged the cool water into her ripe flesh. Her legs parted, inviting him inside. He slipped a finger into her heat and closed his eyes at the way she gripped him.

Opening his eyes to watch the sensations play across her face, he stroked his finger out and then in again, slowly at first. Her thighs widened even more as her body drew him deeper inside. Her hips began to move and he increased his pace, his finger working her with delicate precision.

Her fingers tangled into his hair and she urged him to go faster, but he wasn't close to being finished with her. He withdrew his finger and replaced it with his tongue, sliding into her. Her cry pierced the silence and it was his turn to say, "Shhhh."

Her thighs tensed around him as he licked and ate at her, his lips and tongue working her flesh until her hips moved in a mad frenzy. He added his finger back into the storm and sought the spot inside of her that would drive her over the edge.

Again, she made an animalistic sound, low and desperate, and he knew he had her. He sucked hard on her clit as he pressed against that spot with his finger over and over again. He splayed his hand against her thigh, massaging her, then slipped it beneath her to lift her into his mouth.

Her fingers tightened in his hair and her muscles clenched around his finger as she came hard into his mouth. She let out a series of moans and cries—he could tell she was at least trying to be quiet, but she was too far gone to control herself.

He clutched her backside and held her firmly, letting

his tongue coax her down from the peak of ecstasy. When her orgasm had subsided, he stepped back and used the remaining cloth in the basin to cool himself, wiping his face and chest.

She sat up, her eyes clear and wide. "Thank you. That was . . . even better than last time."

Her tone was exceptionally calm, and her demeanor equally so. Were they . . . finished? "Are you leaving?"

She glanced down at his erection. "Would you like me to finish what I started?"

God, yes, but not as badly as he wanted to make love to her. "No, I want to bury myself so deep inside of you that I don't know where I end and where you begin."

Her lips parted and her gaze softened. She clasped his hand and drew him back onto the bed with her. "Then by all means, please do."

Chapter Nineteen

REASON TOLD HER to end this now, but the desire still curling inside of her demanded she forge ahead. Nothing about this made any sense, but—and maybe it was the heat—she didn't care.

Rhys came over her, his body hot and heavy, but in the most delicious way. He stroked between her thighs, making her shiver despite the sweltering temperature. Then the head of his cock was there, nudging her open. She lifted her hips and opened to him, bringing her hands low on his back to guide him.

With a gentle glide, he slid into her. "Put your legs around me."

She did as he bade, curling her legs around his hips, which brought him further inside of her.

Braced on his hands positioned on either side of her head, he gazed down at her, his eyes nearly black with desire. His face was set in tense lines as he began to move inside of her. Slowly at first with a soft friction. Sensitive from her earlier orgasm, every thrust tingled through her. She teetered at the edge of another tumble into the abyss.

He rotated his hips, plunging deeper than ever before. She dug her fingers into his backside and cried out. His mouth covered hers and swallowed her cries.

His tongue mimicked the wicked thrust of his cock and he was right—she didn't know where he ended and she began.

He drove faster, hitting a spot that made lights

dance behind her shuttered eyes. He broke the kiss, his breathing coming fast and hard. She rose to meet him, welcoming him into her heat. His mouth came down on her collarbone, nipping her flesh and she came apart. Wave after wave of ecstasy broke over her as she came again. The tease of orgasm she'd felt last time he'd been inside her hadn't remotely prepared her for this maelstrom of sensation. She fought to keep her cries to a minimum, but she was a slave to the release sweeping through her.

Vaguely, she was aware that he was still thrusting, his hips moving in a circular motion. Bliss continued to arc over her as he kissed a hot, wet trail up her neck to her ear.

"You're an adventurous woman, are you not?"

"Yes," she breathed, unable to give the word proper volume.

"I'm going to turn you over now."

She opened her eyes, took in the harsh set of his mouth and the ebony luster of his eyes. She nodded.

He pulled out of her and flipped her over. "Get on your knees."

She obeyed him again, her body quivering from the multiple releases, yet still eager for more.

He guided her forward. "Clasp the bed." He pushed her legs apart and caressed the curve of her backside. She moaned as his fingers glided along her sensitive folds. He pressed one inside and pumped her a few times. Then his tongue swept over her and she clenched the headboard as white-hot pleasure burst over her. She didn't know how much more she could stand.

"Rhys. Please."

He came into her then, but this time it wasn't slow

and it wasn't gentle. He drove inside of her, plunging deep and then withdrawing. When he swept forward again, she pushed back, meeting his thrust. Her nerve endings were ultrasensitive—it was as if her previous orgasm hadn't really finished, or he'd coaxed it back. Whatever the reason, her body quivered with rapture.

"God, yes, Margery." He gripped her hips and let himself go, pushing into her with frenzied strokes.

His hand skimmed up her side and around to pinch her nipple. The sensations thrumming through her intensified as another orgasm shot through her. She moaned while he worked her breast and continued his relentless assault. He stiffened, and his low groan filled her senses.

Then he was gone from her and she pushed back, looking for him.

"Had . . . to . . . get . . . out."

Like he had before, right. At last, sanity invaded her haze of delirium. She slowly turned over. He had climbed off the bed and was cleaning himself with one of the towels. He wetted a new one and handed it to her with a smoldering look. "There's no escaping the heat today, I'm afraid."

Apparently not.

He turned from her and she tidied herself, but mostly she enjoyed the cool cloth against her heated skin.

He drew on his small clothes and breeches and picked up her chemise. He offered it to her with an apologetic smile. "I'm afraid it's quite damp."

She took it from him. "So is your bed." She pulled the chemise over her head and realized it was also in pieces—drooping over her breast and missing one sleeve. No matter, it would give Jane something else to do and Margery would simply say it had torn when she removed it.

He buttoned his fall, but didn't move to don his shirt. Not that she blamed him, she couldn't bring herself to put anything on over her chemise. But she held the corner up to keep it from gapping away from her chest.

"You, ah, seemed to know what you were doing," he said. "It's none of my business of course, but I wanted to say you are . . . quite good."

Feminine satisfaction blossomed through her. "Thank you. As are you. It's also none of my business, but I wondered if you'd had a bit of practice, since you attend Lord Trevor's parties."

He coughed. "Ah, perhaps." He sent her a provocative glance. "I was a bit more . . . relaxed at Oxford a decade ago."

She suddenly wished she'd known him then. When he was young and maybe a bit wild. Probably less self-assured. She slid a look at his profile, took in the strong set of his jaw, the ever-present intelligence in his gaze. On second thought, she couldn't imagine him without his flashes of arrogance, and what's more, she didn't want to.

"My aunt told me many things about what happens between men and women."

He wetted a fresh cloth and laid it over the back of his neck. "Were you to be married?"

Margery shrugged. "Not specifically, no. Aunt Agnes chose a . . . different path as a young woman. She explained to me why she'd chosen to become someone's mistress, and she was happy to satisfy my inquisitive nature."

"I see," he murmured. "I appreciate an inquisitive

woman very much."

"As an academic, I'm sure you do." Margery redipped her towel and wiped it over her arms. She was still hot, but the inferno their lovemaking had wrought had passed.

Lovemaking.

Good heavens, what was she doing? She struggled to remember why she'd come into his room in the first place. To demand an answer from him about the treasure. And he'd said he was still thinking about it. That he even considered choosing Septon over her—and that's what it felt like, she realized—threatened to overheat her again. She shouldn't care . . . but she did. Suddenly she wanted to get as far away from him as possible.

She scooped up her clothing.

He bent to help her.

"I don't require your assistance," she snapped, furious with herself for allowing this to happen again.

He stepped back. "What's wrong? Why are you upset?"

She straightened, her arms full of her dress and stays. "You're asking that after what we just did again? This heat affected my brain."

"Your brain? I'm fairly certain that is not the body part—or parts— affected. I can say with ease that my brain didn't figure into the equation at all."

He was right. They'd both surrendered to their desire, something they couldn't seem to avoid. "You're right. I was angry with myself, not you." She softened her tone and relaxed the tension rioting through her shoulders. "I still don't expect or want marriage."

He looked away. "Neither do I. In fact, I think the sooner our association is over, the better."

Margery flinched at the harshness of his tone. Did he really mean that? It was what she wanted, wasn't it, to get back to her life? "Our partnership can end now. You've lost interest in the treasure, and I still plan to find it. You may go your way and I will go mine. I won't need your help to complete my quest and I shall find my own way back to Gloucester." She'd also have to figure out how in the world she'd sell the treasure, but perhaps Digby could assist with that.

Rhys's answering stare was disturbingly penetrating. "What about Penn? You promised to visit him when we returned from this trip."

Oh, dear. She'd quite forgotten about Penn. She was mucking this up horribly, all because she found Rhys Bowen too bloody impossible to resist.

She hugged the clothing tighter to herself. "Penn will understand. I'll write to him."

"I'm sure that will appease a young boy whose mother recently abandoned him."

Margery sucked in sweltering air. Emotions that she kept stringently locked away bubbled to the surface. Turning before she exposed something foolish, she went back to her room, struggling with the door as she juggled her clothes. At last, she managed to get it closed.

Dropping her things in a heap, she went to the open window and vainly sought the slightest breeze to wash away the frustration and desperation curling inside of her.

The door creaked, forcing her to turn. Rhys stepped over the threshold carrying her shoes. "You forgot these." He set them on the floor gently.

She ought to thank him, but she was still fighting with her own inner turmoil.

"I'm sorry about what I said. Penn is not your responsibility; he's mine."

She nodded, appreciating his apology. A slight breeze tickled her neck, but was gone as quickly as it had come.

"Please consider abandoning the search."

She looked at him sharply, surprised he'd ask her, knowing that she needed the treasure.

"Just listen to me," he said. "Your safety is in question. I can't allow you to continue alone."

His presumption fired her temper. She felt raw, vulnerable. "First, I am not your responsibility. Second, I won't be alone." She tried to bite back the words as soon as they left her mouth.

"You won't?" He scrutinized her a long moment while she attempted to behave as if she hadn't just said something she shouldn't. "Do *not* tell me Digby will be helping you."

"I won't."

"But he is." He ran his hand through his hair. "Bloody hell, Margery. We still don't know if Digby is a member of the Order who's gone off on his own."

He was back to that? "I find it highly unlikely. He's an Arthurian enthusiast, not some clandestine steward of a centuries-old group like *your friend*."

He inhaled loudly, as if he were exasperated with her—and he assuredly was. "Yes, Septon is my friend, which is why I trust him more than Digby."

"Yet *Septon* is the one who is actually part of an organization that is seeking to stop us from finding this treasure."

"For good reason." His voice climbed.

She fought to keep her tone even. "So he says. He could very easily be lying in order to obtain the treasure for himself."

Rhys glanced at the ceiling, the muscles in his jaw flexing. "Please consider it. I'll compensate you for your book." He held up his hand. "No, don't tell me you won't take the money. It's my fault it was stolen, and my reimbursing you for its loss doesn't constitute any other sort of *lurid* transaction."

She remembered using that word with him after they'd met. That seemed so long ago now, but it hadn't even been a fortnight. "I can't abandon the search. I won't."

His mouth pressed into a disappointed line. "Then we are at an impasse."

Footsteps sounded in the hallway.

"You have to go," she said.

He hesitated and sweat broke out on her neck—both at the fear of being discovered and because of the tumult in his gaze.

In the end, he turned and left, closing the door firmly behind him.

GETTING FULLY DRESSED was almost painful in the oppressive heat, but it had been necessary in order to leave the inn. And Rhys hadn't been able to suffer another moment in his sweltering room—or next door to Margery.

This afternoon had been an avoidable disaster. They'd both succumbed to a fever brought on by the temperature and their unquenchable desire. At least his was unquenchable. He'd wanted her again as soon as he'd climbed off the bed.

But then things had degraded, and it seemed a repeat of today's blissful events would never come to pass. He scowled, moving into a grove of trees that provided some much-welcome shade. To his left, the inn rose a few hundred yards away. He turned and quickened his pace, eager to put distance between himself and the woman bedeviling his thoughts.

Blast it all, he couldn't let her continue the search for the treasure without him, not when a faceless hazard lurked. He grunted. Not faceless. Digby would be with her, and for now, Rhys considered him a threat. Was that the reason for his distrust of the man—jealousy? Yes, but he had no cause for it since Margery didn't seem interested in a permanent future with either one of them.

He was going to have to maintain the search with her, and Septon would have to keep the Order away from them. Meanwhile, Rhys would work to convince Margery to turn whatever they found over to the Order after they found it. Perhaps he could arrange things to have the Order pay her for the treasure—even if the money actually came from Rhys.

He loosened his cravat, uncaring that he might look less than dressed. Who was he going to encounter anyway?

Bloody Digby.

The gentleman, his own cravat hanging loose, walked toward him. He offered an affable smile. "Deuced hot. This is about the coolest spot to be had, here under the trees." He gestured toward the canopy shading them.

Rhys wasn't interested in Digby's observations or small talk of any kind. His abject frustration boiled over. "What are you really doing in Caerwent?"

Digby stopped short and blinked at him. "I'm not sure what you mean."

"I'm calling your bluff," Rhys said softly, but with enough menace to make the other man's eyes widen. "Are you a member of the Order of the Round Table? And don't pretend you don't know what I'm talking about."

Digby's features relaxed and he inclined his head. "I am not."

Rhys was taken aback by the man's admission, despite having demanded it. Which didn't mean he was trustworthy. He glanced at Digby's calf. "Prove it."

Digby opened his mouth but then closed it abruptly. He walked to the nearest tree, leaned against the trunk, and removed his boot. After dropping it to the ground, he peeled his stocking down to his ankle and revealed his pale, untattooed flesh. "Will this satisfy?"

Damn it all to hell. Rhys would've wagered his library that Digby was a member, particularly if he was actually an Arthurian expert. "You're at least aware of the Order if you knew to show me that."

"I'm an Arthurian enthusiast." He cocked his head as he drew his stocking back up his calf. "I know many things."

Things he'd presumably told Margery if she'd consented to partner with him to find the treasure. When and how had that come about? Likely as soon as Rhys had said he was considering stopping the quest, something he now bitterly regretted. "Tell me some of these things."

Digby drew on his boot, then turned and walked away from the inn. Rhys fell into step beside him, keeping a few feet of distance between them—as much as the copse would allow.

"I became interested in Arthur at Cambridge. I've spent a great deal of time researching everything to do with him and his knights. I've found several mentions of the Order."

Why hadn't Rhys ever heard of them? Because he hadn't ever specialized in Arthurian texts. Not like his father, who'd sought them out periodically. Had he known of the Order? "What do you know of it?"

"It was founded in at least the eighth century—that's the earliest writing I've found that references its existence. However, I believe it may be older."

It was, according to Septon, but Rhys didn't say so. "If you're not a member of the Order, yet you are an Arthurian enthusiast, you must admit your presence here is rather coincidental when we are on a quest for Arthurian treasure."

Digby removed his hat and wiped a handkerchief over his forehead. Like Rhys, he'd forsaken gloves in the heat. "My being here at this particular time is coincidence, I assure you. Caerwent is an important location in Arthurian legend, and I come here from time to time, always hoping I'll see something new or make a discovery." His smile was self-deprecating. "I haven't been successful yet. I should tell you, however, that I tracked the de Valery manuscript to Miss Derrington's aunts. It was the reason I tried to court her several weeks ago."

Rhys gritted his teeth. The man had practically been stalking Margery. "That doesn't exactly substantiate your claim that your being in Caerwent just now is a happy accident. Are you aware Miss Derrington's manuscript has gone missing?"

Digby stopped and turned, the hat still in his hand. "Yes, because I took it."

Rhys rushed forward and grabbed the man by the front of his shirt. He pushed him back against the nearest tree. "Where are they?" he ground out between his teeth.

Digby didn't fight him. "Safe. I planned to tell Miss Derrington as soon as I could speak with her privately."

"Are you aware that one of those books was entrusted to my custody as well as hers?" Rhys tightened his hold. "Why wouldn't you tell me as well?"

"I wasn't sure of your association with the Order. You and Septon are old friends."

"You're a treasure hunter," Rhys spat.

Digby's eyes flashed. He wrapped his hand around Rhys's wrist and tried to extract his grip. "No more than you. I save Arthurian artifacts from the Order. Once it gains possession of something, the members tuck it away, hiding it from the world when the item should be studied and enjoyed."

Rhys couldn't argue with that. In fact, he reluctantly appreciated the other man's opinion. He loosened his hold and let his hand drop away. "You make a habit of going around and plucking up antiquities before the Order finds them?"

Digby smoothed his garments. "What started as a hobby has become a bit of an obsession, I'm afraid."

"And what do you do with these items?"

"It depends. Forgive me if I'd rather not say." Digby didn't trust him.

Rhys begrudgingly admired the man for not being stupid. "I'm not a member of the Order and I don't plan to be." He stepped away from Digby, who relaxed against the tree. "I'm inclined to agree with you regarding keeping these antiquities from being lost or forgotten."

Digby exhaled. "That's relieving to hear. You must realize the Order is dangerous. Are you aware their ranks have included thieves and murderers?"

Despite the heat of the afternoon, a chill snaked down Rhys's spine. The cipher glass suddenly felt heavy in his pocket, and Rhys resisted the urge to touch it to ensure its security. "Who and why have they killed?"

Digby's gaze turned dark. "Anyone who opposes their objective. They tried to kill de Valery and succeeded in killing his brother."

The perspiration along Rhys's back and neck turned cold. "How do you know that?"

"I have a written account of a hanging just after de Valery wrote the manuscripts." He nodded toward the inn. "When we get back, I can show it to you. De Valery's brother was executed by the Order for crafting a device that could be used to decipher a treasure map."

The cipher glass. Rhys's fingers absolutely itched to take it firmly in his grasp. "The Order truly will stop at nothing."

"Including killing their own. You see, de Valery and his brother were members of the Order."

Rhys couldn't prevent his sharp inhalation. "How do you know this?"

"Because the written account is from de Valery himself."

"Where did you find such a thing?" That in itself was practically a treasure.

"As I said, I've made an occupation of locating important Arthurian artifacts. I tracked down some of de Valery's writings several months ago—it's how I determined that Miss Derrington's aunts probably had one of his manuscripts."

Rhys's neck continued to prickle. "Wait. If you took the books, did you also steal the other manuscript from Stratton?"

Digby glanced away. His face was already red from the temperature, but the color deepened. "I did. I was afraid the Order was going to get to it first. But as you know, the book was a fake."

Rhys advanced on him again, but Digby held up his hand in defense. "Were you behind the attempts to steal Miss Derrington's books?" He was going to beat the man senseless if he was.

Confusion marred the other man's features. "What attempts? I only took them yesterday when I saw you arrive at the church."

"On two occasions, someone tried to steal her book, which put her at considerable risk."

Digby frowned. "I understand your consternation, and I feel precisely the same. I guarantee the Order was behind it."

"Septon assures me they weren't."

Blinking, Digby looked at him incredulously. "After what I just told you about the Order, you'd still take his word?"

Rhys had respected Septon enough to listen to his plea, and even be persuaded by it.

"You must also consider that Septon isn't aware of every move the Order makes," Digby warned.

Septon had said there were people above him in the Order. It wasn't only possible that the Order was behind the attempts to steal the book, it suddenly seemed likely. Trepidation mingled with outrage. Rhys was first and foremost a historian and a scholar, and the value of this find was too important to ignore. The Order might try to stop them from finding the treasure, but Rhys was going to do it anyway. He had to—for himself and for Margery.

He turned and started back toward the inn. "What sort of scheme did you and Miss Derrington hatch? And when?" He hadn't meant to say that last bit out loud and kept his other questions to himself.

Had it been this morning during breakfast, or had they met even earlier? Last night, perhaps, while Rhys had gone to Septon's? He couldn't wait to interrogate her about her plan.

Digby strolled beside him and kept his gaze fixed straight ahead. "You should discuss that with her."

Had she promised Digby a share of its worth? As if it were her treasure to control. Yes, one of the books was hers, but the other belonged to Nash and he'd entrusted it to both her and Rhys to use to find the treasure. And they'd found the cipher glass—a necessary tool to their success—together. Not that any of those facts gave them ownership of a still unknown object.

"Do you know what the treasure is?" Rhys asked.

"I don't. Like you, I can only theorize. I think we can assume it's very important."

On that, they agreed. A breeze stirred and Rhys removed his hat to welcome the cooler air. He stopped and pivoted toward Digby. "What do you want?"

"The same as you, I suspect: the truth."

That was precisely what Rhys wanted. Facts and evidence were the tenets of his discipline. "You mentioned a map. There isn't one. Just the code, which Miss Derrington presumably shared with you."

Digby nodded, then a slow smile crept over him.

"There *is* a map. We just have to figure out how to find it."

Chapter Twenty

MARGERY PICKED HER way down the stairs behind Mrs. Powell. The innkeeper's wife had come up to inform her that Mr. Bowen *and* Mr. Digby had requested her presence in the dining room. Nothing good could come from them being together. Nevertheless, she answered the summons and when Mrs. Powell turned to go toward the kitchen, Margery continued to the dining room.

The door was ajar. When she pushed it wider, both men stood from their chairs. An array of refreshments was laid out before them, including a pitcher of lemonade. Margery practically dove for it.

However, Mr. Digby rushed to pour her a glass first, saving her from committing a gauche act. The heat, it seemed, was turning her into a half-wit.

She accepted the glass with a smile and took a sip, though she wanted to down the lot in one gulp. "Thank you."

Mr. Digby gestured to a chair. "Please, join us."

She looked from him to Rhys, who'd moved toward the open window. Both men looked as if they could melt—their cravats lacked their usual starch—but she couldn't say it detracted from Rhys in the slightest. He still managed to appear incredibly masculine, and the moisture at his temples only reminded her of earlier . . . something she'd do better to forget.

Turning from him, she took the chair Digby indicated. "Mrs. Powell said you both wanted to see me?" She sipped her lemonade, hoping it might somehow soothe the knot in her stomach as well as her overheated temperature.

"Yes." Digby glanced at Rhys, who was still looking out the window, his features in profile. "We wanted to discuss the treasure."

Margery smoothed her damp palms over her skirt. She wished she could see Rhys's expression, but sensed he was angry. And if he'd been talking about the treasure with Digby, it seemed likely that he knew she'd already spoken to Digby about it. Anxiety curled through her. She struggled to keep her voice level. "What is it?"

Rhys pivoted, and she saw the ice in his eyes, so at odds with the summer afternoon boiling around them. "Digby and I have decided to work together to find the treasure—something I ascertain you'd already organized for yourself."

Oh, yes, he was furious.

She forced a bright smile that threatened to split her face in two. "How splendid." She longed to ask him what had changed his mind about pursuing the treasure, but suspected it had to do with his rampant jealousy regarding Digby. Although given his obvious anger toward her, that might not be the case any longer.

Rhys strode toward the table, his powerful presence seeming to dominate the room. "Digby, the books."

Digby reached under the table to the chair beside his and lifted a pair of books—the de Valery manuscripts—which he set upon the table.

Margery stood. "My book! Where did you find it?"

"He didn't," Rhys said evenly. "He stole it." The look he cast her clearly said, *see, I told you he wasn't trustworthy*. Yet, he had to have said something to Rhys to persuade him they should work together.

Thoroughly confused, she looked between the two men, ending up glaring at Digby. "Why?"

He gave her an apologetic smile as he stood and came around the table. Taking her hand, he gave her fingers a squeeze. "I'm sorry I didn't say anything last night. I was . . . nervous. Like I told you, I . . ." He lowered his voice, but Margery was fairly certain Rhys could hear him anyway. "I practically swallow my tongue when I'm around you. I'd planned to tell you this morning, but then Bowen came along with us."

She glanced at Rhys, who was watching them with a clenched jaw. She'd never seen his eyes blacker. Extracting her fingers from Digby's grip, she sat back down. "Why did you take the books?"

Digby exhaled, and he looked at the floor for a moment. "I'm not proud that I took them from you, but please know it was for a good purpose."

Rhys cleared his throat. "He gads about taking Arthurian antiquities before the Order can whisk them away and hide them from the world."

"Is that true?" she asked Digby.

He nodded as he went to sit down once more. "Mr. Bowen and I share a passion for antiquities and the desire to ensure that this treasure—whatever it is—isn't lost to the Order. Again, I deeply regret taking your book, Miss Derrington. At the time, I wasn't sure as to your motives."

She didn't forgive him for not telling her straightaway, but if Rhys had decided to work with him, that was good enough for her. Heavens, at what point had she put her faith in Rhys? She wasn't sure, but was surprised by how *good* it felt. "What will you do once you find the treasure?"

"Once *we* find it," Rhys said, "we'll assess its value and determine what to do with it. The primary objective is to find it before the Order."

Margery realized she might not see any reward from finding it, but that had been a risk all along. She thankfully had the book back and could still sell it to Rhys if necessary. She looked at Digby. "Have you formulated a plan for drawing the Order's sentinel from the church?"

Rhys came to stand at the table, between Margery and Digby. "What plan is this?"

"Mr. Digby agrees that the treasure is likely in the church, given the clue, though we're still trying to determine the importance of Anarawd." She was trying not to look at Rhys, but flicked him a glance. "He's a sixth-century scribe who may have known Arthur and his knights."

"Yes, I know." His tone carried that familiar haughtiness that both thrilled and annoyed her. "Septon told me the other night."

"So he lied to us yesterday afternoon when we asked about him?" Margery asked.

"Just as Digby here lied—by omission—about taking your book."

Digby's gaze was anguished as he looked between them. "I'm terribly sorry. I was only trying to protect them from the Order."

"You should have approached us and told us what you knew," Rhys said. "Now, redeem yourself and tell us what you know of this scribe."

"Not as much as I'd like. He may have been the one who recorded the tales in de Valery's manuscripts—from oral stories told by Gareth, one of Arthur's knights." Digby moved Margery's manuscript from the top of the other one. "It seems likely since most of the stories center around his adventures."

Margery itched to have her book back in her possession. And Lord Nash's. "May I?" She reached across and picked hers up. Wrapping her fingers around it securely, she set it down in front of her. Next to her lemonade. She reached for it just as Rhys did the same and their fingers overlapped. A shock of sexual awareness jolted her, but she was careful not to snatch her hand back lest she tumble the glass and ruin her book.

Rhys did the same thing, keeping his fingers tangled with hers. "Shall I remove it, or shall you?"

"I will. You get the tray."

He took his hand away slowly, his hand caressing hers in the process. Was that an accident?

She picked up her glass and moved it to the sideboard as Rhys did the same with the tray. With their backs to Digby, they exchanged looks that felt hotter than the day outside.

He turned and went back to the table, leaving her to rein her wanton attraction to him.

She sat down in front of her manuscript and, absently, she opened it and began to flip the pages.

"Anarawd was a monk at St. Tathyw's monastery," Digby said. "Since St. Tathyw was another part of the code, we assume the link between him and Anarawd, specifically his occupation as a scribe, is likely important."

Rhys scooted his chair closer to Margery's and looked over her shoulder at the book. "I would agree."

The two men went on discussing Anarawd and the other parts of the code while Margery continued leafing through the book. When she got to the last illustration, she paused, her fingertip lingering at the edge of the page.

This was the busiest plate in the book, with a cast of characters filling the illustration. It depicted a feast with a hamper overflowing with food and a bejeweled knife being used to carve a great roasted beast. The detail was incredibly precise, the colors rich—she'd looked at it a hundred times and yet she'd never noticed the man standing in the distance. He was very small, inconsequential and easily dismissed. He wore a light robe so that he almost blended into the background. But it was his activity that now drew her attention. He was writing.

"I think I found him."

The men grew silent.

Rhys leaned over, and she felt his presence more than saw him. "What?"

"Anarawd." She pointed to the man in the picture. "I think this is him. He's writing, like a scribe."

Digby stood abruptly, his chair clattering against the floor, and came around the table to look at the book over her shoulder. "By God."

She turned to look at Rhys, who was fixated on the illustration. "Where's the glass?"

His head came up and he gave her a harsh stare. "The what?"

Had he not told Digby they had it?

"No need to hide it from me, Bowen," Digby said. "I won't try to take it. I'm not worried about you having the device because I know you won't cloak it into nonexistence like the Order would."

Margery held out her hand, knowing he'd have it on his person.

Rhys reluctantly pulled it from his coat pocket and set it securely into her palm, his fingertips grazing her flesh and again eliciting a thrilling sensation that swept her from head to toe.

Pushing aside the irritating persistence of her desire for him, she brought the glass to her eye and regarded the illustration. She gasped as the colors altered.

"You see something?" Digby asked, his voice trilling with excitement.

She turned the glass and the picture changed slightly. It looked like stones, but she couldn't be sure what she was seeing. "Here." She returned the device to Rhys. Frustration curled through her. "Why didn't we notice this before?"

"I think because we failed to study all of the illustrations in your book after the first several revealed nothing. Shoddy investigation on our part." His tone was dark with self-derision. "I need a parchment and ink."

"I'll ask Mrs. Powell." Digby hurried from the room.

"I would've preferred not to use the glass in front of him," Rhys said in a hushed tone.

She was confused. "But you agreed to work with him."

He pressed his lips together. "He has knowledge I don't. I still don't trust him completely."

She couldn't argue with him. She'd only just begun to fully trust Rhys.

Digby returned with the required implements and handed them to Rhys. "We'll need to hurry. Mrs. Powell requires the dining room to set it for dinner."

Margery considered suggesting they move upstairs to Rhys's bedchamber because he had a large enough table for their use, however she was fairly certain that a return to the location of their last . . . *indiscretion* wasn't a good idea. Particularly if his bed was still mussed.

Rhys was already scratching a drawing across the parchment. Alternately looking through the device and sketching, he soon had a rough illustration of the stones in the hidden picture.

"May I look?" Digby asked, showing a patience Margery didn't think she could've managed.

Rhys handed him the glass.

With a reverent nod, Digby put it to his eye and immediately sucked in a breath. "It's extraordinary."

Margery studied the drawing Rhys had made. "What do you think it is?"

"If I'm not mistaken it's the stone floor of the Caerwent church. And this," he pointed to a stone that he'd shaded, "is where the treasure could be located."

Excitement thrummed in Margery's chest. "Do you know which stone that is?"

"It's hard to determine what angle this was drawn from, but it should give us a rough idea." He sat back in his chair and looked from Margery to Digby and back again. "Either way, I think it's safe to say we need to dig beneath the floor of the church."

They were so close! "If we leave now, we might have enough light." Margery glanced out the window at the sun that was rapidly descending toward the horizon.

Rhys shook his head. "No, we can't attempt this until tomorrow morning." He looked at Digby. "After we discuss the plan to remove the Order's sentinel from the equation."

Digby nodded. "I agree. We need to organize our method before rushing in. There's no telling what manner of defense the Order might have in place."

Margery frowned, disappointed at having to wait. "What do you mean?"

Digby set the glass on top of the book. "The Order will go to any lengths to protect the treasure. *Any* lengths." He exchanged a dire look with Rhys.

Margery turned to Rhys, who appeared equally grim. "What about Septon? He's your friend. Why don't you speak with him?"

Rhys shook his head. "You know that Septon asked me not to pursue the treasure."

"Is it even still there?" Margery asked. "Why wouldn't the Order have dug it up and hidden it long ago?"

"I don't think they know its precise location," Digby said. "I think that's why they tried to steal your book." At her inquiring look, he added, "Bowen told me they attacked you." A fierce look entered his eyes, as if he wanted to avenge her. It seemed, despite her telling him that she wasn't interested in courtship, he was still harboring a romantic inclination toward her.

"Does the Order keep someone at the church around the clock?" Rhys asked Digby.

"Yes, they have a few people who take turns watching. I think they must be especially vigilant right now, since they know you're hunting the treasure."

"Which is why the sentinel was inside the church and not just watching from afar, as with de Valery's house." Rhys tapped his finger on the table. "We'll have to lure him outside and somehow distract him."

"Or incapacitate him," Digby offered.

Margery sent him a sharp glance. "I don't want to hurt anyone. We are not the Order."

Digby looked pained. "Of course not, but we can

bind him or lock him up somewhere until we complete our work. If we don't, he could notify others and we'll end up having to defend ourselves from a group."

"Unfortunately, I think Digby's right," Rhys said. He turned to Digby. "We're going to have to subdue and secure him somehow."

"I'll see if I can find some rope."

"We'll also require a blindfold and something to gag him—I'll take care of that."

The entire enterprise made Margery feel a bit queasy. "Is all of this really necessary?"

"I'm afraid so." For the first time since she'd entered the dining room, Rhys looked at her with something akin to concern. "Don't worry, we won't hurt him."

She still didn't like it, but she couldn't think of another way so she nodded.

"I'll go look for that rope. See you at dinner." Digby stood and left.

Rhys pocketed the cipher glass and closed the book. He picked it up and eyed hers. "I suppose you'll be taking yours?"

"I will." She ran her hand over the cover of her book. "What do you think will happen once we find the treasure?"

"Without knowing what it is, I can't say."

She understood there were no guarantees, that there had never been any. The entire endeavor had been a risk. Except that he'd said he would still buy her book, if she wanted to sell it. It seemed she'd had faith in him all along. "You'll still buy my book? If we don't find any treasure."

He answered quickly and warmly. "Of course."

Then their partnership would truly be over. Though

it had brought her more joy than she ever anticipated, she'd always known it was never going to last. Losing her parents had taught her that it was safer to keep her emotions buried in order to protect against the inevitable pain of loss. Like everything in life, this was temporary and nothing she did would change that.

She picked up her book and left.

FOLLOWING AN AWKWARD dinner during which he and Digby discussed Arthurian legend and Margery listened attentively, Rhys stripped his clothing away and stood naked in front of the window. Thank God a decent breeze was blowing tonight, offering a much-needed respite from the stagnant heat of the day.

His gaze roved to the door to Margery's room. He'd been painfully aware of her all night, seated to his left, the ripe apple scent of her bathwater teasing him with every shift of her body. She'd worn a light gown with a wide, green sash that accentuated her slender waist. The neckline had tantalized him with just a hint of her breasts, and he'd had to work to keep from looking at them and imagining them wet and hot as they'd been earlier that afternoon.

His cock rose high and hard as he thought of their erotic play. That he'd never touch or taste her again was like a knife to his heart, but there was nothing to be done about it. If their sparring was any indication, they were simply too hotheaded to enjoy a long-term relationship.

He chuckled softly, amused to be describing himself as short-tempered. However, since he'd met Margery, he'd uncovered a surprisingly passionate nature and for the first time he wondered if he ought to take a wife. And yes, he wondered if it ought to be her.

Watching her with Digby was as excruciating as contemplating a future without her. Perhaps more so. It was one thing to think of her alone and another to think of her with someone else.

He went to the water basin and splashed his face. It didn't help. His thoughts were still full of Margery, his body still tight with desire. He wanted her, and not just for tonight. He wanted her forever. Her body, her mind, her exasperating ability to provoke him—he wanted it all.

Blast, he was in love with her.

He stood in the near dark of his room, a single candle burning in the sconce near the door, and stared into nothing. He'd loved one person his entire life—his father—and he'd always worried that he'd never love another, not necessarily because he wouldn't find someone, but that he wouldn't know how. His father had been harsh, serious, restrained. Rhys had felt love in the sense that his father had been proud of him and pleased with his successes. But emotion had never been discussed or declared, and by the time he'd reached adulthood, Rhys had barely even known love existed.

Now, with Margery, he felt an overwhelming urge to protect and please and honor. He wanted to be a better man, not because his father demanded it, but because Margery deserved it. She brought joy and excitement to his life—things he hadn't realized were missing and now didn't think he could live without.

But could he convince her to spend her life with him? She was slow to trust and even slower to lower her emotional defenses. He suspected it was due to losing her parents at such a young age, but whatever the reason, he wanted to be the one who broke her guard down, the one *she* chose to let inside.

Night sounds carried to him over the wind—insects, the hoot of an owl, the rustle of the leaves on the tree outside his window. Then the opening and closing of a door. Margery's room.

Hopefully that had been Jane leaving for some reason. Locating his banyan on a hook, Rhys put it on and quickly buttoned it closed. Crossing to the door, he opened it slowly. A single candle burned on the small table. He stepped lightly over the threshold, his eyes scanning the room.

Jane was asleep on her pallet in the corner. His gut clenched as he looked at the bed, searching for Margery.

Empty.

Where the devil had she gone? The candlelight illuminated a garment on the coverlet—her nightrail. If she hadn't donned it, that meant she was clothed. It was late. Why wouldn't she have dressed for bed, particularly if her maid was already asleep?

Because she'd gone to the church.

He'd seen the excited glint in her eye when they'd determined the treasure was in the church and the disappointment when he'd said they had to wait until morning. She'd also been resistant to their plan to remove the Order's sentinel from their path. But surely she wasn't foolish enough to attempt to search for the treasure without Rhys, particularly when the Order was guarding it. Besides, it was something they were meant to do together—every move they'd made, every step along the journey had brought them to this place and he couldn't imagine finishing it without her. Maybe, however, she didn't feel the same.

He loved her, but he had no idea if she reciprocated the emotion. Maybe she'd never lower her defenses, and he was fighting a losing battle.

Going back to his room, he dressed quickly, without bothering to don anything over his shirt. He raced down the stairs and completed a cursory search of the common areas. No Margery. He moved outside, his frustration over her lack of sense if she *had* gone to the church warring with his concern that perhaps something else had occurred, something nefarious.

A figure near the corner of the inn drew his attention. With several long strides, he was there in an instant. "Craddock?"

His coachman turned. "Sir, good evening. I was just out for a refreshing walk. Today was a real burner."

Rhys couldn't contain his anxiety. "Have you seen Miss Derrington?"

"Indeed. She came by here not too long ago. Said she was going for a walk."

"Did you see which way?"

"That way, I think." Craddock gestured down the lane, toward the church.

Bloody stubborn female. If she found herself in danger it would serve her right. But that didn't mean Rhys wasn't going to intervene.

He took off toward the church and hoped to hell she hadn't done anything foolish.

Chapter Twenty-one

MARGERY CAME THROUGH the back door of the inn, keeping her tread light so as not to disturb anyone. Unable to sleep due to the heat, she'd gone outside for a brief reprieve.

Why was she lying to herself? She hadn't been able to sleep because she couldn't stop thinking of Rhys and how she longed to steal into his room—into his bed—and put her hands on him.

Securing the door gently closed, she scolded herself. She couldn't keep thinking of him that way. Their partnership was nearly at an end, and he'd made it achingly clear that he was finished with her. Could she blame him? She'd deceived him back in Leominster, dismissed his marriage proposal, and had been too eager to accept Digby's participation. No, she didn't blame him at all.

She'd pushed him away at every opportunity because allowing him to get too close meant that losing him would only hurt that much more. As it was, the thought of never seeing his eyes light at that precise moment of discovery, or hearing his warm laugh, stung deep.

Turning, she stopped short as Craddock stepped toward her. "Good evening, miss," he said, frowning.

"Good evening, Craddock. You're about late."

"I was out for a walk." He was still frowning at her, his head cocked to the side in contemplation.

Her neck prickled. "Is something amiss?"

"I ran into Mr. Bowen a little bit ago. He was looking for you. I told him I saw you taking a walk earlier."

Her neck prickled with apprehension. "Where is Mr. Bowen now?"

"He muttered something about the church. I think he walked there."

She had to go after him. The moon was full and quite high in the sky, but she wanted a lantern to take along. "Craddock, would you mind fetching a light and accompanying me to the church?"

"Of course, miss." He took off toward the back of the inn.

Margery touched the back of her hair, still swept up from her neck. She'd sent Jane to bed without using her assistance, telling her she was going for a short walk in the rear yard. She considered leaving the maid a note, but reasoned the young woman was probably already asleep.

Rhys had to be irate. There was no doubt in her mind that he'd assumed—with reason—that she'd gone to the church to find the treasure. She had to find him and tell him she wouldn't do that without him. But why?

Because she cared about him. More than she wanted to admit. More than she'd even realized. It was, apparently, too late to safeguard her heart. The pain she feared was already at hand.

Craddock returned, carrying a lantern. "Ready?"

She nodded, and they exited the back door. The night was still warm, but a refreshing breeze had picked up, offering a welcome reprieve from the day's sweltering heat. She walked quickly, eager to reach her destination, and Craddock kept up easily.

There was light coming from the interior of the church, but she suspected there were always candles lit, especially since the Order's sentinel had taken up residence of late. She quickened her pace and practically ran onto the porch where the Silurum stone was kept.

As soon as she stepped into the church, she stopped dead.

Rhys was on his knees, using a spade to dig up a stone from the floor.

He hadn't come here to stop her, he'd come to find the treasure himself.

Her blood ran cold, despite the warm night, and she simply stared at him.

He lifted his dark gaze to hers, sweat beading his brow. His linen shirt gaped at the neck so she could see a good portion of his chest. She swallowed and averted her gaze back to his stricken face.

"Margery," he said grimly, "you shouldn't have come."

"I can see that," she snapped, disbelief and hurt swirling inside of her as she comprehended his deception.

He slowly shook his head. "It's not what you think. Craddock, help—"

Margery heard a scuffle behind her. She spun about as a man knocked Craddock in the head with the butt of a pistol. The man caught Craddock and the lantern he carried as he slumped to the floor.

Alarm mingled with the trepidation icing Margery's insides. She didn't recognize the man standing over Craddock, with his pistol pointed at . . . Rhys.

She swung her head around. Rhys had gotten up. His lip was curled with menace, and he looked as if he was about to leap across the cobblestoned floor and attack the man behind her.

From the corner of her eye, she saw Digby step into the church—from the exit to the yard they'd used the other day. Relief eased the turmoil in her gut. "Digby," she murmured, never more grateful to see another person.

But when Rhys didn't react to the baron's presence, her fear rose once more. Something was wrong.

Digby also had a pistol, and he also pointed it at Rhys. *No.*

"What are—"

Digby cut her off. He glanced at the man behind Margery, who was now close enough that she could feel his heat at her back. "Tie him up and throw him in the cupboard with the other one. Miss Derrington, please join me." He offered her his usual lopsided smile, which quickly morphed into a snarl when he looked at Rhys. "Get back to work."

Rhys sent her a dark stare before kneeling once more and digging around the stone.

As Margery moved closer to Digby, she was aware that the other villain—and they truly were villains—had gagged Craddock and was securing his hands and feet together. The coachman was still unconscious.

"Please don't hurt him," Margery said to Digby.

"I won't unless it becomes necessary. I never wish to hurt anyone." He glanced at her regretfully, but kept his focus on Rhys. "If you'd only relinquished your book that first night in Hereford, our paths might never have crossed again."

"You son of a bitch," Rhys rumbled. "You did attack her."

"*I* didn't. My man was told to obtain the book with

as little difficulty as possible. How was I to know Miss Derrington is a fearless hellcat?"

Margery wanted to shout with frustration. She should've listened to Rhys about not trusting Digby, but she'd been too blinded by wanting the treasure. "You're wrong. Our paths would've crossed again because I wasn't going to give up on the treasure that easily." She'd been consumed by it, driven by the need to claim her own future. She'd been blind to the fact that with every step of this adventure—with Rhys—she'd been doing just that.

Digby lifted a shoulder. "No matter, it's all worked out splendidly. Though I was truly hoping you and I could've come to a mutual accord. Your passion and initiative would make us a formidable team."

"He's a treasure hunter, Margery," Rhys said. "He was never going to share it with anyone." He looked up at Digby, his nostrils flaring. "Do you already have a buyer?"

Digby sent Rhys a malevolent glare. "You're stretching my patience, Bowen. Stop talking and dig."

Margery curled her fingers into her hand, longing to hit Digby.

The sound of something being dragged drew her attention, and she watched the other villain shove Craddock into a cupboard, closing it once he was inside. "Will he be able to breathe in there?" she asked, shaking with fear.

"I wouldn't worry about him. Someone will come along, and by then I'll be long gone," Digby said.

"I'll hunt you down," Rhys swore.

"No, you won't, because you'll be dead."

Margery lunged forward. "No! You said you didn't like to hurt anyone."

"Hold her." Digby motioned to his cohort. "I take no pleasure in it," he told Margery, "but as I said, it's sometimes necessary. I can't risk Bowen coming after me for the treasure."

The second man grabbed Margery's arm and dragged her back against his chest. He dug the barrel of his pistol into her side.

An inhuman sound erupted from Rhys's throat, but Digby reached out and grabbed a candlestick from a table and threw it at Rhys, striking him in the head. Digby's face contorted into a mask of rage as he grabbed Rhys by the neck and shoved him face first into the stones. "If you don't find this treasure for me, I'm going to kill her, too, understand?" He waited a beat, then knocked Rhys's forehead against the rock. "I said, do you understand?"

"Yes." Rhys's response was muffled, but audible.

Digby let him go and retreated. He wore a waistcoat over his shirt, which was also open at the collar. He tugged at his garments to reposition them as he aimed his pistol at Rhys.

When Rhys's head came up, blood trickled from his hairline. His face was dark, his eyes darker. Margery had never seen him look so enraged.

Knots of fear formed a chain from her throat to her belly. She was going to be sick. She couldn't let Digby kill him. What were they going to do?

Taking deep breaths, she watched Rhys digging around the stone. Why had he selected that particular one? She tried to make sense of how the map applied to the actual floor, but couldn't. Did Rhys understand it, or was he simply guessing?

At last, the stone came loose. Digby leaned over to look into the space. "There's nothing there. You said it was there."

"No," Rhys said levelly. "I said it *could* be there. Give me the map."

Digby withdrew the parchment Rhys had drawn earlier and tossed it to the floor. "Try again, and this time you'd better be right." He nodded toward the man holding her, who squeezed Margery's arm painfully. She tried not to make a sound, but gave off a whimper, which drew Rhys's frustrated glare.

She couldn't continue like this. "Digby, if I agree to go with you—to marry you—will you let Rhys go?"

Digby's eyes flashed with surprise. His lips parted and he looked between them as if he was trying to detect some sort of plan.

"I'll go with you—happily," she added, though her stomach threatened to empty its contents at the thought.

"Margery, don't." Rhys's quiet plea filled her soul.

"Why would you do that?" Digby asked. "You said you weren't interested in marriage, though there seems to be something between the two of you." His tone was derisive. "Keep digging, Bowen or I'll have Hawkins make another part of you bleed."

Margery clenched her hands into fists and bit her tongue to keep from begging Digby to stop. "There's nothing between me and Mr. Bowen, though I know he'd like there to be. I only care that he doesn't die—I don't want that for anyone." God, this was going to hurt Rhys. "The treasure is what's important to me. It's always been the treasure. And using him to find it was merely a means to an end."

Rhys had flinched when she'd said "using," and Margery's heart constricted. He looked at her, his gaze uncertain, and she knew she was almost there.

She moved toward Digby, but her captor held her fast. "Please, Digby, let me come to you."

Digby stared at her a long moment, then motioned for her to come. With slow, sure steps that belied the fear quaking through her, she made her way to his side. She caressed his cheek and slid her hand to the side of his jaw. Pressing her hand against him, she urged his head down so she could kiss him. Softly, she touched her lips to his and bit her cheek to hide her revulsion.

Digby slipped his tongue into her mouth, but she pulled back and offered a hasty smile. "Not here. There will be plenty of time for that later." She stroked his jaw and prayed he believed her.

With a triumphant grin, Digby turned to Rhys, who was watching them in utter rage. "Miss Derrington has just saved your life. Don't mess it up by not complying with the arrangement she's just negotiated. You still need to find that treasure. Stop fooling around and dig under the correct stone."

Margery realized Rhys had already moved two other stones, to no avail. Had he been stalling? She expected nothing less from a man of his exceptional intelligence.

Rhys's black eyes found hers. "Margery." The single word nearly drove her to her knees.

Squaring her shoulders, she dug for a strength she wasn't sure she had. "Stop calling me that. You are too familiar. Hurry up and find the treasure so we may leave." The hurt in his gaze pulled at her heart and she knew she had to do more. "I need you to understand that I only ever wanted the treasure—only the treasure. Everything I've said, everything I've done has been with that result in mind. Once you accept that, we can finish this and move on."

The fire burning behind his eyes went out. The rich,

dark color hardened to obsidian, and she knew she'd killed whatever feeling he had for her.

And a part of her died too.

RHYS LOOKED AT the map he'd sketched, but the image blurred. He couldn't believe what Margery said. Yet, she'd spoken quite convincingly. Plus, she'd gone and kissed that prick Digby. All for the treasure. He knew she wanted it—no, he knew she *needed* it. But would she really go to such lengths to get it? He thought he'd come to know her, and he'd certainly come to care for her. Hell, he loved her.

While he was nothing to her.

He blinked several times and brought the map into focus. He'd been digging in random spots, trying to delay until he could organize a plan of escape. He'd considered taking Digby by surprise, but with the second bloke—Hawkins was his name—and then Margery's appearance, he hadn't wanted to risk it. He was certain that in a confrontation between just the two of them, he would dominate Digby handily. How he yearned for the chance.

He knew where the stone was located because of the way the rows were laid out. There was a number pattern that allowed him to figure the orientation of the map. But if he found the correct stone and unearthed the treasure now, they'd leave—and regardless of what Digby said, he didn't trust the man not to kill him.

He stood up, still clutching the map.

Digby pointed his pistol at Rhys's chest. "Where are you going?"

"To try another stone."

"You'd better get it right. Margery would rather I didn't kill you, but my patience will only hold for so long." He glanced at Margery. "Sorry, my love, the treasure is all that matters."

She looked at Digby, her lashes fluttering. "Of course." She turned an icy stare on Rhys. "Do yourself a favor and find it *now*."

Something about the way she said the word sparked hope in his chest. Was it possible she was playing an elaborate part? God, he hoped so.

Feeling slightly buoyed, he went to the stone in the northwest corner and counted two rows over and three rows down. He sank to his knees and used the dull tool Digby had provided to pry up the stone. He had to work his fingers around it to loosen the rock—the last one had taken considerable effort. This one, however, seemed to wobble more easily. Excitement stirred in his chest. This could be it . . .

He picked up the rock, it was heavier than the others, and set it aside.

Digby and Margery crept forward, while Hawkins flanked Rhys from the other side.

"Is that a . . . box?" Margery asked breathlessly.

Rhys looked up at her, saw the enthusiasm in her gaze and had to stifle the urge to sweep her against him. This was not how this discovery was supposed to play out. They were supposed to find this together and celebrate . . .

"Open it," Digby demanded, also sounding thunderstruck.

Rhys pried it up from the small nook and set it beside the hole. The box bore a simple latch, which he flicked apart. With a wary glance at his captors, he opened the lid.

Everyone gathered close. "What is it?" Digby asked. "Margery, pick it up."

Rhys withdrew the sheaf of papers crowding the box and held them up to her. She grasped them, her fingers grazing his knuckles. Her gaze found his and again, he had the sense that everything she was currently doing was an act.

Digby peered over her shoulder at the stack of parchment. "What is it?"

"I don't know." She sifted through the papers. "I can't read it."

Digby snatched them from her and scowled at them. "Neither can I. Bowen, what is this?" He thrust the documents at Rhys, who caught the papers before they scattered.

"It's in Latin." Rhys arched a brow at Digby. "They didn't teach you that at Cambridge?" Likely the scoundrel hadn't bothered to learn it.

"I'm afraid I was sent down after my first year."

"Not surprising," Rhys muttered.

Digby pointed his pistol at Rhys's forehead. "What does it say? Does it direct us where to look next?"

Rhys scanned the pages. His chest expanded. It was an extraordinary find—better than any bejeweled heart or magical sword. "No, this *is* the treasure."

"I don't understand." Digby gritted his teeth. "It's a bunch of ancient parchment."

"Sixth-century parchment to be exact." He held up the last page for both of them to see. "Can you read the name there at the bottom?"

Margery's intake of breath filled him with joy. She understood. "Anarawd."

"What?"

She turned to Digby, her features animated with the excitement of the discovery. "The scribe, Anarawd, wrote this."

Digby seized the papers from Rhys and stared at them, as if he'd somehow learned to read Latin in the space of the last two minutes. "Are these the recorded stories . . . from the knights?"

"I wasn't able to read them closely, but yes, it seems they are the source material for de Valery's manuscripts. A series of poems if I'm not mistaken."

Digby looked at him, his gray eyes feverish. "Do they prove the existence of Arthur?"

"I'd have to study them."

"That won't be necessary. I have an associate who will know their worth."

"I thought you were an Arthurian expert," Rhys observed drily.

Digby clenched his teeth. "Don't push my tolerance, Bowen.

"I must say this is disappointing." Digby rolled the vellum, and Rhys nearly threw himself at the bounder to save the artifacts from damage. "It will garner a decent price, but it's no Heart of Llanllwch." He looked at Margery apologetically. "I'm sorry, Margery. The next one will be better."

Rhys couldn't remain silent. "You're a fool, Digby. This is an incredible discovery."

Digby threw him a nasty glare. "It's not the treasure I was hoping to find."

"It's precisely what I wished for—and more." Rhys stared at Margery, the curve of her lip, the brilliant gleam of her hazel eyes, and knew he'd found a treasure worth keeping. A treasure worth fighting for. He held his breath waiting for her response.

She opened her mouth, but Rhys never got to hear what she was going to say. The rough hands of Hawkins pulled him to his feet.

"Bind him," Digby ordered as he went to another pile of rope and tossed some to his henchman.

Hawkins set his pistol down before he grabbed Rhys. It was now or never. Rhys lifted his arm and chopped his hand into Hawkins's nose. Blood flowed, but Hawkins pivoted and took Rhys down hard to the stone floor.

Rhys heard a scuffle, looked up, and saw Digby and Margery hurrying from the church. With a loud cry, he heaved up at his attacker and threw him aside. He scrambled to his feet, but a hand on his ankle pulled him back down.

Hawkins dragged him backward as Rhys kicked at him with his free foot. He dug his fingers into the stones for purchase. But Hawkins was bloody strong, and Rhys slid back. With a burst of strength, he turned himself over so he could see Hawkins. The man had a knife in his hand and swiped up at Rhys's leg, keeping his grip firm around Rhys's boot.

Kicking out, Rhys tried to knock the knife away, but Hawkins had a firm grasp. The knife slashed at Rhys's boot, but only nicked the leather.

Damn it, every moment he tangled with the man was a moment Digby was escaping with Margery. Rhys reached behind him, looking for anything he could find. His fingers met the empty box, a pathetic weapon to be sure, but better than nothing. He lurched upward with it and brought it down on Hawkins's head.

The villain howled, then arced his arm wildly, wielding the knife with careless abandon. A third figure appeared, his head cloaked. He swung out and knocked the knife from Hawkins's hand. The stranger's black robe flowed with his movements, momentarily blocking Rhys's view.

Hawkins's hand released Rhys's ankle. He clambered to his feet and moved around the stranger to look down at Hawkins. The cloaked man had his boot against the villain's throat.

"Go, they're on foot," he said to Rhys. "I've got this one."

Septon. Rhys recognized his friend's voice. He clasped his shoulder. "Thank you."

Rhys sprinted from the church, hoping he wasn't too late to catch them.

Chapter Twenty-two

MARGERY STUMBLED ALONG after Digby, who was pulling her hand as he raced from the churchyard and down the lane toward the main road. She tried to dig her feet into the soft dirt, but Digby was surprisingly strong and she wasn't able to stop his progress.

She ought to go with him—at least for now—but she wanted to ensure Rhys was safe.

"Margery, keep up," Digby snapped. "I have a coach waiting for us in town."

She had to think of something before they reached it. She didn't think he'd just let her go if she said she'd changed her mind.

"Digby, please, can we slow down? My side is aching." It was, but she would endure it if it meant running *away* from him.

"In a moment. We need to get to the coach. Hurry." He tugged her along.

She gasped for breath, the summer night air burning her lungs as she fought to maintain his pace.

At last they began to slow. They were nearing the town's other inn—the aptly named Coach and Horse.

He stopped and leaned over, his breath coming hard and fast. "Wait here." He squeezed her hand and went toward the stable.

She glanced around the yard, the only light the descending moon and a lantern on a post outside the inn. She turned to go back to the church and gasped when Rhys caught her in his arms.

He clasped her upper arm and clamped his palm over her mouth. "Don't scream."

She wrapped her hand around his wrist and looked at him in relief. She smiled, but he couldn't see it behind his grip. Instead, she collapsed against him and slid her arm around his waist.

He loosened his hold. "Are you all right?"

She nodded into his chest, joy flooding her at finding he was unharmed.

The unmistakable cock of a pistol filled the night. "Let her go, Bowen."

Margery turned in Rhys's embrace and saw Digby maybe fifteen feet away, his pistol directed at Rhys's head.

"I may've failed at Cambridge, but I've plenty of other useful skills. I'm a crack shot, for one."

"You're not taking her, Digby. Just go," Rhys said, keeping his arm tight around her. "I won't try to stop you."

"She wants to come with me," Digby said, taking a step forward.

Rhys scoffed. "It was a ploy. Are you really that stupid?"

"Damn you, Bowen." He fired and Margery screamed.

Rhys's arm dropped from her, and he lurched backward. Margery spun to catch him, but he held himself up.

Digby came at them with a roar. Margery positioned herself in front of Rhys so that Digby crashed into her. He did so with enough force to take all of them to the ground. She landed atop Rhys as Digby fell on her.

Rough hands pushed at her, and she realized both men were trying to get at each other through her.

Ultimately, she ended up in a heap in the dirt as the two men tussled. Digby had the upper hand and was driving his fist into Rhys's face.

Margery looked around frantically for a weapon. Her gaze landed on the stable and the hoe leaning against the doorframe. Desperate to help Rhys, she ran and grasped the hoe.

The sounds of the fight—their grunting and exertions—saturated the heavy summer air. Margery approached them, trying to determine how to strike, but they were moving so fast, their arms and legs tangling, she couldn't find an opening.

Rhys landed a solid punch to Digby's face, sending the other man sprawling backward. Margery leapt forward and brought the hoe down on his head. Twice. "Stay down!"

As if he heard her, Digby fell back and didn't get up.

Heaving, Margery turned and knelt beside Rhys, who was lying on his back staring up at the night sky. She dropped the hoe, but kept it in reach. Blood soaked his shoulder, confirming her worst fear—that he'd been shot.

She pulled his shirt aside to look, and he winced. "I know it hurts."

"Quite, but it isn't bad. I don't think the bullet is lodged in the flesh. Digby isn't as good of a shot as he claimed."

She nearly smiled at the surprising humor in his tone. "Thank goodness for that."

The door of the inn opened and a man in a nightcap came ambling out. "Good Lord, what's gone on here?"

A trio of men, also in their nightclothes, followed him outside.

Rhys struggled to sit up, and Margery helped him.

"My apologies, kind sir. This man is a criminal. I had to prevent him from kidnapping this young lady. Furthermore, he stole something that belongs to her."

Anarawd's tales.

Rhys nudged her to go get them. She glanced at him, saw him nod toward Digby, and got up to remove the papers from where he'd tucked them into his waistcoat.

"We'll need to alert the magistrate," she said to the innkeeper. "However, first we need to help Mr. Bowen. He's been shot. Can you help me get him inside?"

The innkeeper rushed forward. "Of course. Though, I'm afraid I don't have any open rooms."

Rhys declined the man's proffered arm. "I can walk. We don't need a room, just a place to tend my wound. A chair and a basin of water will suffice." He looked at the other men standing in the yard. "Can any of you find something to bind Mr. Digby before he regains consciousness and escapes?"

The innkeeper nodded. "Andrew, nip into the stable and fetch some rope."

The young man, perhaps the innkeeper's son or an employee, did as he was bade. One of the other men stepped forward. "I'll stand guard over this one."

"And I'll help," the other offered.

The innkeeper thanked them—these were clearly guests—and led Margery and Rhys inside. She wrapped her arm around Rhys's waist and helped him walk.

He looked down at her. "I really don't need any help."

"I know, but I want to touch you. Is that acceptable?"

His lips teased up. "Perfectly."

The innkeeper directed them to the tidy sitting

room to the right of the entry hall. "Just sit there and I'll fetch some water. Maybe a bit of brandy?"

Rhys nodded. "Thank you."

Margery led Rhys to a small table situated in the corner with a pair of wooden chairs. "Sit."

He did as she commanded, wincing again as he did so. When he was settled, he fixed her with a probing stare. "You're certain you're all right? He didn't hurt you?"

She shook her head. "No, you fared far worse, I'm afraid."

"You were brilliant," he said, his eyes warm and dark.

"I'm sorry I said those things." She sat in the nearest chair, turning on the cushion so she faced him.

He grasped her hand between his long fingers. "I know you didn't mean them." He smiled. "At least, I do now."

"The treasure *was* important to me," she said, her throat clogging. "For so long, it was all I could see, all that mattered. But when I saw you in the church, saw what you were willing to do for me." She swallowed. "No, that isn't right. I think I've known for so long—"

He leaned forward and kissed her, his lips caressing hers. "Shhh. I love you, Margery."

She smiled against his mouth, tears blurring her vision. "I love you." She pulled back and wiped her eyes. "I wasted so much time pushing you away. It was easier. After my parents died, I didn't want to feel. It hurt so much."

He stroked her cheek. "Margery."

"I'm just so . . . afraid. Of losing you, of being alone." Her hands shook as she admitted her fear and awaited his response.

He put his arm around her shoulders and drew her against him. "I know. I am too. I never expected to fall in love and now that I have—and felt the sting of loss, although temporary—I realize it's worth the risk. *You're* worth the risk."

Joy coursed through her. He didn't just accept her as she was, he truly understood. "I couldn't have said it better," she said, resting her forehead against his. "I cast all of my reservations to the wind when I decided to solve the de Valery code with you. The adventure itself, not the end result, is the true treasure."

He kissed her again, their mouths blending together. "I couldn't agree more."

THE FOLLOWING MORNING, Rhys turned over in his bed, disappointed to find he was alone. Margery had cleaned his wound at the Coach and Horse, after which they'd made their way back to their inn, where Craddock had been waiting to greet them. He'd reported that both Digby and Hawkins were being managed by the mysterious cloaked stranger and the other man, the Order's sentinel, who'd been locked in the cupboard with Craddock.

A rap on Rhys's door—the one that led to the hall—drew him to clamber out of bed. His shoulder, tightly bandaged, ached. Though the ball had only grazed the flesh—thankfully, Digby wasn't quite the marksman he'd proclaimed—the cut had been deep enough to bleed profusely and cause him a decent amount of pain.

Not enough to prevent him from making love to

Margery after they'd returned in the middle of the night. He smiled at the memory of her straddling him, insisting that he let her do all of the work. He'd already decided to feign the depth of his injury for the foreseeable future.

A second rap on the door reminded him he was supposed to be putting on clothing instead of fantasizing about his fiancée.

Fiancée.

He liked the sound of that, loved that she'd agreed to marry him.

Grimacing, he pulled on his breeches and plucked up his banyan. Tugging it over his wounded arm was difficult, but he managed. "I'm coming," he called as he made his way to the door.

Septon stood on the other side. Gone was the black cloak from last night, replaced by his usual costume—that of a country gentleman who just happened to be a member of a secret cult.

"How are you?" he asked, stepping into Rhys's room.

"As well as can be expected." Aside from the shoulder injury, he sported a black eye, the wound on his forehead, and several sore ribs.

Septon cracked a smile. "Excellent. May I sit?" He eyed a chair at the table.

Rhys held out his hand. "Of course." He perched on the edge of the bed, while Septon sat. Rhys didn't bother asking why he'd come. He already knew. "I'm not going to give you the poems."

Septon exhaled and laid his palm flat on the table. "I was afraid you were going to say that."

"I have to study them. You understand that, don't you? And I'd be happy to have you study them with me." He couldn't think of anyone he'd rather share the excitement of discovery with. Actually, that wasn't true anymore. He smiled to himself.

"You seem rather pleased this morning," Septon observed.

"I am. Miss Derrington has consented to be my wife."

Septon inclined his head. "Congratulations. I shall look forward to Trevor's inevitable premarital celebration."

"I think I'll eschew the typical bacchanalia."

Septon's mouth crept up into a reluctant smile. "I can't say I'm surprised." His lips flattened. "The Order won't be pleased that you're keeping the poems."

"But they'll allow it?"

"For a time, perhaps, though it depends on what you plan to do. If you want to study them for your own academic pursuit, they won't attempt to obtain them from you. However, if you try to publish a paper or otherwise publicize their existence, the Order will intervene."

"So I may have one of the most important literary finds of the century and no one can know about it?"

Septon inclined his head. "You still have the de Valery manuscript and the Order will not interfere with whatever you choose to do with it—provided you make it clear there is no code and of course no treasure. Nash must agree to do the same when you return his book to him."

"I can live with that, and I'm certain Lord Nash will agree." Bringing Margery's aunts' lost de Valery book to light would establish Rhys as a leading literary scholar, though that goal seemed less important now that he had Margery.

"What of Digby?" Rhys wanted the man imprisoned at the very least—he'd targeted Margery from the very beginning, going to Gloucester and approaching her because he'd traced the book to her aunts, then following her to Monmouth and tracking them as they'd launched their quest.

"The Order will collect any Arthurian items he might still possess and the magistrate will take care of the rest," Septon said.

"The Order won't intervene and take justice into their own hands?" Rhys was reluctant to dampen his blissful mood, but he had to ask Septon about what Digby had told him. "They don't seem to be as benevolent as you claimed."

"I told you there have been members who step outside the Order."

"Is that what happened to de Valery's brother?"

Septon's face darkened. "It was a quarrel between brothers. De Valery the scribe was angry when de Valery the alchemist tried to manufacture his peculiar cipher glass and sell it to other code makers. De Valery the scribe wanted the science for himself alone."

"Badly enough to orchestrate his brother's death?"

"I don't know how it deteriorated to such a macabre ending, but the glass went missing—until you found it. Some in the Order theorize that a third party hid it in an effort to quell the animosity between the brothers, only it backfired and de Valery the alchemist was blamed for the loss of the device and hanged."

Rhys couldn't imagine turning on one's family, not when it was such a precious commodity. "What a sad tale."

"History is full of them, but then you know that." Septon stood. "When you're finished with the poems, I will take them into custody for the Order. Then we shall study them together." He flashed an eager smile.

So Rhys didn't get to keep them permanently. He wouldn't argue, not when he was just glad to have them for a time. "Thank you. What of the device?"

"Its use has been exhausted." Septon shrugged. "Feel free to put it on your desk as a curiosity—without revealing what it ever did, of course."

Everything about their quest was to be kept secret then. "I can do that." Rhys walked his friend to the door. "I'll see you at my wedding?"

Septon clapped him on his good shoulder. "I wouldn't miss it."

Later that morning, Rhys sat in the inn's kitchen garden, enjoying the pleasant summer day. The temperature was still warm, but it wasn't the cloying heat of yesterday.

Margery set a tray on a small table beside him. "Mrs. Powell makes the best lemonade. You must promise that we'll return, if only to enjoy this." She poured two glasses of the pale yellow liquid and handed him one. Taking a hearty drink, she sat in a chair next to his.

"I'll promise you anything, but are you certain you want to return to Caerwent?"

She lifted a shoulder. "Why not? I have many excellent memories." Her gaze fell on his wounded arm, now hidden beneath his layers of clothing, but aching nonetheless. "Perhaps you do not."

"On the contrary, I shall recall the hot summer days of Caerwent with the utmost fondness."

She grinned at him before sipping her lemonade and setting the glass on the table, leaning over him in the process.

He snaked his arm around her waist and pulled her

into his lap.

She tried to pull away, but her sultry smile belied her actions. "Rhys!"

"Now, you're worried about propriety? A woman I greatly admire recently took me to task for such nonsense."

"And she was right to do it."

He captured the back of her head with his palm, holding her captive to his stare. "She is free to lecture me about anything at all. Any time." His lips met hers, and she kissed him with a passion he felt straight to his toes.

After a long moment, she pulled away and laid her head against his unwounded shoulder.

He stroked her hair, enjoying the moment and looking forward to a lifetime of them. "Are you sure you aren't disappointed in how our adventure turned out? The treasure wasn't what you expected."

"No, but neither was the journey." She looked up at him, love shining in her eyes. "And it's far from over."

Epilogue

SEPTEMBER DAWNED WITH a nasty rainstorm. Not that Margery minded, for that meant she would have an excuse to stay indoors and sneak away with her new husband for a few stolen kisses—or more.

Still, disappearing in the middle of the day might be noticed by one of the other people who now inhabited Hollyhaven: Penn or one of Margery's aunts. Convincing them to relocate to Monmouth had taken a bit of cajoling, but they'd both agreed that they preferred to be with Margery than alone in Gloucester. Harker had also been pleased to accompany them and was enjoying her new position as the housekeeper of Hollyhaven, while Mrs. Thomas had been delighted to focus her duties on her true love: cooking.

Margery dodged an orange ball of fur darting up the stairs. Penn appeared at the base and stopped short before pursuing the kitten.

"What's wrong with Felicity?" she asked.

"Fergus was playing a little too rough and she got upset," Penn said. A second kitten, a black cat with orange wisps here and there, padded toward the stairs. Penn scowled down at him. "Naughty boy. Be nicer to your sister."

"Indeed," Margery said to the cat. "Else your mother will see that you're punished."

They'd taken in the family of three—a mama and her two kittens—because really, three cats were better than one.

Aunt Eugenie walked into the hall and looked up as Margery descended the last few steps. "Oh, Margery, there you are. Tea is ready. Or coffee if you're Aggie." She made a moue of distaste.

Margery smiled, thrilled to have everyone she loved within arm's reach. "I'll fetch Rhys."

Aunt Eugenie nodded and strode back toward the drawing room.

Margery crossed the hall and went into Rhys's library, where he was bent over the Anarawd manuscripts laid across his table. He'd translated them and was in the process of making several copies, including one in Latin, so that he'd have the text, if not the original.

Margery came up behind him and massaged his neck. "Your handwriting is so lovely."

"A necessary skill in my occupation. My father made certain I wrote legibly and with an attractive slant."

Of course he had. She'd come to learn just how exacting the elder Bowen had been. "Tea is ready."

He reached back and laid his hand over hers, then brought it around to press a kiss to her palm. "I was thinking that we might take Penn with us when we return Nash's book."

"That's a splendid idea."

"Then we can swing through Caerwent to show him the ruins." Penn had been so upset about not being able to accompany them that they'd promised to take him as soon as possible. Plus, they would deliver the Anarawd poems to Septon. "Are you ready to give them up?" She nodded toward the papers on the table.

He exhaled. "No. And I'm especially reluctant to turn them over to the Order, even if I do agree that keeping their existence quiet is for the best."

They'd discussed this question many times—how the revelation of these works that were contemporary to Arthur and his knights might fuel interest in finding the thirteen treasures. "I thought we agreed that the thirteen treasures were likely lost, if they ever even existed."

"As magical items you mean. I think they're likely extant, but no, I don't believe they can feed an army or tame any beast."

She didn't believe that either. But she was still intrigued by them. It was a shame Anarawd's tales didn't shed any light on where they might be.

Rhys turned his chair and brought her to stand between his legs. His arms encircled her waist and he nuzzled her chest, pressing a kiss to the flesh exposed above her bodice. "I was thinking that the poems might be lost or stolen en route to Septon."

She looked down at him in surprise. "What do you mean?"

He shrugged. "What if Nash held on to them? We once discussed the treasure perhaps belonging to him, since his family commissioned the manuscripts from de Valery in the first place." He looked past her and shook his head. "That's one mystery I'd like to solve, but don't think we ever will."

"Why they commissioned them, you mean?"

He nodded. "I trust Nash to not only keep them safe, but to appreciate the privilege of holding them . . . for his grandson."

"Kersey?" Rhys had told her about Penn's true parentage and she understood the necessity to keep it secret, for now. She also understood how deeply the truth would affect Kersey some day and was sorry for it. Ensuring that his family's legacy, of preserving the work of Anarawd, was passed on to him was the least, and perhaps best, they could do for him. Margery touched her husband's jaw. "Nash will be thrilled . . . and honored."

"But the Order must never know," Rhys said solemnly.

"Know what?" Penn skipped into the room. He flung himself in a chair, having become a comfortable member of the household.

Margery stepped out from between Rhys's legs and stood beside his chair.

"You're still working on this?" Penn picked up one of the sheets Rhys had been copying into Latin. Penn's brow furrowed as he tried to form the words, but he stumbled over the pronunciation.

"Would you like to learn Latin?" Rhys asked, eyeing him with interest, and perhaps hope.

Penn lifted a shoulder. "I s'pose." He turned and looked at Margery, who frowned at his posture and gestured for him to sit up. He complied. "Yes, I'd like to learn Latin."

"And I'd be delighted to teach you."

Penn stood. "You're supposed to come for tea. We can't start without you, and Mrs. Thomas made Shrewsbury cakes." His favorite. And Margery's. She'd fallen in love with this boy as surely as she'd fallen in love with his foster father.

Rhys got up. "All right, we're coming."

Penn darted from the room, and Margery realized a kitten was dogging his heels. She smiled, amazed at how quickly and wonderfully her life had changed.

"He's settled in quite nicely, hasn't he?" Rhys asked, offering her his arm.

She curled her hand around his sleeve and let him

lead her from the library. "Better than we could have hoped. You've never heard from his mother?" They'd both wondered whether she had passed.

Rhys shook his head. "And I suspect we never will. It's all right. He has a mother." He stopped and looked at her with love and joy.

She laid her hand on his chest, adoring this man who filled her life better than she could have dreamed. "And a father."

He kissed her forehead. "And we all have a family."

The end

Thank You!

Thank you so much for reading *Lady of Desire*. I hope you enjoyed it!

Would you like to know when my next book is available? Sign up for my Reader Club at http://www.darcyburke.com/readerclub, follow me on Twitter at @darcyburke, or like my Facebook page at http://facebook.com/DarcyBurkeFans.

Reviews help others find a book that's right for them. I hope you'll consider leaving a review at your favorite online vendor or networking site.

Lady of Desire is the first book in the Legendary Rogues Series. Be sure to read the remaining books to find out what happens with the thirteen treasures and the Order of the Round Table!

Thank you again for reading and for your support. I love to hear from readers, so I hope you'll drop me a note and visit me on Facebook.

xoxox,

Darcy

Author's Note

I chose to set this story in and near Wales both because of the subject matter and because my grandmother, Selma Rita King Finney was born in Cardiff in 1916. I still have family there and was fortunate enough to visit several years ago. It's a beautiful land with charming people, and while the Welsh language is difficult to pronounce, I find it lovely—probably because I can still hear my great-uncle Alec singing it.

The thirteen treasures of Britain are mythical objects that appear in various legends. They have been used in countless stories and in many ways (Harry Potter's Deathly Hallows are somewhat based on them). I adapted them for this series and created the Heart of Llanllwch for purely narrative purposes. The Silurum Stone is real and I plan to visit the Caerwent Church to see it some day.

The Order of the Round Table is a completely fictional group, but is based on the myriad secret societies that have existed for centuries. Edmund de Valery and Anarawd are fictional characters as are the documents they produced.

Of course there is no proof that King Arthur, his knights, the Round Table or any of Arthurian legend is real. I'd like to think it's a little bit history, with a dash of embellishment, and a lot of great storytelling.

Books by Darcy Burke

Historical Romance

Legendary Rogues

Lady of Desire
Romancing the Earl
Lord of Fortune
Captivating the Scoundrel

The Untouchables

The Forbidden Duke
The Duke of Daring
The Duke of Deception
The Duke of Desire
The Duke of Defiance
The Duke of Danger
The Duke of Ice
The Duke of Ruin
The Duke of Lies
The Duke of Seduction
The Duke of Kisses
The Duke of Distraction

Secrets and Scandals

Her Wicked Ways
His Wicked Heart
To Seduce a Scoundrel
To Love a Thief (a novella)
Never Love a Scoundrel
Scoundrel Ever After

Contemporary Romance

Ribbon Ridge

Where the Heart Is (a prequel novella)
Only in My Dreams
Yours to Hold
When Love Happens
The Idea of You
When We Kiss
You're Still the One

Ribbon Ridge: So Hot

So Good
So Right
So Wrong

Praise for Darcy Burke's

Legendary Rogues Series

LADY of DESIRE

"A fast-paced mixture of adventure and romance, very much in the mould of *Romancing the Stone* or *Indiana Jones*."

-All About Romance

"...gave me such a book hangover! ...addictive...one of the most entertaining stories I've read this year!"

-Adria's Romance Reviews

ROMANCING the EARL

"Once again Darcy Burke takes an interesting story and...turns it into magic. An exceptionally well-written book."

-Bodice Rippers, Femme Fatale, and Fantasy

"...A fast paced story that was exciting and interesting. This is a definite must add to your book lists!"

-Kilts and Swords

LORD of FORTUNE

"I don't think I know enough superlatives to describe this book! It is wonderfully, magically delicious. It sucked me in from the very first sentence and didn't turn me loose—not even at the end ..."

-Flippin Pages

"If you love a deep, passionate romance with a bit of mystery, then this is the book for you!"

-Teatime and Books

Secrets & Scandals Series

HER WICKED WAYS

"A bad girl heroine steals both the show and a highwayman's heart in Darcy Burke's deliciously wicked debut."

–Courtney Milan, *NYT* Bestselling Author

HIS WICKED HEART

"Intense and intriguing. Cinderella meets *Fight Club* in a historical romance packed with passion, action and secrets."

–Anna Campbell, *Seven Nights in a Rogue's Bed*

TO SEDUCE A SCOUNDREL

"Darcy Burke pulls no punches with this sexy, romantic page-turner. Sevrin and Philippa's story grabs you from the first scene and doesn't let go. To Seduce a Scoundrel is simply delicious!"

–Tessa Dare, *NYT* Bestselling Author

TO LOVE A THIEF

"With refreshing circumstances surrounding both the hero and the heroine, a nice little mystery, and a touch of heat, this novella was a perfect way to pass the day."

–The Romanceaholic

NEVER LOVE A SCOUNDREL

"A nice mix of intrigue and passion...wonderfully complex characters, with flaws and quirks that will draw you in and steal your heart."

–BookTrib

SCOUNDREL EVER AFTER

"There is something so delicious about a bad boy, no matter what era he is from, and Ethan was definitely delicious."

-A Lust for Reading

The Untouchables Series

THE FORBIDDEN DUKE

"I LOVED this story!!" 5 Stars

-Historical Romance Lover

"This is a wonderful read and I can't wait to see what comes next in this amazing series..." 5 Stars

-Teatime and Books

THE DUKE of DARING

"An unconventional beauty set on life as a spinster meets the one man who might change her mind, only to find his painful past makes it impossible to love. A wonderfully emotional journey from attraction, to friendship, to a love that conquers all."

-Bronwen Evans, USA Today Bestselling Author

THE DUKE of DECEPTION

"...an enjoyable, well-paced story ... Ned and Aquilla are an engaging, well-matched couple – strong, caring and compassionate; and ...it's easy to believe that they will continue to be happy together long after the book is ended."

-All About Romance

"This is my favorite so far in the series! They had chemistry from the moment they met...their passion leaps off the pages."

-Sassy Book Lover

THE DUKE of DESIRE

"Masterfully written with great characterization...with a flourish toward characters, secrets, and romance... Must read addition to "The Untouchables" series!"

-My Book Addiction and More

"If you are looking for a truly endearing story about two people who take the path least travelled to find the other, with a side of 'YAH THAT'S HOT!' then this book is absolutely for you!"

-The Reading Cafe

THE DUKE of DEFIANCE

"This story was so beautifully written, and it hooked me from page one. I couldn't put the book down and just had to read it in one sitting even though it meant reading into the wee hours of the morning."

-Buried Under Romance

"I loved the Duke of Defiance! This is the kind of book you hate when it is over and I had to make myself stop reading just so I wouldn't have to leave the fun of Knighton's (aka Bran) and Joanna's story!"

-Behind Closed Doors Book Review

THE DUKE of DANGER

"The sparks fly between them right from the start... the HEA is certainly very hard-won, and well-deserved."

-All About Romance

"Another book hangover by Darcy! Every time I pick a favorite in this series, she tops it. The ending was perfect and made me want more."

-Sassy Book Lover

THE DUKE of ICE

"Each book gets better and better, and this novel was no exception. I think this one may be my fave yet! 5 out 5 for this reader!"

-Front Porch Romance

"An incredibly emotional story...I dare anyone to stop reading once the second half gets under way because this is intense!"
-Buried Under Romance

THE DUKE of RUIN

"This is a fast paced novel that held me until the last page."
-Guilty Pleasures Book Reviews

" ...everything I could ask for in a historical romance... impossible to stop reading."

-The Bookish Sisters

THE DUKE of LIES

"THE DUKE OF LIES is a work of genius! The characters are wonderfully complex, engaging; there is much mystery, and so many, many lies from so many people; I couldn't wait to see it all uncovered."

-Buried Under Romance

"..the epitome of romantic [with]...a bit of danger/action. The main characters are mature, fierce, passionate, and full of surprises. If you are a hopeless romantic and you love reading stories that'll leave you feeling like you're walking on clouds then you need to read this book or maybe even this entire series."

-The Bookish Sisters

Ribbon Ridge Series

A contemporary family saga featuring the Archer family of sextuplets who return to their small Oregon wine country town to confront tragedy and find love...

The "multilayered plot keeps readers invested in the story line, and the explicit sensuality adds to the excitement that will have readers craving the next Ribbon Ridge offering."
-Library Journal Starred Review on YOURS TO HOLD

"Darcy Burke writes a uniquely touching and heart-warming series about the love, pain, and joys of family as well as the love that feeds your soul when you meet "the one."
-The Many Faces of Romance

I can't tell you how much I love this series. Each book gets better and better.
-Romancing the Readers

"Darcy Burke's Ribbon Ridge series is one of my all-time favorites. Fall in love with the Archer family, I know I did."
-Forever Book Lover

Ribbon Ridge: So Hot

SO GOOD

" ...worth the read with its well-written words, beautiful descriptions, and likeable characters...they are flirty, sexy and a match made in wine heaven."

-Harlequin Junkie Top Pick

"I absolutely love the characters in this book and the families. I honestly could not put it down and finished it in a day."

-Chin Up Mom

SO RIGHT

"This is another great story by Darcy Burke. Painting pictures with her words that make you want to sit and stare at them for hours. I love the banter between the characters and the general sense of fun and friendliness."

-The Ardent Reader

" ...the romance is emotional; the characters are spirited and passionate... "

-The Reading Café

SO WRONG

"As usual, Ms. Burke brings you fun characters and witty banter in this sweet hometown series. I loved the dance between Crystal and Jamie as they fought their attraction."

-The Many Faces of Romance

"I really love both this series and the Ribbon Ridge series from Darcy Burke. She has this way of taking your heart and ripping it right out of your chest one second and then the next you are laughing at something the characters are doing."

-Romancing the Readers

Acknowledgments

This book was so much fun to write, especially during the epic writing week I spent with Joan Swan/Skye Jordan and Elisabeth Naughton. There was so much good writing mojo that it transformed this book from a novella to a novel! Researching Arthurian legend and creating aspects to enhance the story was great fun and I want to thank Joan, Elisabeth, and Rachel Grant for helping me plotstorm.

I also want to thank Rachel, Elisabeth, and Janice Goodfellow for reading drafts. Your feedback is always spot-on and helpful. Special thanks to Janice and Emma Locke for their help with blurb-writing.

Sending hugs and thanks to Erica Ridley, Lila DiPasqua, and Erica Monroe because they're awesome and they make life fun.

Most of all, thank you to my family who inspire me to come up with happily ever afters—it's easy to do when you're living one.

About the Author

Darcy Burke is the USA Today Bestselling Author of hot, action-packed historical and sexy, emotional contemporary romance. Darcy wrote her first book at age 11, a happily ever after about a swan addicted to magic and the female swan who loved him, with exceedingly poor illustrations.

A native Oregonian, Darcy lives on the edge of wine country with her guitar-strumming husband, their two hilarious kids who seem to have inherited the writing gene. They're a crazy cat family with two Bengal cats, a small, fame-seeking cat named after a fruit, and an older rescue Maine Coon who is the master of chill and five a.m. serenading. In her "spare" time Darcy is a serial volunteer enrolled in a 12-step program where one learns to say "no," but she keeps having to start over. Her happy places are Disneyland and Labor Day weekend at the Gorge. Visit Darcy online at http://www.darcyburke.com and sign up for her newsletter, follow her on Twitter at http://twitter.com/darcyburke, or like her Facebook page, http://www.facebook.com/darcyburkefans.

CPSIA information can be obtained
at www.ICGtesting.com
Printed in the USA
LVHW111519310520
657057LV00004B/1157